D0457547

Smooth Talking Stranger

Also by Lisa Kleypas

Seduce Me at Sunrise

Blue-Eyed Devil

Mine Till Midnight

Sugar Daddy

WALLFLOWER SERIES

A Wallflower Christmas

Scandal in Spring

Devil in Winter

It Happened One Autumn

Secrets of a Summer Night

Lisa Kleypas

Smooth Talking Stranger

St. Martin's Press New York

This is a work of fiction. All of the characters, organizations, and events portrayed in this novel are either products of the author's imagination or are used fictitiously.

For information, address St. Martin's Press, 175 Fifth Avenue,
New York, N.Y. 10010.

www.stmartins.com

Library of Congress Cataloging-in-Publication Data

Kleypas, Lisa.
Smooth talking stranger / Lisa Kleypas. — 1st ed.
p. cm.
ISBN-13: 978-0-312-35166-3
ISBN-10: 0-312-35166-6
1. Millionaires—Texas—Fiction. 2. Abandoned children—Fiction.
3. Birth fathers—Fiction. I. Title.
PS3561.L456S66 2009
813'.54—dc22 2008050528

First Edition: April 2009

10 9 8 7 6 5 4 3 2 1

To Greg

because every day I spend with you is the perfect day

love always,

L.K.

Smooth Talking Stranger

ONE

"DON'T GET IT," I SAID AS I HEARD THE RINGTONE of our apartment phone. Call it a premonition, paranoia, but something about that sound severed every comfortable feeling I had managed to stitch around myself.

"It's a 281 number," my boyfriend Dane said, sautéing tofu in a pan, dumping in a can of organic tomato sauce. Dane was a vegan, which meant we used soy protein in place of ground beef in our chili. It was enough to make any native-born Texan cry, but for Dane's sake I was trying to get used to it. "I can see it on the caller ID."

281. Houston. Those three digits were enough to start me hyperventilating. "It's either my mother or my sister," I said desperately. "Let the machine pick up." I hadn't spoken to either of them in at least two years.

Ring.

Pausing in the act of stirring a handful of frozen veggie crumbles into the sauce, Dane said, "You can't run away from your fears. Isn't that what you always tell your readers?"

I was an advice columnist for *Vibe*, a magazine about relationships and sex and urban culture. My column, called "Ask Miss Independent," had started at a student-run publication, and I had quickly developed a following. Upon graduating, I'd taken Miss Independent to *Vibe*, and they offered me a weekly feature. Most of my advice was posted publicly, but I also sent private paid-for replies to those who requested it. To supplement my income, I also did occasional freelancing for women's magazines.

"I'm not running away from my fears," I told Dane. "I'm running away from my relatives."

Ring.

"Just pick it up, Ella. You always tell people to face their problems."

"Yes, but I prefer to ignore mine and let them fester." I sidled closer to the phone and recognized the number. "Oh God. It's Mom."

Ring.

"Go on," Dane said. "What's the worst that could happen?"

I stared at the phone with fearful loathing. "In the space of thirty seconds, she could say something that would send me back to therapy indefinitely."

Ring.

"If you don't find out what she wants," Dane said, "you'll worry about it all night."

I let out an explosive breath and snatched up the phone. "Hello?"

"Ella. This is an emergency!"

To my mother, Candy Varner, everything was an emergency. She was a shock-and-awe parent, the ultimate drama queen. But she had covered it up so adeptly that few people suspected what went on behind closed doors. She had demanded her daughters' collusion in the myth of our happy family life, and Tara and I had given it to her without question.

At times Mom wanted interaction with my younger sister and me, but she quickly became impatient and surly. We learned to watch for every sign that would indicate the fluctuations of her mood. We had been storm chasers, trying to stay close to the twister without getting swept up in it.

I headed to the living room, away from Dane and the clatter of pans. "How are you, Mom? What's going on?"

"I just told you. An emergency! Tara came to visit today. Just appeared with no warning. She has a baby."

"Her own baby?"

"What would she be doing with someone else's baby? Yes, it's hers. You didn't know she was pregnant?"

"No," I managed to say, groping for the back of the sofa. I propped myself against it, half-sitting, half-leaning. I felt sick to my stomach. "I didn't. We haven't been in touch."

"When was the last time you picked up the phone to call her? Have you thought about either of us, Ella? Your only family? Do we have *any* place on your list of priorities?"

I was struck mute, my heart pounding like a dryer full of wet sneakers as an awful-familiar feeling from my childhood settled over me. But I was no longer a child. Reminding myself that I was a woman with a college degree, a career, a steady boyfriend, and a circle of good friends, I managed to answer calmly, "I sent cards."

"They weren't sincere. That last Mother's Day card didn't say one word about all the things I did for you while you were growing up. All the happy times."

I clasped my hand to my forehead in the hopes that it would keep my brain from exploding. "Mom, is Tara there now?"

"Would I be calling you if she was? She—" My mother was cut

off by the angry wail of an infant in the background. "Can you hear what I'm dealing with? She left it here, Ella! She's gone! What am I supposed to do?"

"Did she say when she was coming back?"

"No."

"And there was no guy with her? Did she say who the father was?"

"I don't think she knows. She has ruined her life, Ella. No man will ever want her after this."

"You might be surprised," I said. "A lot of unmarried women have babies nowadays."

"There's still a stigma. You know what I went through to keep that from happening to you and Tara."

"After your last husband," I said, "I think we would have preferred the stigma."

Her tone turned icy. "Roger was a good man. That marriage would have lasted if you and Tara had ever learned to get along with him. It wasn't my fault that my own children drove him away. He loved you girls, and you never gave him a chance."

I rolled my eyes. "Roger loved us a little too much, Mom."

"What do you mean?"

"We had to sleep with a chair wedged against the door to keep him out of our bedroom at night. And I don't think he was planning to straighten our covers."

"That's all in your own mind. No one believes you when you say things like that, Ella."

"Tara believes me."

"She doesn't remember anything about Roger," my mother informed me triumphantly. "Not anything at all."

"Does that strike you as normal, Mom? To have large episodes of your childhood blocked out completely? Don't you think she should remember *something* about Roger?"

"I think it's a sign that she's been doing drugs or drinking. Those things run on your father's side."

"It's also a sign of childhood trauma or abuse. Mom, are you sure Tara didn't just go to the store?"

"Yes, I'm sure. She left a goodbye note."

"Have you tried her cell phone?"

"Of course I did! She won't answer." My mother was nearly choking with impatience. "I gave up the best years of my life taking care of you. I'm not going through it again. I'm too young to have a grand-baby. I don't want anyone to know about this. You come get it before anyone sees him, Ella! Do something with this baby or I'll give it to Social Services."

I blanched as I heard the edge in her voice, knowing it wasn't an empty threat. "Don't do anything," I said. "Don't give the baby to anyone. I'll be there in a few hours."

"I'm going to have to cancel a date tonight," she said darkly.

"I'm sorry, Mom. I'm coming. I'm leaving right now. Just hold down the fort. *Wait*, okay?"

The phone clicked. I was anxious and trembling, the air-conditioned breeze glancing off my neck and making me shiver.

A baby, I thought miserably. *Tara's baby*.

I trudged into the kitchen. "Until this moment," I said, "I thought the worst thing that could happen tonight was your cooking."

Dane had taken the skillet off the burner. He was pouring something bright orange into a martini glass. Turning, he handed it to me, his green eyes warm with friendly sympathy. "Have some."

I took a swallow of gingery-sweet gruel and grimaced. "Thanks. I was just thinking I needed a good stiff slug of carrot juice." I set aside the glass. "But I'd better take it easy. I have to drive tonight."

As I looked into Dane's concerned face, the calmness of him, the sanity of him, was like being wrapped in a soft blanket. He was casually handsome, blond, and lean, with the perpetual toasted-and-salted scruffiness of someone who had just come in from the beach. Most of the time Dane dressed in denim and hemp and enviro-sandals, as if he were perpetually ready for a spontaneous trip to some equatorial region. If you'd asked Dane to describe his perfect vacation, it would have been some survivalist trek through an exotic jungle, equipped with only a nylon water bag and a pocket knife.

Although Dane had never met my mother or sister, I had told him a lot about them, furtively unearthing memories like fragile artifacts. It wasn't easy to talk about my past, any part of it. I had managed to trust Dane with the basics: my parents had divorced and my father had left us when I was five. All I heard of my dad after that was that he had gotten a new wife, new children, and there was no place for Tara and me in his second time around.

Regardless of his failure as a dad, I could hardly blame him for wanting to escape. It bothered me, however, that my father knew what kind of parent he had left us alone with. Maybe he reasoned that daughters were better off with their mothers. Maybe he had hoped my mother would get better over time. Or maybe he feared one or both of his daughters would turn out exactly like her, and that was not something he could handle.

There had been no significant man in my life until I had met Dane at the University of Texas. He was always gentle, reading my signals, never demanding too much. He made me feel safe for the first time ever.

And yet for all that, there was something missing between us, something that nagged at me like a pebble that had worked its way into my shoe. Whatever that missing thing was, it kept Dane and me from reaching absolute closeness.

As we stood in the apartment kitchen, Dane put a warm hand on my shoulder. The shaky-cold feeling began to subside. "From what I was able to hear," Dane said, "Tara dumped off a surprise baby with your mother, who's planning to sell it on eBay."

"Social Services," I said. "She hasn't thought of eBay yet."

"What does she expect you to do?"

"She wants me to take the baby off her hands," I said, wrapping my arms around myself. "I don't think she's given much thought to anything beyond that."

"No one knows where Tara is?"

I shook my head.

"Want me to go with you?" he asked gently.

"No," I said, almost before he could finish the question. "You have too much to do here." Dane had started his own environmental monitoring equipment company, and business was expanding almost too fast for him to handle. It would be difficult for him to take the time off. "Besides," I said, "I don't know how long it will take to find Tara, or what shape she'll be in when I do."

"What if you get stuck with this kid? No, let me rephrase—what are you going to do to *avoid* being stuck with this kid?"

"Maybe I could just bring it here for a few days? Just long enough to—"

Dane was shaking his head firmly. "Don't bring it here, Ella. No babies."

I gave him a dark look. "What if it were a baby polar bear or a baby Galápagos penguin? I bet you'd want it then."

"I'd make an exception for endangered species," he allowed.

"This baby is endangered. It's with my mother."

"Go to Houston and take care of the situation. I'll be waiting for you when you come back." Dane paused and added firmly, "Alone." Turning to the stove, he picked up the pan of veggie sauce and dumped it over a bowl of whole-grain pasta. He sprinkled shredded soy cheese over the top. "Eat something before you go—this'll give you sustained energy."

"No, thanks," I said. "I've lost my appetite."

A wry grin crossed his lips. "Like hell you have. Ten minutes after you leave, you're heading to the drive-through window of the nearest Whataburger."

"You think I'd cheat on you?" I demanded with all the innocent outrage I could muster.

"With another guy, no. With a cheeseburger . . . in a heartbeat."

TWO

I HAD ALWAYS HATED THE THREE-HOUR DRIVE BE-tween Austin and Houston. But the long stretch of quiet time gave me the opportunity to sift through childhood memories, and try to figure out what had led Tara to have a baby she wasn't ready to care for.

I had realized early in life that too much of anything wasn't good for you, and that included beauty. I'd had the good luck to be born moderately pretty, with blue eyes and blond hair, and a milk-colored complexion that, when exposed to the cruel blaze of the Texas sun, went straight to sizzling-red. ("You have no melatonin," Dane had once marveled. "It's like you were meant to live in the library.") At five-four I was average height with decent measurements and good legs.

Tara, however, belonged in the realm of goddesses. It was as if nature, having done the necessary experimentation with me, had decided to create the pièce de résistance. Tara had hit the genetic jackpot with her fine-chiseled features, luxuriant platinum hair, and pillowy lips that no amount of collagen could mimic. At five-ten, she was a long-stemmed size two and was often mistaken for a supermodel. The only reason Tara hadn't gone on that predestined career path was that even the minimal stores of discipline and ambition required of a model were beyond her.

For those and other reasons, I had never envied Tara. Her beauty, the sheer magnitude of it, simultaneously distanced people and invited them to take advantage of her. It caused people to assume she was stupid, and truth be told, it had not exactly driven Tara to prove her intellectual mettle. A gorgeous woman was never expected to be smart, and if she was, most people found it off-putting. There was only so much good fortune a normal person could forgive in another. So a surfeit of beauty had only earned trouble for my sister. When I'd last seen Tara, there had already been too many men in her life.

Just like our mother.

Some of Mom's boyfriends had been nice men. They had first seen her as a beautiful and vivacious woman, a single working mom who was devoted to her two daughters. Eventually, however, they came to understand what she was, a woman who badly needed love and yet was unable to return it . . . a woman who struggled to control and dominate the people who tried to get close to her. She drove them all away and brought in new ones, a constant and exhausting turnover of lovers and friends.

Her second husband, Steve, had only lasted four months before he'd filed for divorce. He'd been a kind and rational presence in our household, and even that short time of living with him had shown me that not all adults were like Mom. When he had said goodbye to Tara and me, he had told us regretfully that we were good girls, and he wished he could take us with him. But later Mom had said that Steve had left *because* of Tara and me. We would never have a family, she had added, if we didn't behave better.

When I was nine, Mom had married Roger, the last husband, without even telling Tara and me about it beforehand. He was charismatic and good-looking, and he took such a friendly interest in his new stepdaughters that at first we loved him. But before long the man who read us bedtime stories was also showing us pages from porn magazines. He was fond of playing tickling games that went on too long and were not at all what grown men should have been doing with little girls.

Roger took a particular interest in Tara, taking her on father-daughter outings and buying her special presents. Tara began to have nightmares and nervous tics, and she picked at her food without eating. She asked me not to leave her alone with Roger.

Mom went into a fury when Tara and I tried to tell her. She even punished us for lying. We were afraid to tell anyone outside the family, certain that if our own mother wouldn't believe us, no one else would, either. The only option I had was to protect Tara as much as I could. When we were at home, I stayed with her every minute. She slept next to me at night, and I kept a chair against the door.

One night Roger tapped at the door for nearly ten minutes.

"Come on, Tara. Let me in, or I won't buy you any more presents. I just want to talk to you. Tara—" He pushed harder at the door, and the chair creaked in protest. "I was nice to you the other day, wasn't I? I told you I loved you. But I won't be nice anymore if you don't move that chair out of the way. Open it, Tara, or I'll tell your mama you've been acting up. You'll get punished."

My little sister curled into a ball against me, trembling. She put her hands over her ears. "Don't let him in, Ella," she whispered. "Please."

I was scared, too. But I pulled the covers around Tara and got out of bed. "She's sleeping," I said, loud enough for the monster at the door to hear.

"Open it, you little bitch!" The hinges rattled as he pushed harder. Where was my mother? Why wasn't she doing anything?

In the feeble glow of a Rainbow Brite night-light, I frantically rummaged beneath the bed for the craft box where we kept our art supplies. My fingers curved around the cold handles of a pair of metal scissors. We used them to cut out paper dolls, pictures from magazines, and cereal box tops.

I heard the thud of impact as Roger put his shoulder to the door, so hard that the chair began to crack. Between each thud, I heard the sound of my sister weeping. Adrenaline raced through me, sending my heartbeat into a drumming fury. Panting, I went to the door, gripping the scissors. Another thud, another, with sounds of wood vibrating and splintering. Light from the hallway shot into the room as Roger shoved the door wide enough to get his hand in. But as he began to push the chair aside, I darted forward and stabbed his hand with the pair of scissors. I felt the sickening give of metal penetrating something pliant. There was a muted roar of pain and fury, and then . . . nothing . . . except the sound of retreating footsteps.

Still gripping the scissors, I got back into bed with Tara. "I'm scared," my little sister had wept, soaking the shoulder of my nightgown with her tears. "Don't let him get me, Ella."

"He won't," I had said, stiff and shaking. "If he comes back, I'll stick him like a pig. You go to sleep, now."

And she had slept huddled against me all night, while I stayed awake, my heart jolting every time I heard a noise.

In the morning, Roger had left our house for good.

Mom never asked either of us about that night, or what had happened, or how we felt about Roger's abrupt departure from our lives.

The only thing she ever said about it was, "You will never get a new daddy. You don't deserve one."

There had been other men after that, some of them bad, but never quite as bad as Roger.

And the strangest part of all was that Tara didn't remember Roger, or the night I had stabbed his hand with the scissors. She was bewildered when I told her about it a few years later. "Are you sure?" she had asked with a puzzled frown. "Maybe you dreamed it."

"I had to wash the scissors the next morning," I told her. It frightened me that she looked so blank. "There was blood on them. And the chair was cracked in two places. You don't remember?"

Tara had shaken her head, mystified.

After that experience, after the parade of men who never stayed, I was leery and gun-shy, afraid to trust any man. But as Tara had gotten older, she had gone the other way. For her there were innumerable partners, and prolific sex. And I wondered how much real pleasure, if any, she had gotten out of it.

The urge to protect and care for Tara had never left me. During our teen years, I had driven to strange places in the night to pick her up where a boyfriend had stranded her . . . I had given her my waitressing money to buy a prom dress . . . I had taken her to the doctor to get birth control pills. She had been fifteen at the time.

"Mom says I'm a slut," Tara whispered to me in the doctor's waiting room. "She's mad because I'm not a virgin anymore."

"It's your body," I had whispered back, holding her icy hand in mine. "You can do what you want with it. But don't get pregnant. And . . . I think you shouldn't let a boy do that to you unless you're sure he loves you."

"They always say they love me," Tara had told me with a bitter smile. "How do you know when one of them actually means it?"

I shook my head helplessly.

"Are you still a virgin, Ella?" Tara had asked after a moment.

"Uh-huh."

"Is that why Bryan broke up with you last week? 'Cause you wouldn't do it with him?"

I shook my head. "I broke up with him." Glancing into her soft blue eyes, I tried for a rueful smile, but it felt more like a grimace. "I came home from school and found him with Mom."

"What were they doing?"

I hesitated for a long moment before replying. "Drinking together," was all I said. I thought I'd cried until no more tears were left, but my eyes watered again as I nodded. And although Tara was younger than me, she put her hand on my head and pulled it down to her narrow shoulder, offering comfort. We had sat together like that until the nurse came and called Tara's name.

I didn't think I would have survived my childhood without my sister, or she without me. We were each other's only link to the past . . . that was the strength of our bond, and also our weakness.

To be fair to Houston, I would have liked it a lot more if I hadn't been viewing it through a prism of memories. Houston was flat, humid as a wet sock, and surprisingly green in parts, dangling at the end of a belt of heavy forestland that extended from East Texas. There was a furious amount of development in every crevice of its spider-web layout—condos and apartments, retail and office buildings. It was an intensely alive city, flashy and spectacular and filthy and busy.

Gradually the summer-braised pastures turned into oceans of smoking-hot asphalt with islands of strip malls and big-box stores. Here and there a lone high-rise shot up like a plant runner sent out from the main growth of central Houston.

Mom lived in the southwest region, in a middle-class neighborhood built around a town square that had once harbored restaurants and shops. Now the square had been taken up by a large home-improvement store. My mother's house was a two-bedroom colonial ranch style fronted with skinny white columns. I drove along the street, dreading the moment I would pull up in the drive.

Stopping in front of the garage, I hopped out of my Prius and hurried to the front door. Before I even had a chance to ring the doorbell, Mom had opened the door. She was talking to someone on the phone, her voice low and seductive.

". . . promise I'll make it up to you," she cooed. "Next time." She laughed at little. "Oh, I think you know how . . ." I closed the door and waited uncertainly while she continued to talk.

Mom looked the same as always: slim, fit, and dressed like a teen pop star, no matter that she was pushing fifty. She wore a tight black tank top, a denim miniskirt cinched with a rhinestone-encrusted Kippy belt, and high-heeled sandals. Her forehead was as taut as the skin on a grape. Her hair had been bleached Hilton blonde, falling to her shoulders in meticulously sprayed waves. As she glanced over me, I knew exactly what she thought of my plain white cotton camp shirt, a practical garment that buttoned down the front.

While listening to the person on the other end of the line, Mom gestured toward the hallway that led to the bedrooms. I nodded and went in search of the baby. The house smelled like air-conditioning and old carpets and tropical air freshener, the rooms dark and silent.

A small dressing-table lamp had been left on in the master bedroom. My breath quickened in anxious wonder as I approached the bed. The baby was in the center of it, a lump no larger than a loaf of bread. A boy. He was dressed in blue, his arms out-flung, his mouth clamped tight as a powder compact as he slept. I crawled onto the bed beside him, staring at this defenseless creature with his little-old-man face and tender pink skin. His eyelids were so fragile they were tinted blue as they lay closed over his sleeping eyes. The small skull was covered with soft black hair, and his fingers were tipped with nails as tiny and sharp as bird claws.

The baby's absolute helplessness made me intensely anxious. When he woke up, he was going to cry. And leak. He was going to need things, mysterious things that I knew nothing about and had no desire to learn.

I could almost sympathize with Tara for having foisted this overwhelming problem on someone else. Almost. But mainly I wanted to kill her. Because my sister had known that leaving him with Mom was a stupid idea. She had known that Mom would never keep him. And she had been aware that I would probably be recruited to do something about it. I had always been the family's problem-solver, until I had opted out in an act of self-preservation. They still hadn't forgiven me for that.

Since then I had often wondered how and when I might be able to reunite with my mother and sister, if we all would have changed enough that we could have some kind of workable relationship. I hoped maybe it would turn out like one of those Hallmark movies, a lot of soft-focus hugging and laughing as we sat on a porch swing.

That would have been nice. But it wasn't my family.

As the baby slept, I listened to his soft kitten-breaths. His smallness, his aloneness, caused an invisible weight to settle over me, sadness mixed with anger. I wasn't going to let Tara run from this, I vowed grimly. I was going to find her, and for once she would have to deal with the consequences of her actions. Failing that, I was going to find the baby's father and insist that he bear some responsibility.

"Don't wake him up," my mother said from the doorway. "It took me two hours to put him down."

"Hi, Mom," I said. "You look great."

"I've been working with a personal trainer. He can hardly keep his hands off me. You've put on weight, Ella. You'd better be careful . . . you get your figure from your daddy's side, and his people always ran to fat."

"I exercise," I countered, annoyed. I was not at all fat. I was curvy and strong, and I took yoga three times a week. "And I get no complaints from Dane," I added defensively, before I could stop myself. Immediately I was tempted to smack myself in the head. "But it doesn't matter what anyone thinks of my figure, as long as I'm happy with it."

My mother ran a dismissive glance over me. "You're still with him?"

"Yes. And I'd like to get back to him as soon as possible, which means we need to find Tara. Can you tell me again what happened when you saw her?"

"Come to the kitchen."

Easing myself from the bed, I left the room and followed her.

"Tara showed up without calling first," my mother explained as we reached the kitchen, "and said, 'Here's your grandbaby.' Just like that. I let her in, and I poured some tea, and we sat down to talk. Tara said she's been living with your cousin Liza, and working at a temp agency. She got pregnant by one of her boyfriends, and she says he's not in a position to help. You know what that means. Either he doesn't have two nickels to rub together, or he's already married. I told Tara she should put the baby up for adoption, and she said she didn't want to do that. So I said, 'Your life will never be the same. Everything changes after you have a baby.' And Tara said she was starting to figure that out. Then she mixed some formula for the baby and fed him while I went to the back room to take a nap. When I got up, Tara was gone and the baby was still here. You'll have to get him out of here by tomorrow. My boyfriend can't know about this."

"Why not?"

"I don't want him to think of me as a grandmother."

"Other women your age have grandchildren," I said in a matter-of-fact tone.

"I'm not my age, Ella. Everyone thinks I'm a lot younger." She seemed offended by my expression. "You should be happy about that. To know what's in your future."

"I don't think I'll look like you in the future," I said wryly. "I don't even look like you now."

"You might if you put some effort into it. Why is your hair so short? You don't have the right face for that style."

I lifted a hand to my chin-length bob, which was the only practical style for my straight, fine hair. "Can I see the note Tara left?"

Mom brought a manila folder to the kitchen table. "It's in here along with the hospital papers."

I opened the folder and found a piece of notebook paper on top. The sight of my sister's handwriting, all loopy and uneven, was painfully familiar. The words had been dug deep by a ballpoint pen that had nearly perforated the paper with its desperate force.

Dear Mom,

I have to go somewhere and figure things out. I don't know when I'll be back. I hereby give you or my sister Ella the authority to take care of my baby and be his guardian until I'm ready to come get him.

Sincerely,

Tara Sue Varner

"Hereby," I murmured with a wretched smile, leaning my forehead on my hand. My sister had probably thought a legal-sounding word would make it more official. "I think we're supposed to get in touch with Child Protective Services and let them know what's happened. Otherwise someone could claim the baby has been abandoned."

Sorting through the contents of the folder, I found the birth certificate. No father listed. The baby was exactly a week old, and his name was Luke Varner. "Luke?" I asked. "Why did she name him that? Do we know anyone named Luke?"

Mom went to the refrigerator and pulled out a can of Diet Big Red. "Your cousin Porky—I think his real name is Luke. But Tara doesn't know him."

"I have a cousin Porky?"

"Second cousin, once removed. He's one of Big Boy's sons."

One of the legions of extended family that we'd never had anything to do with. Too many explosive personalities and disorders to put in one room together—we were a living catalog of the DSM-IV, the doctor's manual of mental disorders. Returning my attention to the certificate, I said, "She had him at Women's Hospital. Do you know who was with her? Did she say anything about it?"

"Your cousin Liza was with her," came my mother's sour reply.

"You'll have to call her to get the details. She won't tell me anything."

"I will. I . . ." Dazedly I shook my head. "What's going on with Tara? Did she seem depressed to you? Did she seem scared? Did she look sick?"

Mom poured the Big Red over ice, watching the pink foam rise to the rim of the glass. "She was heavy. And she looked tired. That was all I noticed."

"Maybe this is some kind of postpartum problem. She may need antidepressants."

Mom poured a shot of vodka into the Big Red. "Doesn't matter what pills you give her. She'll never want that baby." After taking a swallow of the fizzy-bright liquid, she said, "She's not cut out for having kids any more than I was."

"Why did you have children, Mom?" I asked softly.

"It was what women did when they got married. And I did my best. I made sacrifices to give you the best childhood I could. And neither of you seems to remember any of it. It's a shame, how ungrateful children are. Especially daughters."

I couldn't begin to reply. I had no way to describe how I had struggled to collect every good memory possible. How every moment of my mother's affection—a hug, a bedtime story—had been a gift from heaven. But mostly how my childhood, and Tara's, had seemed like a rug pulled out from under us. And how her complete lack of motherly instinct—even the basic urge to protect her offspring—had made it difficult for Tara and me to have relationships with people.

"I'm sorry, Mom," I managed to say, my voice thick with regret. But I was fairly certain my mother didn't understand what I was sorry for.

A high, mewling cry came from the bedroom. The sound chilled me. He needed something.

"Time for his formula," my mother said, going to the refrigerator. "I'll heat it up. Go get him, Ella."

Another cry, this one sharper. It made my back teeth hurt like I'd just bitten into tin foil. I sped to the bedroom and saw a small form on the bed, wriggling like a baby seal. My heart went so fast that I couldn't feel any spaces between the beats.

I leaned over, reaching tentatively, uncertain how to pick him up. I wasn't good with children. I had never wanted to hold my friends' babies—they had never appealed to me. I slid my hands beneath the small flopping body. And the head. I knew you were supposed to support the head and neck. Somehow I gathered him up against me, his weight somehow fragile and solid at the same time, and the crying paused, and the infant looked up at me in a squinty Clint-Eastwood sort of way, and the crying started again. He was so unprotected. Helpless. I had only one coherent thought as I went to the kitchen, and it was that no one in my family, including me, should be trusted with one of these.

I sat and clumsily readjusted Luke in my arms, and Mom brought a bottle to me. Cautiously I put the silicone nipple—which wasn't shaped anything like a normal human one—against the tiny mouth. He latched on and went quiet, intent on feeding. I hadn't realized I was holding my breath until I let it out with a sigh of relief.

"You can stay here tonight," Mom said. "But you have to leave tomorrow and take him with you. I am much, much too busy to deal with this."

I clenched my teeth to hold back a burst of protests—this wasn't fair . . . none of it was my fault . . . I was busy, too . . . I had my own life to get back to. But what kept me silent, aside from the knowledge that my mother didn't care, was the fact that the person who was really getting the raw deal was the one who couldn't speak up for himself. Luke was a hot potato, doomed to be tossed back and forth until someone was forced to keep him.

And then it occurred to me: what if the father was a cokehead or a criminal? How many guys had Tara slept with, and was I going to have to track them all down and have them tested? What if some of them refused? Was I going to have to hire a lawyer?

Oh, this was going to be fun.

MOM SHOWED ME HOW TO BURP HIM AND TO CHANGE the diaper. Her competence surprised me, especially since she had never been a baby person, and it had undoubtedly been a long time since she had last done such a thing. I tried to picture her as a young mother, patiently attending to the never-ending tasks of caring for a baby. I couldn't imagine she had enjoyed any of it. My mother, with only a baby for company, a needy, noisy, inarticulate creature . . . no, it was impossible to envision.

I brought in my bags from the car, changed into my pajamas, and took the baby into the guest bedroom.

"Where is he going to sleep?" I asked, wondering what you did when there was no crib available.

"Put him next to you on the bed," Mom suggested.

"But I might roll over onto him, or accidentally push him over the side."

"Then make a pallet on the floor."

"But—"

"I'm going to bed," my mother said, striding from the room. "I am worn out. I've had to look after that baby all day."

While Luke waited in his plastic carrier, I made a pallet for both of us on the floor. I rolled up a quilt to make a bolster between us. After laying Luke on his back on one side of the pallet, I sat on the other side and flipped open my cell phone to call my cousin Liza.

"Are you with Tara?" Liza demanded as soon as I said hello.

"I was hoping she was with you."

"No. I've tried calling her a thousand times and she won't pick up."

Although Liza was my age, and I had always liked her, we'd never had much to do with each other. Like most of the women on my mother's side, Liza was blond and leggy, and possessed a perpetual appetite for male attention. With her long face and slightly horsy grin, she wasn't as pretty as my sister Tara, but she had *it*, the unmistakable quality that men couldn't resist. You would walk through a restaurant with her, and men would literally turn in their chairs to watch her go by.

Through the years Liza had managed to get access to some fast circles. She dated rich Houston guys and their friends, becoming sort of a playboy-groupie, or to put it more unkindly, a local starfucker of sorts. There was no doubt in my mind that if my sister had been living with Liza, she had been the eager recipient of Liza's leftovers.

We talked for a few minutes, and Liza said that she had a few ideas about where Tara might have gone. She would make some calls, she said. She felt sure Tara was okay. She hadn't seemed depressed or crazy. Just ambivalent.

"Tara was going back and forth about the baby," Liza said. "She wasn't sure she wanted to keep it. She changed her mind so many times the past few months, I gave up trying to figure out what she was going to do."

"Did she get any kind of counseling?"

"I don't think so."

"What about the father?" I demanded. "Who is he?"

There was a long hesitation. "I don't think Tara is all-the-way sure."

"She must have *some* idea."

"Well, she thought she knew, but . . . you know Tara. She's not very organized."

"How organized do you have to be to know who you're sleeping with?"

"Well, we were both partying a lot for a while . . . and the timing's not easy to work out, you know? I guess I could put together a list of the guys she went out with."

"Thank you. Who are we putting at the top of the list? Who did Tara say the most likely father was?"

There was a lengthy hesitation. "She said she thought it was Jack Travis."

"Who's that?"

Liza gave an incredulous laugh. "Doesn't that name mean anything to you, Ella?"

My eyes widened. "You mean a *Travis* Travis?"

"The middle son."

The head of the well-known Houston family was Churchill Travis, a billionaire investor and financial commentator. He was on the golden Rolodexes of media people, politicians, and celebrities. I'd seen him on CNN more than a few times, and in all the Texas magazines and papers. He and his children inhabited the small world of powerful people who rarely faced the consequences of their actions. They were above the economy, above threats from men or governments, above accountability. They were their own species.

Any son of Churchill Travis had to be a privileged, spoiled jerk.

"Great," I muttered. "I'm assuming it was a one-night stand?"

"You don't have to sound so judgmental, Ella."

"Liza, I can't think of any way to ask that question without sounding judgmental."

"It was a one-night stand," my cousin said shortly.

"So this will be coming out of left field for Travis," I mused aloud. "Or not. It's possible he gets this all the time. Surprise babies popping up like daisies."

"Jack dates a lot of women," Liza admitted.

"Have you ever gone out with him?"

"We've hung out in the same circles. I'm friends with Heidi Donovan, who goes out with him sometimes."

"What does he do for a living, aside from waiting for Big Daddy to kick the bucket?"

"Oh, Jack's not like that," Liza protested. "He's got his own company . . . something about property management . . . it's at 1800 Main. You know that glass building downtown, the one with the funny-looking top?"

"Yes, I know where that is." I loved that building, all glass and art deco flourishes with a segmented glass pyramid on top. "Could you get his number for me?"

"I could try."

"And in the meantime, you'll work on that list?"

"I guess. But I don't think Tara would be too happy about that."

"I don't think Tara is especially happy about anything these days," I said. "Help me find her, Liza. I need to see if she's okay and figure out what to do for her. I also want to find out who the father is and to work out some kind of plan for this poor abandoned baby."

"He wasn't abandoned," my cousin protested. "A baby isn't abandoned if you know where you left him."

I considered explaining the flaws in her logic, but it was clearly a waste of time. "Please work on the list, Liza. If Jack Travis doesn't turn out to be the father, I'm going to have to force every man Tara slept with last year to take a paternity test."

"Why go stirring up trouble, Ella? Can't you just take care of the baby for a while like she asked?"

"I . . ." Words failed me for a moment. "I have a *life*, Liza. I have a job. I have a boyfriend who wants nothing to do with babies. No, I can't sign on indefinitely as Tara's unpaid nanny."

"I was just asking," Liza said defensively. "Some men like babies, you know. And I didn't think your job would get in the way . . . it's mostly typing, right?"

I had to smother a laugh. "It definitely involves typing, Liza. But I have to do a little bit of thinking, too."

We talked for a few more minutes, mostly about Jack Travis. Apparently he was a man's man who hunted and fished, drove a little too fast, lived a little too hard. Women were lined up from Houston to Amarillo in hopes of being his next girlfriend. And from what Heidi had confided to Liza, Jack Travis would do absolutely anything in bed, and had an insane amount of stamina. In fact—

"TMI," I told Liza at that point.

"Okay. But let me tell you this: Heidi said that one night he took off his tie and used it to—"

"*TMI*, Liza," I insisted.

"Aren't you curious?"

"No. My column gets all kinds of letters and e-mails about bedroom issues. Nothing can shock me anymore. But I'd rather not know about Travis's sex life if I'm going to have to face the guy and ask him to take a paternity test."

"If Jack is the father," Liza said, "he'll help out. He's a responsible guy."

I wasn't buying it. "Responsible men don't have one-night stands and get women pregnant."

"You'll like him," she said. "All women do."

"Liza, I never like the kind of guy that all women like."

After I got off the phone with my cousin, I stared at the baby. His eyes were round blue buttons, and his face was puckered with a disarming expression of concern. I wondered what his impression of life was after his first week in the world. A lot of coming and going, car rides, changing faces, different voices. He probably wanted his mother's face, his mother's tone. At his age, a little consistency wasn't too much to ask. I cupped my hand lightly over the top of his skull, smoothing the black fluff. "One more call," I told him, and flipped open the phone again.

Dane picked up on the second ring. "How's Operation Baby Rescue going?"

"I've rescued the baby. Now I'd like someone to rescue me."

"Miss Independent never needs to be rescued."

I felt the hint of a genuine smile appear on my face, like a crack in the winter ice. "Oh, right. I forgot." I told him everything that had happened so far, and about the possibility that Jack Travis was the father.

"I'd approach that claim with some healthy skepticism," Dane commented. "If Travis is the sperm donor, don't you think Tara would have gone to him by now? From what I know of your sister, getting knocked up by a billionaire's son is the highest pinnacle of achievement."

"My sister has always operated from a system of logic that is nothing like ours. I can't begin to guess why she's behaving this way. And when I find her, I'm not at all certain she'll be capable of taking care of Luke. When we were younger, she couldn't even keep a goldfish alive."

"I've got connections," Dane said quietly. "I know some people who can help place him with a good family."

"I don't know." I glanced at the baby, whose eyes were closed. I wasn't sure I could live with the idea of giving him to strangers. "I have to figure out what's best for him. *Someone* has to put his needs first. He didn't ask to be born."

"Get a good night's sleep. You'll figure out the right answer, Ella. You always do."

THREE

IT WAS A MARK OF DANE'S UNFAMILIARITY WITH babies that he had suggested, without irony, that I get a good night's sleep. My nephew was a living, breathing sleep disorder. It was without exception the worst night I had ever spent, a series of harsh awakenings and crying and formula-mixing and feeding and burping and diaper-changing, and then after about five minutes of rest it all started again. I didn't know how anyone could live through months of this. After one night, I was a wreck.

In the morning I showered, turning the water up to near-scalding in the hopes that it would ease my aching muscles. Wishing I'd had the foresight to bring a more impressive outfit, I dressed in the only clean clothes I had: a pair of jeans, a fitted cotton shirt, and leather flats. I brushed my hair until it was neat and smooth, and looked at my haggard, stone-white face. My eyes were so irritated and dry that I didn't bother with my contact lenses. I decided to wear my glasses, a pair of sensible rectangular wire-rims.

It didn't improve my mood when I went to the kitchen, bringing Luke in his carrier, and saw my mother sitting at the table. Her fingers were knobbed with rings, her hair curled and sprayed. She wore shorts, her legs smooth and tan, and one of the pedicured toes that peeped from her wedge sandals sparkled with a tiny crystal toe ring.

I set Luke's carrier on the floor at the other side of the table, away from her.

"Does the baby have any other clothes?" I asked. "His one-piece is dirty."

Mom shook her head. "There's a discount store down the street. You can buy some things for him there. You'll need a big pack of diapers—they go through them fast at this stage."

"No kidding," I said wearily, heading for the coffeepot.

"Did you talk to Liza last night?"

"Uh-huh."

"What did she say?"

"She thinks Tara's okay. She's going to make some calls today to try and find her."

"What about the baby's daddy?"

I had already decided not to tell her anything about Jack Travis's possible involvement. Because if there was any way to ensure my mother's interest and unwanted involvement, it was to mention a rich man's name.

"No idea yet," I said casually.

"Where are you going today?"

"It looks like I'm going to find a hotel room." I didn't say it in an accusatory way. I didn't need to.

Her slim body stiffened in the chair. "The man I'm seeing can't find out about this."

"Because you're a grandmother?" I took a perverse pleasure in seeing her twitch at the word. "Or because Tara wasn't married when she had the baby?"

"Both. He's younger than me. Conservative, too. He wouldn't understand there's only so much you can do with rebellious children."

"Tara and I haven't been children for a while, Mom." I took a sip of black coffee, the bitter brew eliciting a judder of revulsion. Living with Dane, I had grudgingly accustomed myself to softening the brew with soy milk instead. *What the hell,* I thought, and reached for the carton of half-and-half on the counter. I poured a liberal dollop into the coffee.

Mom's lipstick-coated mouth pressed into thin, dry ribbons. "You've always been a know-it-all. Well, you're about to find out how much you *don't* know."

"Believe me," I muttered, "I'm the first one to admit that I have no clue about any of this stuff. I had nothing to do with it. This isn't my baby."

"Then give it to Social Services." She was getting agitated. "Whatever happens to him will be your fault, not mine. Get rid of him if you can't handle the responsibility."

"I can handle it," I said, my voice quiet. "It's okay, Mom. I'll take care of him. You don't have to worry about anything."

She subsided like a child who had just been mollified by a lollipop. "You'll have to learn the way I did," she said after a moment, reaching down to adjust her toe ring. A hint of satisfaction edged her tone as she added, "The hard way."

THE DAY WAS ALREADY BLAZING. I TOOK LUKE INTO the discount store, while he squalled up and down the aisles, writhing angrily in the ragged foam-lined infant seat that was bolted to the handles of the basket. Luke finally quieted when we left, soothed by the vibration of the basket wheels as they rattled over the rough asphalt of the parking lot.

The outside air was roasting-hot, while the indoors' were chilled by Arctic air-conditioning. As you went outside and inside, alternately sweating and drying, you were eventually covered in an invisible film of sticky salt. Luke and I were heated to the pink of boiled shrimp.

And this was how I was going to meet Jack Travis.

I called Liza, hoping she had managed to get his phone number.

"Heidi wouldn't give it to me," Liza said, sounding disgruntled. "Talk about insecure—I think she's scared I'm going to make a move on him! I had to bite my tongue to keep from telling her about all the times I could have gone after him but didn't on account of our friendship. 'Sides, she knows as well as anyone that there's plenty of Jack Travis to go around."

"It's a wonder the man gets any sleep."

"Jack's upfront about not being able to commit to one woman, so no one expects it of him. But Heidi's been seeing him so long, I think she's convinced herself she can get him to cough up an engagement ring."

"Like a hairball," I said, entertained. "Well, good luck to her. But in the meantime, how am I going to get in touch with him?"

"I don't know, Ella. Short of just barging in there and asking to see him, I can't think of anything."

"Fortunately I have excellent barging skills."

"I'd be careful," my cousin said warily. "Jack's a nice guy, but he's not the kind you can push around."

"I wouldn't think so," I agreed, while my stomach tightened in a spasm of nerves.

* * *

THE TRAFFIC IN HOUSTON HAD ITS OWN MYSTERIOUS patterns. Only keen familiarity and vast experience would allow you to maneuver through them. Naturally, Luke and I got caught in stop-and-start traffic that turned a fifteen-minute drive into a forty-five-minute one.

By the time we reached the artful, glittering structure of 1800 Main, Luke was howling and a foul smell had filled the car, demonstrating that a baby will inevitably have a dirty diaper at the worst possible time in the worst possible place.

I drove to the underground parking garage, the commercial half of which was completely full, and I had to drive out again. As I drove farther down the street, I found a public paying lot. After parking in one of the street-level spaces, I managed to change Luke's diaper in the back seat of the Prius.

The baby carrier seemed to weigh about a thousand pounds as I lugged it along the street to the building. Icy air hit me in a controlled blast as I entered the luxurious lobby, all marble and brushed steel and gleaming wood. After glancing at a glass-shielded directory of the office floors, I walked briskly by the reception desk. I knew there was no way they were going to let an unidentified woman with no appointment and no connections simply breeze through to the elevators.

"Miss—" One of the men behind the desk gestured for me to approach him.

"Someone's coming down to meet us," I said brightly. Reaching into the bag hanging from my shoulder, I pulled out the Ziploc bag containing the dirty diaper. "We had a little emergency; is there a restroom nearby?"

Blanching at the sight of the bulging baggie, the man hastily directed me toward a restroom on the other side of the elevator bank.

Passing the reception desk, I lugged Luke to the center of the double row of elevators. As soon as a door opened, we stepped inside along with four other people.

"How old is she?" a woman in a smart black skirt suit asked with a smile.

"It's a he," I said. "A week old."

"You're getting around so well, considering."

I briefly considered explaining that I wasn't the mother, but that might have led to another question, and I wasn't about to explain any part of the circumstances that Luke and I had found ourselves in. So I just smiled and murmured, "Yes, thanks, we're doing great." For the next several seconds, I brooded about how Tara might be getting around, if she was healing properly after giving birth. We reached the eleventh floor, and I carried Luke out of the elevator and past the doors of Travis Management Solutions.

We went into a serene area decorated in natural colors, with a small grouping of contemporary upholstered furniture. I set down Luke's carrier, rubbed my aching arm, and approached the receptionist. Her face was a polite mask. The black eyeliner on her upper lids had been extended so it formed little checkmarks at the corners of her eyes, as if they had been part of a list she had gone through that morning. *Right eye? . . . check. Left eye? . . . check.* I gave her a smile that I hoped conveyed that I was a woman of the world.

"I know this is out of the blue," I said, pushing up my glasses, which had started to slip down my nose, "but I need to see Mr. Travis about an urgent matter. I don't have an appointment. I just need five minutes. My name is Ella Varner."

"Are you acquainted with Mr. Travis?"

"No. I was referred by the friend of a friend."

Her face remained carefully expressionless. I half-expected her to reach under the desk and press a button for security. Any second now, men in beige polyester uniforms would burst through the doors and haul me off.

"What do you want to see Mr. Travis about?" the receptionist asked.

"I'm sure he wouldn't want me to tell anyone until he hears it first."

"Mr. Travis is in a meeting."

"I'll wait for him."

"A long meeting," she said.

"That's fine. I'll catch him when he takes a break."

"You'll have to make an appointment and come back later."

"When's his next opening?"

"His schedule is full for the next three weeks. There may be something at the end of the month—"

"This can't wait until the end of the *day*," I insisted. "Look, all I need is five minutes. I'm here from Austin. I'm dealing with a pressing matter that Mr. Travis needs to know about—" I broke off as I saw her blank face.

She thought I was crazy.

I was beginning to think so, too.

Behind me, the baby started crying.

"*You've got to keep him quiet,*" the receptionist said with biting urgency.

I went to Luke, picked him up, and grabbed a bottle of chilled formula from the side of the diaper bag. I had no way to warm it, so I pushed the nipple into his mouth.

But my nephew didn't like his formula cold. Pulling his mouth from the plastic nipple, he began to wail.

"Miss Varner—" the receptionist said in agitation.

"His bottle's cold." I gave her an apologetic smile. "Before you send us off, would you mind warming it? Just put it in a cup of hot water for a minute? Please?"

She let out a short, sharp sigh. "Give it to me. I'll take it back to the coffee station."

"Thank you." I offered her a placating smile, which she ignored as she left.

I wandered around the reception area, bouncing Luke gently, humming, doing anything I could think of to soothe him. "Luke, I can't take you anywhere. You always make a scene. And you never listen to me. I think we should start seeing other people."

Aware of a figure approaching from one of the hallways that branched out from the reception area, I turned gratefully. I assumed it was the receptionist, back with the bottle. Instead I saw three men walking out, all dressed in dark, expensive-looking suits. One of them was fair and slim, the other short and a bit portly, and the third was the most striking man I had ever seen.

He was tall and big-framed, all hard muscle and easy masculinity, with dark eyes and heavy well-cut black hair. The way he carried himself—the confidence in his walk, the relaxed set of his shoulders—proclaimed that he was accustomed to being in charge. Pausing in mid-conversation, he gave me an alert look, and my breath caught. A blush crept over my face, and a hectic pulse began at the front of my throat.

One glance and I knew exactly who and what he was. The classic alpha male, the kind who had spurred evolution forward about five million years ago by nailing every female in sight. They charmed, seduced, and behaved like bastards, and yet women were biologically incapable of resisting their magic DNA.

Still staring at me, the man spoke in a deep voice that raised gooseflesh on my arms. "I thought I heard a baby out here."

"Mr. Travis?" I asked crisply, jostling my whimpering nephew.

He gave a short nod.

"I hoped I might catch you between meetings. I'm Ella. From Austin. Ella Varner. I need to talk to you briefly."

The receptionist came from another hallway, plastic bottle in hand. "Oh God," she muttered, hurrying forward. "Mr. Travis, I'm sorry—"

"It's okay," Travis said, gesturing for her to give me the bottle.

I took it, shook a few lukewarm drops on my wrist as my mother had told me to do, and shoved the nipple into the baby's mouth. Luke grunted in satisfaction and fell into a busy, sucking silence.

Looking back up into Travis's eyes, which were as dark and rich as blackstrap molasses, I asked, "May I speak with you for a few minutes?"

Travis studied me thoughtfully. I was struck by the contradictions about him, the expensive clothes and bold good looks, the sense of unpolished edges. He was unapologetically masculine in a way that suggested you should either scramble to get on his good side or get the hell out of his way.

I couldn't help contrasting him with Dane, whose golden handsomeness and jaw-softening stubble had always been so soothing and approachable. There was nothing soothing about Jack Travis. Except maybe his deep sugar-maple baritone.

"Depends," Travis said easily. "You gonna try to sell me something?" He had a heavy Texas accent, the kind in which dropped *G*'s hit the floor like summer hailstones.

"No. It's a personal matter."

A touch of offhand amusement lurked in the corners of his mouth. "I usually save personal matters for after five."

"I can't wait that long." I took a deep breath before adding boldly, "And I should warn you that if you get rid of me now, you'll have to deal with me later. I'm very persistent."

The trace of a smile lingered on his lips as he turned to the other men. "Would y'all mind waiting for me at the bar on the seventh floor?"

"No hardship," one of them said in a brisk British accent. "We never mind loitering in the bar. Shall I order for you, Travis?"

"Yeah, I don't expect this'll take long. Dos Equis, lime wedge, no glass."

As the men left, Jack Travis turned his full attention to me. Although I was medium height, hardly a short woman, he towered over me. "My office." He motioned for me to precede him. "Last door on the right."

Carrying Luke, I went to the corner office. A large fanned wedge of windows revealed the skyline, where relentless sunlight ricocheted off a stand of glass-skinned buildings. In contrast to the sterile reception area, the office was comfortably cluttered, with deep leather chairs, and piles of books and folders, and family pictures in black frames.

After positioning a chair for me, Travis half-sat on his desk, facing me. His features were emphatically defined, the nose straight and substantial, the jaw nearly lacerating in its precision.

"Let's make this fast, Ella-from-Austin," he said. "I got a deal on the stringer, and I'd rather not keep those guys waiting."

"You're going to manage property for them?"

"Hotel chain." His gaze flickered to Luke. "You might want to tilt that bottle—she's getting air."

I frowned and adjusted the bottle upward. "It's a boy. Why does everyone assume he's a girl?"

"He's wearing Hello Kitty socks." There was a distinct note of disapproval in his voice.

"They were the only ones available in his size," I said.

"You can't put a boy in pink socks."

"He's only a week old. Do I have to worry about gender bias already?"

"You really are from Austin, aren't you?" he asked wryly. "How can I help you, Ella?"

The task of explaining was so considerable, I hardly knew where to start. "Just so you're prepared," I said in a businesslike tone, "the story I'm going to tell you ends with a stinger."

"I'm used to that. Go on."

"My sister is Tara Varner. You went out with her last year." Seeing that the name didn't ring a bell, I added, "You know Liza Purcell? . . . She's my cousin. She fixed you up with Tara."

Travis thought for a moment. "I remember Tara," he finally said. "Tall, blond, leggy."

"That's right." Seeing that Luke had finished the bottle, I put the empty container in the diaper bag and draped the baby over my shoulder to burp him. "This is Tara's son. Luke. She gave birth to him, left him with my mother, and took off somewhere. We're trying to locate her. Meanwhile I'm trying to secure some kind of situation for the baby."

Travis was very still. The atmosphere in the office took on a hostile chill. I saw that I had been identified as a threat, or perhaps just a nuisance. Either way, his mouth was now edged with contempt.

"I think I get the stinger you're working around to," he said. "He's not mine, Ella."

I forced myself to hold that unnerving black gaze. "According to Tara, he is."

"The Travis name inspires a lot of women to notice a likeness between me and their fatherless children. But it's not possible for two reasons. First, I never have sex without holstering the gun."

Despite the seriousness of the conversation, I wanted to smile at the phrase. "You're referring to a condom? That method of protection has an average failure rate of fifteen percent."

"Thank you, professor. But I'm still not the father."

"How can you be sure?"

"Because I never had sex with Tara. The night I took her out, she drank too much. And I don't sleep with women in that condition."

"Really," I said skeptically.

"Really," came the soft reply.

Luke burped, and settled into the curve of my neck like a sack of pinto beans.

I thought of what Liza had told me about Jack Travis's hyperactive love life, his near-legendary womanizing, and I couldn't prevent a cynical smile. "Because you're a man of high principles?" I asked acidly.

"No, ma'am. It's just that I prefer the woman to participate."

For just a moment I couldn't stop myself from imagining him with a woman, what kind of participation he required, and I was disgruntled to feel scalding color rushing over my face. It only got worse when he gave me a coolly interested glance, as if I were an inept criminal he had just collared.

That made me increasingly determined to stand my ground. "Did you have anything to drink the night you were out with Tara?"

"Probably."

"Then your judgment was impaired. And possibly your memory.

There's no way you can be absolutely certain that nothing happened. And there's no good reason for me to believe you."

Travis was silent, still staring at me. I realized that no detail escaped his notice—the dark circles under my eyes, the scurf of dried baby spit-up on my shoulder, the unthinking way I had curved my hand over Luke's head.

"Ella," he said quietly, "I can't be the only guy you're approaching with this."

"No," I admitted. "If it turns out that you're not the father, then I'm going to have the other lucky candidates served and made to take paternity tests. But I'm giving you the chance to get it done right now, with no fuss and no publicity. Take the test, and if it goes your way, you're out of the picture."

Travis looked at me like I was one of those tiny green lizards that loved to skitter across the thresholds of Texas homes. "I got lawyers who could make you run around in circles for months, honey."

I gave him a mocking smile. "Come on, Jack. Don't deprive me of the pleasure of watching you donate a DNA sample. I'll even pay for it."

"That offer might interest me," he said, "if it involved anything more exciting than a buccal swab."

"I'm sorry. I wish I could take your word about not having slept with Tara. But if you did, you don't have much incentive to admit it, do you?"

He stared at me with eyes the color of burnt coffee. A hot, unfamiliar riff of sensation chased down my spine.

Jack Travis was a big, sexy tomcat, and there was no doubt in my mind that my sister would have given him anything and everything he wanted. And I didn't care if Travis had holstered his gun, double-bagged it, or tied it in a knot. He could probably get a woman pregnant just by winking at her.

"Ella, if you'll allow me . . ." He stunned me by reaching out and gently pulling the glasses from my face. I looked at him through the bewildered blur, and perceived that he was cleaning the smudged lenses with a tissue. "There," he murmured, and replaced them on my face with care.

"Thank you," I managed to whisper, now seeing him in new, breathtaking detail.

"What hotel are you staying at?" I heard him ask, and I struggled to collect my thoughts.

"I don't know yet. I'm going to find something after I leave here."

"No, you won't. There are two conventions going on in Houston. Unless you've got some strings to pull, you'll have to drive clear to Pearland to get a room."

"No strings," I admitted.

"Then you need help."

"Thanks, but I don't—"

"Ella," he interrupted, his tone uncompromising. "I don't have time to argue with you. Complain all you want later, but for now, shut up and follow me." Standing, he reached for the baby.

Mildly startled, I clutched Luke a little more closely.

"It's okay," Travis murmured. "I got him."

His large hands slid between me and the baby, deftly cradling Luke's slumped body and transferring him to the carrier on the floor. I was surprised by the ease with which Travis handled the baby, and also by my own intense awareness of him. The scent of him, fresh like cedar and clean earth, sent pleasure signals to my brain. I saw the shadow of whisker-grain that even the closest shave would never completely remove, and the way the thick locks of black hair had been cut in short, no-nonsense layers.

"You've obviously had experience with babies," I said, fumbling for the diaper bag, making certain the zipper was closed all the way.

"I have a nephew." Travis strapped Luke in securely and lifted the heavy carrier with ease. Without asking permission, he led the way to the front of the office, pausing at one of the doors in the hallway. "Helen," he said to the auburn-haired woman seated at a desk piled with folders, "this is Miss Ella Varner. I need you to find her a hotel room for the next couple of nights. Something close by."

"Yes, sir." Helen gave me a neutral smile and picked up her phone.

"I'm paying for it," I interjected. "Do you need my credit card number, or—"

"We'll take care of the details later," Travis said. He guided me out to the reception area, set Luke down beside a chair, and gestured for me to sit. "Wait here like a good girl," he murmured, "while Helen makes the arrangements."

Good girl? The deliberate chauvinism caused my jaw to drop. My gaze shot up to his, but my indignant reply was forestalled as I saw that he had known exactly what my reaction would be. He also knew that I wasn't in a position to take offense.

Reaching for his wallet, Travis pulled out a business card and handed it to me. "My cell number. I'll be in touch later this evening."

"So you're agreeing to the paternity test?" I asked.

Travis slanted a look at me, his eyes filled with a simmer of challenge.

"I wasn't aware I had a choice," he said, and left the office with long, easy strides.

FOUR

THE HOTEL ROOM HELEN HAD RESERVED FOR ME WAS a luxurious suite with a separate sitting area and a kitchenette outfitted with a sink and a microwave. One look at the hotel—a European-style resort located in the Galleria area—and I knew my credit-card balance was going to be maxed out in a matter of hours. Maybe minutes.

But the suite was gorgeous, the floors thickly carpeted, the bathroom lined with marble tiles and stocked with spa products.

"Time to party," I told Luke. "Let's raid the minibar." I opened the cans of formula I had brought up from the car, made several bottles, and stocked them in the tiny fridge. After lining the sink with a white towel, I filled it with warm water and gave Luke a bath.

When he was clean and fed and drowsy, I laid him in the center of the king-sized bed. As I pulled the curtains over the windows, the afternoon blaze was extinguished by a shroud of slick, heavy brocade. Relishing the cool and quiet of the hotel room, I headed toward the bathroom to take a shower. But I paused as I glanced at the baby again.

Luke was so alone and small, blinking up at the ceiling with quiet forbearance. I couldn't bring myself to leave him while he was still awake. Not while he was waiting so patiently for whatever would happen to him next. I crawled onto the bed and lay next to him, stroking the dark fluff on his head.

Living with Dane, I had heard and discussed and pondered any number of injustices in the world. But it hardly seemed that there could be anything worse than an unwanted child. Lowering my head, I pressed my cheek against his pale baby skin, and kissed the fragile curve of his skull. I watched his lashes lower, and his mouth compress like a grumpy old man's. His hands rested on his chest like tiny pink starfish. I touched one of them with my finger, and his hand closed around it with surprising tightness.

He fell asleep holding my finger. It was an intimacy unlike anything I had ever felt before. And an unfamiliar, sweet pain spread in my chest, as if my heart were cracking open.

I dozed for a little while. After that I took a long shower and dressed in an oversized gray T-shirt and a pair of denim cutoffs. Returning to the bed, I opened my laptop and checked my e-mail. There was one from Liza:

> dear ella, this is a list of guys i know for sure tara went out with. i'll send you more names when i remember them. i feel awful doing this behind tara's back. she has a right to privacy you know . . .

"Like hell," I murmured aloud, reflecting that my sister had given up her right to privacy as soon as she'd left her baby at my mother's house.

. . . i think i know where tara might be, but i'm waiting for someone to call me back before i know for sure. i'll let you know some time tomorrow.

"Liza," I said ruefully, "didn't anyone ever show you how to push the shift key to make a capital letter?"

I opened the attachment containing the list of names and shook my head with a groan, wondering how the file had made it past the size restrictions of the e-mail provider.

I closed and saved it.

Before I got to my other e-mails, I clicked on Google and looked up Jack Travis, curious about what it would bring up.

There was a long list of results, cluttered with references to the father, Churchill Travis, and the oldest brother, Gage.

But there were a few interesting links to Jack, one of them to an article in a national business magazine. It was titled "A Son Also Rises."

Until recent years, Jack Travis, middle son of billionaire Churchill Travis, has had a higher profile on Houston's club scene and nightlife than in the business community. All that is about to change as Jack Travis comes into his own with a slew of projects and public-private ventures that promise to launch him into the top ranks of Texas developers.

Although he is in a different trade from his father, Jack Travis has proved the rule that the apple never falls far from the tree. Yet when asked about his ambitions, Travis presents himself as an accidental businessman. The facts tend to belie his laid-back demeanor and what some label as false modesty.

Exhibit A: Travis Capital, a recently formed subsidiary of Travis Management Solutions, just acquired Alligator Creek, a 300-acre golf course in South Florida for an undisclosed amount after months of negotiations. The course will be managed by a Miami partner company.

Exhibit B: TMS is currently developing a section of downtown Houston, the equivalent of ten Manhattan blocks, into office buildings, apartment buildings, a retail concourse, and a cinema complex, all of which will be managed by a newly formed TMS division. . . .

The article went on to describe other projects in the works. Going back to the results list, I saw a row of thumbnail pictures and clicked on a few of them. My eyes widened as I beheld a photo of a shirtless Jack waterskiing, his body lean and powerful, his stomach a virtual abacus of muscle. Another of Jack and a popular sitcom actress lounging on a Hawaiian beach. Jack and a female news anchor, dancing at a local charity event.

"You're a busy boy, Jack," I murmured.

Before I could open any more pictures, I was interrupted by the ring of my cell phone. Scrambling for my purse, I fished out the phone, hoping the noise wouldn't wake the baby.

"Hello?"

"How's it going?" Dane asked.

I relaxed at the familiar voice. "I'm having a fling with a younger man," I told him. "He's kind of short for me, and there's a little incontinence problem . . . but we're working to get beyond all that."

Dane chuckled. "Are you at your mom's?"

"Ha. She kicked me out first thing this morning. But Luke and I are staying at a chichi hotel. Mr. Travis had his secretary find it for us. I think the per-night cost would just about cover my monthly car payment." As I went on to describe the events of the day, I poured a cup of coffee for myself. I couldn't help grinning privately as I emptied a couple of tiny presealed containers of half-and-half into the brew.

"So Travis agreed to take a paternity test," I finished, sipping the coffee. "And Liza's still trying to track down Tara. And my column is late, so I'm going to have to finish it up tonight."

"You think Travis was lying when he said he didn't sleep with Tara?"

"Maybe not deliberately lying. But I think there's a chance he's mistaken. And obviously he thinks so, too, otherwise he wouldn't have agreed to the paternity test."

"Well, if it is his kid, it'll be a lottery win for Tara, won't it?"

"She would probably look at it that way." I felt a frown tug between my eyebrows. "I hope she won't try to use Luke to get money out of the Travises whenever she wants it. He deserves more than to be treated like an ATM card." I glanced at the small, sleeping form on the bed. Luke was twitching as he slept and dreamed. I wondered what kind of dreams you had when you were only a week old.

Carefully I leaned over and adjusted the baby blanket higher over his chest. "Dane," I said softly, "remember that thing you told me about the duck and the tennis ball? About how baby ducks get attached to the first thing they see after they're born?"

"Imprinting."

"How does that work again? . . ."

"After the duckling is hatched, there's a window of time during which another creature, or even an inanimate object, is stamped onto his nervous system, and he becomes bonded to it. In the study I read, a duckling became imprinted to a tennis ball."

"How long is the window of time?"

Dane's voice was half-wary, half-amused. "Why? Are you afraid you're the tennis ball?"

"I don't know. It's possible Luke is the tennis ball."

I heard him swear softly. "Don't get attached to him, Ella."

"I won't," I said quickly. "I'm coming back to Austin as soon as possible. I'm certainly not going to—" I was interrupted by a knock at the door. "Wait just a second," I told Dane. Padding barefoot through the suite, I unlatched the door and opened it.

Jack Travis stood there, his tie knot loosened and his hair rumpled in waves that fell partially over his forehead. He glanced over me, cataloguing my clean-scrubbed face, my bare legs and feet. Slowly his gaze traveled back up to mine. I felt a dart of heat low in my stomach.

My fingers clenched on the cell phone. "It's room service," I said to Dane. "Let me call you later."

"Sure, babe."

Closing the phone, I took an awkward step back and gestured for Jack to enter the suite. "Hi," I said. "When you said you would be in touch, I was sort of expecting a phone call."

"I'll make it quick. I just dropped off my clients. They're staying here, too. Both of 'em are jet-lagged and ready to call it a day. Your room okay?"

"Yes. Thanks."

We stood facing each other in the thickening silence. My bare, unpolished toes dug into the velvet-pile carpet. I felt at a disadvantage being dressed in shorts and a T-shirt while he was in his business clothes.

"My doctor will see us tomorrow morning for the paternity test," Jack said. "I'll pick you up in the lobby at nine."

"Do you have any idea how long it will take to get the results?"

"Usually three to five days. But the doc's going to fast-track it, so the results might be in as early as tomorrow night. Any word on your sister yet?"

"I think I'll hear something soon."

"If you have any problems, I've got a guy who can find people pretty fast."

"A private detective?" I regarded him doubtfully. "I don't know if he could do anything—there's not much to go on at this point."

"If your sister has a cell phone with her, it would take about fifteen minutes to locate her."

"What if the phone is turned off?"

"If it's one of the newer ones, you can still track it. And there are other ways to get a bead on someone . . . ATM transactions, SSN trace, credit-card records . . ."

Something about his cool, rational tone made me uneasy. He had the mind-set of a hunter, I thought.

Thinking of Tara, worrying, I rubbed my sore temples and closed my eyes for a few seconds. "If I can't reach her by tomorrow," I said, "I'll start thinking along those lines."

"Have you eaten yet?" I heard Jack ask.

"Other than snack food from the minibar, no."

"Do you want to go out to dinner?"

"With you?" Caught off guard by the question, I looked at him in surprise. "You must be having a slow night. Don't you have a harem to get back to or something?"

Jack regarded me with narrowed eyes.

I was instantly contrite. I had not meant to sound bitchy. But in my current state of physical and mental exhaustion, I had no conversational red flags left.

Before I could apologize, Jack asked in a low voice, "Have I done something to you, Ella? Other than help you get a hotel room, and agree to take an unwarranted paternity test?"

"I'm paying for the room. And the paternity test. And if it was all that unwarranted, you wouldn't be taking it."

"I may back out of it now. There's only so much I'll put up with, even for a free buccal swab."

An apologetic grin pulled at the corners of my mouth. "I'm sorry," I said. "I'm hungry and sleep-deprived. I've had no time to prepare for any of this. I can't find my sister, my mother is crazy, and my boyfriend is in Austin. So I'm afraid you're dealing with all my accumulated frustration. And I think on a subconscious level, you represent all the guys who might have knocked up my sister."

Jack gave me a sardonic glance. "It's a lot easier to knock up someone when you actually have sex with her."

"We've already established that you're not one hundred percent certain whether you slept with Tara or not."

"I am one hundred percent certain. The only thing we've established is that you don't believe me."

I had to bite back another smile. "Well, I appreciate the dinner offer. But as you can see, I'm not dressed to go out. And not only am I tired of lugging around this eighty-five-pound baby but there's no place you could take me to because I'm a vegan, and no one in Houston knows how to cook without animal products."

The mention of dinner must have revved up my appetite, because my stomach chose that moment to emit a loud, embarrassing growl. Mortified, I clutched a hand over my midriff. At the same time, an impatient mewl came from the bed, and I looked toward the sound. Luke was awake, his tiny arms waving.

I hurried to the fridge, got a bottle, and put it into a sink of hot water. While the formula was warming, Jack went to the bed and picked up Luke. Holding him in a secure and competent grip, Jack murmured softly to the baby. It made no difference. Luke started squalling, his mouth wide open and his eyes screwed shut.

"There's no use in trying to quiet him." I rummaged in the diaper bag for a burp cloth. "He just screams louder and louder until he gets what he wants."

"Always works for me," Jack said.

After a couple of minutes I took the bottle from the sink, tested it, and went to an upholstered chair. Jack brought Luke to me, settling him in my waiting arms. The baby clamped his gums on the silicone nipple and began to feed.

Jack stood over me, his gaze shrewd. "Why are you a vegan?"

I had learned from experience that a conversation beginning with that question never tended to go well.

"I'd rather not go into that."

"Not an easy diet to stick to," Jack said. "Especially in Texas."

"I cheat," I confessed. "Just in little ways. A pat of butter here, a French fry there."

"You can't have French fries?"

I shook my head. "You never know if they've been cooked in the same oil as fish or meat." I looked down at Luke, brushing my fingertip over the tops of the miniature hands that had clamped on the sides of the bottle. My stomach growled again, even more loudly than the first time. I flushed in embarrassment.

Jack's brows lifted. "Sounds like you haven't eaten in days, Ella."

"I'm starving. I'm always hungry." I sighed. "The reason I eat vegan is because my boyfriend Dane does. I never feel full for more than twenty minutes, and it's hard to keep up my energy."

"Then why do you do it?"

"I like the health benefits. My cholesterol and blood pressure are really low. And my conscience feels better when I eat an animal-free diet."

"I know of some good remedies for an active conscience," he said.

"I'm sure you do."

"It sounds like if it weren't for your boyfriend, you'd be eating meat."

"Probably," I admitted. "But I agree with Dane's take on the issues, and most of the time it's not a problem for me. Unfortunately, I'm temptable."

"I like that in a woman. It almost makes up for your conscience."

I had to laugh at that. He was a rascal, I thought. It was the first time I had ever found that quality appealing in a man. As our gazes caught, he gave me a dazzling grin that could have qualified as a fertility-enhancing treatment. My stomach paused in mid-growl.

Magic DNA, I reminded myself ruefully.

"Jack, you should probably go now."

"I'm not going to leave a starving woman with nothing to eat except stale chips from the minibar. And you sure as hell won't find anything vegan in this hotel."

"There's a restaurant downstairs."

"It's a steakhouse."

"I'm sure they'll have a green salad. And maybe a fruit plate."

"Ella," he chided, looking me over. "Surely you've got a bigger appetite than that."

"Yes. But I have principles. And I try to live by them. Besides, I've learned that every time I fall off the wagon, it's a lot harder to get back on."

Jack stared at me with the smile playing on his lips. Slowly he reached for his tie, pulled the knot free, and removed it. A flush climbed up to my hairline as I watched him. He folded the tie in a leisurely manner and tucked it into the pocket of his suit jacket.

"What are you doing?" I managed to ask.

Jack shrugged out of his jacket and draped it over the arm of a nearby chair. He had the build of an avid outdoorsman, his body lean and tough-looking. Without a doubt there was some serious muscle packed beneath the conservative business attire. As I stared at the robust male in front of me, I felt the involuntary pull of millions of years of evolutionary baggage.

"I'm finding out how temptable you really are."

I let out an unsteady laugh. "Listen, Jack, I don't—"

Holding up a silencing finger, he went to the phone. He dialed, waited a moment, and flipped open the leather-bound guest-services book. "Room service for two," he said into the phone.

I blinked in surprise. "I'm not really comfortable with that idea."

"Why not?"

"Your playboy reputation."

"I had a misspent youth," he conceded. "But it makes me an interesting dinner companion." He returned his attention to the phone. "Yeah, charge it to the room."

"I'm not comfortable with that idea, either," I said.

Jack glanced at me. "Too bad. I'm making it a condition of my doctor's visit tomorrow. If you want a sample of my inner cheek cells, you're going to buy me dinner."

I considered that for a moment. Dinner with Jack Travis . . . alone in a hotel room.

I looked at Luke, who was smacking busily at his bottle. I was holding a baby, I was tired and cranky, and I couldn't remember the last time I had brushed my hair. God knew I was not going to inspire any sexual interest from Jack Travis. He'd had a long day, and he was hungry. He was probably the kind of person who didn't like to eat by himself.

"Okay," I said reluctantly. "But no meat, fish, or dairy for me. That includes butter and eggs. And no honey."

"Why? Bees aren't animals."

"They're arthropods. Just like lobsters and crabs."

"For God's sake—" His attention was diverted by the person on the phone. "Yeah. We'll have a bottle of the Hobbs cabernet."

I wondered how much that was going to cost me. "Could you find out if it's made with animal-derived fining products?"

Jack ignored that and continued to order. "We'll start with the slow-cooked duck eggs on a bed of chorizo sausage. And two bone-in cowboy rib eyes of grass-fed Angus. Medium."

"What?" My eyes went huge. "What are you doing?"

"I'm ordering a couple of slabs of USDA Prime beef," he informed me. "It's called protein."

"You sadistic bastard," I managed to say, while saliva spiked in my mouth. I couldn't remember the last time I'd had a steak.

Reading my expression, Jack flashed a grin and turned his attention back to the phone. "Baked potatoes," he said. "The works. Sour cream, bacon . . ."

"And cheese," I heard myself say dazedly. Real cheese that actually melted. I swallowed hard.

"And cheese," Jack repeated. He glanced at me, an evil gleam in his eyes. "What about dessert?"

All thoughts of resistance fled. If I was going to break every vegan rule and dietary principle, betraying Dane in the process, I might as well do a thorough job of it.

"Something chocolate," I heard myself say breathlessly.

Jack scanned the menu. "Two pieces of chocolate cake. Thanks." Setting the phone down, he sent me a triumphant glance.

It still wasn't too late. I could insist that he cancel my half of the order and replace it with a green salad, a plain potato, and steamed vegetables. But I had gone weak-kneed at the thought of a rib eye.

"How long until they bring my steak?" I asked.

"Thirty-five minutes."

"I should have told you to go to hell," I muttered.

He smiled smugly. "I knew you wouldn't."

"How?"

"Because women who are willing to cheat a little can always be talked into cheating a lot." Jack laughed as I frowned at him. "Relax, Ella. Dane never has to know."

FIVE

A PAIR OF WAITERS BROUGHT A FEAST TO THE HOTEL room and arranged it in the sitting area. They unfolded the hot cart into a table, draped it in white linen, and brought out silver-domed plates. By the time the wine was poured and all the dishes were uncovered, I was trembling with hunger.

Luke, however, became fractious after I changed his diaper, and he howled every time I tried to set him down. Holding him against one shoulder, I contemplated the steaming grilled steak in front of me and wondered how I was going to manage with only one hand.

"Let me," Jack murmured, and came to my side of the table. He cut the steak into small, neat bites with such adroitness that I gave him a look of mock-alarm.

"You certainly know how to handle a knife."

"I hunt whenever I get the chance." Finishing the task, Jack set down the utensils and tucked a napkin into the neckline of my shirt. His knuckles brushed my skin, eliciting a shiver. "I can field-dress a deer in fifteen minutes," he told me.

"That's impressive. Disgusting, but impressive."

He gave me an unrepentant grin as he returned to his side of the table. "If it makes you feel better, I eat anything I catch or kill."

"Thanks, but that doesn't make me feel better in the least. Oh, I'm aware that meat doesn't magically appear all nicely packaged in foam and cellophane at the grocery store. But I have to stay several steps removed from the process. I don't think I could eat meat if I had to hunt the animal and . . ."

"Skin and gut it?"

"Yes. Let's not talk about that right now." I took a bite of the steak. Either it was the long period of deprivation, or the quality of the beef, or the skill of the chef . . . but that succulent, lightly smoked, melting-hot steak was the best thing I had ever tasted. I closed my eyes for a moment, my tonsils quivering.

He laughed quietly at my expression. "Admit it, Ella. It's not so bad being a carnivore."

I reached for a chunk of bread and dabbed it in soft yellow butter. "I'm not a carnivore, I'm an opportunistic omnivore." I bit into the dense bread and savored the sweet richness of fresh butter. I had forgotten how good food could taste. Sighing, I forced myself to go slowly and appreciate it.

His gaze didn't stray from my face. "You're a smart woman, Ella."

"Are you intimidated by a woman with a big vocabulary?"

"Hell, yes. Any woman with an IQ higher than room temperature, and I'm gone. Unless she's paying for dinner."

"I could play dumb and *you* could pay for dinner," I offered.

"Too late. You already used a five-syllable word."

Feeling how heavy Luke had gotten, I realized he was asleep. Time to put him down. "Excuse me . . ." I tried to push away from the table. Instantly Jack was by my side, pulling back the chair.

I went to the bed and gently laid the baby down, covering him with a knit blanket. Returning to the table, where Jack was still standing, I sat while he pushed the chair in for me. "This experience with Luke," I said, "has confirmed everything I've ever thought about motherhood. Mainly that it's something I'll never be ready to do."

"So if you marry Dane, you'll wait awhile before having one of those?" He nodded in Luke's direction.

I dug into my potato, picking up a forkful of fluffy white starch saturated with butter and covered with melted aged cheddar. "Oh, Dane and I won't ever get married."

Jack gave me an alert glance. "Why not?"

"Neither of us believes in it. It's just a piece of paper."

He appeared to consider that. "I've never understood why people say something is just a piece of paper. Some pieces of paper are worth a hell of a lot. Diplomas. Contracts. Constitutions."

"In those cases, I agree the paper is worth something. But a marriage contract and all that goes with it, the ring, the big meringue-puff wedding dress, doesn't mean anything. I could make Dane a legal promise that I would love him forever, but how can I be certain I will? You can't legislate emotions. You can't own someone else. So the union is basically a property-sharing agreement. And of course if there are children, you have to work out the terms for co-parenting . . . but all of that can be handled without marriage. The institution has outlived its usefulness." I took a bite of buttery cheese-topped potato, which was so rich and delicious that eating it seemed like something I should be doing in private with the shades down.

"It's natural to want to belong to someone," Jack said.

"One person can't belong to another person. At best, it's an illusion. At worst, it's slavery."

"No," he said. "Just a need for attachment."

"Well . . ." I paused to take another bite of the potato. "I can feel plenty attached to someone without needing to turn it into a legal agreement. In fact, I could argue that my perspective is a more romantic one. The only thing keeping two people together should be love. Not legalities."

Jack drank some wine and leaned back, watching me speculatively. He continued to hold the glass, his long fingers curved lightly around the crystal bowl. It was not at all what I would have expected a rich man's hand to look like, brown and roughed-up, nails clipped close to the quick. Not a graceful hand, and yet attractive in its calloused power . . . holding the fragile glass so gently. . . . I couldn't help staring.

And for one second I imagined the touch of those blunt-tipped fingers on my skin, and I was instantly, disgracefully aroused.

"What do you do in Austin, Ella?"

The question ripped me away from the dangerous thoughts. "I'm an advice columnist. I write about relationships."

Jack's face went blank. "You write about relationships and you don't believe in marriage?"

"Not for myself. But that doesn't mean I disapprove of marriage for other people. If that's the format they choose for their commitment, I'm all for it." I grinned at him. "Miss Independent gives great advice to married people."

"Miss Independent."

"Yes."

"Is it some kind of male-bashing column?"

"Not at all. I like men. I'm a big fan of your gender. On the other hand, I often remind women that we don't need a man to feel complete."

"Shit." He was shaking his head and smiling faintly.

"You don't like liberated women?"

"I do. But they take a lot more work."

I wasn't sure what kind of work he was talking about. And I certainly wasn't going to ask.

"So I guess you know all the answers." Jack leveled a steady gaze at me.

I made a face, disliking the implication of arrogance in that. "I would never claim to know all the answers. I just want to help other people find answers, if possible."

We talked about my column, and then discovered that we had both graduated from UT, although Jack's class had been six years ahead of mine. We also found that we shared an appreciation for Austin jazz.

"I used to go listen to the Crying Monkeys whenever they played the Elephant Room," Jack said, referring to the famous basement room on Congress Street, where some of the top musicians in the world performed. "My friends and I would sit there for hours, taking in that easy-sprawl jazz and drinking straight Jim Beam . . ."

"And picking up women left and right."

His mouth tightened. "I date a lot of women. But I don't have sex with everyone I go out with."

"That's a relief," I said. "Because if you did, you should probably get more than your inner cheek cells tested at the doctor's office."

"I have other interests besides chasing women."

"Yes, I know. You also chase terrified deer."

"And again, for the record, I did not sleep with your sister."

I sent him a skeptical look. "She said you did. Your word against hers. And you wouldn't be the first guy to duck and dodge a situation like this."

"She wouldn't be the first woman to lie about who knocked her up."

"You took her out. You can't deny that you were interested in her."

"Sure, I was interested. At first. But five minutes after the date started, I knew I wasn't going to sleep with her. There were warning signals."

"Such as?"

His gaze turned contemplative. "It was like she was trying too hard. Laughing too loud. Constantly nervous. The questions and answers didn't connect."

I understood what he was trying to express. "Hyper-vigilant," I said. "Manic. Like any little thing might make her jump out of her skin. Like she was always trying to think two steps ahead."

"Exactly."

I nodded as I sorted through memories that were never far below the surface. "It's because of how we were raised. My parents divorced when I was five and Tara was three, and after that Dad was out of the picture. So we were left alone with my mother, who makes everyone around her crazy. Explosions. Drama. There was no such thing as a normal day. Living with her all those years trained Tara and me to expect disaster at any moment. We both developed a lot of coping mechanisms, including hyper-vigilance. It's a hard habit to get rid of."

Jack watched me intently. "You did, though."

"I had a lot of counseling in college. But mostly I'm okay because of Dane. He taught me that living with another person doesn't have to mean daily chaos and drama. I don't think Tara has ever had someone stable like Dane in her life." I nudged my wineglass toward him, and he obligingly refilled it. Staring moodily into the inky depths of cabernet, I continued. "I feel guilty for not staying in touch with her the past couple of years. But I was tired of trying to save her. It was all I could do to save myself."

"No one could blame you for that," he murmured. "You're not your sister's keeper. Let it go, Ella."

I was puzzled by a sense of connection, of being understood, that made no sense at all. He was a stranger. And I was telling him far too much. I decided I must have been even more tired than I'd thought. I tried to summon a casual smile. "I have to work up my daily quota of guilt over something. Today it might as well be Tara." Picking up my wine, I took a swallow. "So," I said, "what's a guy from a family of financial gurus doing in property management? Are you the black sheep?"

"No, just the middle sheep. I can't stand talking about investment strategies, leveraging, buying on margin. . . . None of it interests me. I like building things. Fixing things. I'm a nuts-and-bolts guy."

It occurred to me as I listened to Jack that he and Dane had one rare quality in common: each man knew exactly who he was, and was entirely comfortable with it.

"I started working at a management company out of college," Jack continued, "and eventually got a loan and bought the business."

"Did your dad help you?"

"Hell, no." A rueful grin. "I made mistakes he probably would have steered me away from. But I didn't want anyone saying he'd done it for me. I took responsibility for all the risk. And I had a lot to prove, so I sure as hell didn't want to fail."

"Obviously you didn't." I studied him. "Interesting. You seem like the alpha male type, but you're the middle son. Usually middle children are more laid-back."

"For a Travis, I am laid-back."

"Eek." I grinned and began on my chocolate cake. "I'm kicking you out after dessert, Jack. I have a long night ahead of me."

"How often does the baby wake up?"

"About every three hours."

We finished dessert and the rest of the wine. Jack went to the phone, dialed for room service to collect the table, and picked up his jacket.

Pausing at the door, he looked down at me. "Thanks for dinner."

"You're welcome. And I warn you, if you back out of the doctor's visit after this, I'm going to take out a hit on you."

"I'll pick you up at nine." Jack didn't move. We were standing close, and I was disconcerted to feel my breath quicken. Although his posture was relaxed and easy, he was so much bigger than me that I had a subtle sense of being physically dominated. What surprised me was that the feeling wasn't entirely unpleasant.

"Is Dane the alpha type?" he asked.

"No. Beta all the way. I can't stand alphas."

"Why? Do they make you nervous?"

"Not at all." I gave him a mock-threatening glance. "I eat alpha males for breakfast."

There was a spark of mischief in his dark eyes. "I'll be over here early, then." And he left before I could manage a reply.

SIX

I WOULDN'T HAVE BELIEVED IT POSSIBLE, BUT MY second night with Luke was even worse than the first. The glow of contentment I'd gotten from an amazing steak dinner, fine wine, and lively conversation was completely gone by the second feeding. "You're a real mood-killer, Luke," I told the baby, who didn't seem concerned in the least. I lost count of how many times he woke and how many diapers I changed, but it seemed like I didn't get more than twenty minutes of continuous sleep. When the wake-up call came at seven-thirty, I crawled painfully out of bed and staggered to the bathroom to brush my teeth and to take a shower.

A fifteen-minute shower and two cups of stale-tasting coffee from the miniature countertop coffeemaker revived me somewhat. I dressed in khakis and a light blue shirt with elbow-length sleeves, and flat braided-hemp sandals. I debated whether or not to blow-dry my hair, afraid the noise would wake the baby, and then I decided grimly that he would damn well have to cry.

After drying my hair into a smooth bob, I switched off the appliance.

Silence.

Had something happened to Luke? Why was he so quiet? I rushed into the bedroom and checked on him. He was lying peacefully on his back, his chest rising and falling, cheeks watercolor-pink. I touched him just to make sure he was okay. He yawned and closed his eyes more tightly.

"*Now* you want to sleep," I muttered. I sat beside him, staring at the remarkably fine skin, the delicate lashes, the tiny drowsing features. His eyebrows were so sparse and silky, they were almost invisible. He looked like Tara. I could make out the resemblance in the shape of the nose and mouth—although the hair was inky-dark. Like Jack Travis's, I thought, fingering the soft strands.

Leaving the bed, I went to detach my cell phone from its plug-in charger. I dialed my cousin Liza.

She picked up immediately. "Hello?"

"It's Ella."

"How's the baby?"

"He's fine. Have you made any progress on finding Tara? Because if not—"

"I found her," Liza said triumphantly.

My eyes widened. "What? Where is she? Did you talk to her?"

"Not directly. But there's this guy she goes to sometimes when she's having a tough time . . ."

"Goes to?" I repeated warily. "You mean, like dating?"

"Not dating, exactly. He's married. Anyway, I thought Tara might have gone to him. So I found his number and left a message for him, and he finally called me back. He says she's okay, and she's been with him the past couple of days."

"Who is this guy?"

"I can't tell you. He wants his name kept out of this."

"I'll bet he does. Liza, I want to know exactly what is happening to my sister, and where she is, and—"

"She's at a clinic in New Mexico."

My heartbeat accelerated to a pace that made me light-headed. "What kind of clinic? Rehab? Is she doing drugs?"

"No, no, it's not drugs. I think she had a breakdown or something."

The word "breakdown" scared me, making my voice ragged as I asked, "What's the name of the place?"

"Mountain Valley Wellness."

"Did this guy you mentioned check her in? Did she check herself in? What kind of shape is she in?"

"I don't know. You'll have to ask her yourself."

My eyes screwed shut as I forced myself to ask, "Liza . . . she . . . didn't try to hurt herself, did she?"

"Oh, nothing like that. From what I can tell, having the baby was too much for her to handle. Maybe she needs a vacation."

That drew a mirthless smile from me as I reflected that Tara needed a lot more than a vacation.

"Anyway," my cousin said, "here's the number of the place. And I think you can reach her by cell now."

I took down the information, ended the call, and headed straight for my laptop.

A Google search of the clinic revealed that it was a short-term residential treatment center located in a small town near Santa Fe. The pictures on the Web site made it look more like a spa or a vacation resort than a mental health clinic. In fact, a few holistic therapies and nutritional classes were mentioned. But the place also appeared to have a certified and licensed professional staff and intensive psychiatric services. The "treatments" page described an emphasis on mind and body wellness, with the goal of using minimal or no medication.

Mountain Valley Wellness looked kind of lightweight for a person who might have had a breakdown. Did they have the resources to help her? Did they dispense psychological advice along with facials and pedicures?

Although I badly wanted to call the admissions office, I knew there was no way they would violate the confidentiality of one of their patients.

Sitting at the desk in the corner of the room, I clasped my head in my hands. I wondered how messed up my sister was. Fear, pity, anguish, anger, all tangled inside me as I reflected that it would be nearly impossible for most people to function well, having been brought up the way we had.

I thought of my mother's histrionic fits, the bizarre twists of logic, the wild impulses that had confused and frightened us. All those men coming and going, all part of Mom's desperate search to make herself happy. But no one and nothing ever had. Our lives had not been normal, and our efforts to pretend otherwise had imposed a bitter isolation on Tara and me. We had grown up knowing we were different from everyone else.

Neither of us seemed able to be close to anyone. Not even each other. Closeness meant the one you loved the most would cause you the most damage. How did you unlearn that? It was woven deep between every fiber and vessel. You couldn't cut it out.

Slowly I picked up the phone and dialed Tara's cell number. This time, unlike all my previous efforts, she picked up. "Hello?"

"Tara, it's me."

"Ella."

"Are you okay?"

"Yeah, I'm fine." My sister's voice was high and wavering. The voice of a young child. The sound brought back a thousand memories. I remembered the child she had been. I remembered reading to her those days and nights when we had been left alone for far too long, when there wasn't enough to eat and we had no idea where our mom was. I had read books about magical creatures, intrepid children, adventurous rabbits. And Tara had listened and listened, gathered tightly against my side, and I hadn't complained even though we were both hot and sweaty because there was no air-conditioning.

"Hey," I said softly. "What's going on with you?"

"Oh . . . not much."

We both snickered. I was relieved that even if my sister had possibly lost her mind, she still had a sense of humor.

"Tara Sue . . ." I wandered to the bed to glance at Luke. "You're the only person I know who hates surprises as much as I do. Is a little advance warning too much to ask? You could have called me. E-mailed. Sent me a 'what I did over summer vacation' essay. Instead, I get a call from Mom the night before last."

A long silence passed. "Is she mad at me?"

"She's always mad," I said reasonably. "If you want to know how she reacted to Luke . . . well, I think if it had ever occurred to her that either of us would have ever committed the unpardonable sin of making her a grandmother, she would have had us both sterilized before puberty. Luckily for Luke, Mom's not much of a long-term thinker."

Now Tara sounded tearful. "Is he all right?"

"He's great," I said at once. "Healthy and eating well."

"I guess . . . I guess you're wondering why I dropped him off with Mom."

"Yes. But before you tell me about that, where are you? At that clinic Liza told me about?"

"Yes, I got here last night. It's a nice place, Ella. I have a private room. I can come and go any time I want. They're saying I should probably stay at least three months."

I was struck silent. Why three months? How did they know that was the necessary amount of time to deal with Tara's problems? Had they taken stock and concluded she was only three months' worth of crazy? Surely if she were suicidal or psychotic, they'd want to keep her longer. Or was it possible they didn't want to reveal the truth to Tara, that she had been enrolled in their extended residency program? There were about a dozen questions I wanted to ask at once, all of them so urgent that they bottlenecked and I couldn't get out a sound. I cleared my throat, trying to relieve it of clotted words that tasted like salt.

As if she sensed my helplessness, Tara said, "My friend Mark bought me a plane ticket and made the arrangements."

Mark. The married man.

"Do you want to be there?" I asked gently.

A whisper. "I don't want to be anywhere, Ella."

"Have you talked to anyone yet?"

"Yes, a woman. Dr. Jaslow."

"Do you like her?"

"She seems nice."

"Do you feel like she can help you?"

"I think so. I don't know."

"What did you talk about?"

"I told her how I'd dropped Luke off with Mom. I didn't mean to do it, just leaving the baby there like that."

"Can you tell me why you did it, sweetie? Did something happen?"

"After I left the hospital with Luke, I went home to the apartment with Liza for a couple of days. But everything was weird. The baby didn't seem like mine. I didn't know how to act like a parent."

"Of course not. Our parents didn't act like parents. You had no example to go by."

"It was like I couldn't stand one more second of being in my own skin. Every time I looked at Luke, I didn't know if I was feeling what I was supposed to feel. And then it was like I was floating outside my body and I was fading away. Even after I came back into myself, I was in a fog. I think I'm still in it. I hate it." A long silence, and then Tara asked tentatively, "Am I going crazy, Ella?"

"No," I said immediately. "I had the same problem a few times. The therapist I saw in Austin told me that spacing-out like that is sort of an escape route we work out for ourselves. A way to get past trauma."

"Do you still get it sometimes?"

"That detached out-of-body feeling? . . . Not for a long time. A therapist can help you get to where you stop doing it."

"You know what's making me crazy, Ella?"

Yes. I knew. But I asked, "What?"

"I try to think about what it was like for us, living with Mom and all her conniptions, and all those men she brought in the house . . . and the only parts I can remember clearly are the times I was with you . . . when you made me dinner in the toaster oven, and when you read stories to me. Stuff like that. But the rest of it is a big blank. And when I try to remember things, I start to feel scared and dizzy."

My voice, when I could reply, came out thick and halting, like heavy frosting I was trying to spread on a fragile cake. "Did you tell Dr. Jaslow any of the things I told you about Roger?"

"I told her some of it," she said.

"Good. Maybe she can help you remember more."

I heard a shaky sigh. "It's hard."

"I know, Tara."

There was a long silence. "When I was little, I felt like a dog living with electric fencing. Except that Mom kept moving the fencing around. I was never sure where to go to keep from being zapped. She was crazy, Ella."

"Was?" I asked dryly.

"But no one ever wanted to hear about it. People didn't want to believe a mother could be like that."

"I believe it. I was there."

"But you haven't been around for me to talk to. You went to Austin. You left me."

Until that moment I had never felt guilt so intensely that all my nerves screamed simultaneously with the hurt of it. I had been so desperate to escape that smothering life, with all its soul-destroying patterns, that I had left my sister behind to fend for herself. "I'm sorry," I managed to say. "I—"

There was a knock at the door.

It was nine-fifteen. I was supposed to have been in the lobby with Luke, waiting for Jack Travis.

"Shit," I muttered. "Wait a second, Tara—it's housekeeping. Don't hang up."

"Okay."

I went to the door, opened it, and gestured for Jack Travis to come in with a sharp motion of my hand. I was in a flurry, feeling as if I were about to fly apart.

Jack entered the room. Something about his presence quieted the hard-thumping clamor in my ears. His eyes were black and fathomless. He gave me an alert glance, taking full measure of the situation. With a short nod that conveyed *Everything's cool*, he went to the bed and looked down at the sleeping baby.

He was dressed in slightly baggy jeans and a green polo shirt with slits on the sides, the kind of outfit a man could only wear if he had a perfect physique and didn't give a damn about appearing taller, more muscular, leaner, because he already was all those things.

My senses stung with primal warning as I saw the powerfully built male standing over the baby, who was too helpless even to roll over on his own. For a split second I was amazed by my own protective instincts over a child who wasn't even mine. I was a tigress, ready to pounce. But I relaxed as I saw Jack rearrange the baby blanket over Luke's tiny chest.

I sat on an ottoman, positioned by an overstuffed chair. "Tara," I said carefully, "I'm a little confused about your friend Mark's involvement in this. Is he paying for your stay at the clinic?"

"Yeah."

"I want to pay for it. I don't want you to owe him anything."

"Mark would never ask me to pay it back."

"I meant owing him something in an emotional sense. It's hard to say no to someone after they've dropped this kind of money on you. I'm your sister. I'll take care of it."

"It's okay, Ella." Her voice was bruised with annoyance and exhaustion. "Forget about it. That's not what I need from you."

I was prying as gingerly as I could. It was like trying to remove petals from the heart of a flower without making the whole thing fall apart. "Is he the baby's father?"

"The baby doesn't have a father. He's just mine. Please don't ask about it. With all the shit I'm dealing with right now—"

"Okay," I said hastily. "Okay. It's just . . . if you don't establish paternity for Luke, he won't be legally entitled to any support from the father. And if you ever want to apply to the state for any kind of financial assistance, they're going to insist on knowing who the other parent is."

"I won't need to do that. Luke's daddy is going to help out when I need it. But he doesn't want any custody or visitation or anything like that."

"You know that for sure? He said so?"

"Yes."

"Tara . . . Liza said you told her it was Jack Travis."

I saw Jack's back tense, rows of sturdy muscle flexing beneath the fine green mesh of his shirt.

"It's not," she said flatly. "I only told her that because she kept on asking about it, and I knew that would shut her up."

"Are you sure? Because I was ready to make him take a paternity test."

"Oh, God. Ella, do *not* bother Jack Travis with this. He's not the father. I never even slept with him."

"Why did you tell Liza you did?"

"I don't know. I guess it made me embarrassed, him not wanting me, and I didn't want to admit it to Liza."

"I don't think there was any reason for you to feel embarrassed," I said softly. "I think he was being a gentleman." Out of the corner of my eye, I saw Jack sit on the edge of the bed. I felt his gaze on me.

"Whatever." My sister sounded exhausted and aggrieved. "I have to go."

"No. Wait. Just a couple of things. Tara, would you mind if I talk with Dr. Jaslow?"

"Okay."

I was surprised by her ready acceptance. "Thank you. Tell her it's okay to talk to me. She'll want written permission. And the other thing . . . Tara . . . what do you want done with Luke while you're at the clinic?"

There was a silence so prolonged and absolute, I wondered if the phone connection had been broken.

"I thought you would take care of him," Tara finally said.

My forehead felt like it had been tacked against my skull. I rubbed it, moving the tight skin, pressing hard into the little shallow where the top of my nose fused into orbital bone. I was trapped. Cornered. "I don't think I could talk Dane into that."

"You could move in with Liza. Take up my half of the rent."

I stared blindly at the hotel room door and thought it was probably a good thing Tara couldn't see the look on my face. I was already paying half of a monthly rent with Dane. And the idea of moving in with my cousin, who would be bringing men into the apartment at all hours . . . not to mention Liza's reaction to living with a screaming infant . . . no, that would never work.

Tara spoke again, every word pulled tight, like a string of rattling cans. "You have to figure it out. I can't think about it. I don't know what to tell you. Hire someone. I'll ask Mark to pay for it."

"Can I talk to Mark?"

"No," she said vehemently. "Just decide what you want to do. But all I need is for you to take care of the baby for three months. Three months out of your whole life, Ella! Can't you do that for me? It's the only thing I've ever asked from you! Can't you help me, Ella? Can't you?"

Her voice was hemmed with panic and fury. I heard my mother's tone as Tara spoke, and it frightened me.

"Yes," I said gently. I repeated it until she subsided. "Yes . . . yes."

And then we were both wordless, breathing into the phone.

Three months, I thought bleakly, for Tara to come to terms with an entire screwed-up childhood and all its crippling echoes. Could she do it? And could I keep my own life from imploding until then?

"Tara . . . ," I said after a few moments, "if I'm a part of this, I'm a part of this. You'll let me talk to Dr. Jaslow. And you'll let me talk to *you*. I won't call often, but when I do, don't avoid me. You'll want to hear how the baby's doing, right?"

"Okay. Yes."

"And for the record," I couldn't resist adding, "this isn't the only thing you've ever asked of me."

Her papery laugh rustled in my ear.

Before Tara hung up, she told me her room number and a landline I could use to reach her at the clinic. Although I wanted to talk to her longer, she ended the conversation abruptly. I closed the cell phone and wiped its sweaty surface against my jeans, and set it aside with undue care. Dazed, I tried to catch up with everything that was happening. It was like running after a moving car.

"Who the hell is Mark?" I wondered aloud.

I was paralyzed. I didn't move or look up even when Jack Travis's shoes came into my line of vision. Rugged leather slip-ons with heavy stitching. He held something between his fingers . . . a folded slip of paper. Without a word he gave it to me.

Opening the paper, I saw the address of the New Mexico clinic, and below it, the name *Mark Gottler*, accompanied by a phone number and an address for the Fellowship of Eternal Truth.

Bewildered, I shook my head. "Who is he? What does a church have to do with this?"

"Gottler is the associate pastor." Jack lowered to his haunches in front of me, bringing our faces level. "Tara checked into the clinic with one of his credit card numbers."

"My God. How did you—" I broke off, passing my palm across the sweaty surface of my forehead. "Wow," I said unsteadily. "Your investigator really *is* good. How did he get this information so fast?"

"I called him yesterday right after I met you."

Of course. With the unimaginable resources at his disposal, Jack would have had everything checked out. No doubt he'd had me checked out as well.

I glanced down at the paper again. "How did my sister get involved with a married church pastor?"

"Seems the temp agency she works for sends her there from time to time."

"To do what?" I asked bitterly. "Pass around the collection plate?"

"It's a megachurch. Big business. They hire MBAs, offer investment counseling, run their own restaurant. It looks damn near like Disneyland. Thirty-five thousand members and rising. Gottler's on TV whenever the main pastor needs a substitute." He watched as I plaited my fingers together, letting the addresses and phone numbers flutter to the floor. "My company has a couple of maintenance contracts with Eternal Truth. I've met Gottler a couple of times."

I looked at him sharply. "Really? What is he like?"

"Smooth. Friendly. Family guy. Doesn't seem like the kind who'd step out on his wife."

"They never do," I muttered. Before I realized what I was doing, I had formed my hands into the children's game—*here is the church . . . here is the steeple. . . .* I pulled my fingers apart and knotted my hands into fists. "Tara wouldn't admit that he was the father. But why else would he be doing this for her now?"

"Only one way to know for sure. But I doubt he'd be willing to take a paternity test."

"No," I agreed, trying to absorb it all. "Bastard children aren't exactly career-boosters for TV preachers." The air-conditioning seemed to have dropped the room temperature to sub-zero. I was shivering. "I need to meet with him. How would I go about that?"

"I wouldn't advise waltzing in there without an appointment. My office is pretty laid-back about stuff like that. But you'd never get past the front door of Eternal Truth."

I decided to be more direct. "Could you help me get a meeting with Gottler?"

"I'll think about it."

That meant no, I thought. My nose and lips were numb. I looked past Jack's shoulder to the bed, wondering if the baby was cold.

"He's okay," Jack said gently, as if he could read my thoughts. "Everything's going to be okay, Ella."

I jumped a little as I felt his hand close over one of mine. I gave him a round-eyed glance, wondering what he wanted. But there was nothing suggestive in his touch or his gaze.

His hand was startling in its strength and heat. Something about that vital grip animated me like a drug injected straight into my bloodstream. Such an intimate thing, the clasp of hands. The comfort and pleasure I derived from it were unspeakably disloyal to Dane. But before I could object or even fully absorb the sensation, the warm touch was withdrawn.

All my life, I'd had to grapple with the needs engendered by the lack of a father. It had left me with a deeply buried attraction to strong men, men with the capacity to dominate, and that terrified me. So I had always gone in the other direction, toward men like Dane who made you kill your own spiders and carry your own suitcase. That was exactly what I wanted. And yet someone like Jack Travis, unimpeachably male, so damned sure of himself, held a secret, nearly fetishistic allure to me.

I had to lick my dry lips before I could speak. "You didn't sleep with Tara."

Jack shook his head, his gaze locked on mine.

"I'm sorry," I said humbly. "I was certain you had."

"I know."

"I don't know why I was so stubborn about it."

"Don't you?" he murmured.

I blinked. I could still feel the part of my hand he had gripped. My fingers flexed to retain the sensation. "Well," I said, oddly out of breath, "you're free to go now. Cancel the doctor's visit, you're off the hook. I promise never to bother you again."

I stood, and so did Jack, and his body was so close I could almost feel the solid warmth of him. Too close. I would have stepped back, except the ottoman was right behind me.

"You're taking care of the baby until your sister is back on her feet," he said rather than asked.

I nodded.

"How long?"

"She said three months." I tried to sound collected. "I'm going to be optimistic and assume it won't be any more than that."

"You gonna take him to Austin?"

My shoulders hitched in a helpless shrug. "I'll call Dane. I'll . . . I don't know how this will work."

It wasn't going to work. I knew Dane well enough to be certain that there was serious trouble ahead for us.

It occurred to me that I might lose him over this.

The day before yesterday, my life had been great. Now it was falling apart. How was I going to make room in my life for a baby? How was I going to get my work done? How was I going to hold on to Dane?

A little cry floated from the bed. Somehow that sound brought everything into focus. Dane didn't matter at the moment. Logistics, money, careers, none of it mattered. Right now the only important thing was the hunger of a helpless infant.

"Call me when you decide what to do," Jack said.

Heading to the minibar, I rummaged for a bottle of chilled formula. "I'm not going to bother you anymore. Really. I'm just sorry I—"

"Ella." He came to me in a couple of relaxed strides, catching me by the elbows as I straightened. I tensed at the feel of it, being lightly gripped by those warm rough-cast fingers. He waited until I could bring myself to look up at him.

"You're not involved," I said, trying to sound grateful but dismissive. Absolving him.

Jack wouldn't let me look away. "Call me when you decide."

"Sure." I had no intention of ever seeing him again, and we both knew it.

His lips twitched.

I stiffened. I didn't like it when someone found me amusing.

"Later, Ella."

And he was gone.

Luke squawked from the bed.

"I'm coming," I told him, and hurried to get his bottle ready.

SEVEN

I FED LUKE AND CHANGED HIS DIAPER. CALLING Dane would have to wait until Luke was ready to rest again. I realized I was already starting to arrange my life according to Luke's patterns. His eating and sleeping and periods of wakefulness formed the structure around which everything else had to be interpolated.

Settling him on his back, I hung over him, crooning bits and pieces from nursery songs, dredging them up from childhood memory. Luke bobbed and arched, following me with his mouth, his eyes. I took one of his waving hands and pressed it to my cheek. His palms were the size of quarters. He kept his hand on me, staring in absorption at my face, seeking the connection as much as I did.

I had never been so wanted or needed by anyone on earth. Babies were dangerous . . . they made you fall in love before you knew what was happening. This small, solemn creature couldn't even say my name, and he depended on me for everything. Everything. I'd known him for little more than a day. But I would have thrown myself in front of a bus for him. I was shattered by him. This was awful.

"I love you, Luke," I whispered.

He looked completely unsurprised by the revelation. *Of course you love me,* his expression seemed to say. *I'm a baby. This is what I do.* His hand flexed a little on my cheek, testing its pliancy.

His fingernails were scratchy. How did you trim a baby's nails? Could you do it with regular adult clippers, or did you need some special tool? I lifted his feet and kissing the little pink soles, innocently smooth as kitten paws. "Where's your instruction manual?" I asked him. "What's the baby customer-service number?"

I realized I had not given my married friend Stacy nearly enough respect or understanding when she'd had her baby. I had tried to work up some sympathetic interest, but I'd had no idea what she'd been faced with. You couldn't until you faced it yourself. Had she felt this overwhelmed, this ill equipped for the responsibility of growing a person? I'd always heard that women possessed an instinct for this, some hidden cache of maternal wisdom that unlocked when you needed it.

No such feeling was coming to me.

The only thing I could identify was a powerful urge to call my best friend Stacy and whine. And having always believed in the therapeutic value of the occasional good, thorough whine, I called her. I was in new territory, the perils and pitfalls of which were entirely familiar to Stacy. She had dated Dane's best friend Tom for years, which was how I'd gotten to know her. And then she'd accidentally gotten pregnant by Tom, and he'd done the expected thing and married her. The baby, a girl named Tommie, was now three. Stacy and Tom both swore it was the best thing that had ever happened to them. Tom even seemed to mean it.

Dane and Tom were still best friends, but I knew that privately Dane thought of Tom as a sell-out. Once, Tom had been a liberal activist and rugged individualist, and now he was married and owned a minivan with stained seat-belt straps and a floor littered with empty juice boxes and Happy Meal toys.

"Stace," I said urgently, relieved when she picked up the phone. "It's me. Do you have a minute?"

"Sure do. How are you, girl?" I pictured her standing in the kitchen of her small renovated arts-and-crafts house, eyes bright as lollipops in her smooth mocha complexion, intricately braided hair knotted up to bare the back of her neck.

"Doomed," I told her. "I am absolutely doomed."

"Problems with the column?" she asked sympathetically.

I hesitated. "Yes. I have to come up with advice for a single woman whose younger sister had a baby out of wedlock and wants her to take care of it for at least three months. Meanwhile, the younger sister is going to stay in a mental health clinic and try to get sane enough to be a mother."

"That's tough," Stacy said.

"It gets worse. The older sister lives in Austin with a boyfriend who's already told her she can't bring the baby back to live with them."

"Asshole," she said. "What's his reason?"

"I think he doesn't want the responsibility. I think he's afraid it will interfere with his plans to save the world. And maybe he's afraid this might change their relationship and the girlfriend will start wanting more from him than she has in the past."

Finally Stacy got it. "Oh. My. Lord. Ella, are you talking about you and Dane?"

It was a pleasure to download on someone like Stacy who, as a loyal friend, automatically took my side. And even though I was changing the rules on Dane by trying to bring a baby into our lives, Stacy's sympathies were entirely with me.

"I'm in Houston with the baby," I told her. "We're in a hotel room. He's right next to me. I don't want to do this. But he's the first guy I've said 'I love you' to since high school. Oh, Stace, you wouldn't believe how cute he is."

"All babies are cute," Stacy said darkly.

"I know, but this one is above average."

"All babies are above average."

I paused to make a face at the baby, who was blowing bubbles. "Luke is in the top one percent of above average."

"Hold it. Tom's home for lunch. I want him in on this. *Tooooooom!*"

I waited while Stacy explained the situation to her husband. Of Dane's considerable number of friends, Tom had always been my favorite. There was never any boredom or melancholy when Tom was around . . . wine flowed, people laughed, conversation coursed easily. When Tom was around, you felt witty and smart. Stacy was the taut and dependable clothesline from which the colorful Tom was free to wave and beckon.

"Can you put Tom on the other line?" I asked Stacy.

"At the moment we only have one phone. Tommie dropped the other one in the potty. So . . . have you talked to Dane yet?"

My stomach lurched. "No, I wanted to call you first. I'm stalling because I know what Dane is going to say." A stinging haze came over my eyes. My voice came out thin and emotion-cluttered. "He won't go for this, Stace. He's going to tell me not to come back to Austin."

"Bullshit. You come right back here with that baby."

"I can't. You know Dane."

"I do, and that's why I think it's time for him to step up to the plate. This is a grown-up responsibility, and he needs to handle it."

For some reason I felt compelled to take Dane's side. "Dane is a grown-up," I said, blotting my eyes on my sleeve. "He has his own company. A lot of people rely on him. But this is different. Dane has always been clear on not wanting anything to do with babies. And just because I'm being forced into a situation I didn't see coming doesn't mean Dane has to suffer as well."

"Of course it does. He's your partner. And having a baby is not suffering. It's—" She paused at a comment from her husband. "Shut up, Tom. Ella, when a baby comes into your life, you have to give a lot. But you get even more than you give. You'll see."

Luke had begun to blink slowly as the need for sleep crept over him. I kept my hand on his tummy, feeling the small digestive gurgle against my palm.

". . . had a terrific childhood," Stacy was saying, "and he's at the right age to settle down. Everyone who knows him thinks he'd make a wonderful father. You need to force the issue, Ella. Once Dane sees how fantastic it is to have children, how much they add to your life, he'll be ready to make a commitment."

"He can barely commit to owning socks," I said. "He has to have total freedom, Stacy."

"No one can have total freedom," she pointed out. "The whole point of a relationship is to have someone there when you need him. Otherwise it's just a . . . wait a minute." She paused, and I heard a muffled voice in the background. "Do you want Tom to talk to him? He says he'd be glad to."

"No," I said quickly. "I don't want Dane to be pressured."

"Why should he be spared?" Stacy asked indignantly. "*You're* being pressured, aren't you? *You're* having to face a tough situation—why shouldn't he have to help you with it? I swear, Ella, if Dane doesn't do right by you, I'm going to give him such shit—" She paused at a comment from her husband. "I mean it, Tom! For God's sake, what if Ella had gotten pregnant the way I did? You stepped up to handle the responsibility—don't you think Dane should? I don't give a damn if it's his baby or not. The fact is, Ella needs his support." She returned her full attention to me. "No matter what Dane says, come back to Austin with the baby, Ella. Your friends are here. We'll help you with him."

"I don't know. I'd be running into Dane . . . it would be weird living near him but not with him. Maybe I should just try to find a furnished apartment here in Houston. It's only for three months."

"And go back to Dane when the problem is solved?" Stacy asked, outraged.

"Well . . . yes."

"I guess if you got cancer you'd have to take care of it all by yourself, too, so you wouldn't inconvenience him? Make Dane part of this. You should be able to rely on him, Ella! You're . . . here, Tom wants to say something."

I waited until I heard his resigned voice. "Hey, Ella."

"Hey, Tom. Before you say anything . . . don't tell me what Stace wants me to hear. Tell me the truth. You're his best friend and you know him better than anyone. Dane's not going to budge, is he?"

Tom sighed. "It's all a trap to him, anything that smacks of the house, the dog, the wife, and the two-point-five kids. And unlike Stacy and apparently everyone else we know, I don't think Dane would make a wonderful father. He's not nearly enough of a masochist."

I smiled with rueful sadness, knowing Tom was going to catch hell from Stacy for his honesty. "I know that Dane would rather try to save the world than try to save one baby. But I can't figure out why."

"Babies are tough customers, Ella," Tom said. "You get a lot more credit for trying to save the world. And it's easier."

EIGHT

"I'VE BEEN PUT IN A SITUATION I CAN'T WALK AWAY from," I told Dane on the phone. "So I'll tell you what I want to do, and after you hear me out, you can tell me what choices I have. Or not."

"My God, Ella," he said quietly.

I frowned. "Don't say 'My God, Ella' yet. I haven't even told you my plan."

"I know what it is."

"You do?"

"I knew the moment you left Austin. You've always been the clean-up crew of your family." Dane's resigned kindness was only one step away from pity. I would have preferred hostility. He made me feel as if life was a circus and I had been permanently assigned to walk behind the elephant.

"No one's forcing me to do anything I don't want to do," I protested.

"As far as I know, taking care of your sister's baby has never been on your list of life goals."

"She only had the baby a week ago. I'm allowed to revise my list of life goals, aren't I?"

"Yes. But that doesn't mean I have to revise mine, too." He sighed. "Tell me everything. Believe it or not, I'm on your side."

I explained what had happened, the conversation with Tara, and I finished with a defensive, "It's only three months. And the baby's hardly any trouble at all." *Unless you happen to like sleep*, I thought. "So I'm going to look for a furnished apartment in Houston, and stay here until Tara gets better. I think Liza might help out, too. And then I'll go back to our apartment in Austin. To you." I went for a brisk finish. "Sound like a good plan?"

"It sounds like *a* plan," he said. I heard the soft, slow expulsion of a pent-up breath, one from the bottom of his lungs. "What do you want me to say, Ella?"

I wanted him to say, *Come home. I'll help with the baby*. But I told him, "I want to know what you're really thinking."

"I think you're still locked in all the old patterns," Dane said quietly. "Your mother snaps her fingers or your sister screws up, and you put your own life on hold to take care of everything. But it's not just three months, Ella. It could be three *years* before Tara is able to screw her head on straight. And what if she has more kids? Are you going to take them all in?"

"I've already thought of that," I admitted with difficulty. "But I can't worry about what might happen in the future. Right now there's only Luke, and he needs me."

"What about what you need? You're supposed to be writing a book, aren't you? And how will you keep the column going?"

"I don't know. But other people manage to work and take care of their children."

"This isn't your child."

"He's part of my family."

"You don't have a family, Ella."

Although I had made similar comments in the past, it rankled to hear him say it. "We're individuals bound by a pattern of reciprocal obligation," I said. "If a group of chimps in the Amazon can be called a family, I think the Varners qualify."

"Considering the fact that chimps occasionally cannibalize each other, I might agree with that."

I reflected that I shouldn't have confided quite so much about the Varners to Dane. "I hate arguing with you," I muttered. "You know too much about me."

"You'd hate it even more if I let you make the wrong decision without saying anything about it."

"I think it's the right decision. The way I'm looking at it, it's the only decision I can live with."

"Fair enough. But *I* can't live with it."

I took a deep breath. "So where does it leave us if I go ahead and do this? What happens to a four-year relationship?" It was hard for me to believe the person I had depended on more than anyone, a man I trusted and cared for deeply, was drawing such a definitive line in the sand.

"I suppose we could consider this a hiatus," Dane said.

I considered that while cold distilled worry seeped through my veins. "And when I come back we'll pick up where we left off?"

"We can try."

"What do you mean *try*?"

"You can stick something in the freezer and thaw it out three months later, but it's never exactly the same."

"But you'll promise to wait for me, right?"

"Wait for you how?"

"I mean you won't sleep with someone else."

"Ella, neither of us can promise not to sleep with someone else."

My jaw dropped. "We can't?"

"Of course not. In a mature relationship there are no promises and no guarantees. We don't own each other."

"Dane, I thought we were exclusive." I realized that for the second time that day, I was whining. A new thought occurred to me. "Have you ever cheated on me?"

"I wouldn't call it cheating. But no, I haven't."

"What if I slept with someone else? Wouldn't you feel jealous?"

"I wouldn't deny you the chance to experience other relationships freely, if that was what you wanted. It's a matter of trust. And openness."

"We have an open relationship?"

"If you want to label it that way, yes."

I had rarely, if ever, been so stunned. The basic assumptions I had made about Dane and me were being casually overturned. "My God. How can we have had an open relationship when I didn't know it? What are the rules for that?"

Dane sounded vaguely amused. "There are no rules for us, Ella. There never have been. That's the only reason you've stayed with me this long. The minute I tried to confine you in any way, you'd have been out of there."

My head was filled with arguments and demands. I wondered if he was right. I was afraid he was. "Somehow," I said slowly, "I've always thought of myself as a conventional person. Way too conventional for a relationship with no structure."

"Miss Independent is," he said. "The advice she gives other people follows a definite set of rules. But as Ella—no, you're not conventional."

"But I'm Miss Independent *and* Ella," I protested. "Where's the real me in all of that?"

"Apparently the real you is in Houston," he said. "And I wish you'd come back."

"I'd like to bring the baby home for just a few days, until I figure things out."

"That doesn't work for me," Dane said promptly.

I scowled. "It's my apartment, too. I want to stay in my half."

"Fine. I'll crash somewhere else until you and the baby are gone. Or I'll move out and you can have the whole place—"

"No." Instinctively I knew that if Dane were forced out because I had chosen to take care of Luke, I might lose him for good. "Never mind, you stay there. I'll find a temporary place for me and Luke."

"I'll help any way I can," Dane said. "I'll assume your share of the monthly rent for as long as you need."

I was annoyed by the offer. And I was as irate as a flank-strapped bull because of his refusal to accept Luke. But most of all I was frightened by the revelation that we were in a relationship with no rules and no promises. Because it meant I was no longer certain of him.

Or of me.

"Thanks," I said sullenly. "I'll let you know where we end up."

"THE FIRST THING WE HAVE TO DO," I TOLD LUKE the next day, "is find a nice place we can rent or sublet. Should we focus on the downtown area? Montrose? Or would you be open to finding something close by in Sugar Land? We could always go to Austin, but we'd have to take care to avoid you-know-who. And it's a *lot* more expensive to rent in Austin."

Luke looked contemplative, sucking slowly on the bottle as if he were mulling the possibilities.

"Are you thinking it over?" I asked him. "Or are you working on another dirty diaper?"

I had spent the previous evening doing a lot of Googling, mostly on infant care. I had read pages on diapering dos-and-don'ts, milestones for the first month of life, and schedules of pediatric visits. I had even found directions on how to trim a baby's nails. "It says here, Luke," I had reported, "that you're supposed to be sleeping fifteen to eighteen hours a day. You need to work on that. It also says I'm supposed to sanitize all the stuff you put your mouth on. And it says you're going to learn how to smile by the end of the month."

I had spent several minutes with my face right over his, smiling at him and hoping for a response. Luke had responded with such a solemn grimace that I had told him he looked like Winston Churchill.

After bookmarking a dozen baby-care sites, I had started to check out available furnished apartments in the Houston area. The ones I could afford looked cheap and depressing, and the ones I liked were astronomical. Unfortunately, it was difficult to find something in a decent location and nicely decorated that was also offered at a mid-range price. I had gone to sleep feeling anxious and depressed. Perhaps out of mercy, Luke had only woken three times during the night.

"We've got to find something today," I told him. "And get out of this expensive hotel room." I decided to spend the morning targeting possibilities on the Net, and going to see a few places in the afternoon. As I wrote down the first address and telephone number, my phone rang.

Travis, the display read. I felt a little tumble of nerves and curiosity as I picked it up. "Hello?"

"Ella." I heard Jack's distinctive baritone, fluid as molten pennies. "How are you?"

"Great, thanks. Luke and I are apartment-hunting. We've decided to move in together."

"Congratulations. You looking in Houston, or are you heading back to Austin?"

"We're staying here."

"Good." A brief hesitation. "Do you have lunch plans?"

"No."

"Let me pick you up at noon."

"I can't afford to have another meal with you," I said, and he laughed.

"This one's on me. There's something I want to talk to you about."

"What could you possibly want to talk to me about? Give me a hint."

"You don't need a hint, Ella. All you need is to say yes."

I hesitated, thrown off-guard by the way he talked to me, friendly and yet insistent, in the way of a man who was not accustomed to being told no.

"Could it be a casual place?" I asked. "At the moment Luke and I don't have anything nice to wear."

"No problem. Just don't put pink socks on him."

To my surprise, Jack picked us up in a small hybrid SUV. I had expected a gas-guzzling monster, or maybe a hideously expensive sports car. I certainly hadn't bargained on something that Dane or one of his friends would have felt comfortable driving.

"You, in a hybrid," I said in wonder, struggling to strap the base of Luke's car seat in the back row. "I thought you'd drive a Denali or a Hummer or something."

"A Hummer," Jack repeated with a snort, handing me Luke in his carrier and gently nudging me aside. He reached in to secure the car-seat base himself. "Houston's got enough toxic emissions. I'm not going to add to the problem."

I raised my brows. "That sounds like something an environmentalist would say."

"I am an environmentalist," Jack said mildly.

"You can't be, you're a hunter."

Jack smiled. "There're two kinds of environmentalists, Ella. The kind who hugs trees and thinks a single-cell amoeba is as important as a Nova Scotian elk . . . and then there's my kind, which thinks of regulated hunting as part of responsible wildlife management. And since I like to be out in nature as much as possible, I'm against pollution, overfishing, global warming, deforestation, or anything else that messes with my stomping grounds."

Jack took Luke's carrier from me and carefully locked it onto the base. He paused to murmur to the baby, who was strapped in like a mini-astronaut ready for a dangerous mission.

Standing back and a little to the side, I couldn't help appreciating the view as Jack bent into the car's interior. He was a powerfully built man, tight-loomed muscles encased in boot-cut denim jeans, his big shoulders flexing beneath a light blue shirt with rolled-up sleeves. He had the kind of form ideal for a quarterback, heavy enough to take a hit from a rusher, tall enough to throw an accurate pass over linemen, lean enough to be limber and fast.

As was often the case in Houston, a drive that should have taken fifteen minutes lasted almost a half hour. But I enjoyed the ride. Not only was I happy to be out of the hotel room, but Luke was sleeping, lulled by the air-conditioning and the motion of the car.

"What happened with Dane?" Jack asked casually. "Did you break up?"

"No, not at all. We're still together." I paused uncomfortably before adding, "But we're on . . . hiatus. Just for three months, until Tara comes for her baby and I go back to Austin."

"Does that mean you're free to see other people?"

"We've always been free to see other people. Dane and I have an open relationship. No promises, no commitments."

"There is no such thing. A relationship *is* promises and commitments."

"To conventional people, maybe. But Dane and I believe you can't own someone."

"Sure you can," Jack said.

I raised my brows.

"Maybe it's different in Austin," Jack continued. "But in Houston, a dog doesn't share his bone."

He was so outrageous, I couldn't help laughing. "Have you ever gotten serious with anyone, Jack? Really serious, like getting engaged?"

"Once," he admitted. "But it didn't work out."

"Why not?"

"Why?"

The hesitation before his reply was long enough that I realized this was a subject he seldom discussed. "She fell in love with someone else," he finally said.

"I'm sorry," I said sincerely. "Most of the letters I get for my column are from people on the down side of a relationship. Men trying to hang on to unfaithful women, women in love with married men who are always promising to leave their wives but never do. . . ." My voice trailed away as I watched his thumb move in a restless stroke against the gleaming leather steering wheel, as if there were a rough patch he was trying to smooth out.

"What would you tell a man whose girlfriend slept with his best friend?" Jack asked.

I understood immediately. I tried to keep my sympathy concealed, sensing that he wouldn't like it. "Was it a one-time thing, or did they start dating?"

"They got married," he said grimly.

"That stinks," I said. "It's the worst when they get married, because then everyone thinks it absolves the couple of all wrongdoing. 'Oh, well, they cheated on you, but they got married so that makes everything all right.' So that leaves you having to swallow the bitter pill and send an expensive wedding present, otherwise you look like a jerk. It's a screw job on multiple levels."

His thumb stilled on the steering wheel. "That's right. How did you know?"

"Madame Ella knows all," I said lightly. "I would further guess that their marriage isn't going well now. Because relationships that start out that way always have cracks in the foundation."

"But you don't disapprove of cheating," he said. "Because one person can't own another, right?"

"No, I strongly condemn cheating when the rules aren't understood by both parties. Unless you agree that you're having an open relationship, there is an implicit promise that you're going to be faithful. There's nothing worse than breaking a promise to someone who cares about you."

"Yes." His voice was quiet, but the single word was weighted with an emphasis that revealed how much it resonated with him.

"So am I right about their marriage?" I pressed. "It's not going well?"

"Lately," he admitted, "it looks a little worse for wear. They'll probably get divorced. And that's a shame, because they have two kids."

"When she becomes available again, do you think you'll be interested in her?"

"Can't say I haven't thought about it. But no, I won't go down that path again."

"I have a theory about men like you, Jack."

That seemed to lighten his mood. He slid me an amused glance. "What is your theory, Ella?"

"It's about why you haven't committed to anyone yet. It's really a matter of efficient market dynamics. Most of the women you date are basically the same. You show them a good time, and then it's on to the next, leaving them to wonder why it didn't last. They don't realize that no one ever outperforms the market by offering the same thing everyone else is offering, no matter how well packaged. So the only thing that's going to change your situation is when something random and unexpected occurs. Something you haven't seen on the market before. Which is why you're going to end up with a woman who's completely different from what you and everyone else expects you to go for." I saw him smile. "What do you think?"

"I think you could talk the ears off a chicken," he said.

The restaurant Jack drove us to may have been casual by his standards, but it had valet parking, luxury cars in the front, and a crisp white canopy leading up to the door. We were shown to an excellent table by a window. Judging from the pristine and tasteful décor and the trickle of elegant piano music in the background, I expected Luke and me to be thrown out about halfway through the meal. But Luke surprised me by behaving well. And the food was delicious, and I had a glass of chardonnay that struck a chord of pleasure on my tongue, and Jack was possibly the most charming man I had ever met. After lunch, we drove to downtown Houston and into the underground parking garage of 1800 Main.

"We're going up to your office?" I asked.

"To the residential side, where my sister works."

"What does she do?"

"She handles financial operations and contracts, mostly. Some day-to-day operations, stuff I can't always get to."

"Am I going to meet her?"

Jack nodded. "You'll like her."

We took an elevator up to a small, gleaming marble-lined lobby featuring a contemporary bronze sculpture and a stately concierge desk. The concierge, a young man in a meticulously tailored suit, smiled at Jack and looked subtly askance at the sleeping baby. Jack had insisted on carrying him, for which I was grateful. My arms had not yet accustomed themselves to the new responsibility of hauling Luke and his paraphernalia everywhere.

"Tell Miss Travis we're heading up," Jack told him.

"Yes, Mr. Travis."

I followed Jack through a set of etched glass doors that slid apart with a soft *whoosh*, and we went to a pair of elevators. "Which floor is the office on?" I asked.

"Seventh. But Haven's going to meet us in her apartment on the sixth."

"Why there?"

"It's a furnished non-rev unit—one of the perks of Haven's job.

But her fiancé lives in a three-bedroom on an upper floor, and she's already moved most of her stuff to his place. So her apartment is sitting there empty."

As I realized what he was leading up to, I gave him a bemused look. My stomach swooped, although I wasn't certain if it was from the motion of the elevator or from sheer surprise. "Jack, if your idea has something to do with me and Luke living *here* for the next three months . . . I appreciate that, but it's just not possible."

"Why?" We stopped, and Jack gestured for me to precede him from the elevator cab.

I decided to be blunt. "I can't afford it."

"We'll find a number you can live with."

"I don't want to owe you anything."

"You wouldn't. This is between you and my sister."

"Yes, but you own the building."

"No, I don't. I just manage it."

"Don't split hairs. It's Travis-owned."

"Okay." Amusement edged his tone. "It's Travis-owned. Still, you wouldn't owe me. This is just a matter of timing. You need a place to stay and there's an available apartment."

I continued to frown. "*You* live in this building, don't you?"

He looked mocking. "I don't have to hand out apartment deals to get a woman's attention, Ella."

"I wasn't implying that," I protested, while humiliation sent a wash of scarlet from head to toe. The truth was, I had been implying it. As if I, Ella Varner, were so irresistible that Jack Travis would go to extraordinary lengths to have me live in the same building. Good Lord, from what part of my ego had *that* emerged from? I struggled to come up with a save. "I just meant that you couldn't be happy about the prospect of having a noisy newborn in your building."

"I'd make an exception for Luke. After the start he's gotten in life, he's due for a good turn." Jack led the way to an apartment near the end of a gray-carpeted hallway, part of an H-shaped layout. He pushed the buzzer, and the door opened.

NINE

HAVEN TRAVIS WAS SLENDER AND SO MUCH SMALLER than her brother that it seemed questionable they had come from the same parents. But the Gypsy-dark eyes were identical. She was fair and black-haired and delicately beautiful. Her expression was vibrant with intelligence and yet there was something about her . . . a hint of bruised vulnerability in a way that suggested she had not gone unscathed from life's sharper edges.

"Hey, Jack." Her attention was instantly captured by the sleeping baby in the carrier. "Oh, what a cute baby." She had a distinctive voice, bright and warm, a little raspy, as if she'd just taken a swallow of expensive liquor. "Give that carrier to me—you're jostling him."

"He likes it," Jack returned calmly, ignoring her efforts to take Luke. He bent his head for a kiss. "Ella Varner, this bossy woman is my sister, Haven."

She shook my hand in a firm and confiding grip. "Come in, Ella. This is such a coincidence—I just started reading your column a few weeks ago."

Haven welcomed us into her apartment, a small one-bedroom unit

decorated in shades of white and cream and distressed dark woods. The disciplined color scheme was enlivened by a few jolts of fresh botanical green. A Swedish wooden floor clock occupied the corner. The main living space was filled with a few simple pieces of furniture—antique French chairs, an overstuffed sofa covered in black-and-cream toile.

"My best friend Todd decorated it," Haven told me, noticing my interest.

"It's wonderful. It looks like something out of a magazine."

"Todd says the mistake some people make with decorating small spaces is that they choose too many delicate pieces. You need something substantial like that sofa, or there's nothing to anchor the room."

"It's still too small," Jack said as he set the baby carrier on the low, wide coffee table.

Haven smiled. "None of my brothers," she informed me, "think a sofa is comfortable unless it's the size of a pickup flatbed." She went to the sleeping baby and regarded him with tender concern. "What's his name?"

"Luke." As I answered, I was surprised to feel a flush of pride.

"Jack told me a little about your situation," Haven said. "I think it's terrific, what you're doing for your sister. Obviously it's not the easy road to take." She smiled. "But it's exactly what I'd expect Miss Independent to do."

Jack looked at me speculatively. "I'd like to read some of your stuff."

"There are a couple of issues of *Vibe* on the side table," Haven told him. "It might be a nice change from *Troutmaster Digest*."

To my dismay, Jack picked up the most recent issue, which contained one of my more provocative columns.

"Maybe you shouldn't . . ." I began, but my voice trailed away as he paged through the periodical. I could tell the moment he found my page, with its cartoon portrait of me wearing cartoon high heels and a fashionable swing coat. And I knew exactly what he was reading even before his brows began to inch toward his hairline.

Dear Miss Independent,

I'm dating a fantastic guy—handsome, successful, caring, and good in bed. But there's a problem. He's built on the petite side, sexually speaking. I've always heard that size doesn't matter, but I can't help wishing he had more to offer in that department. I want to stay with him in spite of the fact that he's hung like a cocktail weenie, but how can I stop wishing for a kielbasa?"

—Length Lover

Dear Length Lover,

Despite the claims made by a barrage of spam in Miss I.'s mailbox, it is not possible to increase a man's genital size. But here are a few relevant facts to consider: there are approximately 8,000 nerve endings in the clitoris, and a lesser concentration in the outer third of the vagina, and virtually none in the inner two-thirds. Therefore, a shorter penis is able to provide all the necessary stimulation that a longer one can.

For most women, a partner's skills are far more important than his size. Try various positions and techniques, emphasize foreplay, and keep in mind that many roads lead to Rome.

Finally, if you want something big to play with during intercourse, bring some toys to bed. Think of it as outsourcing.

—Miss Independent

Jack's expression was faintly bemused, as if he were attempting to reconcile the persona of Miss Independent with what he had observed of me so far. Lowering to the small moss-green sofa, he continued to read.

"Come see the kitchen," Haven told me, tugging me toward a tiled area with granite countertops and stainless-steel appliances. "Would you like something to drink?"

"Yes, thanks."

She opened the refrigerator. "Mango iced tea, or raspberry basil?"

"Mango, please." I sat on a stool at the island.

Jack ripped his attention away from the magazine long enough to protest, "Haven, you know I can't stand that stuff. Just give me the regular kind."

"I don't have the regular kind," his sister retorted, pulling out a pitcher of citrus-colored tea. "You can try some of the mango."

"What's wrong with tea-flavored tea?"

"Quit complaining, Jack. Hardy tried this a few times and he likes it."

"Honey, Hardy would like it if you picked up grass clippings from the yard and brewed them. He's pussy-whipped."

Haven bit back a smile. "I dare you to say that to his face."

"Can't," came the laconic reply. "He's pussy-whipped, but he could still kick the crap out of me."

My eyes widened as I wondered what kind of man could manage to kick the crap out of Jack Travis.

"My fiancé used to be a welder on a drilling rig and he's tough as hell," Haven informed me, her eyes twinkling. "Which is a good thing. Otherwise my three older brothers would have run him off by now."

"We've done everything short of giving him a medal for taking you on," Jack retorted.

From their easy manner with each other, it was clear they enjoyed each other's company. Continuing to bicker companionably, Haven brought some tea to her brother and came back to the kitchen.

After giving me a glass, Haven leaned her forearms on the top of the kitchen island. "Do you like the apartment?" she asked.

"Yes, it's terrific. But there are issues—"

"I know. Here's the deal, Ella," she said with disarming frankness. "I've never paid rent for this apartment, since it came with the job. And after I get married, I'm moving into Hardy's place on the eighteenth floor." A self-conscious smile crossed her face as she added, "Most of my things are there already. So what we've got is an empty furnished apartment. I don't see why you shouldn't stay here with Luke for the next few months—taking care of your own utilities, of course—until it's time for you to go back to Austin. I wouldn't charge you anything, since the apartment would go unused in any case."

"No, I'd have to sublet it," I said. "I couldn't take it for free."

She made a little grimace and ran a hand through the layers of her hair. "I don't know how to put this delicately . . . but whatever you paid me would be nothing more than a symbolic gesture. I don't need the money."

"I still wouldn't consider it otherwise."

"Then take the amount you'd like to pay in rent and invest it for Luke."

"Can I ask why you're not turning this apartment into a revenue-producing property?"

"We've talked about it," she admitted. "There's a waiting list. But we're still not sure what we're ultimately going to do with it. When or if we hire a new manager, he or she will have to live on-site, so we'll need to keep this unit available."

"Why would you need a new—" I began, but I thought better and shut my mouth.

Haven smiled. "Hardy and I will probably try to start a family soon."

"A man who actually wants a baby," I said. "What a concept."

There was no sound from Jack. I heard the rustling of glossy magazine pages.

I looked at Haven and hitched my shoulders in a helpless shrug. "I'm amazed that you're willing to do this for a complete stranger."

"You're not a *complete* stranger," she said reasonably. "After all, we know your cousin Liza, and Jack did go out with your sister Tara—"

"Once," he interjected from the other room.

"Once," Haven repeated with a grin. "So you count as the friend of a friend. Also . . ." Her expression turned reflective. "Not long ago I was having a tough time, going through a nasty divorce. A few people, including Jack, helped me get through it. So I want to keep the good Karma going."

"I wasn't trying to help you," Jack said. "I needed cheap labor."

"Stay here, Ella," Haven urged. "You can move in immediately. All you need is a crib for the baby, and you're set."

I felt uncertain and awkward. I was not used to asking for help or receiving it. I had to figure out the possible complications. "If I could have just a little time to think about it? . . ."

"Sure." Her brown eyes sparkled. "Out of curiosity, what would Miss Independent say?"

I smiled. "I don't usually ask her advice."

"I know what she'd say." Jack came into the kitchen, bringing his empty tea glass. He braced one hand on the edge of the island, standing so close that I was tempted to shrink away. But I stayed still, nerve endings collecting movement with the acuity of cat's whiskers. The scent of him was fresh and dry, underpinned with a cedary masculine spice that I wanted to breathe in again and again.

"She'd tell you to do what was best for Luke," Jack said. "Wouldn't she?"

I nodded and leaned against the counter, cupping my elbows with my palms.

"So do it," he murmured.

He was pushing again, more insistent than any man had ever been with me. And for some reason, instead of pushing back, I wanted to relax into it.

Since I felt another blush coming on, I didn't dare glance up at him but instead turned my attention to Haven. She was watching her brother with an intense gaze, as if something he had just said or done had not been entirely in character. And then she busied herself with taking her empty glass to the sink, and said it was time for her to get back upstairs to the office, something about contracts and appointments. "I'll leave you to lock up," she said cheerfully. "Take as long as you need to think it over, Ella."

"Thanks. It was nice to meet you."

Neither Jack nor I moved as she left. I tensed on the stool, my toes hooking around one of the lower rungs. He leaned over me until I almost thought I could feel his breath stirring my hair.

"You were right," I said huskily. "I do like her." I sensed rather than saw Jack's brief nod. His silence impelled me to continue. "I'm sorry she had to go through a divorce."

"My only regret is she didn't do it sooner. And that I didn't get to wipe him off the face of the earth." There was no bravado in his tone, only a dead-serious calm that made me uneasy. I looked up at him then.

"You can't always protect the people you love," I said.

"So I've learned."

He didn't ask if I was going to stay. Somehow we both knew.

"This is very different from my life," I said after a moment. "I don't ever get to visit these kinds of places, much less live in one. I don't belong here, and I have nothing in common with anyone who does."

"Where do you belong? Back in Austin with Dane?"

"Yes."

"Appears he doesn't think so."

I scowled. "That's a cheap shot."

Jack was unrepentant. "The people in this building are like everyone else, Ella. Some are nice and some aren't. Some are smart, and others are about as bright as a wet match in a dark cave. In other words, pretty normal. You'll get along fine." His voice gentled. "You'll find friends here."

"I'm not going to stay here long enough to get to know anyone. I'll be busy with Luke, obviously, and trying to help Tara get better. And I'll be working, of course."

"Are you going to drive to Austin to get your things, or will Dane bring them here?"

"I don't have a lot of stuff, actually. I think Dane can box up most of my clothes and UPS them. Maybe in a couple of weeks he'll drive over to visit."

I heard Luke waking up in the next room. Automatically I hopped off the stool. "Food and diaper time," I said, striding to the baby carrier.

"Why don't you stay here with Luke and relax while I go to the hotel and get your bags? I'll check you out now so you won't get charged for another night."

"But my car . . ."

"I'll take you to pick it up later. For now, rest."

That sounded good. The last thing I wanted was to get back in the car with Luke and go anywhere, especially in the worst heat of the day. I was tired, and the apartment was cool and serene. I looked at Jack ruefully. "I already owe you too many favors."

"One more won't make a difference, then." He watched as I unbuckled Luke and scooped him up from the carrier. "You got everything you need?"

"Yes."

"I'll be back in a little while. You've got my cell number."

"Thank you. I . . ." Feeling grateful, I reached into the insulated pocket of the diaper bag and pulled out a cold bottle. "I don't know why you're doing all this. Especially after the trouble I put you to. But I appreciate it."

Jack paused at the door and glanced back at me. "I like you, Ella. I respect what you're doing for your sister. Most people in your situation would back down rather than take the risk. I don't mind helping someone who's trying like hell to do the right thing."

WHILE JACK WAS GONE, I TOOK CARE OF LUKE AND then carried him around the apartment. We went into the bedroom, which was decorated with a brass bed covered in antique white lace, a rattan chest used as a nightstand, and a Victorian glass globe lamp. I settled Luke on the bed and sat next to him with my cell phone in hand.

I dialed Tara's number, got her voice recording, and left a message.

"Hi, sweetie . . . Luke and I are doing great. We're staying in Houston for the next three months. I was just thinking about you. Wondering how you were. And Tara . . ."—my throat tightened with compassion and tenderness—"I have some idea of what you're going through. How hard it is to talk about . . . well, about Mom and the past and all that stuff. I'm proud of you. You're doing the right thing. You're going to be okay."

As I hung up, I felt hot pressure behind my eyes. But the gathering tears vanished when I saw that Luke had turned his head to watch me with an innocently inquiring gaze. I inched closer and nuzzled his skull, the dark hair flat and silky as bird feathers. "You're going to be okay, too," I told him. And as the warmth of our bodies collected, we dozed together, Luke slipping into his innocent dreams, I into my unruly ones.

I slept far more heavily than I had expected or intended, waking when the room was dark. Surprised that Luke hadn't made a sound, I reached for him and felt a thrill of panic as my hand found nothing but empty space.

"Luke!" I scrambled upward, gasping.

"Hey . . ." Jack entered the room and turned on the light. "Easy. It's okay, Ella." His voice was soothing and soft. "The baby woke up before you did. I took him to the other room to let you get a little more sleep. We've been watching a game."

"Did he cry?" I asked thickly, rubbing my eyes.

"Only when he realized the Astros were having another first-round play-off flameout. But I told him there's no shame in crying over the Astros. It's how we Houston guys bond."

I tried to smile, but I was exhausted and not yet fully awake. And to my horror, as Jack approached the bed I had a terrible instinctive urge to lift my arms to him. But he was not Dane, and it was inappropriate, very nearly appalling, to think of him in the same context. It had taken four years of hard-won confidences and emotional risk for Dane and me to reach the intimacy we now shared. I couldn't imagine having that with any other man.

Before I could move, Jack came to stand beside the bed, looking down at me with soft dark eyes. I fell back a little, my stomach clenching with pleasure as I imagined for a split-second that he was about to lower over me, and his weight would be so hard and satisfying—

"Your car will be at the residents' garage in a couple of hours," he murmured. "I paid a guy at the hotel to drive it over here."

"Thank you, I . . . I'll pay you back. . . ."

"No need."

"I don't want to be even more in debt to you than I already am."

He shook his head, looking amused. "Sometimes, Ella, you can relax and let someone do something nice for you."

I blinked as I heard chamber music coming from the other room. "What are you listening to?"

"I picked up a DVD for Luke while I was out. Something with Mozart and sock puppets."

A grin rose to my lips. "At this stage I don't think Luke can see more than ten inches beyond his face."

"That explains his lack of interest. I thought maybe he preferred Beethoven."

He extended a hand to help me from the bed. I hesitated before taking it. I could certainly get off the bed on my own. But it seemed uncivil to ignore the gesture.

My hand felt exactly right in his, his long thumb crossing over mine, our palms converging gently. I pulled away from him as soon as I was upright. I tried to remember if my attraction to Dane had been this immediate and direct. No . . . it had developed gradually, a slow and patient unfolding. I had a solid dislike of fast-moving things.

"Your suitcase is in the other room," Jack told me. "If you're hungry, you can order something from the restaurant on the seventh floor. You need anything else, call Haven. I put her number beside the phone. I won't see you for a few days—I'll be out of town."

I wanted to ask where he was going, but instead I nodded. "Travel safely."

His eyes glinted with humor. "Thanks."

He left with friendly dispatch, his matter-of-fact departure a relief and yet oddly anticlimactic. I went into the main room and found my suitcase, and noticed that the hotel receipt, tucked into a crisp white envelope, had been left on top. Opening it, I saw the final tally, and I cringed. But as I scanned the itemized list of expenses, I noticed something was missing: the room-service dinner.

He must have paid for it, I thought. We had agreed that I would. Why had he changed his mind? Was it pity? Maybe he thought I couldn't afford it? Or maybe he'd never had any intentions of letting me pay for it. Mystified and vaguely annoyed, I set aside the hotel bill and went to gather Luke in my arms. I watched the sock-puppet show with the baby and tried not to think about Jack Travis. Most of all, I tried not to wonder when he would come back.

TEN

IN THE DAYS THAT FOLLOWED I CALLED ALL MY friends to tell them what had happened. It seemed I repeated the story of my sister's surprise baby at least a hundred times until I got good at telling the expurgated version. While most of them were supportive, some like Stacy were not at all pleased that I had chosen to stay in Houston. I felt guilty knowing that Dane was getting more than his share of calls and comments. It seemed that our friends' reactions were divided among gender lines. The women said that of course I'd had no choice but to take care of Luke, whereas the men were far more understanding of Dane's decision not to take responsibility for a baby he'd had nothing to do with.

Unfathomably, some of the discussions drifted into a referendum on whether or not I should have gotten Dane to marry me before now, as that would have made the situation very different.

"How exactly would it be different?" I asked Louise, a personal trainer whose husband, Ken, was a Lake Travis paramedic. "Even if Dane had married me, he still wouldn't want babies."

"Yes, but he would have *had* to help you with Luke," Louise replied. "I mean, a man can't exactly kick his wife out in these circumstances, could he?"

"He didn't kick me out," I said defensively. "And I could never force Dane into doing something he didn't want just because we were married. He would still have the right to make his own choices."

"That's ridiculous," Louise said. "The whole reason you get married is so you can take away their choices. And they're happier that way."

"They are?"

"Definitely."

"Does marriage take away our choices, too?"

"No, it gives us more choices, plus security. That's why women want to get married more than men."

I was perplexed by Louise's views on marriage. And I reflected that marriage could devolve into a very cynical arrangement if love was taken from the equation. Like a brick wall with the mortar crumbling out, it would eventually collapse.

Reluctantly I called my mother to update her on Tara, the baby, and the fact that I was staying in Houston for a while to help her.

"After all the years you spent running around in Austin," my mother said, "you have no right to complain."

"I'm not complaining. And I wasn't running around. I was working and studying and—"

"It's drugs, isn't it? Tara was so innocent. She got pulled into that glamorous lifestyle with all her rich friends . . . all that cocaine dust floating around, she probably inhaled some by accident, and then—"

"There's no such thing as secondhand cocaine snorting, Mom."

"She was *pressured*," my mother snapped. "You have no idea what it's like to be beautiful, Ella. All the problems it can bring on."

"You're right, I wouldn't know. But I'm pretty certain Tara wasn't doing drugs."

"Well, your sister just wants attention. You make sure she knows I'm not paying a cent for her to have a three-month getaway. I need a getaway a lot worse than anyone else, let me tell you. All the stress this has caused me—why hasn't anyone thought about sending me to a spa?"

"No one's expecting you to pay for it, Mom."

"Who is, then?"

"I don't know yet. But the main thing to concentrate on now is helping Tara to get better. And taking care of Luke. He and I are staying in a nice little furnished apartment."

"Where is it?"

"Oh, inside the loop somewhere. Nothing special." I repressed a grin as I gazed at my luxurious surroundings, knowing if she found out I was living at 1800 Main, she'd be there within the half hour. "The place needs some work. Do you want to help me fix it up? Maybe tomorrow—"

"I'd like to," she said hastily, "but I can't. I'm too busy. You'll have to do it on your own, Ella."

"Okay. Would you like me to stop by with Luke sometime? I'm sure you want some bonding time."

"Yes . . . but my boyfriend likes to drop in unexpectedly. I don't want him to see the baby. I'll call you when I have a free day."

"Good, because I could use some babysitting—"

She hung up the phone.

When I called Liza and told her that I was staying in an apartment at 1800 Main, she was impressed and wildly curious. "How did you get a deal like that? Did you sleep with Jack or something?"

"Of course not," I said, offended. "You know me better than that."

"Well, I think it's weird, the Travises letting you stay there like that. But I guess they all have so much money, they can afford to make nice gestures. To them, maybe it's like tithing."

THE PERSON WHO HELPED ME THE MOST, NOT ONLY IN an emotional but a practical sense, was Haven Travis. She guided me through the process of having the utilities changed over, told me where to go for things I needed, and even recommended a babysitter her sister-in-law liked.

Haven made no judgments, nor did she want to interfere in anyone else's business. She was a good listener, and she had a quick sense of humor. I felt comfortable around her—nearly as comfortable as I did with Stacy—and that was saying something. I reflected that for all the people you lost touch with or couldn't hold on to, life occasionally made up for it by giving you the right person at the right time.

We had lunch and shopped for baby supplies one afternoon, and walked together a couple of mornings before the daytime heat accumulated. As we cautiously exchanged the details of our lives, we discovered this was one of those rare friendships in which everything was instantly understood. Although Haven didn't say much about her failed marriage, she indicated there had been some kind of abuse. I knew what courage it had taken for her to leave the relationship and rebuild her life, and the process of recovering would take a long time. And whoever she had been before, she was now different in significant ways.

The abusive marriage had distanced Haven from her old friends, some of whom were too uncomfortable to face the issue, and others who wondered what she had done to cause it. And then there had been others who had chosen not to believe her at all, thinking a rich woman couldn't be abused. As if money was a shield against all manner of violence or ugliness.

"Someone said behind my back," Haven told me, "that if I'd been knocked around by my husband, it must have been because I'd wanted it."

We were both quiet as the stroller wheels rattled over the pavement. Although Houston was not a walking city by anyone's definition, there were a few places you could walk comfortably, especially Rice Village, where there were shade trees. We passed eclectic shops and boutiques, restaurants and clubs, salons, and a children's retail store. The prices made me dizzy. It was unbelievable how much you could spend on children's fashion.

Contemplating what Haven had just told me, I wished I could think of some consoling reply. But the only solace I could offer was to reassure her that I believed her. "It scares people to think that they could be hurt or abused for no reason," I said. "So they'd rather think you caused it somehow, and then they can reassure themselves that they're safe."

Haven nodded. "But I think it must be even worse when it's done by a parent to a child. Because then the child thinks he or she deserves it, and carries that around forever."

"That's Tara's problem."

She gave me an astute glance. "Not yours?"

I shrugged uncomfortably. "I've had a few years to work on it. I think I've whittled it down to a manageable size. I'm not nearly as anxious as I used to be. On the other hand . . . I have attachment problems. It's hard for me to be close to people."

"You've formed an attachment to Luke," she pointed out. "And that's just been a few days, right?"

I considered that and nodded. "I guess babies are exempt."

"What about Dane? . . . You've been with him for a long time."

"Yes, but lately I've realized . . . the relationship works but it isn't going anywhere. Like a car left running in the driveway." And I told her about our open relationship, and what Dane had said, that if he'd tried to confine me in any way, I would have left him.

"Would you have?" Haven asked, opening the door of a coffee shop while I pushed the stroller inside. A life-giving blast of cold air surrounded us.

"I don't know," I said earnestly, my forehead wrinkling. "He may be right. Maybe I can't handle anything more than that. I could be allergic to commitment." I parked the stroller beside a tiny table, lifted the accordion-pleated top, and peeked at Luke, who was kicking his legs happily in response to the coolness.

Still standing, Haven surveyed the chalkboard menu for coffee specials. Her dazzling grin reminded me of her brother. "I don't know, Ella. It might be some deep-seated psychological issue, or . . . it's possible you just haven't found the right guy yet."

"There is no right guy for me." Bending over the baby, I murmured, "Except for you, formula-breath." I caught a tiny bare foot and kissed it. "There is only you, and my passion for your sweaty little feet."

I felt Haven pat my back lightly as she moved around the table. "You know what I think, Ella . . . aside from the fact that I'm going to have an iced mint mochaccino topped with whipped cream and chocolate shavings? I think in the right circumstances, you could pull that car out of the driveway any time you want to."

* * *

JACK FEATURED PROMINENTLY IN MANY OF HAVEN'S childhood stories. In the manner of older brothers, he had alternately been the hero and the villain. Most often the villain. But now in adulthood, in a family with complex dynamics, a close bond had formed between them.

According to Haven, their older brother Gage had always been the focus of their father's greatest demands, highest praise, and deepest ambitions. The only child of Churchill Travis's first marriage, Gage had worked hard to please his father, to become the perfect son. He had been serious, driven, hyper-responsible, distinguishing himself at an elite boarding school, later graduating from UT and Harvard Business School. But Gage was not nearly the hard-ass their father had been. He had an innate kindness, an allowance for human frailty, that Churchill Travis found difficult to summon.

Churchill's second marriage had lasted until the death of his wife, Ava, and had produced three children: Jack, Joe, and Haven. Since Gage already shouldered the main burden of expectation and responsibility, Jack had the opportunity to play, experiment, run wild, make friends. He had always been the first to jump into a fight and the first to shake hands afterward. He'd played every sport, charmed his teachers into giving him better grades than he deserved, and dated the prettiest girls in school. He was a loyal friend who paid his debts and never broke his word. Nothing made Jack madder than when someone made a deal with him and wouldn't keep their side of it.

When Churchill had decided his young sons needed to be reminded what hard labor was, he set them to laying sod in the blistering south Texas sun, or building a hand-cut stone fence along the edge of their property, until their muscles were on fire and a dark tan had saturated their skin several layers down. Of the three boys, only Jack had truly enjoyed the outside labor. Sweat, dirt, physical exertion—had all felt purifying to him. His basic need to test himself against the land, and nature, manifested in a lifelong love of outdoor pursuits: hunting, fishing, anything that took him away from the air-conditioned opulence of River Oaks.

Haven had been spared these particular life lessons from her father. Instead, she had been subjected to her mother's notions of how to bring up a girl to be ladylike. Naturally Haven had been a tomboy, forever trailing after her three brothers. Because of the significant age difference between Gage and Haven, he had assumed a vaguely paternal role, intervening on her behalf when he deemed it necessary.

But Jack had warred with Haven on many occasions, such as when she had gone uninvited into his room or played with his train set without asking. For revenge, he had given her Indian burns, and when she had tattled on him, their daddy had beaten him with his belt until Haven had cried. Schooled in the Texan art of manliness, Jack had prided himself on not shedding one tear. Afterward, Churchill had told his wife Ava that Jack was the most stubborn boy alive. "Too damn much like me," the father had said, frustrated that he could not motivate the rebellious Jack the way he had with Gage.

Haven told me she had been miserable when Gage, her champion, had been sent away to school. But contrary to all expectations, Jack had not persecuted her in their brother's absence. When she came home crying one day because a boy at school was bullying her, Jack had listened to the whole story, and rode off on his bike to take care of the problem. The bully never bothered Haven again. Never came near her, as a matter of fact.

They had lost touch for a while after Haven married a man her father hadn't approved of. "I didn't let anyone know what I was going through," she said ruefully. "I'm pretty stubborn, too. And I was too proud to let everyone find out what a mistake I'd made. And by then my husband had crushed my self-confidence until I was too afraid and ashamed to ask anyone for help. But eventually I broke away, and Jack offered me a job to help me get back on my feet. We became friends . . . buddies, sort of . . . in a way we never had before."

I was curious about the "eventually I broke away" part, knowing something pretty major had happened. But that was a conversation that would take place in its own time.

"What do you think about his love life?" I couldn't resist asking. "Will he ever settle down?"

"Absolutely. Jack likes women—I mean *truly* likes them, not in some misogynistic notch-on-the-bedpost way. But he's not going to commit until he finds someone he's sure he can trust."

"Because of the woman who married his best friend?"

She shot me a wide-eyed glance. "He told you about that?"

I nodded.

"Jack hardly ever mentions her. It was a huge deal for him. When a Travis falls for someone, he falls hard. They get really intense. Not everyone is ready for a relationship like that."

"Certainly not me," I said with a stale laugh, while something in me recoiled at the idea. Jack Travis getting all intense was not something I'd ever care to see.

"I think he's lonely," Haven said.

"But he's so busy."

"I think the busiest people are often the loneliest."

I changed the subject at the first opportunity. Talking about Jack made me restless and vaguely irritable, the way I felt when I wanted something I knew was bad for me.

I TALKED WITH DANE ON THE PHONE EVERY NIGHT, telling him about my new surroundings and about Luke. Although Dane didn't want to have anything to do with a baby personally, he certainly didn't mind hearing about Luke and the experience of caring for him.

"Do you think you'll ever want one?" I asked Dane, relaxing on the sofa with Luke draped on my chest.

"I can't say no definitively. There might be another phase in my life when I might . . . but it's hard to imagine. The things I'd get out of it, I'm already getting now from my environmental work and the charity groups."

"Yes, but what about raising a child who will care about those things, too? That's a way to make the world a better place."

"Come on, Ella. You know that's not what would happen. Any child of mine would end up being a Republican lobbyist or a chemical company CFO. Life always screws your best intentions."

I chuckled, envisioning a toddler—Dane's toddler—dressed in a miniature three-piece suit and carrying a calculator. "You're probably right."

"Are you thinking about having one someday?"

"No, God no," I said at once. "I'm trying to hang on until I can give Luke back to Tara. I'm dying for a good night of sleep. Or an uninterrupted meal. And just once, I'd like to go out without all this paraphernalia. It's insane. The stroller, the diapers, wipes, burp cloths, binkies, bottles . . . I've forgotten what it's like to just pick up the keys and walk out the door. And there are all these pediatric visits I've had to schedule—developmental assessments and screenings and shots—so it's a good thing I'm not sleeping, because I'll need the extra time to work."

"Maybe the best part is that you're finding all this out now, so you'll never have to wonder."

"I think it's like rhubarb," I said. "You either love it or you hate it. But you can't ever make yourself acquire a taste for it if you're not naturally predisposed."

"I hate rhubarb," Dane said.

BY THE END OF MY FIRST FULL WEEK AT 1800 MAIN, I was still mastering the trick of carrying a bag of groceries and pushing a stroller while getting through doorways. It was early Friday evening. The traffic was so bad that instead of driving anywhere, I had decided to walk a quarter of a mile to an Express grocery and deli, and back. After the short walk in the heat, Luke and I were parboiled. The plastic handles of the grocery bags were slipping in my wet palm and the diaper bag threatened to slide off my shoulder as I maneuvered the stroller into the lobby. And the baby was making fretful noises.

"You know, Luke," I said breathlessly, "life's going to be a lot easier for all of us when you can walk. No, damn it . . . don't start crying, there's no way I can pick you up right now. God. Luke, *please* hush. . . ." Swearing and sweating, I pushed the stroller past the concierge desk.

"Miss Varner, do you need help?" the concierge asked, beginning to rise.

"No, thanks. Got it. We're fine." I lurched past the etched glass doors and reached an elevator just as it opened.

Two people stepped out, a gorgeous redhead wearing a skimpy white dress and strappy gold sandals . . . and Jack Travis in a lean black suit, a crisp white shirt open at the throat, and sleek black oxfords. In one glance he took in my dilemma. Simultaneously, he reached for the grocery bags and used his foot to keep open the elevator door. His dark brown eyes sparkled. "Hey there, Ella."

My breath stuck in my throat. I found myself smiling at him idiotically. "Hi, Jack."

"You heading up? Looks like you could use a hand."

"No, I'm fine. Thank you." I pushed the stroller onto the elevator.

"We'll help you get to your apartment."

"Oh, no, I can manage—"

"It'll only take a minute," he said. "You don't mind, do you, Sonya?"

" 'Course not." The woman seemed friendly, and nice, giving me a wide-open smile as she stepped back into the elevator. I couldn't fault Jack's taste. Sonya was a stunner, with gleaming perfect skin, vivid red hair, and a magnificent figure. As she bent over to coo at the fussy baby, the combination of her abundant cleavage and beautiful face was enough to make Luke quiet. "Oh, he's the cutest little thing," she exclaimed.

"He's cranky from being out in the heat."

"Look at all that dark hair . . . he must take after his daddy."

"I think so," I said.

"How have you been?" Jack asked me. "Settling in okay?"

"We couldn't be better. Your sister has been great—I don't know what we would have done without her."

"She says the two of you have been getting along."

As Sonya listened to the brief conversation, she gave me a quick, wary glance, as if she were assessing what kind of connection I might have with Jack. I saw the exact second that she decided I was no competition. With my face shiny-clean, my hair cut in a plain bob, and my figure obscured by an oversized T-shirt, my fashion look screamed "new mom."

The elevator stopped at the sixth floor, and Jack held the door while I pushed the stroller out. "I'll take the bags," I said, reaching for the groceries. "Thanks for the help."

"We'll walk you to your door," Jack insisted, keeping hold of the bags.

"Have you moved in recently?" Sonya asked me as we proceeded down the hallway.

"Yes, about a week ago."

"You're so lucky to live here," she said. "What does your husband do?"

"I'm not married, actually."

"Oh." She frowned.

"I have a boyfriend in Austin," I volunteered. "I'm moving back there in about three months."

Sonya's frown cleared. "Oh, that's *wonderful.*"

We reached my door, and I pushed the combination on the keypad. While Jack held open the door, I wheeled the stroller inside and lifted Luke out. "Thanks again," I said, watching Jack set the grocery bags on the coffee table.

Sonya cast an admiring glance around the apartment. "Great decorating."

"I can't take any credit for that," I said. "But Luke and I are making our contribution." With a wry grin, I gestured to the corner of the room, where a large cardboard box and rows of wooden and metal pieces had been laid out.

"What are you putting together?" Jack asked.

"A crib with a changing table attachment. I bought it at Rice Village the other day when I was out with Haven. Unfortunately, they charge a hundred bucks extra if you want it assembled, so I said I'd rather do it myself. The delivery guys brought this box of parts with some instructions, and so far I'm still trying to figure it out. I think it would be easier if I could read the manual. So far I've found the Japanese, French, and German pages, but nothing in English. Now I sort of wish I'd gone ahead and paid the extra hundred bucks." Realizing I was chattering, I smiled and shrugged. "But I like a challenge."

"Let's go, Jack," Sonya urged.

"Right." But he didn't move, just looked from me and Luke to the pile of crib parts. The odd moment of expectant silence caused my heart to lurch with an extra thud. His gaze returned to mine, and he gave me a brief nod that held an implicit promise: *Later.*

I didn't want that. "You two go on," I said brightly. "Have fun."

Sonya smiled. "Bye." Taking Jack's arm, she tugged him from the apartment.

THREE HOURS LATER LUKE WATCHED FROM AN INFANT bouncy seat while I sat on the floor surrounded by crib parts. I was finished with dinner, which had consisted of spaghetti with tomato sauce, ground beef, and fresh basil. When the leftovers were cool, I was going to freeze them in individual-size portions.

Having grown tired of Mozart and the sock puppets, I had hooked up my iPod to the speakers. The air was filled with the raw, sexy purr of Etta James. "The thing that's great about the blues," I told Luke, pausing to sip from my glass of wine, "is that it's about feeling, loving, wanting without the brakes on. No one's brave enough to live that way. Except maybe musicians."

I heard a knock at the door. "Who could that be? Did you invite someone without telling me?" Rising with my wineglass in hand, I padded barefoot to the apartment entrance. I was wearing a set of pajamas the color of pink cotton candy. I had taken out my contacts and put on my glasses. Standing on my toes, I looked through the peephole. My breath quickened as I saw the familiar outline of a man's head.

"I'm not dressed for company," I said through the door.

"Let me in anyway."

I unlatched the door and opened it to reveal Jack Travis, now wearing jeans and a white shirt, holding a small canvas case that was frayed from heavy use. His gaze coursed slowly over me. "Got that crib put together yet?"

"Still working on it." I tried to ignore the heavy pounding of my heart. "Where's Sonya?"

"We had dinner. I just took her back home."

"Already? Why didn't you stay out later?"

He shrugged a little, staring at me. "Can I come in?"

I wanted to refuse him. I sensed there was something between us, something that required negotiation, compromise . . . but I wasn't ready for it. I couldn't think of a reason to keep him out. I took an uncertain step back. "What's in the bag?"

"Tools." Jack walked inside the apartment and closed the door. His movements seemed cautious, as if he were venturing into some new environment that might present hidden dangers. "Hey, Luke," he murmured, lowering beside the baby. Gently he set the bouncy seat bobbing, and Luke gurgled and kicked enthusiastically. With his attention remaining on the baby, Jack said, "You're listening to Etta James."

I tried to sound flippant. "In assembly-required situations, I always play the blues. John Lee Hooker, Bonnie Raitt . . ."

"You ever listen to any of the Deep Ellum boys? Texas blues . . . Blind Lemon Jefferson, Leadbelly, T-Bone Walker?"

I was slow to respond, my attention snared by the way his shirt had tightened across his broad shoulders and powerful back. "I've heard of T-Bone Walker, but not the others."

Jack glanced up at me. "Ever heard 'See That My Grave Is Kept Clean'?"

"I thought that was a Bob Dylan song."

"No, that was just a cover. It came from Blind Lemon. I'll burn a CD for you—he's not always easy to find."

"I wouldn't have thought a River Oaks boy would know so much about the blues."

"Ella, darlin' . . . the blues is all about a good man feelin' bad. Plenty of that in River Oaks."

It was crazy, how much I loved his voice. The baritone drawl seemed to reach inside and linger in impossible-to-reach places. I wanted to sit on the floor beside him and run my hand over the thick, efficiently short layers of his hair and let my fingers rest against the hard nape of his neck. *Tell me everything*, I would say. *All about the blues, and the time your heart was broken, and what scares you the most, and the thing you've always wanted to do but haven't yet.*

"Something smells good," he said.

"I made spaghetti earlier."

"Is there any left?"

"You just went out to dinner."

Jack looked aggrieved. "It was one of those fancy places. I got a piece of fish the size of a domino, and maybe a spoonful of risotto. I'm starving."

I laughed at his pitiful expression. "I'll fix you a plate."

"While you do that, I'll work on the crib."

"Thanks. I laid out all the pieces according to the diagram, but without the directions in English—"

"No need for directions." Jack glanced at the diagram briefly, tossed it aside, and began sorting through the painted wood pieces. "This is pretty straightforward."

"Straightforward? Did you see how many different kinds of screws are in that plastic bag?"

"We'll figure it out." He opened the canvas bag and pulled out a cordless power drill.

I frowned. "Do you know that forty-seven percent of all hand injuries are caused by using power tools at home?"

Jack expertly inserted a drill bit into the chuck. "A lot of people get hurt getting their hand closed in the door, too. But that doesn't mean you should stop using doors."

"If Luke starts crying because of the noise," I said sternly, "you'll have to use a regular screwdriver."

His brows lifted. "Doesn't Dane use power tools?"

"Not usually. Except one summer when he helped build homes in New Orleans with Habitat for Humanity . . . and that was because he was three hundred and fifty miles away and I couldn't reach him."

A slight smile rose to his lips. "What's your problem with electric drills, darlin'?"

"I don't know. I'm not used to them, that's all. They make me nervous. I didn't grow up with a brother or a father who used stuff like that."

"Well, you missed out on some important protocol, Ella. You can't stand between a Texan and his power tools. We like them. Big ones that drain the national grid. We also like truck-stop breakfasts, large moving objects, Monday night football, and the missionary position. We don't drink light beer, drive Smart Cars, or admit to knowing the names of more than about five or six colors. And we don't wax our chests. Ever." He hefted the drill. "Now let me do the guy stuff while you go to the kitchen. Trust me, it's a perfect arrangement."

"Luke's going to cry," I said darkly.

"No, he won't. He'll love it."

To my disgust Luke didn't make a sound, watching contentedly as Jack built the crib. I heated a plate of spaghetti and sauce, and set a place for Jack at the kitchen island. "C'mon, Luke," I said, picking up the baby and carrying him into the kitchen. "We'll entertain Cro-Magnon while he has his dinner."

Jack dug into the steaming pasta with gusto, making appreciative noises and finishing at least a third of it before coming up for air. "This is great. What else can you cook?"

"Just the basics. A few casseroles, pasta, stew. I can roast a chicken."

"Can you do meat loaf?"

"Yep."

"Marry me, Ella."

I looked into his wicked dark eyes, and even though I knew he was joking, I felt a wild pulse inside, and my hands trembled. "Sure," I said lightly. "Want some bread?"

After dinner, Jack was back on the floor, putting together the crib with a deftness born of vast experience. He was good with his hands, confident and capable. I had to admit, I enjoyed watching as he rolled up his sleeves over hair-dusted forearms and knelt in front of the wooden frame, his body athletic and superbly conditioned. I sat nearby with a glass of wine and handed screws to him. Every now and then he got close enough that I caught the scent of him, a sexual incense of male sweat and clean skin. He swore a couple of times as a couple of screws were stripped, the fluent profanity immediately followed by a beg-pardon.

Jack Travis was a novelty in my experience, an old-fashioned man's man. None of the boys I had gone to college with had been anything more than that, just boys trying to figure out who they were and what their place in the world was. Dane and his friends were sensitive, environmentally aware guys who rode bikes and had Facebook accounts. I couldn't imagine Jack Travis ever blogging or worrying about finding himself, and it was pretty certain that he didn't give a damn about whether or not his clothes were sustainably produced.

"Jack," I said thoughtfully, "do you think of women as equals?"

He fitted a support bar against the frame. "Yes."

"Do you ever let a woman pay for dinner?"

"No."

"Is that why the room-service meal wasn't on my hotel bill?"

"I never let a woman pay for my food. I just said dinner was on you because I knew it was the only way you'd let me stay."

"If you think of women as equals, why didn't you let me buy you dinner?"

"Because I'm the man."

"If you had a choice between hiring a man or a woman to manage one of your projects, but you knew the woman was childbearing age, would you choose the man over her?"

"No. I'd choose the best person."

"If they were equal in every way . . . ?"

"I wouldn't hold the potential for pregnancy against her." Jack gave me a quizzical smile. "What are you trying to find out?"

"I'm wondering where to put you on the evolutionary scale."

He tapped a screw into place. "How high have I gotten so far?"

"I haven't decided yet. What's your stand on political correctness?"

"I'm not against it. But a little goes a long way. Hold on a minute—" The drill whirred and screeched as Jack attached a frame bracket. He paused and looked up at me with an expectant grin. "What else?"

"What are you looking for in a woman?"

"Someone who's loyal. Loving. Likes to spend time together, especially outdoors. And I sure wouldn't mind if she hunts."

"Are you sure you wouldn't be happier with a Labrador retriever?" I asked.

It seemed to take Jack no time at all to finish the crib. I helped to hold the large sections together while he attached them and even added extra reinforcing. "I think a baby elephant could sleep in that crib without breaking it," I said.

"Want it here or in the bedroom?" Jack asked.

"The bedroom's so small, I'd rather keep it in here. Is that weird, having a crib in the main room?"

"Not at all. It's Luke's apartment, too."

With Jack's help, I moved the crib beside the sofa and put a sheet over the mattress. Gently, I lowered the drowsy baby into the crib and covered him with a blanket, and started a mobile playing overhead. Bears and honeypots circled slowly, accompanied by a gentle lullaby.

"Looks comfortable," Jack whispered.

"Doesn't it?" Seeing how cozy Luke was, how safe, I felt a rush of gratitude. The dark city was seething outside, scored with traffic, people swarming, drinking, dancing, while the ground slowly released the heat of the day. But we were tucked away in this cool, protected place, everything as it should be.

I needed to fill Luke's bottles, and get ready for the night. We had a routine. I found something deeply comforting in the rituals of bath and bedtime.

"It's been a long time since I was in the habit of taking care of a child," I said, barely aware I was speaking aloud. My hand gripped the top of the crib rail. "Not since I was a child."

For reply, Jack slid his hand over mine, engulfing it with warm pressure. Before I could look up at him, he let go and went to pack up his tools. Methodically, he dumped all the scraps of cardboard and plastic into the flat rectangular box the crib had come in. Lifting the box with one hand, he carried it to the door. "I'll take this out for you."

"Thank you." Smiling, I went to see him out. "I appreciate this, Jack. Everything. I—"

The wine must have eradicated every last atom of common sense I possessed, because I reached up to give him a hug in the same way I would have done with Tom or one of Dane's other friends. A buddy hug. But every nerve from head to toe screamed *"Mistake!"* as soon as the front of my body met his, adhering like wet cottonwood leaves.

Jack's arms went around me, clasping me against a wall of muscle,

and he was so big and warm, and it felt so scary-good that I stiffened all over. The hot drift of his breath against my cheek made my heartbeat go crazy, and instant arousal filled the space between every thump. I gasped, ducking away, my face crammed against his shoulder.

"Jack . . ." I could hardly speak. "I wasn't making a pass at you."

"I know." One hand slid to the back of my head, fingers lacing through the silky-fine locks. Gripping gently, he guided me to look at him. "It's not at all your fault that I'm taking it that way."

"Jack, don't—"

"I like these," he murmured, touching the rectangular rim of my glasses, carefully grasping an earpiece. "A lot. But they're in the way."

"Of what?" I tensed as he pulled off my glasses and set them aside.

"Hold still, Ella." And his head lowered.

ELEVEN

IF I'D BEEN THINKING RATIONALLY, I NEVER WOULD have allowed it. Jack's mouth brushed slowly over mine before settling with gentle pressure. I moved against his unyielding weight until I found some perfect, unexpected alignment that sent heat jolting through me. My knees gave out, but it didn't matter because he was holding me so securely. One of his hands came up to my jaw with extreme care.

Every time I tried to finish the kiss, he pressed harder, coaxing me to stay open, tasting slowly. This was so different from what I was accustomed to, it seemed like something other than kissing. I realized that my kisses with Dane had become a form of punctuation, the quotations or the hasty dash at the end of a conversation. This was softer, more urgent and relentless. Wild, fresh, tumbling kisses, eroding my balance. I groped Jack's shoulders, my fingers curving over the hard nape of his neck.

He took a quick breath and reached down, his hand sliding over my pajama bottoms as he coaxed my hips high and tight. The full-on pressure of him was stunning, galvanic. He was unbelievably hard.

Everywhere. He was in control, infinitely stronger, and he wanted me to know it.

He kissed me until the sensations flowed in directions I couldn't go, spilling and sliding darkly. As I felt a desperate ache cambering low in my body, I finally understood that if I slept with this man, he would take everything. All the defenses I had built would be destroyed.

Shaking, I pushed at him and managed to turn my head long enough to gasp, "I can't. No. That's enough, Jack."

He stopped at once. But he kept me against him, his chest moving hard and fast.

I couldn't look at him. My voice was hoarse as I said, "That shouldn't have happened."

"I've wanted this since the first second I saw you." His arms tightened, and he bent over me until his mouth was close to my ear. Gently he whispered, "You did, too."

"I didn't. I don't."

"You need some fun, Ella."

I let out an incredulous laugh. "Believe me, I don't need fun, I need—" I broke off with a gasp as he pressed my hips closer to his. The feel of him was more than my dazzled senses could handle. To my mortification, I hitched up against him before I could stop myself, heat and instinct winning out over sanity.

Feeling the reflexive response, Jack smiled against my scarlet cheek. "You should take me on. I'd be good for you."

"You are *so* full of yourself . . . and you would not be good for me, with your steaks and power tools and your attention-deficit libido, and . . . I'll bet you're a card-carrying member of the NRA. Admit it, you are." I couldn't seem to shut up. I was talking too much, breathing too fast, jittering like a wind-up toy that had been wound to the limits of its mechanism.

Jack nuzzled into a sensitive place behind my ear. "Why does that matter?"

"Is that a yes? It must be. *God.* It matters because—stop that. It matters because I would only go to bed with a man who respected me and my views. My—" I broke off with an inarticulate sound as he nibbled lightly at my skin.

"I respect you," he murmured. "And your views. I think of you as an equal. I respect your brains, and all those big words you like to use. But I also want to rip your clothes off and have sex with you until you scream and cry and see God." His mouth dragged gently along my throat. I jerked helplessly, muscles jolting with pleasure, and his hands gripped my hips, keeping me in place. "I'm gonna show you a good time, Ella. Starting with some take-no-prisoners sex. The kind when you can't remember your own name after."

"I've been with Dane for four years," I managed to say. "He understands me in a way you don't."

"I can learn you."

It seemed as if something inside me had started to unravel, weakness spreading, all my body tightening against it. I closed my eyes and bit back a whimper. "When you offered me the apartment," I said weakly, "you implied you had no ulterior motives. I don't appreciate the position this puts me in, Jack."

His head lifted, and his lips brushed the tip of my nose. "What position would you prefer?"

My eyes flew open. Somehow I managed to twist away from him. Half-sitting, half-leaning on the arm of the sofa, I pointed to the door with a trembling finger. "Go, Jack."

Jack looked as sexy as hell, rumpled and aroused. "You're kicking me out?"

I could hardly believe it myself. "I'm kicking you out." I went to get my glasses, fumbling to put them back on.

His mouth had turned sullen. "There's more we need to talk about."

"I know. But if I let you stay, I don't think we'll do much talking."

"What if I promise I won't touch you?"

As our gazes caught, it seemed the entire room was filled with volatile heat. "You'd be lying," I said.

Jack rubbed the back of his neck and scowled. "You're right."

I tilted my head toward the door. "Please go."

He didn't move. "When can I see you again? Tomorrow night?"

"I have work."

"The day after?"

"I don't know. I've got a lot of stuff to do."

"Damn it, Ella." He went to the door. "You can put it off for now, but you'll just have to deal with it later."

"I'm a big believer in putting things off," I told him. "In fact, I even put off procrastinating."

He gave me a smoldering glance and left, carrying the empty crib box with him.

Slowly I cleared away the clutter in the kitchen and wiped the counters, and made Luke's bottles. I kept stealing glances at the phone—it was about time for my nightly talk with Dane—but it remained silent. Was I obligated to tell him what had happened between me and Jack? . . . Did an open relationship allow for secrets? And if I confessed to Dane about the attraction I felt for Jack Travis, what good could possibly come of it?

As I pondered the situation, I decided the only reason to tell Dane about the kiss was if it was leading to something. If I was becoming involved with Jack. And I wasn't. The kiss was meaningless. Therefore, the wisest option—not to mention the easiest one—was to pretend it had never happened.

And put off talking about it until the whole thing was forgotten.

THE NEXT DAY I CALLED MY SISTER. I WAS FRUSTRATED but not especially surprised that Tara was dragging her feet on giving Dr. Jaslow permission to talk to me.

"You know I'm not going to do anything that's against your interests," I told her. "I want to help."

"I'm doing fine by myself. You can talk to my doctor later. Maybe. But it's not something I need right now." There was a defensive brittleness to Tara's tone that I understood all too well. I had felt that, lived in that feeling, for a year or so after I had started therapy. Once you started to realize that you had a right to your own privacy, you became rabidly protective of it. Of course, Tara didn't want my interference. On the other hand, I needed to know what was going on.

"Can you tell me just a little about what you've been doing?"

An unenthusiastic silence passed before Tara replied. "I've started taking an antidepressant."

"Good," I said. "Can you tell a difference?"

"It's not supposed to kick in for a few weeks, but I think it's helping already. And I've been talking with Dr. Jaslow a lot. She says the way we were raised was definitely not normal or healthy. And when your own mother is crazy and neglects you and competes with you, you have to figure out what that did to you as a child, and then you need to work on fixing it. Or . . ."

"Or we might end up repeating some of her patterns," I said softly.

"Yeah. So Dr. Jaslow and I are talking about some of the things that have always bothered me."

"Like . . ."

"Like the way Mom always said I was the pretty one and you were the smart one . . . that was wrong. It made me believe I was dumb and there was no chance of getting smarter. And I made a lot of stupid mistakes because of that."

"I know, sweetie."

"Maybe I'll never be a brain surgeon, but I'm smarter than Mom thinks."

"She doesn't know either of us, Tara."

"I want to confront Mom, try to make her understand what she did to us. But Dr. Jaslow says Mom will probably never get it. I could explain and explain, but Mom would deny it or say she doesn't remember."

"I agree. All you and I can do is work on our own issues."

"I'm doing that. I'm finding out a lot I didn't know. I'm getting better."

"Good. Because Luke misses his mommy."

Tara responded with a shy eagerness that touched me. "Do you really think so? I had him for such a short time, I don't know if he'll remember me."

"You carried him for nine months, Tara. He knows your voice. Your heartbeat."

"Does he sleep through the night?"

"I wish," I said ruefully. "Most nights he wakes up about three times at least. I'm getting used to it—I've started to sleep so lightly that as soon as he makes any noise at all, I'm instantly awake."

"Maybe it's better that he's with you. I've never been good at waking up fast."

I chuckled. "He gets loud in a hurry. Believe me, he'll have you popping out of bed like a toaster waffle." Pausing, I asked cautiously, "Do you think Mark will want to see him at some point?"

Abruptly the warm communication stopped. Tara's voice turned flat and cold. "Mark's not the father. I told you, there is no father. Luke's just mine."

"I'm not buying that Luke came from the cabbage patch, Tara. I mean, *someone* participated. And whoever it was, he owes you some help, and more importantly he owes Luke."

"That's my business."

It was difficult to keep from pointing out that since I'd been recruited to take care of Luke at my own expense, it was partly my business, too. "There are a lot of practical considerations we haven't begun to talk about, Tara. If Luke's daddy is helping you, if he's made promises . . . well, those promises need to be made legal. And someday Luke's going to want to know—"

"Not now, Ella. I've got to go—I'm late for an exercise class."

"But if you'll just let me—"

"Bye." The phone went dead in my hand.

Fuming and worried, I went to a pile of bills and catalogs on the kitchen island, and found the piece of paper Jack had given me with the number for the Fellowship of Eternal Truth.

I wondered what my responsibility was. It was clear to me that Tara was not at the point at which she could make decisions about the future. She was vulnerable, and she was probably being deceived by Mark Gottler into thinking that he would take care of her, that he would provide for her and the baby indefinitely. Maybe he had preyed upon her and taken advantage, thinking there would be no repercussions because she had virtually no family to speak of.

But she had me.

TWELVE

FOR THE NEXT TWO DAYS I CALLED THE FELLOWSHIP of Eternal Truth, requesting a meeting with Mark Gottler. I got nothing but evasions, silences, or implausible excuses.

I was being stonewalled. I knew it would be impossible for me to get a meeting with Gottler on my own. He was way up in the adminisphere of the church, secluded and sheltered from the reach of mere mortals.

When I told Dane about the problem, he said he might have a helpful connection. The church had an extensive network of charities, and an old friend of his had something to do with Eternal Truth's Central American outreach. Unfortunately those efforts fell through, and I was left at square one again.

"You should ask Jack," Haven said on Friday after she got off work. "This is the kind of problem he's really good with. He knows everyone. He's not shy about calling in favors. And if I'm not mistaken, I think the company has a couple of contracts with that church."

We were having drinks in the apartment she shared with her fiancé, Hardy Cates. Haven had made a pitcher of white sangria, stirring Riesling together with chunks of peaches, oranges, and mangoes, and a liberal splash of Peach Schnapps.

The three-bedroom apartment featured a wall of floor-to-ceiling glass windows that overlooked Houston. It was decorated in a sophisticated natural palette, with oversized furniture covered in rich fabrics and soft leather.

I had only seen that kind of apartment on TV shows and in movies. I distrusted the pleasure I got from being in such beautiful surroundings. It had nothing to do with reverse prejudice or envy. It was just that I understood how temporary my presence was in this world, and I didn't want to get used to it. Although I had never considered myself an ambitious person, I was discovering the terrible allure of luxury. With a private grin, I thought of how much I needed Dane to readjust my priorities.

Luke lay on a blanket on the floor, resting on his tummy. I watched, fascinated, as he briefly lifted his head. He was getting stronger, focusing more on his surroundings. It seemed he changed a little every day. I knew he wasn't doing anything that millions of babies didn't already do, that most people would have said he was ordinary . . . but to me he was amazing. I wanted so much for him. I wanted Luke to have every advantage in the world, and instead he had gotten less than average. No family, no home, not even a mother yet.

Patting his diapered rear end, I considered what Haven had just said about Jack. "I know he could help," I said. "But I'd rather find some other way around it. Jack has done enough for me and Luke."

Haven brought her own glass of sangria and sat on the floor beside us. "I'm sure he wouldn't mind. He likes you, Ella."

"He likes all women."

That drew a wry smile from Haven. "I won't argue with that. But you're different from the usual buckle-bunnies I've seen him with."

I shot her a quick glance and opened my mouth to protest.

"Oh, I know you're not *with* him," she said. "But it's obvious there's interest. At least on his part."

"Really?" I struggled to keep my tone and expression neutral. "I haven't gotten that. I mean, Jack's been really nice about helping me get settled in here . . . but he definitely understands that I'm going back to Dane, and that I'm not available, and . . . what's a buckle-bunny?"

She grinned. "It used to be a description of the girls who hung around rodeo cowboys looking to hook up. Now it means any Texas gold digger who's looking for a sugar daddy."

"I'm not a gold digger."

"No, you advise them in your column. You tell them to support themselves and get their priorities straight."

"Everyone should listen to me," I said, and Haven laughed, lifting her glass.

I shared the toast, and took a sip.

"Have as much as you want, by the way," Haven told me. "Hardy won't touch it. He says he'll only have a fruity drink if we're on a tropical beach and no one we know is looking."

"What is it with Houston guys?" I asked in bemusement.

Haven grinned. "I don't know. I have an old college friend from Massachusetts who visited recently, and she swore the men around here were a subspecies."

"Did she like them?"

"Oh, yes. Her only complaint was that they didn't talk enough for her taste."

"Obviously she didn't get them started on the right subjects," I said, and Haven snickered.

"No kidding. Last week I had to listen to Hardy and Jack discuss all the ways you can start a fire without matches. They came up with seven."

"Eight," came a deep voice from the doorway, and I turned to see a man walking into the apartment. Hardy Cates had the rangy, muscular build of a roughneck, a surplus of sex appeal, and the bluest eyes I had ever seen. His hair wasn't the inky black of Jack's, but a rich mink brown. Setting down a bulging leather briefcase, he went to Haven. "We remembered," he continued laconically, "that you could polish the bottom of a Coke can with toothpaste and use the reflection to light tinder."

"Eight, then," Haven said, laughing, and lifted her face as he bent over her for a kiss. When he lifted his head, she said, "Hardy, this is Ella. The woman who's staying in my apartment."

Hardy bent and extended a hand to me. "Nice to meet you, Ella." His smile widened as he saw Luke. "How old is he?"

"About three weeks."

He gave the baby an approving glance. "Good-looking boy." Loosening his tie, Hardy glanced at the pitcher of pale liquid on the coffee table. "What are y'all drinking?"

"Sangria." Haven smiled at his expression. "There's beer in the fridge."

"Thanks, but tonight I'm starting with something stronger."

Haven watched alertly as her fiancé went to the kitchen. Although Hardy seemed relaxed, Haven must have been keenly attuned to his moods, because a furrow corrugated her forehead. She got up and went to him. "What is it?" she asked, while he poured a shot of Jack Daniel's.

Hardy sighed. "Had it out with Roy today." Glancing over at me, he explained, "One of my partners." His attention returned to Haven. "He's been analyzing cuttings from an old well, and he thinks we're going to hit a good pay zone if we keep on drilling. But the fingerprints on the cuttings—that's a way of measuring the quality of the oil—show that even if we find a reservoir, it's not going to be worth it."

"Roy doesn't agree?" Haven asked.

Hardy shook his head. "He's fighting to keep the checkbook open. But I told him the budget's gonna stay ribs-and-dick until—" Pausing, he threw me an apologetic grin. "Pardon, Ella. My language gets kind of rough when I've been out with the field guys."

"No problem," I said.

Haven ran a light hand over his arm after he tossed back the shot in one swallow. "Roy should know better than to argue with you," she murmured. "Your instinct for finding oil is practically legendary."

Setting aside the glass, Hardy gave her a rueful smile. "According to Roy, so is my ego."

"Roy's full of it." She leaned closer to him. "Need a hug?"

I leaned over Luke and played with him, trying to ignore what was quickly becoming a private moment.

I heard Hardy murmur something to the effect that he would get what he needed later, followed by absolute silence. Glancing at them, I saw his head bent over hers. Quickly I returned my attention to the baby. They should have some time alone, I thought.

As they came into the living room, I began to pack up the diaper bag. "Time for us to go," I said brightly. "Haven, that was the best sangria I've ever—"

"Oh, stay for dinner," she exclaimed. "I've already made a ton of chicken *escabeche*—it's a cold Mediterranean salad. And we'll have some tapas and olives and Manchego cheese."

"She's a great cook," Hardy said, crossing an arm around her front and pulling her against him. "Stay, Ella, or I'll end up having to drink that damn sangria with her."

I looked at them doubtfully. "Are you sure you don't want some privacy?"

"We wouldn't have it even if you left," Hardy said. "Jack's coming up here."

"He is?" Haven and I asked at the same time. A jolt of anxiety went through me.

"Yeah, I saw him in the lobby, told him to come up for a beer. He's in a great mood. He just met with some zoning lawyer about the building renovations for the McKinney Street property."

"They can bypass the restrictions?" Haven asked.

"The lawyer says so."

"I told Jack not to worry. Houston zoning is a myth. It never actually happens." Haven gave me an encouraging glance. "This'll work out perfectly, Ella. You can ask Jack about getting into Eternal Truth."

"You want Jack to go to church?" Hardy asked blankly. "Honey, he'd be struck by lightning as soon as he went in the front door."

Haven grinned at him. "Compared to you, Jack is a choirboy."

"Since he's your big brother," he told her kindly, "I'll let you keep your illusions."

The doorbell rang, and Haven went to answer it. I was annoyed to feel my pulse beginning to drum. The kiss meant nothing, I told myself. The feel of his body against mine had meant nothing. The sweet intimate taste of him, the heat—

"Hey, boss." Standing on her toes, Haven hugged Jack briefly.

"You only call me boss when you want something," Jack said, following her into the apartment. He stopped as he saw me, his expression inscrutable. He must have taken a moment to change clothes after work, because he was wearing faded jeans and a fresh T-shirt that seemed to glow optic-white against his cinnamon tan. I was unnerved by a response that cut deeply into my composure. He had an irresistible combination of vitality, confidence, and masculinity, blended like some perfectly proportioned cocktail. "Hey, Ella," he murmured, giving me a brief nod.

"Hi," I said feebly.

"You and Ella are staying for dinner," Haven informed him.

Jack glanced alertly at her and then back at me. "Are we?"

I nodded, reaching for my sangria, managing by some miracle not to knock it over.

Easing down to the floor beside me, Jack picked Luke up and tucked him against his chest. "Hi, little guy." The baby looked up at him intently, while Jack played with his tiny hand. "How's the crib working out?" Jack asked me, his attention still focused on Luke.

"It's great. Very sturdy."

He met my gaze then. We were sitting very close. The irises of his eyes were amazingly clear and brown, like some exotic spice dissolved in brandy. *You need a challenge*, he had told me, and I found it right there in his gaze, along with the promise that not only was I going to lose but I would enjoy it.

"Ella has a problem we were hoping you could help with," Haven said from the kitchen, opening the refrigerator.

Jack stared at me steadily, while one corner of his mouth curled upward. "What's your problem, Ella?"

"You want a beer, Jack?" came Hardy's voice.

"Yeah," Jack replied. "Lime wedge if you got it."

"I'm trying to get a meeting with Mark Gottler," I told Jack. "To talk with him about my sister."

His expression softened. "Is she okay?"

"Yes, I think so. But I don't think she's doing anything to secure her own interests, or Luke's. I need to meet with Gottler and pin him down on a few things. He's not going to pay Tara's clinic bill and dust his hands and think he's through with the whole thing. He's going to have to do right by Tara and Luke."

Settling Luke back onto the blanket, Jack picked up a little stuffed bunny and dangled it over him, causing Luke to kick his legs in enjoyment. "So you want me to get you in there," he said.

"Yes. I need to see Gottler privately."

"I can arrange a meeting, but the only way you'll get in there is by going embedded."

I gave him an outraged glance, incredulous that he would have propositioned me within earshot of his sister. "If you think I'm going to sleep with you just so I can see Gottler—"

"I said *embedded*, Ella. Not 'in bed.' "

"Oh," I said, chastened. "You meant like a computer virus?"

Jack nodded, looking sardonic. "I'll come up with some reason to meet with him and take you along. No sex required. Although if you're feeling grateful . . ."

"I'm not that grateful." But I couldn't help smiling, because I had never met a man who could have exuded such barely leashed sexiness while holding a stuffed bunny.

Jack followed my gaze to the toy in his hand. "What kind of stuff are you buying him? This isn't for boys."

"He likes it," I protested. "What's wrong with bunnies?"

Haven sat on a nearby ottoman, smiling ruefully. "Our brother Gage is the same," she told me. "Very definite ideas on what's appropriate for boys. Although I don't think he would have had a problem with the bunny, Jack."

"There's a bow on its tail," came Jack's grim observation. But he made do with the toy, hopping it across Luke's chest and making it swoop over his face.

Haven and I laughed at Luke's entranced expression. "Men and women relate to children so differently," Haven said. "Gage plays much rougher with Matthew, tosses him in the air, surprises him, and the baby seems to love it. I guess that's why it's good to have both—" She broke off and colored swiftly, recalling too late that Luke didn't have a father to speak of. "Sorry, Ella."

"It's okay," I said immediately. "Obviously Luke's going to be a little short on male influence for a while. But I'm hoping my sister will meet a good man at some point, and maybe Luke will have a stepfather someday."

"He'll be fine," Jack said, holding the bunny still while Luke grasped its ear. "God knows our dad was hardly ever around. And when he was, we could hardly wait to get rid of him. We grew up without a father, most of the time."

"And look how we turned out," Haven said. They glanced at each other, she and Jack, and burst out laughing as if at some absurdity.

We had a casual dinner, and everyone took turns holding Luke. Haven continued to pour the sangria, and I drank until I was pleasantly giddy. I laughed more than I had in weeks. Months. I wondered what it meant, however, that I could enjoy the company of people who were so different from Dane and my friends in Austin.

I was certain that Dane would find much to criticize about Hardy and Jack, both of them well versed in backroom deals and bending the rules. They were older than the men I was accustomed to, and far more cynical, and probably ruthless when it came to getting what they wanted. And yet so damnably charming.

That was the danger, I thought. The affable manners and the charm, blinding you to what they really were. The kind of man who could control you, steer you into compromise after compromise, and make you think you were happy doing it. And only after you had walked into the trap would you realize the mistake you had made. The revelation was that even knowing this, I could be so attracted to a man like Jack Travis.

I sat next to him on one of the deep velvet sofas, trying to identify the feeling that was stealing over me. I finally realized it was relaxation. I had never been an especially relaxed person, always wound tight and waiting for an emergency to strike. But tonight I was strangely at ease. Maybe it was because I was in a situation in which I had no need to protect myself or prove anything. Maybe it was the sleeping baby, warm and safe in my arms.

As I settled back with Luke, I found myself tucked against Jack's warm side, one of his arms extended along the sofa back. Closing my eyes, I let my cheek rest on his shoulder. Just for a moment. One of his hands came up to the side of my face, stroking my hair.

"What did you put in that goddamn sangria, Haven?" I heard him ask mildly.

"Nothing," she said in a defensive tone. "White wine, mostly. I've had just as much as Ella, and I'm fine."

"I'm fine, too," I protested, screwing my eyes open. "Just a li'l—" I paused, having to concentrate to form the words right. My tongue felt like it had been Scotchguarded. "Shleep-deprived."

"Ella, honey . . ." There was a tremor of laughter in Jack's voice, and his hand moved over my hair. His fingers delved through the light, loose strands to my scalp and stroked tenderly. I closed my eyes again and held still, hoping he wouldn't stop.

"What time is it?" I mumbled, yawning.

"Eight-thirty."

I heard Haven ask, "Should I make coffee?"

"No," Jack said before I could reply.

"Liquor can hit you like an anvil when you're tired," Hardy said, sounding sympathetic. "It was like that on the rig. A couple of weeks on with a night shift thrown in, and you were so exhausted one beer would lay you flat."

"I'm still getting used to Luke's schedule," I said, rubbing my bleary eyes. "He's not what you'd call a good sleeper. Even for an infant."

"Ella," Haven said, her face kind and concerned, "we've got an extra bedroom. Why don't you crash here tonight? I'll take care of Luke so you can get some rest."

"No. Oh, that's so nice, you're so . . . but I'm fine. I jus' need to . . ." I paused to yawn, and forgot what I'd been saying. "Need to find the elevator," I said vaguely.

Haven came to me, lifting the baby from my arms. "I'll put him in his carrier."

I wished I could have just five more minutes of resting against Jack. The muscles beneath his T-shirt pillowed my cheek so firmly, so perfectly. "Li'l longer," I mumbled, burrowing deeper. I sighed and drowsed, dimly aware of the murmured conversation around me.

". . . hard, what she's doing," Haven was saying. "To put your life on hold . . ."

"What's the deal with the Austin guy?" Hardy asked.

"Wouldn't man up," Jack replied in a tone of unqualified disdain. And although I wanted to say something in Dane's defense, I was too exhausted to make a sound. Either I dozed more heavily or a long silence passed, because I didn't hear anything for a while.

"Ella," I eventually heard, and I shook my head in annoyance. I was so comfortable, and I wanted the voice to go away. "Ella." Something soft and hot brushed my cheek. "Let me take you down to your apartment."

I was mortified to realize that I had fallen sound asleep in front of all three of them, and that I was practically in Jack's lap. "Okay. Yes. I'm sorry." I struggled upward, tried to find my balance.

Jack reached out to steady me. "Lightweight."

Red-faced and groggy, I scowled. "I didn't have that much to drink."

"We know you didn't," Haven said soothingly, and she shot her brother a warning glance. "You're the last person who has any right to tease, Mr. Sleep Inertia."

Jack grinned and told me, "I get up at seven every morning, but I'm not really awake 'til noon." He kept a supportive arm around my shoulder. "Come on, blue eyes. I'll help you find the elevator."

"Where's the baby?"

"I just fed and changed him," Haven said. Hardy lifted Luke's carrier and gave it to Jack, who took it with his free hand.

"Thank you." I gave Haven a woeful glance as she handed me the diaper bag. "I'm sorry."

"For what?"

"For falling asleep like that."

Haven smiled and reached out to hug me. "There's nothing to be sorry about. What's a little narcolepsy among friends?" Her body was slim and strong, one small hand patting my back. The gesture surprised me in its naturalness and ease. I returned the embrace awkwardly. Haven said over my shoulder, "I like this one, Jack."

Jack didn't answer, only nudged me out into the hallway.

I trudged forward, nearly blind with exhaustion, staggering with it. It took extreme focus to keep one foot in front of the other. "I don't know why I'm so tired tonight," I said. "It's all caught up with me, I guess." I felt Jack's hand descend to the center of my back, guiding me forward. I decided to talk to keep myself awake. "You know, chronic sleep deper . . . dep . . ."

"Deprivation?"

"Yes." I shook my head to clear it. "It gives you memory problems and raises your blood pressure. And it results in occupational hazards. It's lucky I can't get hurt doing my job. Unless I fall forward and hit my head on the keyboard. If you ever see QWERTY imprinted on my forehead, you'll know what happened."

"Here we go," Jack said, loading me onto the elevator. I squinted at the row of buttons and reached for one. "No," he said patiently, "that's the nine, Ella. Press the upside-down one."

"They're all upside-down," I told him, but I managed to find the 6. Propping myself up in the corner, I wrapped my arms around my midriff. "Why did Haven tell you 'I like this one'?"

"Why shouldn't she like you?"

"It's just . . . if she says it to you, it implies . . ."—I tried to wrap my foggy brain around the idea—". . . something."

A quiet laugh escaped him. "Don't try thinking just now, Ella. Save it for later."

That sounded like a good idea. "Okay."

The elevator door opened, and I tottered out while Jack followed.

Due to luck rather than coordination, I pushed the right combination on the keypad of my door. We went into the apartment. "Have to make the bottles," I said, lurching toward the kitchen.

"I'll take care of that. Go put on your pajamas."

Gratefully I went into the bedroom and changed into a T-shirt and flannel pants. By the time I finished washing my face and brushing my teeth, and went to the kitchen, Jack had already filled the bottles, put them in the refrigerator, and had settled Luke in the crib. He smiled as I approached him hesitantly. "You look like a little girl," he murmured, "with your face all clean and shiny." He touched my face with one hand, his thumb stroking beneath one of my dark-circled eyes. "Tired girl," he whispered.

I flushed. "I'm not a child."

"I know that." He eased me closer, his arms warm and secure, shoring my balance. "You're a strong, smart woman. But even strong women need help sometimes. You're wearing yourself out, Ella. Yeah, I know you don't like advice unless you're giving it. But you're getting some anyway. You need to start thinking long-term about what you're going to do with Luke."

I was amazed that I could reply coherently. "This isn't a long-term situation."

"You don't know that. Especially if it all depends on Tara."

"I know that people can change."

"People can change their habits, maybe. But not who they are deep down." Jack began to rub my back and shoulders, and squeezed the sore muscles at the nape of my neck. I let out a faint moan at the exquisite pressure of his fingers. "I hope to hell that Tara will be able to solve her problems and turn into a half-decent parent and let you off the hook. But I'd be damn surprised if that happens. I think this situation is more permanent than you'd like to admit. You're a new mother, whether or not you had a chance to get ready for it. You're going to burn out if you don't take care of yourself. You need to sleep when the baby sleeps. You need to find daycare, or get a nanny or a go-to babysitter."

"I won't be here that long. Tara will come for him, and then I'm going back to Austin."

"Back to what? A guy who bails on you when you need him? What's Dane doing now that's more important than helping you? Fighting for the rights of endangered ferns?"

I stiffened and pushed away from him, irritation jolting me out of my fugue-state. "You have no right to judge Dane or my relationship with him."

Jack made a scoffing sound. "That half-assed excuse for a relationship was over the moment Dane told you not to bring the baby to Austin. You know what he should have said? . . . 'Hell, yes, Ella, I'll stand by you no matter what you do. Shit happens. We'll make it work. Come home now and get in bed.' "

"There was no way Dane could have handled this and kept his company going, and you have no idea how many causes he has, how many people he helps—"

"His woman should be his number-one cause."

"Spare me the bumper-sticker philosophy. And quit taking cheap shots at Dane. When have you ever put a woman first?"

"I'm about to put you first right now, darlin'."

That comment could have been construed a few different ways, but the gleam in his eyes gave it a positively filthy spin. My thoughts scattered and my pulse went crazy. It wasn't fair for him to make a move on me when I was exhausted. But apparently on Jack Travis's list of priorities, fairness ranked a lot lower than sex. And it was sex we were circling around. It had been since the beginning. There was no way either of us could take it out of the equation.

I found myself scooting behind the coffee table like the outraged virgin in some Victorian melodrama. "Jack, this isn't a good time. I'm really tired and I'm not thinking straight."

"That's what makes it a great time. If you were rested and sober, it'd be a hell of a lot harder to argue with you."

"I don't do things on impulse, Jack. I don't—" I broke off with a swift in-drawn breath as he reached across the space between us and snatched my wrist in his hand. "Let go." There was no force to my voice at all.

"How many guys you been with, Ella?" he asked softly, drawing me around the coffee table.

"I don't believe people should tell each other their numbers. In fact, I once wrote a column—"

"One, two?" he interrupted, bringing me close again.

I was trembling. "One and a half."

A smile touched his lips. "How can you have sex with half a guy?"

"I was dating him in high school. We were experimenting. I was working up to going all the way with him, but before that happened, I came home one day and found him in bed with my mother."

With a sympathetic sound, Jack held me close, the embrace so careful and protective that I had no chance in hell of resisting it.

"I'm over it now," I added.

"Right." He continued to hold me.

"Sex has always been great with Dane. I've never needed to look anywhere else."

"Okay."

"Basically I'm not really driven in that regard."

"Sure." His arms tightened until I had no choice but to rest my head on his shoulder. I relaxed slowly. It was so quiet in the room, nothing but the sound of his breathing, and mine, and the hum of the air-conditioning vent.

Sweet Lord, he smelled good.

I wanted nothing to do with any of this. It was like being strapped into a roller-coaster seat, waiting for the ride to start, knowing it was going to be awful. Death-defying drops. Hematoma-inducing G-forces.

"Ever wonder what it would be like with someone else?" Jack asked gently.

"No."

I felt his mouth brush over my hair. "You never had a spontaneous moment when you said, 'What the hell,' and went for it?"

"I don't have spontaneous moments."

"Here's one for you, Ella." Jack's lips found mine, following insistently as I tried to evade him. His hand curled around the back of my neck, his fingers strong. A shock went through me, spurring my heart into a fast, frantic beat. He kissed me repeatedly, long indecent kisses, all slippery friction and hot silk. I gasped at the abrasion of his shaven jaw and cheeks, the insistent exploration of his tongue.

Blindly I reached for his wrists, one behind my neck, one at my side, and I gripped hard, the tips of my nails digging into dense muscle. I didn't know if I was trying to pull his hands away or push them closer. He kept kissing me, exploring roughly, expertly. I let go of his wrists and molded against the arousing terrain of his body. I had never existed in such a purely physical compass, thinking nothing, aware of nothing. Only needing. Craving.

He slid one hand to my bottom, urging me against the stiff, enticing pressure of his erection, and I was panting, arching in a desperate effort to keep him right there. His kisses gentled, his mouth absorbing the sounds that rose in my throat. I strained against him, sensation collecting, muscles tightening as his hand pressed me in a subtle rhythm. Nothing had ever been so delicious as his mouth, his body, the hands that urged me forward until our hips were rubbing in a lazy exact pulse.

The tension gathered in a surge that promised release . . . wrenching, out-of-control, in-heat spasms that would cause me to die of humiliation. All that from a kiss and a fully clothed embrace. *Not going to happen,* I thought in panic, tearing my mouth from his.

"Wait," I said with difficulty, my fingers tangling helplessly in his shirt. My body throbbed in every extremity. My mouth felt swollen. "I have to stop."

Jack looked down at me, his eyes heavy lidded, his cheekbones and the bridge of his nose burnished with high color. "Not yet," he said thickly. "We're just getting to the best part." Before I could make another sound, he bent to take my mouth again. This time there was intent in the rhythm, a shameless grinding deliberateness. He was pushing me, teasing, letting my squirming body carry the momentum.

Taste, movement, hot rhythmic stroking, all pulled the ecstatic sensations into one forward direction. I jerked against him, giving a low cry. The rush was so powerful that I couldn't keep up with my own heartbeat. I shivered and hunched and clenched my hands in his shirt. And Jack prolonged the pleasure, maintaining the unhurried sliding rhythm, knowing exactly what he was doing. As the last few twitches left my body, dissolving in a white-hot glow, I whimpered and sagged against him. "Oh no. Oh God. You shouldn't have done that."

Jack nipped at my chin, my scarlet cheek, the tender skin of my throat. "It's okay," he whispered. "It's all good, Ella."

We both fell silent, waiting for me to catch my breath. Pressed as close as we were, I could hardly keep from noticing that he was still aroused. What was the sexual etiquette for this? I had an obligation to reciprocate, didn't I? "I guess," I faltered after a long moment, "I should do something for you now."

Jack's midnight eyes were bright with amusement. "That's okay. My treat."

"That's not fair to you."

"Get some rest. Later you can tell me what's on the menu."

I looked at him uncertainly, wondering what he might expect from me. I'd had a normal healthy sex life with Dane, but we had never strayed into what anyone would consider exotic territory. "My menu is pretty limited."

"Considering how much I liked the appetizer, I wouldn't complain." Jack released me cautiously, keeping one hand on my shoulder as I swayed. "Want me to carry you to bed?" His tone was teasing and gentle. "Tuck you in?"

I shook my head.

"Go on, then," Jack murmured. I felt him pat my bottom.

And he left the apartment while I stared after him, feeling dazed and elated and horribly guilty. I bit my lip to keep from calling him back.

I checked on Luke, who was deep in slumber, and then I went to the bedroom and crawled beneath the covers. As I lay in the darkness, my battered conscience crawled out of a trench, waving a little white flag.

I realized Dane and I hadn't talked the previous night, or this one. The familiar pattern of my life was fading like a rub-on tattoo.

I'm in trouble, Dane. I think I'm going to make a terrible mistake. I can't seem to stop it from happening.

I'm losing my way.

Let me come home.

Had I not been so exhausted, I would have called Dane. But I knew I wouldn't be coherent. And in some obdurate, bruised corner of my heart, I wanted Dane to call me.

But the phone stayed silent. And when I fell asleep, Dane had no part of my dreams.

THIRTEEN

Dear Miss Independent,

I just started going out with a guy I have nothing in common with. He's a few years younger than me and we have different tastes in just about everything. He likes the outdoors, I like to stay inside. He likes sci-fi and I like knitting. In spite of all that, I have never been so crazy about anyone. But I'm afraid that since we're so different, the relationship is doomed to fail. Should I break it off now before we get any more involved?

—Worried in Walla Walla

Dear Worried,

Sometimes when we're not paying attention, relationships happen. There is no rule that requires two people in love to be exactly alike. In fact, there is some scientific evidence to suggest that on a genetic level, the people who are the most opposite are the most likely to have a healthy and long-lasting pairing. But really, who can explain the mysteries of attraction? Blame it on Cupid. The moon. The shape of a smile. Both of you can thrive on your differences, as long as you respect them. You say tomato, he says tomahto. Let it happen, Worried. Dive in headfirst. We usually learn the most about ourselves from people who are different from us.

—Miss Independent

I stared at my computer screen. "Let it happen?" I muttered. I hated to let things happen. I never went anywhere new without MapQuesting it. Whenever I bought something, I sent in the registration and warranty cards. When Dane and I had sex, we used condoms, spermicide, *and* the pill. I never ate foods containing red dye. I wore sunscreen with double digit SPF.

You need some fun, Jack had told me, and subsequently proved that he was more than capable of supplying it. I had a feeling that if I ever let go with him, there would be a lot of seriously adult fun involved. Except that life wasn't about fun, it was about doing the right thing, and if fun was an occasional by-product, you were lucky.

I cringed at the thought of the next time I saw Jack, wondering what I would say to him. If only I could confide in someone. Stacy. But I knew she would tell Tom, who would make some comment to Dane.

Halfway through the day, the phone rang, and I saw Jack's number on the caller ID. I reached for the phone, snatched my hand back, then reached again cautiously.

"Hello?"

"Ella, how's it going?" Jack sounded relaxed and professional. An office voice.

"Pretty good," I said warily. "You?"

"Great. Listen, I made a couple of calls to Eternal Truth this morning, and I want to bring you up to date. Why don't you meet me for lunch at the restaurant?"

"The one on the seventh floor?"

"Yeah, you can bring Luke. Meet me there in twenty minutes."

"Can't you just tell me now?"

"No, I need someone to eat with."

A slight smile rose to my lips. "Am I supposed to believe that I'm your only option?"

"No. But you're my favorite option."

I was glad he couldn't see the color that swept over my face. "I'll be there."

Since I was still wearing my pajamas, I dashed to the closet and grabbed a beige twill jacket, a white shirt, jeans, and sandals with wedge heels. I spent the rest of the time getting Luke ready, changing him into a fresh onesie and baby jeans that snapped along the insides of the legs.

When I was certain we were presentable, I put Luke in his carrier and slung the diaper bag over my shoulder. We went up to the restaurant, a contemporary bistro with black leather chairs and glass tables, and colorful abstract artwork on the walls. Most of the diners were business people, women in conservative dresses, men in classic suits. Jack was already there, talking with the hostess. He was lean and handsome in a dark navy suit and French blue shirt. Ruefully I reflected that Houston, unlike Austin, was a place where people dressed for lunch.

Jack saw me and came forward to take Luke's carrier. He disconcerted me by pressing a brief kiss on my cheek.

"Hi," I said, blinking. I was annoyed to discover that I was embarrassed and breathless, as if I'd been caught watching an adult cable channel.

Jack seemed to know exactly what I was thinking. He smiled slowly.

"Don't look so smug," I told him.

"I'm not smug. This is just my way of smiling."

The hostess led us to a corner table by the windows, and Jack set Luke's carrier on the chair beside mine. After seating me, Jack handed me a small blue paper bag with string handles.

"What's this?" I asked.

"It's for Luke."

I reached in the bag and pulled out a small stuffed truck made for infants. It was soft and pliant, sewn with different textured fabrics. The wheels made a crinkling noise when you squished them. I shook the toy experimentally and heard a rattling sound. Smiling, I showed the toy to Luke and placed it on his chest. He immediately began to grope the interesting new object with his tiny fingers.

"That's a truck," I told the baby.

"An articulated front loader," Jack added helpfully.

"Thanks. I guess we can get rid of that sissy bunny now."

Our gazes held, and I found myself smiling at him. I could still feel the place on my cheek where he had kissed me.

"Did you talk to Mark Gottler personally?" I asked.

Jack's eyes glinted with humor. "Do we have to start with that?"

"What else would we start with?"

"Couldn't you ask me something like, 'How did your morning go?' or 'What's your idea of the perfect day?' "

"I already know what your idea of the perfect day is."

He arched a brow as if that surprised him. "You do? Let's hear it."

I was going to say something flip and funny. But as I stared at him, I considered the question seriously. "Hmmn. I think you'd be at a cottage at the beach . . ."

"My perfect day includes a woman," he volunteered.

"Okay. There's a girlfriend. Very low-maintenance."

"I don't know any low-maintenance women."

"That's why you like this one so much. And the cottage is rustic, by the way. No cable, no wireless, and you've both turned off your cell phones. The two of you take a morning walk along the beach, maybe go for a swim. And you pick up a few pieces of seaglass to put in a jar. Later, you both ride bikes into the town, and you head for the outfitters shop to buy some fishing stuff . . . some kind of bait—"

"Flies, not bait," Jack said, his gaze not moving from mine. "Lefty's Deceivers."

"For what kind of fish?"

"Redfish."

"Great. So then you go fishing—"

"The girlfriend, too?" he asked.

"No, she stays behind and reads."

"She doesn't like to fish?"

"No, but she thinks it's fine that you do, and she says it's healthy for you to have separate interests." I paused. "She packed a really big sandwich and a couple of beers for you."

"I like this woman."

"You go out in your boat, and you bring home a nice catch and throw it on the grill. You and the woman have dinner. You sit with your feet up, and you talk. Sometimes you stop to listen to the sounds of the tide coming in. After that, the two of you go on the beach with a bottle of wine, and sit on a blanket to watch the sunset." I finished and looked at him expectantly. "How was that?"

I had thought Jack would be amused, but he stared at me with dis-

concerting seriousness. "Great." And then he was quiet, staring at me as if he were trying to figure out some sleight-of-hand trick.

The waiter approached us, described the specials, took our drink orders, and left us with a bread basket.

Reaching for his water glass, Jack rubbed his thumb over the film of condensation on the outside. Then he shot me a level glance as if taking up a challenge. "My turn," he said.

I smiled, having fun. "You're going to guess my perfect day? That's too easy. All it would involve is earplugs, blackout shades, and twelve hours of sleep."

He ignored that. "It's a nice fall day—"

"There's no fall in Texas." I reached for a cube of bread with little shreds of basil embedded in it.

"You're on vacation. There's fall."

"Am I by myself or with Dane?" I asked, dipping a corner of the bread into a tiny dish of olive oil.

"You're with a guy. But not Dane."

"Dane doesn't get to be part of my perfect day?"

Jack shook his head slowly, watching me. "New guy."

Taking a bite of the dense, delicious bread, I decided to humor him. "Where are New Guy and I vacationing?"

"New England. New Hampshire, probably."

Intrigued, I considered the idea. "I've never been that far north."

"You're staying in an old hotel with verandas and chandeliers and gardens."

"That sounds nice," I admitted.

"You and the guy go driving through the mountains to see the color of the leaves, and you find a little town where there's a crafts festival. You stop and buy a couple of dusty used books, a pile of handmade Christmas ornaments, and a bottle of genuine maple syrup. You go back to the hotel and take a nap with the windows open."

"Does he like naps?"

"Not usually. But he makes an exception for you."

"I like this guy. So what happens when we wake up?"

"You get dressed for drinks and dinner, and you go down to the restaurant. At the table next to yours, there's an old couple who looks like they've been married at least fifty years. You and the guy take turns guessing the secret of a long marriage. He says it's lots of great sex. You say it's being with someone who can make you laugh every day. He says he can do both."

I couldn't help smiling. "Pretty sure of himself, isn't he?"

"Yeah, but you like that about him. After dinner, the two of you dance to live orchestra music."

"He knows how to dance?"

Jack nodded. "His mother made him take lessons when he was in grade school."

I forced myself to take another bite of bread, chewing casually. But inside I felt stricken, filled with unexpected yearning. And I realized the problem: no one I knew would have come up with that day for me.

This is a man, I thought, *who could break my heart.*

"Sounds fun," I said lightly, busying myself with Luke, repositioning the truck. "Okay, what did Gottler say? Or did you talk with his secretary? Do we have a meeting?"

Jack smiled at the abrupt change of subject. "Friday morning. I spoke with his secretary. When I mentioned maintenance contract issues, she tried to switch me over to another department. So I implied that it was a personal matter, that I might want to join the church."

I regarded him skeptically. "Mark Gottler would agree to have a private meeting with you in the hopes of getting you to join the congregation?"

"Of course he would. I'm a public sinner with a ton of money. Any church would want me."

I laughed. "Don't you already belong to one?"

Jack shook his head. "My parents were from two different churches, so I was raised Baptist and Methodist. With the result that I've never been sure if it's okay to dance in public. And for a while I thought Lent was something you brushed off your jacket."

"I'm agnostic," I told him. "I'd be an atheist, except I believe in hedging my bets."

"I'm a fan of small churches, myself."

I gave him an innocent glance. "You mean being in a hundred and seventy-five thousand square foot broadcast studio with gigantic I-mag screens and integrated sound and production-lighting systems doesn't make you feel closer to God?"

"I'm not sure I should bring a little heathen like you into Eternal Truth."

"I bet I've led a more virtuous life than you."

"First, darlin', that's not saying much. Second, getting to a higher spiritual level is like increasing your credit score. You get a lot more points for sinning and repenting than if you have no credit history at all."

Reaching over to Luke, I played with one of his sock-covered feet. "For this baby," I said, "I would do anything including jump into the baptismal fountain."

"I'll keep that in mind as a bargaining point," Jack said. "Meanwhile, put your wish list for Tara together, and we'll see if we can stick it to Gottler on Friday."

* * *

THE FELLOWSHIP OF ETERNAL TRUTH HAD ITS OWN Web site and Wikipedia page. The main pastor, Noah Cardiff, was a handsome man in his forties, married with five children. His wife, Angelica, was a slender, attractive woman who wore enough eyeshadow to recoat an RV roof. It quickly became apparent that Eternal Truth was more of an empire than a church. In fact, it was referred to in the *Houston Chronicle* as a "giga church," owning a small fleet of private jets, an airstrip, and real estate that included mansions, sports facilities, and its own publishing company. I was astonished to learn that Eternal Truth also had its own oil and gas field, run by a subsidiary company called Eternity Petrol Incorporated. The church employed over five hundred people and had a twelve-member board of directors, five of whom were Cardiff's relatives.

I couldn't find any clips of Mark Gottler on YouTube, but I did find some of Noah Cardiff. He was charismatic and charming, making the occasional self-deprecating joke, assuring his worldwide congregation of all the good things their Creator had in store for them. He looked angelic, with his black hair and fair skin and blue eyes. In fact, watching the YouTube clip made me feel so good that if a collection plate had been passing by at that moment, I would have dropped twenty bucks in it. And if Cardiff had that effect on a feminist agnostic, there was no telling what a true believer might have been moved to donate.

On Friday, the babysitter arrived at nine. Her name was Teena, and she seemed friendly and competent. I had gotten her name from Haven, who said Teena had done a great job with her nephew. I was worried about leaving Luke in anyone else's care—it was the first time we had ever been separated—but it was also something of a relief to have a break.

As we had agreed, I met Jack downstairs in the lobby. I was a few minutes late, having lingered to give a few last-minute instructions to Teena. "Sorry." I quickened my stride as I walked toward Jack, who was standing by the concierge desk. "I didn't mean to be late."

"It's fine," Jack said. "We still have plenty of—" He broke off as he got a good look at me, his jaw slackening.

Self-consciously I reached up and tucked a lock of my hair behind my right ear. I was wearing a slim-fitting black suit made of summer-weight wool, and black high-heeled pumps with delicate straps that crossed over the front. I had put on some light makeup: shimmery brown eye shadow, a coat of black mascara, a touch of pink blush, and lip gloss.

"Do I look okay?" I asked.

Jack nodded, his gaze unblinking.

I bit back a grin, realizing he had never seen me dressed up before. And the suit was flattering, cut to show my curves to advantage. "I thought this was more appropriate for church than jeans and Birkenstocks."

I wasn't certain Jack heard me. It looked like his mind was working on another track altogether. My suspicion was confirmed when he said fervently, "You have amazing legs."

"Thanks." I gave a modest shrug. "Yoga."

That appeared to set off another round of thoughts. I thought Jack's color seemed a little high, although it was difficult to tell with that rosewood tan. His voice sounded strained as he asked, "I guess you're pretty flexible?"

"I wasn't the most flexible in class by any means," I said, pausing before adding demurely, "but I can put my ankles behind my head." I repressed a grin when I heard a hitch in his breathing. Seeing that his SUV was out in front, I walked past him. He was at my heels immediately.

The Eternal Truth campus was only five miles away. Even though I had done research and had seen pictures of the facilities, I felt my eyes widen in amazement as we pulled through the front gate. The main building was the size of a sports arena.

"My God," I said, "how many parking spaces are there?"

"Looks like at least two thousand," Jack replied, driving through the lot.

"Welcome to church in the twenty-first century," I muttered, preparing to dislike everything about Eternal Truth.

When we went in, I was stunned by the grandeur of the place. The lobby was dominated by a gigantic LED screen showing film clips of happy families having picnics, walking through sunny neighborhoods, parents pushing children on swings, washing the dog, going to church together.

Towering fifteen-foot-high statues of Jesus and the disciples stood near entrances to a food court and an atrium space lined with emerald glass. Panels of green malachite and warm cherry wood lined the walls, and acres of immaculate patterned carpeting covered the floor. The bookstore on the other side of the lobby was filled with people. Everyone seemed upbeat, people pausing to talk and laugh, while feel-good music wafted through the air.

I had read that Eternal Truth was both admired and criticized for its health-and-wealth gospel. Pastor Cardiff emphasized often that God wanted his congregation to enjoy material prosperity as well as spiritual advancement. In fact, he insisted that the two went hand-in-hand. If one of the church members was having financial difficulty, he needed to pray harder for success. Money, it seemed, was a reward for faith.

I didn't know nearly enough about theology to engage in a competent discussion. But I instinctively distrusted anything that was this slickly packaged and marketed. On the other hand . . . the people here seemed happy. If the doctrine worked for them, if it satisfied their needs, did I have any right to object? Perplexed, I stopped with Jack as a smiling greeter came to us.

After a brief murmured consultation, the greeter serenely directed us beyond a set of massive marble columns to an escalator, and we went upward into an airy space of sunlight and emerald glass, and a limestone cornice engraved with scripture: I CAME THAT THEY MAY HAVE LIFE AND HAVE IT ABUNDANTLY. JOHN 10:10

A secretary was already waiting for us at the top of the escalator. She led us to an executive suite with a spacious conference room. There was a twenty-foot-long keystone table made of exotic woods, with a strip of colored printed glass running along the center.

"Wow," I said, surveying the leather executive chairs, the large mounted flat screen TV, the data ports and individual monitors set up for video conferencing. "Quite a setup."

The secretary smiled. "I'll tell Pastor Gottler you're here."

I glanced at Jack, who half-sat, half-leaned on the edge of the table. "You think Jesus would have hung out here?" I asked as soon as the secretary left.

He gave me a warning glance. "Don't start."

"According to what I've read, Eternal Truth's message is that God wants all of us to be rich and successful. So I guess you're a little closer to heaven than the rest of us, Jack."

"If you want to blaspheme, Ella, I'm all for it. *After* we leave."

"I can't help it. Something about this place bothers me. You were right—it *is* like Disneyland. And in my opinion they're feeding their flock spiritual junk food."

"A little junk food never hurt anyone," Jack said.

The door opened, and a tall blond man entered the room.

Mark Gottler was good-looking and swathed in an air of gentility. He was stocky and full-cheeked, well fed, well groomed. Gottler had an air of being above the flock, calmly accepting their reverence. You couldn't imagine him being at the mercy of normal bodily functions.

This was the man my sister had slept with?

Gottler's eyes were the color of melted Kraft caramels. He looked at Jack and went straight for him with an outstretched hand. "Good to see you again, Jack." With his free hand, he briefly covered their clasped ones, making it a two-handed shake. One could take that either as a controlling gesture, or one of exceptional warmth. Jack's pleasant expression didn't change.

"I see you've brought a friend," Gottler continued with a smile, reaching for me next. I shook his hand and was accorded the same two-handed grip.

I pulled back irritably. "My name is Ella Varner," I said before Jack could introduce us. "I think you know my sister, Tara."

Gottler let go of me, staring. The glaze of politeness remained intact, but the air became cold enough to freeze vodka. "Yes, I'm acquainted with Tara," he said, summoning a faint smile. "She did some work in our administrative offices. I've heard a little about you, Ella. You're a gossip columnist, right?"

"Close enough," I said.

Gottler looked at Jack, his eyes opaque. "I was led to believe you were coming to me for counsel."

"I am," Jack said easily, pulling out a chair from the table and gesturing for me to sit. "There is a problem I want to talk to you about. It just doesn't happen to be mine."

"How do you and Miss Varner know each other?"

"Ella's a good friend of mine."

Gottler looked directly at me. "Does your sister know you're here?"

I shook my head, wondering how often he talked with her. Why would a married man in his profession take the risks that he had, having an affair with an unstable young woman and getting her pregnant? It frightened me to comprehend that tens of millions of dollars—more—were at risk because of this situation. A sex scandal would be a huge blow to the church, not to mention the ruin of Mark Gottler's career.

"I told Ella," Jack said, "that I thought you might have some ideas about how we could help Tara." A deliberate pause. "And the baby." Taking the chair beside mine, he leaned back comfortably. "Have you seen him yet?"

"I'm afraid not." Gottler went to the opposite side of the conference table. He took his time about settling into a chair. "The church does what it can for our brothers and sisters in need, Jack. It may be that in the future I'll have a chance to speak with Tara herself about what assistance we can provide for her. But that's a private matter. I think Tara would rather keep it her own business."

I didn't like Mark Gottler at all. I didn't like his smoothness, his smug self-assurance, his perfect hair. I didn't like the way he had fathered a child and hadn't even bothered to see him. There were too many men in the world who had gotten away with abandoning responsibility for the children they had fathered. My own father had been one of them.

"As you know, Mr. Gottler," I said evenly, "my sister isn't in a position to handle her own business. She's vulnerable. Easy to take advantage of. That's why I wanted to talk to you myself."

The pastor smiled at me. "Before we get into this any further, let's take a moment to pray."

"I don't see why—" I began.

"Sure," Jack interrupted, nudging my leg under the table. He sent me a warning glance. *Take it easy, Ella.*

I scowled and subsided, lowering my head.

Gottler began. "Dear Heavenly Father, Lord of our hearts, Giver of all good things, we pray for Your peace today. We ask You to help us turn any moments of negativity into opportunities to find Your way and resolve our differences . . ."

The prayer went on and on, until I came to the conclusion that Gottler was either stalling or trying to impress us with his elocution. Either way, I was impatient. I wanted to talk about Tara. I wanted decisions to be made. As I lifted my head to steal a glance at Gottler, I found that he was doing the same with me, sizing up the situation, assessing me as an adversary. And still he kept talking. ". . . since You created the universe, Lord, You can surely make things happen for our sister Tara, and—"

"She's my sister, not yours," I snapped. Both men glanced up at me in surprise. I knew I should have kept my mouth shut, but I couldn't stand it any longer. My nerves were as tight as the teeth on a pocket comb.

"Let the man pray, Ella," Jack murmured. His hand settled high on my shoulders, his thumb rubbing the nape of my neck. I stiffened but fell silent.

I understood. Rituals had to be observed. We wouldn't get anything by going *mano a mano* with the pastor. I dropped my head and waited while he continued. I occupied myself with taking a few yoga breaths from deep down, continuous and easy. I felt Jack's thumb at the back of my neck, circling with agreeable pressure.

Finally, Gottler finished with, "May You grant us wisdom and profiting ears, almighty and merciful Lord. Amen."

"Amen," Jack and I both murmured, and we looked up. Jack's hand slid away from me.

"Mind if I talk first?" Jack asked Gottler, who nodded.

Jack slid a questioning glance at me.

"Sure," I muttered acidly. "You guys just talk things over while I listen."

Relaxed and soft-voiced, Jack said to Gottler, "Don't see the need to spell out the particulars of the situation, Mark. I think we all know what's under the porch. And we want to keep things private as much as you do."

"Good to hear," Gottler said with unmistakable sincerity.

"I figure we're all after the same thing," Jack continued. "For Tara and Luke to get situated, and everyone to go on with business as usual."

"The church helps a lot of people in need, Jack," Gottler said reasonably. "I'm sorry to say there are many young women in Tara's situation. And we do what we can. But if we help out Tara more than we do others, I'm afraid it's going to draw some unwanted attention to her situation."

"What about a court-ordered paternity test?" I asked tautly. "That would draw some attention, too, wouldn't it? What about—"

"Easy, honey," Jack murmured. "Mark's working around to something. Give him a chance."

"I hope he is," I retorted, "because paying for Tara's stay at the clinic is only the beginning. I want a trust fund for the baby, and I want—"

"Miss Varner," Gottler said, "I had already decided to offer Tara an employment contract." Faced with my ill-concealed scorn, he added meaningfully, "With benefits."

"Sounds interesting," Jack commented, gripping my thigh beneath the table and pushing me fully into my seat. "Let's hear the man out. Go on, Mark . . . what kind of benefits? Are we talking some kind of housing deal?"

"That is definitely on the table," the pastor allowed. "Federal tax law allows ministries to provide parsonages for their employees, so . . . if Tara works for us, it wouldn't violate any prohibitions against personal benefit." Gottler paused thoughtfully. "The church has a ranch in Colleyville that includes a private gated community with about ten houses on it. Each one is fenced with a pool, on an acre lot. Tara and the baby could live there."

"By themselves?" I asked. "With things like utilities, landscaping, maintenance all taken care of?"

"That might be possible," he allowed.

"For how long?" I persisted.

Gottler was silent. Clearly there were limits to what Eternal Truth was willing to do for Tara Varner, no matter that one of its chief clergy had knocked her up. Why did I have to be here prying something out of Mark Gottler that he should have already offered?

My thoughts must have shown on my face, because Jack interceded quickly.

"We're not interested in temporary solutions, Mark, since the baby is now a permanent part of Tara's life. I think we're going to have to work out some kind of promissory contract with assurances for both sides. We can offer a guarantee that there'll never be any talking to the media, the child won't be submitted to genetic testing to determine parentage . . . whatever you need to feel comfortable. But in return Tara will need a car, a monthly expense account, health insurance, maybe a 529 for the baby . . ." Jack made a gesture to indicate the list was longer than he cared to enumerate.

Gottler made a comment about having to get clearance from his board of directors, and then Jack smiled and said he couldn't picture Gottler having a problem there, and for the next few minutes I listened, half-impressed and half-disgusted. They finished with the acknowledgment that both sides were going to let their lawyers hash out the details.

". . . have to let me work on this," Gottler was telling Jack. "You did spring it on me with no advance notice."

"We sprang it on you?" I repeated, incredulous and surly. "You had nine months to consider all this. It hasn't occurred to you until now that you might be obligated to do something for Luke?"

"Luke," Gottler said, looking strangely preoccupied. "Is that his name?" He blinked a couple of times. "Of course."

"Why 'of course'?" I demanded, but he only responded with a humorless smile and a shake of his head.

Jack urged me to stand with him. "We'll let you get on with your business now, Mark. Let's keep that timetable in mind. And I'd like an update as soon as you talk to the board members you mentioned."

"Sure thing, Jack."

Gottler ushered us out of the conference room, past sets of double doors and columns and portraits and plaques. I read the plaques as we walked by, my attention caught by a huge arch of limestone over black walnut doors with stained-glass insets. The stone was engraved : FOR WITH GOD NOTHING SHALL BE IMPOSSIBLE. LUKE 1:37

"Where does that door lead?" I asked.

"To my offices, actually." A man had approached the door from another direction. He paused and turned to face us, smiling.

"Pastor Cardiff," Gottler said quickly. "This is Jack Travis, and Miss Ella Varner."

Noah Cardiff shook Jack's hand. "A pleasure, Mr. Travis. I had the chance to meet your father recently."

Jack grinned. "Hope you didn't catch him on an ornery day."

"Not at all. He's a fascinating gentleman. Old-school. I tried to talk him into attending one of my services, but he said he wasn't finished sinning yet, and he'd let me know when he was." Laughing quietly, Cardiff turned to me.

He was dazzling. A big man, though not quite so tall as Jack, and built on a more slender scale. Whereas Jack looked and moved like an athlete, Noah Cardiff had the grace of a dancer. It was striking to see the two side by side, Jack with his sexy, earthy appeal, and Cardiff, refined and austerely beautiful.

The pastor's complexion was fair, the kind that blushed easily, and his nose was narrow and high-bridged. The smile was angelic and slightly rueful, the smile of a mortal man who was all too aware of human frailty. And the eyes were those of a saint, benevolent light blue, his gaze making you feel annointed in some way.

As he stepped close enough to shake my hand, I caught the scents of lavender and amber spice. "Miss Varner. Welcome to our worship facility. I hope your appointment with Pastor Gottler went well?"

Pausing, he sent a quizzical smile to Gottler. "Varner . . . didn't we have a secretary . . . ?"

"Yes, her sister, Tara, helped us out from time to time."

"I hope she's well," Cardiff told me. "Please give her my regards."

I nodded uncertainly.

Cardiff held my gaze for a moment, seeming to read my thoughts. "We'll pray for her," he murmured. With a graceful hand, he gestured to the plaque over his doors. "My favorite verse, from my favorite of the disciples. It's true, you know. Nothing is impossible in the Lord."

"Why is Luke your favorite?" I asked.

"Among other reasons, Luke is the only disciple who relates the parables of the Good Samaritan and the prodigal son." Cardiff smiled at me. "And he's a strong supporter of women's roles in the life of Christ. Why don't you come to one of our services, Miss Varner? And bring your friend Jack with you."

FOURTEEN

As jack and I went outside, I went over the meeting in my mind. I rubbed my temples, feeling as if rubber bands had been wrapped tight around my skull.

Jack opened the SUV door for me and went to the other side. We both stood with the doors open, letting the heat pour out before we got into the vehicle.

"I can't stand Mark Gottler," I said.

"Really? I couldn't tell."

"While he was talking, I was overwhelmed by the realization that here is this hypocritical asshole who took advantage of my sister, and I'd like to . . . well, I don't know, shoot him or something . . . but instead there we were, negotiating."

"I know. But he's stepping up to the plate. Let's give him points for that."

"He's only doing it because we're forcing him to." I frowned. "You're not on his side, are you?"

"Ella, I just spent the last hour and fifteen minutes with my boot up his ass. No, I'm not on his side. All I'm saying is, the situation isn't all his fault. Okay, we can get in now." Jack turned on the car. The air-conditioning huffed ineffectually in the scorching heat.

I buckled my seat belt. "My sister is in a clinic with a nervous breakdown after being seduced by a married church pastor—are you somehow claiming that this is *her* fault?"

"I'm saying there's enough blame to go around. And Tara wasn't seduced. She's a full-grown woman who uses her body to get what she wants."

"Coming from you, that's a little hypocritical, don't you think?" I asked, smarting.

"Here's the facts, Ella: your sister's about to get a house, a new car, and an allowance of fifteen thousand dollars a month, all for the simple reason that she managed to get knocked up by a guy with money. But no matter how good a deal the lawyers work out, she'll have to find another sugar daddy someday. Problem is, it won't be as easy next time. She'll be older."

"Why don't you think she'll get married?" I asked, increasingly irritated.

"She won't settle for a regular guy. She wants a rich one. And she's not the kind they marry."

"Yes, she is. She's beautiful."

"Beauty is a depreciating asset. And that's the only thing Tara brings to the table. In trading terms, that makes her a short sale, not a buy-and-hold."

The blunt assessment took my breath away. "Is that how rich guys really think?"

"Most of us."

"My God." I was fuming. "You must assume every woman you meet is after your wallet."

"No. But let's just say it's easy to spot the ones who would drop me in a red-hot minute if something happened to the money."

"I don't give a shit about your money—"

"I know that. It's one of the reasons I—"

"—and if you hate my sister so much, why are you bothering to help her?"

"I don't hate her. Not at all. I just see her for what she is. I'm doing all this for Luke's sake. And yours."

"For my sake?" Startled out of my rising anger, I gave him a round-eyed glance.

"There's not much I wouldn't do for you, Ella," he said quietly. "Haven't you figured that out yet?"

While I sat there in stunned silence, he pulled the SUV out of the parking space.

Disgruntled and riled and roasting—it would be a while before the air-conditioning would make any headway against the braised interior of the car—I was quiet for a while. I saw my sister differently than Jack did. I loved her. But did that prevent me from seeing the truth? Did Jack have a better grasp of the situation than I did?

I heard my cell phone ring. Reaching for my handbag, I dug around until I found the phone. "It's Dane," I said tersely. He rarely called during the day. "Do you mind if I take this?"

"Go right ahead." Jack continued to drive, his gaze on the midday traffic. Vehicles lurched and clotted like cells pushing through a hardened artery.

"Dane. Is everything okay?"

"Hi, sweetie, everything's great. How did the meeting go?"

I gave Dane the in-a-nutshell version, and he listened with reassuring sympathy, making none of the judgments that Jack had. It was a relief to talk to someone who didn't push my buttons. I found myself relaxing, the air-conditioning blowing over me like the breath of a glacier.

"Hey, I was wondering," Dane said, "are you up for some company tomorrow night? I'm driving over to pick up a flowmeter from Katy for a system we're building. I'll take you out to dinner and spend the night. Meet this guy you've been spending so much time with."

I froze until Dane added with a laugh, "But I won't change his diaper."

My answering laugh was a shade too high-pitched. "No diaper-changing required. Yes, we'd love to see you. I can't wait."

"Good, I'll be there around four or five tomorrow. Bye, sweetie."

"Bye, Dane."

Closing the phone, I saw that we were back at 1800 Main, pulling into the underground garage.

Jack found a place near the elevator bank, and he stopped the SUV. He turned off the car and stared at me in the shadowy interior.

"Dane's coming to visit tomorrow," I said, aiming for a matter-of-fact tone but only managing to sound tense.

Jack's expression was unreadable. "Why?"

"He's picking up some monitoring equipment in Katy. And since he's going to be in the area, he wants to see me."

"Where's he going to stay?"

"With me, of course."

Jack was quiet for a long moment. It might have been my imagination, but I thought his breathing had acquired a rough edge. "I can get him a hotel room," he finally said. "I'll pay for it."

"Why would you . . . what? . . ."

"I don't want him staying overnight with you."

"But he's my—" I stopped and stared at him in disbelief. "What is this? Jack, I live with him."

"Not anymore. You live here. And—" A short, gouging pause. "I don't want you to have sex with him."

At first I was more bewildered than angry. Jack seemed to have reverted to knuckle-dragging mode, which I had never seen before, certainly not with Dane. That Jack felt possessive, that he wanted a say in when I had sex or whom I had it with, was no less than astonishing. "You don't get to be part of that decision," I said.

"I'm not going to stand by while he takes what's mine."

"*Yours?*" I shook my head, letting out a helpless sound, something between a laugh and a protest. My fingers crept to my mouth and lay over it lightly, like a lace curtain on an open window. It was a painstaking process to collect enough words to reply. "Jack, my boyfriend is coming to visit me. I may or may not have sex with him. But it's not your business. And I don't like games like this." I took an extra breath, and found myself repeating, "I don't like games."

Jack's voice was soft, but it contained a savage note that caused all the hairs on my body to rise. "I'm not playing games. I'm trying to tell you how I feel."

"Got it. Now I'd like some space."

"I'll give you all the space you want. As long as he does, too."

"What does that mean?"

"Don't let him stay in that apartment with you."

I was being given orders. I was being controlled. Suffocating panic rolled over me, and I opened the car door, needing air. "Back off," I said. I climbed out and headed to the elevators, while Jack followed.

I jabbed my finger so hard at the elevator button that I nearly sprained it. "You see, this is why I will always choose Dane, or someone like him, over you. I will *never* be told what to do. I'm an independent woman."

"Chicken shit," I heard him mutter. His breathing wasn't any better than mine.

In a rage, I whirled to face him. *"What?"*

"This doesn't have fuck-all to do with independence. You're scared because you know if you start something with me, it'll go to a place you and Dane never went. He won't stand by you—he's already proved it. He went pussy on you. And now he gets laid for that?"

"Shut up!" I had had enough. And I, who had never struck anyone in my life, hit the side of Jack's arm with my handbag, which happened to be a heavy leather hobo. It made a loud *thwack,* but he didn't appear to notice.

The elevator door opened, the empty cab shedding light over gray concrete and tile. Neither of us made a move to get in, just stood and glared at each other as the argument gathered force.

Taking me by the wrist, Jack hauled me around the side of the elevator bank, into a dark corner scented with exhaust and oil. "I want you," he muttered. "Get rid of him and take me. The only risk is losing someone you don't have anyway. He's not what you need, Ella. I am."

"Unbelievable," I said in disgust.

"What's unbelievable?"

"Your ego. It's surrounded by its own cloud of antimatter. You're a black hole of . . . of hubris!"

Jack stared at me through the shadows, and then he averted his face, and I thought I saw the white flash of a grin.

"Are you *amused*?" I demanded. "What the hell is so funny?"

"I was just thinking if the sex with you is one-tenth as fun as arguing with you, I'll be one happy bastard."

"You'll never find out. You—"

He kissed me.

I was so infuriated that I tried to hit him again with my bag, but it dropped to the ground and I lost my balance on my high heels. Jack grabbed me and kept kissing me, opening my mouth with his. I tasted warmth, the sweet permeation of a breath mint . . . I tasted Jack himself.

Despairing, I wondered why it wasn't like this with Dane. But the way Jack's mouth caught at mine, the firm damp articulation of each kiss, each succulent impact, was too insanely good to resist. He pulled me close and searched slowly with his tongue. The deeper he went, the more heavily I sagged against him, my entire body saturated with lust.

His hands went over my black suit, fondling and gripping lightly. My skin turned hot beneath the layer of delicate wool. He brought his fingers up to my face, stroking back my hair, and I felt a tremor in his hand, the vibration of intense desire. Reaching behind my head, he tangled his fingers in my hair and kissed me. I shivered as I felt his free hand working at the three fabric-covered snaps that held the front of my jacket together. The garment parted, revealing a stretchy cream-colored camisole, held up by two threadlike straps.

Jack muttered something—an imprecation, a prayer—and he reached beneath the camisole to find the soft, fine skin of my waist. We were both shaking now, too absorbed and ravenous to stop. He jerked the fabric upward to reveal private skin that gleamed eggshell-white in the shadows. His head bent to one breast, his mouth hunting for the tip. I drew in a hissing breath as I felt the sinuous glide of his tongue, a firm wet tug. Every pull and stroke sent a shot of pleasure to the pit of my stomach. I leaned my head back against the cold, hard wall, simmering, my hips writhing in a forward tilt.

Jack stood and took my mouth aggressively, his hand sliding over my breast. Long, erotic kisses . . . bites and licks of kisses, until I was drunk on sensation. My arms curled around his neck, pulling his head harder over mine, and he took the offering with a low, savage sound. I had never known such desperate excitement, wanting more, wanting to tell him, *Do anything, anything, I don't care, do it now.* I groped over the front of his body, the powerful muscles covered in a smooth elegant suit, and that excited me even more, the thought of what was beneath those civilized layers.

He gripped my skirt, pulled roughly, and I gasped as I felt the air on my legs, cool against the torturous hot ache of my skin and nerves. He pried beneath the elastic of my panties, searching between my thighs, the humid flesh opening to the invasion of his fingers. I felt him breathing against my neck, the brutal muscles of his upper arm flexing beneath my hand. He slipped a finger inside me, and another. I closed my eyes, going weak as his thumb skated tenderly over my clit, his fingers massaging deep and sure. With each flexing stroke, the knobs of his knuckles gently rubbed a maddening place inside. The pleasure was disorienting . . . disabling . . . crazy.

For the first time in my life, I wanted something more than safety. I wanted Jack with an intensity that went beyond choice or thought. I fumbled with his belt, zipper, button, opening his pants. I gripped him, the shape of him huge and rearing.

Withdrawing his fingers, Jack tugged my underwear and skirt out of the way. He lifted me with shocking ease. The realization of how strong he was sent a flood of anxious excitement through me. Helplessly I wrapped my arms around his neck and dropped my head on his shoulder. *Yes. Yes.* He entered me, and I squirmed at the impossible thickness of him. Kissing my neck, he murmured for me to relax, he would take care of me, just let him do it, let him in. . . . He brought my full weight down until my toes grazed the floor, and the luscious force opened me inexorably.

It was stunningly erotic, having sex while fully clothed, tightly impaled, whimpering against his greedy kisses. Jack set the steady upward-plunging cadence, and every time he went in, my muscles clenched on the pleasure of it, pulling helplessly, taking more and more of him. I was spasming, riding the heat, my limbs tightening around that big driving body until the sheer plenitude of feeling tipped me over into a rich, nearly unendurable orgasm. Jack took my choked cry into his mouth, muffling the sounds I made. He drove deep and held and shuddered, his breath breaking as he found his own release.

A long time passed before either of us moved. I was clasped against him, intimate flesh moistly locked, my head lolling on his shoulder. I felt drugged. I knew that very soon, when my mind started functioning again, I was going to feel some things I badly wanted to avoid. Starting with shame. There were so many inappropriate things about what we'd done that I was actually awed.

And the worst part was how good it had felt, still felt, with his body wedged inside mine, his arms secure around me.

One of his hands clasped my head more firmly against his shoulder, as if he were trying to protect me from something. I heard a quiet curse.

"We just did it in a garage," I said weakly.

"I know, darlin'," he whispered. He began to move, lifting me off himself, and I made a sound of distress. I was wet, and a little sore, and all my muscles were trembling. Leaning against the wall, I let him pull my clothes back into place and snap my jacket back up. After fastening his own clothes, he found my handbag and gave it to me. I couldn't look at him, even when he took my head in his hands.

"Ella." The scent of his breath and the salty essence of sex and hot skin mingled in a sublime erotic perfume. I wanted more of him. The realization brought frustrated tears to my eyes. "I'm going to take you up to my apartment," Jack murmured. "We'll take a shower, and—"

"No, I . . . I need to be by myself."

"Sweetheart. I didn't mean for it to happen like this. Come to my bed. Let me make love to you the right way."

"That's not necessary."

"Yes. It is." His tone was low and urgent. "Please, Ella. This wasn't what I planned for our first time. I can make it so much better for you. I can—"

I touched his lips with my fingers. His breath was searing and soft. I would have spoken, but the elevator doors opened with a ding. I jumped at the sound. A man exited and went to his car, his footsteps a hollow-sounding echo on the concrete.

I waited until the car had left the parking garage before I spoke to Jack. "Listen to me," I said unsteadily. "If what I want or what I feel means anything at all to you . . . you've got to give me some space. Right now I've reached the limits of what I can handle. This is the first time I've had sex with anyone besides Dane. I've got to have time to think." Hesitantly I reached up to stroke his taut jaw. "You don't need to show me any more fireworks," I added. "In fact, the thought is sort of terrifying."

"Ella—"

"You have to back off," I told him. "I'll let you know when or if

I'm ready for anything more. Until then . . . I don't want to see or hear from you. The person I need to see right now is Dane. The person I need to make decisions with is Dane. If there's any room for you in my life after that, you'll be the first to know."

It was a fairly safe assumption that no woman had ever spoken to Jack Travis that way before. But it was the only way I knew how to handle him. Otherwise I was pretty sure I would be naked in his bed within the next ten or fifteen minutes.

Jack caught my wrist, pulling my caressing hand away from his face, and he skewered me with a wrathful stare. "Damn it." He hauled me into his arms and held me close, breathing hard. "I've got about ten things I want to say to you right now. But at least nine of them would make me sound like a psycho."

In spite of the seriousness of the situation, I nearly smiled. "What's the tenth thing?" I asked his shirtfront.

He paused, considering it. "Never mind," he grumbled. "That one would make me sound like a psycho, too."

Guiding me to the elevator, he pressed the button. We rode up in silence. Jack drew his hands over my shoulders, my waist, my hips, as if he couldn't keep from touching me. I wanted to turn against him and let him hold me, and go up to his apartment. Instead I got off the elevator when we reached the sixth floor, and Jack followed me.

"You don't have to walk me to the door," I said.

He scowled and stayed with me until we got to the apartment. I was about to enter the combination on the keypad, when Jack took my shoulders and turned me to face him. The way he stared at me brought a flush to every visible inch of skin. His hand slid behind my neck.

"Jack—"

He kissed me roughly. My lips parted at the demanding pressure.

It was a lewd, scorching, brain-demolishing kiss . . . not that there was much left to demolish. I pushed against him, trying to end it, but he kept on until I went boneless against him. Only then did he pull his head back, glancing down at me with hunger and a flash of belligerent male triumph.

Apparently he felt he had made some kind of point.

It flashed through my mind that this entire event had been a form of territory-marking. "Men are like dogs," Stacy was fond of saying. And she usually went on to add that, like dogs, they all took up too much space on the bed, and they always went for the crotch.

Somehow I pushed the correct combination on the keypad and went into the apartment.

"Ella—"

"I'm on the pill, by the way," I said.

Before he could reply, I closed the door firmly in his face.

"Hi, Ella," the babysitter, Teena, said cheerfully. "How'd your meetin' go?"

"Just fine. How's Luke?"

"All clean and fed. I just put him in the crib."

The mobile was playing gently, bears and honeypots turning in a lazy circle.

"Any problems while I was gone?" I asked.

"Well, he was a little fussy right after you left, but then he calmed down." Teena laughed. "Boys never like to see Mommy go off without 'em."

My heart skipped a beat. *Mommy*. I thought about correcting her, but it didn't seem worth the effort. I gave Teena some cash, let her out of the apartment, and I went to take a shower.

The hot water soothed and relaxed me, easing my aches and

twinges. It did nothing for my guilt, however. For the first time I experienced the two-pronged remorse of having cheated on someone . . . remorse for having done it in the first place, and also for having enjoyed it so much.

Sighing, I wrapped a towel around my hair, put on a robe, and went to check on Luke. The mobile had stopped, and everything was quiet.

Tiptoeing to the side of the crib, I peeked in, expecting to see the baby sleeping. But he was staring up at me in that somber way of his.

"Aren't you asleep yet, Luke?" I asked softly. "What are you waiting for?"

The second he saw me, he moved and kicked, and his mouth curled in a baby-grin.

His first smile.

It startled me, that spontaneous reaction to seeing me. *It's you. I've been waiting for you.* And I felt a lovely ache that went right down to my soul, and I forgot everything except that moment. I had earned that smile. I wanted to earn a million more from him. Without thinking I reached for Luke and lifted him from the crib, exuberantly kissing his warm little face, his smiling mouth. I inhaled his powdery, diapery, innocent smell.

I had never known such happiness.

"Look at you," I murmured, nuzzling into his neck. "Look at that smile. Oh, you are the sweetest boy, the sweetest baby . . ."

My boy. My Luke.

FIFTEEN

"WOW," DANE SAID WHEN HE WALKED INTO THE apartment, after a prolonged hug at the door. He glanced at the designer decorating, the big windows and show-off view, and gave an appreciative whistle.

"It is pretty cool, isn't it?" I asked with a grin.

Dane was the same as always, warm and easygoing and handsome. He was shorter and leaner than Jack, with the result being that we fit together perfectly when we hugged. Seeing him reminded me instantly of all the reasons I had gotten together with him in the first place. He was the man who knew me better than anyone, who never set me off-balance. It was rare to find people in life you knew were never going to hurt you, or screw you over with moral manipulations. Dane was one of them.

I showed Luke to him, and he admired the baby dutifully, watching as I settled Luke into his baby bouncer. I attached a hoop of interesting toys for Luke to look at, and sat next to Dane on the sofa.

"I had no idea you were so good with babies," Dane said.

"I'm not." I took Luke's hand and showed him how to push a plastic puppy from one side of the hoop to the other. Luke flailed at it with a grunt. "I'm getting pretty good with this one, though. He's training me."

"You look different," Dane observed, settling in the corner of the sofa to get a better vantage.

"Tired," I agreed ruefully. "Dark circles."

"No, not that way. You look great. Kind of . . . bright-eyed."

I laughed. "Thanks. I can't imagine why. Probably because I'm so happy to see you. I've missed you, Dane."

"I missed you, too." He reached out and pulled me over him until I was half-sprawled, my hair falling into his face. The top two buttons of his hemp shirt were undone, revealing his smooth golden chest. I got a familiar clean, acrid whiff of his salt rock deodorant. Affectionately I bent to kiss him, those lips I had kissed so many thousands of times. But the gentle contact didn't bring the same sweetness and comfort it always had. In fact, it produced a strange ticklish aversion.

I lifted my head. Dane pulled me closer, and that sent a thrill of something *un*familiar and not at all pleasant through me.

How was that possible?

Feeling the way I stiffened, Dane loosened his arms and looked at me quizzically. "What, not in front of the baby?"

I drew away from him in confusion. "I guess. I . . ." My throat had cinched tight. My lashes closed in a few peppery blinks. "I have some stuff to tell you," I said hoarsely.

"Okay." His tone was gently encouraging.

Did I have to tell him what I had done with Jack? How could I explain any of it? Helplessly I sat there and stared at him. It seemed as if every pore in my body went through a quick-freeze and a rapid thaw, drawing out an uncomfortable film of sweat.

Dane's expression changed. "Sweetie, I'm pretty good at reading between the lines. And I can't help but notice that every time you and I talk, someone else's name keeps coming up in the conversation. So let me start this off for you: 'Dane, lately I've been spending a lot of time with Jack Travis . . . ' "

"Lately I've been spending a lot of time with Jack Travis," I said, and a couple of tears spilled over.

Dane looked patient and unsurprised. He took one of my hands and held it in both of his. "Tell me. I can be your friend, Ella."

I sniffled. "You can?"

"I've always been your friend."

I hopped up and went to the kitchen for a paper towel, and came back blowing my nose. I nudged Luke's bouncy chair until it bobbed, and he stared alertly at the jiggling toys on the hoop. "Everything's fine, Luke," I told the baby, even though he was oblivious to my emotional crisis. "Grown-ups cry, too, sometimes. It's a very natural and n-normal process."

"I think he's handling it okay," Dane said, looking into my woeful face with a wry smile. "Come here and let's talk."

I sat next to him and let out a wobbly sigh. "I wish you were a mind-reader. I want you to know everything but I don't want to have to tell you. Because there are some things I don't want to say out loud."

"There's nothing you can't tell me. You know that."

"Yes, but I've never had to explain about an involvement with another guy. I feel so guilty, I can hardly stand it."

"Your guilt threshold's always been pretty low," he said kindly.

"It's wrong to want Jack, and it's stupid, but I can't make myself stop. I'm so sorry, Dane. I'm sorrier than I could ever imagine being—"

"Wait. Before you go on . . . no apologies. Especially no apologies for your feelings. Feelings are never wrong, they're just feelings. Now tell me."

I didn't tell Dane everything, of course. But I said enough for him to understand that my carefully considered approach to life was unraveling, and I was obsessively attracted to a man I should never have been attracted to, and I was at a complete loss to know why.

"Jack's smart," I said, "but he can be crude. And he's macho and traditional. He's like the football jock in high school that all the girls lined up for, and I always hated that kind of guy."

"Me too."

"But Jack surprises me sometimes with a comment or insight that's just dead-on. And he's honest, and talkative, and curious, and possibly the least self-conscious person I've ever met. He makes me laugh. He says I need to be more spontaneous."

"He's right."

"Well, there's a time and a place for spontaneity. And this is not a phase of my life when I need to think about fun. I have a lot of responsibility."

"What does he think about the baby?"

"Jack likes him. He likes kids."

"Being a traditional guy, he probably wants a family of his own," Dane commented, watching me closely.

"I've already told Jack how I feel about marriage and family. So he knows that would never happen with me. I think the attraction is that I'm a novelty. I'm a turn-on mainly because I'm not chasing after him."

"You'd be a turn-on for anyone, Ella. You're a beautiful woman."

"Really?" I looked at him with a shy grin. "You've never told me that."

"I'm not good about that stuff," Dane admitted. "But you are. In a hot librarian kind of way."

My smile turned wry. "Thanks. I guess it works for Jack."

"How much do you have in common with this guy?"

"Not much. Basically we're polar opposites. But do you want to know the main attraction, the weird part? . . . It's the talking."

"Talking about what?"

"About anything," I said earnestly. "We get started and it's like sex, this back-and-forth, and we're both so *there*, do you know what I mean? We rattle each other. And some conversations seem to be happening on a few different levels at once. But even when we're disagreeing on something, there's a weird kind of harmony in it. A connection."

Dane stared at me thoughtfully. "So if the talking's like sex, what is the sex like?"

"I—"

My mouth opened and closed. Chagrined, I contemplated various ways to explain that so far we'd had what could only have been described as one hell of a good-night kiss, and also a parking-garage quickie. And both times had been spectacular. No, there were no words.

"Classified information," I said sheepishly.

For a moment we sat silently, both of us a little taken aback that I was withholding something, when I had always told Dane everything without reserve. Our relationship had always been completely transparent. This was new, this concept that there was some part of my life Dane couldn't casually riffle through.

"You're not angry?" I asked. "Not jealous?"

"Jealous, maybe," Dane admitted slowly, as if it surprised him. "But not angry. And not possessive. Because it comes down to this: I don't want a traditional relationship and I never will. But if you want to explore that with Travis, you should. You don't need permission, and it's not mine to give. And you're going to do it anyway."

I couldn't help but reflect on the contrast between Dane and Jack, who was infinitely more demanding and possessive. So much more to contend with. A jolt of uneasiness went through me. "To be honest," I half-whispered, "I don't feel as safe with him as I do with you."

"I know."

A ghost of a smile touched my lips. "How do you know?"

"Think about what safety is, Ella."

"Trust?"

"Yes, partly. But also an absence of risk." He unstuck a strand of hair from my damp cheek and tucked it back. "Maybe you need to take a risk. Maybe you need to be with someone who rattles you a little."

I crawled over to him and put my head on his chest. We sat like that for a while, still except for the occasional sigh. Both of us were quiet with the recognition that something was ending, and something was beginning.

Dane touched my chin and lifted my face upward, and kissed me gently. Only then did I understand that Dane had always been a friend I had slept with, and how entirely different that was from having a lover who could be a friend.

"Hey," Dane said softly. "You think we should do it one more time, for old times' sake? As a send-off? A bon voyage?"

I looked at him with a rueful grin. "Couldn't I just hit you with a bottle of champagne instead?"

"By God, let's at least open some," he said, and I got up to get us a couple of drinks we badly needed.

* * *

I TRIED CALLING JACK THE NEXT DAY. AFTER LEAVING two messages on his cell phone, I realized he was in no hurry to call me back. That worried and annoyed me.

"I knew something was going on," Haven said when I called her in the afternoon. "Jack's been in a bitch of a mood. In fact, everyone in the office was relieved when he left to go to a construction site for a project he's managing. Otherwise I think his secretary Helen was going to knock him unconscious with the laminating machine."

"I had to resolve a couple of things with Dane when he came to visit," I said. "So I asked Jack for a little space. Guess he didn't take it well."

Haven's voice was laced with amusement. "No, he did not. But I've never gotten the impression that he's especially good at backing off when he wants something."

"Well, he's backing way the hell off now," I said ruefully. "He's not returning my calls."

"Ella, I probably shouldn't stick my nose in Jack's business, since I've always been so pissed off when he's done that to me—"

"Go ahead," I urged. "I'm asking for your opinion. It's not sticking your nose in when you've been invited."

"Okay," Haven said cheerfully. "I think Jack is so twisted up and turned around, he doesn't know what to do. He's not used to feeling jealous about anyone. He always plays it cool, always has the upper hand, and I think you've gotten to him in a major way. And I have to say, I'm enjoying this."

"Why?" I asked, giddy with hope and nerves.

"I've always seen Jack go out with the career heiress types, or airhead actresses or models, and I think it's because he wanted to avoid *this* . . . being completely crazy about someone, and being vulnerable. Travis men *hate* that. But I think a little suffering might be good for Jack, shake things up in a good way."

"Can I tell you something confidential?"

"Yes, what?"

"Jack made a huge deal out of the fact that Dane was staying at my apartment. He wanted Dane to stay in a hotel room."

"Well, that's stupid. You've lived with Dane for years. If you wanted to have sex with the guy, it wouldn't have made a difference whether he stayed at your place or a hotel room."

"I know. But Dane did stay at my apartment last night. And I'm wondering if Jack might have found out."

Haven chuckled. "Ella, nothing goes on in this building that Jack doesn't know about. He probably told the concierge to let him know the exact time Dane left."

"I didn't have sex with Dane," I said defensively.

"You don't have to explain anything to me."

"It was terrible. Dane started off sleeping on the sofa, but the baby's crying kept him awake, until finally I sent Dane into the bedroom and then I stayed on the sofa. I can tell you with authority that after last night, Dane will never voluntarily reproduce. So now Dane's fled back to Austin, and Jack apparently isn't speaking to me."

Haven laughed. "Poor Ella. My guess is that Jack is just trying to figure out his next move."

"If you get a chance, will you tell him to call me?"

"No, I've got a better idea. My dad's birthday is tomorrow night. The woman he's dating—Vivian—is throwing a party for him at the family home in River Oaks. All the Travises are going to be there, including Jack and my other brothers and my sister-in-law. Come with me and Hardy."

"I don't want to crash a family event," I said uneasily.

"You'll be my guest. But even if you weren't, half of Houston is crashing."

"I don't have a present for your dad."

"Vivian requested that in lieu of presents, everyone make donations to one of Dad's favorite charities. I'll give you a list and you can donate online if you want to."

"You're really sure it's okay?" I was dying to go to the party. I was wildly curious to meet the rest of Jack's family, and to see the home he had grown up in.

"Yes. It's semicasual—do you have a cute dress to wear?"

"I have a light blue wrap dress."

"*Yes*. That's his favorite color. Oh, Ella, this is going to be fun."

"For you, maybe," I said dourly, and Haven snickered.

THE ONLY CONCEIVABLE ZIP CODE IN HOUSTON FOR Churchill Travis to live in was 77019, since you couldn't move up from River Oaks. Located in the geographical center of Houston, it was one of the wealthiest communities in the nation. According to Haven, FOR SALE signs were never allowed in River Oaks. When a home became available it usually received multiple offers and sold within days. Lawyers, businessmen, hedge-fund operators, surgeons, and sports stars had all elected to live in the pine-and-oak-shaded paradise, which was close to the Galleria and Rice, and the best private schools in Texas.

Some of the houses in 77019 were thirty thousand square feet or more, but the Travis mansion was relatively small in its category, at twelve thousand square feet. It was blessed, however, with a remarkably good view of the board-flat city, being located on a bluff by the bayou. As we passed lush gardens and esplanades, all glowing in the light of a wine-colored sunset, my eyes widened at the rows of neo-Georgians, Taras, colonial revivals, Tuscan villas, and French chateaus. There didn't seem to be one indigenous Houston style, but rather a sampling of time periods and places, all built on a grand scale.

"You'll enjoy this, Ella," Haven said reassuringly, twisting around from the front seat of Hardy's Mercedes sedan. "Vivian throws great parties—the food and music are always terrific. She's only had one bomb that I know of, and it was so epic that it actually ended up being sort of cool."

"Why was it a bomb?"

"Well, Peter Jackson was one of the guests of honor, so Vivian did a *Lord of the Rings* homage. She dug up the whole backyard and had it redone with waterfalls and rock formations."

"That doesn't sound so bad," I said.

"No, the bad part was that Vivian got a local Boy Scout group to dress like Hobbits and wander through the party. They shed all over the house, and Dad was allergic to the fur. He complained for weeks." Haven paused. "But I'm sure she won't do anything like that tonight."

"Start drinking as soon as you get there," Hardy advised me.

The Travis mansion, a stately European stone structure, occupied a three-acre lot. We passed through a set of open iron gates and approached a parking area filled with pricey vehicles. A massive garage with huge glass remote-control doors that displayed a Bentley, a Mercedes, a Shelby Cobra, and at least seven other cars, looked like some gigantic vending-machine-of-the-gods. White-coated valets steered the shining vehicles into neatly marked places with the tenderness of parents tucking beloved children into bed.

I was a little dazed as I accompanied Haven and Hardy along the walkway to the milling, glittering crowd. Live music filled the air, a boisterous horn section backing a well-known big-band singer who had recently won acclaim as a supporting actor in a Spielberg movie. The singer, still in his twenties, was crooning "Steppin' Out With My Baby" in a silky semiscat patter.

I felt like I had stepped into some alternate reality. Maybe a movie set. The scene was gorgeous, but it seemed bizarre that people really lived this way, that such excess was commonplace to them.

"I've been to parties before . . ." I started, and fell silent, afraid of sounding gauche.

Hardy glanced down at me, his blue eyes gleaming with humor. "I know." I realized that he really did understand, that while this scene was entirely familiar to Haven, it was a far cry from the east-of-Houston trailer park he had grown up in.

They were an interesting couple, Hardy so big and all-American, Haven petite and exquisite. For all their size difference, however, they seemed remarkably well matched. Any outsider couldn't help but be aware of the glimmering chemistry between the two, a feisty appreciation of each other's intelligence, a mutually provocative awareness. But also tenderness. I saw it especially when Hardy stole glances at Haven while her attention was focused elsewhere. He looked like he wanted to carry her away and keep her all to himself. I envied their ability to stay so close and yet not feel trapped or suffocated.

"Let's get Dad out of the way first," Haven said, leading the way into the house. She looked amazing in a short dress made of crinkled bronze organza, the skirt festively tacked and gathered in a style that could only be worn by an extremely slender woman.

"Do you think Jack is here yet?" I asked.

"No, he never comes to a party early."

"Did you tell him you'd invited me?"

Haven shook her head. "I didn't get a chance. He's been out of reach most of the day."

Jack had called me in the morning, but I had been in the shower and let the machine pick up. He had left a curt message that he had a meeting at the Woodlands north of Houston, and would be gone most of the day. By the time I called back, I had gotten his voice mail. I didn't leave a message, figuring he deserved some payback after he'd avoided my calls the previous day.

It took a while for us to make our way through the main circuit of rooms. Between the two of them, Haven and her fiancé knew everyone. A waiter came by with a tray of champagne in iced glasses. I took one and drank gratefully, the vintage dry and sparkling-crisp on my tongue. Standing near an original Frida Kahlo painting, I took in my surroundings while Haven skillfully fended off a woman who was determined to have her join the Houston Orchid Society.

The guests encompassed a wide variety of ages, the women all wearing perfect makeup and impossibly high heels, the men carefully groomed and well dressed. I was glad I was wearing my best dress, a fluid pale blue knit that wrapped across my breasts in a figure-flattering vee. It was a simple, classic dress that made me look voluptuous, the knee-length hem showing off my legs. I was wearing silver high-heeled sandals, which I had worried were a little over the top until I saw what the other women were wearing. The Houston definition of semicasual seemed to include a generous quantity of jewelry and embellishment, in contrast to Austin semicasual, which basically entailed wearing a shirt and shoes.

I had put on more eye makeup than usual, using smoky gray eyeshadow and two coats of mascara. My lips were slicked with delicate pink gloss. I had turned the ends of my bob up into a neat flip, which I could feel swinging against my cheeks every time I turned my head. There had been no need for blush—my cheeks were touched with a natural flush that was fever-colored in its intensity.

I knew something was going to happen that night, something either very good or very bad.

"He's outside," Hardy reported to Haven, who gestured for me to come with them.

"Jack?" I asked bemusedly.

"No, my dad." Haven grinned and made a comical face. "Come on, you're going to meet some Travises."

We pushed our way through the back of the house out to a vast landscaped lawn. Trees had been webbed with white lights, glittering canopies stretched high over a crowded dance floor. Guests sat on chairs and swarmed around food-laden buffet tables. I was awestruck by the sight of the birthday cake positioned on its own table, a four-foot-tall chocolate creation tied with gum paste ribbons and littered with fondant butterflies.

"Wow," I remarked to an older man who had just turned away from a group. "That's what I call a birthday cake. You think someone's going to jump out of that thing?"

"Hope not," he said in a gravelly voice. "They might catch fire from all the candles."

I laughed. "Yes, and all that frosting would make the stop, drop, and roll so messy." Turning toward him, I extended my hand. "Ella

Varner, from Austin. Are you a friend of the Travises? Never mind, of course you are. They wouldn't invite one of their enemies, would they?"

He smiled as he shook my hand. His teeth were a scrupulous shade of white I always found mildly startling in a person his age. "They would *especially* invite one of their enemies." He was a good-looking old guy, not much taller than me, his steel-colored hair cut short, his skin leathery and sun-cured. Charisma clung to him as if it had been rubbed in like sunscreen.

Meeting his gaze, I was arrested by the color of his eyes, the bittersweet dark of Venezuelan chocolate. As I stared into those familiar eyes, I knew exactly who he was. "Happy birthday, Mr. Travis," I said with an abashed grin.

"Thank you, Miss Varner."

"Call me Ella, please. I think my crashing your party puts us on a first-name basis, doesn't it?"

Churchill Travis continued to smile. "You're a lot prettier than my usual crashers, Ella. Stick with me and I'll make sure they don't throw you out."

The flirty old fox. I grinned. "Thank you, Mr. Travis."

"Churchill."

Haven came up to her father and stood on her toes to kiss his cheek. "Happy birthday, Dad. I was just telling Vivian what a great job she's done with the party. I see you found Ella. You can't have her, though. She's for Jack."

A new voice entered the conversation. "Jack doesn't need another one. Give her to me."

I turned to the man who was just behind me. I was startled to see a younger, lankier version of Jack, still on the early side of his twenties.

"Joe Travis," he said, shaking my hand firmly. He was nearly a head taller than his father. Joe hadn't yet grown into the seasoned masculine prime that his older brother Jack had attained, but he was a charmer, and a head-turner, and he knew it.

"Do not trust him, Ella," Haven said severely. "Joe's a photographer. He got his start by taking embarrassing candid shots of the family—me in my underwear, for example—and bribing us for the negatives."

Hardy heard the last comment as he joined the group. "You got any of those negatives left?" he asked Joe, and Haven elbowed him sharply.

Joe kept my hand in his and gave me a soulful glance. "I'm here alone. My girlfriend left me to work at a hotel in the French Alps."

"Joe, you fink," Haven told him, "don't even think of hitting on your brother's girlfriend."

"I'm not Jack's girlfriend," I said hastily.

Joe shot his sister a triumphant glance. "Looks like she's fair game."

Hardy interrupted the brewing squabble by handing a leather double-finger cigar case to Churchill Travis. "Happy birthday, sir."

"Thank you, Hardy." Opening the case, Travis drew out one of the cigars and sniffed with an appreciative sound.

"There's a full box of those for you in the house," Hardy told him.

"Cohíbas?" Churchill asked, inhaling the fragrance as if it were the finest perfume.

Hardy admitted nothing, just regarded him with a devilish glint in his blue eyes. "All I know is they got Honduran wrappers. Can't account for the insides."

Definitely contraband Cuban cigars, I thought, amused.

Serenely the old man tucked the cigar case inside his jacket. "We'll share a couple of these on the porch later, Hardy."

"Yes, sir."

Glancing around Joe's shoulder, I caught sight of someone standing beside one of the open French doors, and my heart clutched. It was Jack, his lean athletic form clad in a black knit shirt and black pants. He looked sexy, lithe, ready to commit some hi-tech heist. Although his posture was relaxed, one hand shoved casually into a pocket, the tense dark line of his body cleaved the sparkling scene like a rip in a glossy magazine photograph.

Jack's mouth held a brooding tension as he conversed with the woman who stood with him. I felt a little sick as I watched the two of them. She was one of the most beautiful women I had ever seen, with a long fall of buttermilk-colored hair, and sculpted screen-goddess features, and an ultra-slim body displayed in a tiny scrap of a black dress. They appeared to be together.

Joe followed my gaze. "There's Jack."

"He's brought a date," I managed to say.

"No, he hasn't. That's Ashley Everson. She's married. But she heads for Jack like a barracuda whenever she sees him."

"Is she the one who broke his heart?" I whispered.

Joe's head bent. "Uh-huh," he whispered back, "and she's having problems with her husband, Peter. Headed for divorce. Serves 'em right, after what they did to Jack."

"Do you think he . . ."

"No," Joe said instantly. "Jack wouldn't have her on a silver platter, honey. You got no competition."

I was about to protest that I wasn't competing, but at that moment Jack looked up and saw me. I couldn't even breathe. His midnight eyes widened. His gaze dragged slowly down to my silver sandals and back up again. Straightening, he pulled his hand from his pocket and started toward me.

Looking perturbed, Ashley Everson caught at his arm and said something to him, and he paused to reply.

"Ella." Haven's voice drew my attention.

Someone new had joined the group, yet another tall dark-haired man, who could only have been a Travis. The oldest, Gage. Although he bore his father's stamp, he didn't resemble the other two sons nearly as much. There was nothing of the cowboy in him . . . his features were refined and reserved, his handsomeness nearly prodigal. The eyes were not coffee-brown but an unusual light gray, the color of dry ice contained in dark rims. When he smiled, I felt as if I'd been given a reprieve from something.

"Gage Travis," he introduced himself, and put his arm around a woman who had just come to him. "My wife, Liberty."

She was a gorgeous woman with a perfect oval face and an easy smile, her skin a pale, shimmery butterscotch. As she leaned forward to shake my hand, her dark hair moved around her shoulders like liquid. "Nice to meet you, Ella," she said. "I hear you're dating Jack."

I certainly didn't want to present myself as Jack's girlfriend. "We're not *dating*, exactly," I said uncomfortably. "I mean, he's a terrific guy, but I wouldn't presume to . . . you see, we've only known each other for a few weeks, so I wouldn't claim that we were *together* in any way, but—"

"We're together," I heard Jack say behind me, his voice quiet but firm.

I turned toward him, my pulse rioting.

A strong arm slid around my back. Jack's head lowered, his lips brushing my cheek in a social kiss. Nothing untoward, just two friends meeting. But then he moved lower and brushed a brief, hot kiss at the side of my throat. It was unspeakably personal, a declaration of intimacy.

Astonished that Jack would do such a thing in front of his family's collective gaze, I felt myself turn white then scarlet, my face changing colors like a neon sign in a diner window. Shaken, I saw Haven and Liberty exchange a quick, significant glance.

Keeping an arm around me, Jack reached out to shake his father's hand. "Happy birthday, Dad. Brought you a present—it's in the house."

The Travis patriarch looked at us both speculatively before saying, "You know what present I want? For you to settle down and get married, and give me some grandbabies."

Jack greeted this outrageous lack of tact with an equanimity that revealed such complaints were nothing new. "You've already got a grandson," he pointed out calmly.

"I'd like more before I go."

Jack looked sardonic. "Where you planning on going, Dad?"

"All I'm saying is, I'm not gettin' any younger. And if you want the next generation of Travises to have my influence, you'd better get busy."

"Good Lord, Dad," Joe said. "If Jack got any busier in that department, he'd have to carry around a deli-counter ticket machine—"

"Joe," Gage murmured, and that was enough to quiet the youngest brother.

Churchill cast a pointedly approving glance at me. "Maybe you'll be the one to bring Jack up to scratch, Ella."

"I'm not the marrying kind," I said.

Churchill's brows lifted as if he'd never heard a woman say such a thing. "Why not?"

"I'm very into my career, for one thing."

"Too bad," Jack said. "The first requirement of marrying a Travis is, you have to give up your dreams."

I laughed. Jack's expression softened as he looked down at me, and he stroked back a strand of light, glinting hair that had fallen over my forehead. "You want to dance," he murmured, "or stay here for more grilling?" Without waiting for an answer, he began to draw me away with him.

"I wasn't grilling her," Churchill protested. "I was having a conversation."

Jack paused and shot him an ironic glance. "It's only a conversation when more than one person is doing the talking, Dad." As he pulled me away, Jack said, "I'm sorry."

"About your father? . . . No, don't be sorry. I liked him." I glanced uneasily at his hard profile. This was a version of Jack I hadn't seen before. He had always had a sort of I-don't-give-a-shit cockiness, an air of not letting anything matter too deeply. But that was gone. Right now he was angry all the way down to the marrow. Something mattered very much.

We reached the dance floor. Jack took me into his arms in a natural, experienced movement. The band was playing "Song for You," as if they were all having the same long, bluesy dream. Jack's shoulder was hard beneath my hand, his arms steady as he led me without hesitancy. He was a seriously good dancer, his movements fluid but not showy. I wished I could have told his mother that those long-ago dance lessons had paid off handsomely.

I concentrated on relaxing and following him, keeping my gaze on the place where his shirt collar opened. The lowest point of the vee revealed a tantalizing hint of chest hair.

"Dane spent the night with you," Jack said flatly.

I was relieved at this blunt opening gambit, eager to get things resolved. "He slept at the apartment, yes. Although there wasn't much sleeping involved. You see, the—*oof!*"

Jack had stopped abruptly, and I had walked straight into him. Glancing up at his face, I realized what conclusion he had drawn. "Because of the baby," I said hastily. "Luke was crying. I stayed on the sofa, and Dane was in the other room. Jack, you're hurting my hand."

He loosened his grip immediately and tried to moderate his breathing. We resumed dancing for a full minute before he brought himself to ask, "Did you have sex with him?"

"No."

Jack nodded slightly, but the set of his face remained austere, rigid, as if it had been fired in a kiln.

"No more Dane," he eventually said with unnerving finality.

I tried to be funny. "I can't decide if that means you don't want me to see him again or if you're planning to kill him."

"It means if the first thing happens, the second thing is likely to follow."

I was privately amused. And I was aware of a new kind of power, a seductive power, over someone who was stronger, worldlier, more unpredictable, more testosterone-fueled than any man I'd ever known before. It was like sitting behind the wheel to test a race car. Scary and exhilarating all at once, especially for someone who had never liked to travel fast.

"You're a big talker, Jack Travis. Why don't you take me home and back up those words with some action?"

He glanced down at me sharply. I didn't think either of us could believe I had said it.

And from the look in his eyes, it was clear I was about to get all the action I could handle.

SIXTEEN

THE MUSIC FLOWED INTO A SLOW MOLTEN-GLASS version of "Moondance." Jack eased me closer until I felt his breath at my temple, and the brush of his thighs against mine. We danced and I followed blindly, a little unsteady, as if we were on the deck of a ship rather than solid ground. But his hold on me was secure, and he balanced every subtle pitch of my weight. Breathing deeply, I drew in the spicy richness of his scent. A light mist of perspiration bloomed over me everywhere, all at once, as if my skin were coming alive.

The song ended. The applause and the beginning of a new, energetic set was intrusive. In fact, it was like being awakened with a dash of cold water in the face. Blinking, I went with Jack through the densely packed crowd. We were obligated to stop frequently to chat with Jack's acquaintances. He knew everyone. And he turned out to be far more adept than I was at putting on a friendly social mask. But I felt the ferocious tension in his arm as he guided me through the gathering, finding narrow channels of unoccupied space through which we could move.

The birthday cake was lit, and the band accompanied the crowd to a tipsy but vigorous version of "Happy Birthday to You." Slices of cake stuffed with ganache and jam and whipped cream were passed around. I could only eat a bite, the rich fluff sticking in my throat. After I washed it down with a few swallows of champagne, my mood was bright-leavened with sugar and alcohol. I followed easily as Jack led me by the hand.

We paused to say goodbye to Churchill and his lady-friend Vivian, caught sight of Joe in a corner with a young woman who appeared to have great sympathy for his girlfriend-gone-to-France story, and I waved to Haven, Hardy, Gage, and Liberty across the room.

"I feel like we should give them some kind of excuse about leaving early," I said to Jack. "Tell them I need to check on the baby, or—"

"They know why we're leaving."

There wasn't much conversation on the way back to 1800 Main. The feelings between us were too raw. I hadn't yet known Jack long enough to feel much comfortable ease with him—our relationship needed to be broken in.

But I did tell Jack about the talk I'd had with Dane, and he listened closely. I realized that although Jack comprehended Dane's views, on a visceral level he didn't get him at all. "He should have fought for you," Jack said. "He should have tried to hand me my own ass."

"What would that have accomplished?" I asked. "It's ultimately my choice, isn't it?"

"Yeah, you get the choice. But that doesn't change the fact that he should have come after me like a damn Viking for taking his woman."

"You haven't *taken* me," I protested.

He slid me a purposeful glance. "Yet."

And my heart lurched in a ramshackle rhythm.

We went up to his apartment, which I had never seen before. It was several floors up from mine, big windows open to a view of Houston, city lights glittering like diamonds scattered on velvet.

"What time did you tell the babysitter you'd be back?" Jack asked, while I investigated the apartment. It was stylish and spare, with dark leather furniture, a couple of pieces of graphic statement art, a few touches of deco design, fabrics in shades of chocolate, cream, and blue.

"I said about eleven." I touched the edge of a blue Depression-glass bowl imprinted with a swirly pattern. My fingers were trembling visibly. "This is a nice apartment."

Coming up behind me, Jack touched my shoulders with his palms and let them coast down my upper arms, the warmth of his hands making the cool skin prickle pleasantly. He took one of my hands in his. Folding my icy fingers more tightly in his, Jack lowered his mouth to the vulnerable curve of my neck. There was a sensual promise in the way his lips grazed my skin.

He continued to kiss me there, searching for the most acute place, and when he found it, I backed up against him reflexively.

"Jack . . . You're not still mad because Dane slept over, are you?"

His hand wandered along my front, charting every curve and plane, pausing at every flicker of response. My body caught a tense, pleasured arch. Dimly I realized he was gathering information, softly winnowing out the pulses and twitches from all the places I was most vulnerable.

"Actually, Ella . . . every time I think about it, I want to bend a crowbar in half."

"But nothing happened," I protested.

"That's the only reason I haven't hunted him down and dropped him."

I couldn't tell how much of the macho bravado was for show, or how much Jack actually meant. I strove for a reasonable, ironic tone, which was difficult as I felt his fingers slip beneath the edge of my neckline. "You're not going to take it out on me, are you?"

"Afraid so." His breath fractured as he discovered I wasn't wearing a bra. "Tonight you're in for it, blue eyes." With indecent slowness, his hand slid over the round, cool weight of my breast. I leaned back against him, teetering on the heels of my silver shoes. The tip of my breast pricked up between his fingers, and he fondled it tenderly, his thumb spurring it into a resilient bud.

He turned me around to face him. "Beautiful," he whispered. His hands went lower, following the clingy knit of my dress. His expression was intent, his lashes half-lowered until jagged shadows scored down his lean cheeks. And he breathed another word so softly I almost didn't hear it. "Mine."

Mesmerized, I stared into those dark eyes and shook my head slowly.

"Yes," Jack said, and he brought his mouth to mine. I responded helplessly, my hands clutching the front of his shirt. His fingers threaded through my hair, fitting over the curve of my scalp, and he concentrated on my mouth, finding deeper angles, more intimate tastes, until my entire body was radiating heat.

Taking my hand, Jack pulled me to the bedroom. He flipped on one of a trio of light switches, and a discreet glow filled the room from some unidentifiable source. I was too unstrung to register much about the surroundings, other than to note that the bed was big and covered in amber quilts and miles of white linen.

I cleared my throat and tried to sound casual, like this was no big deal. "I don't even get cheesy seduction music?"

Jack shook his head. "I usually do this a cappella."

"You mean unaccompanied?"

"No, I haven't done this unaccompanied since I was fourteen."

My breathless laugh ended with a gasp as Jack reached out and tugged gently at the tiny snaps that held the front of my dress closed. The sides listed open, unveiling the full round shapes of my breasts, my white silk panties.

"Look at you," he whispered. "It's a crime for you to wear clothes." He eased the dress off my shoulders until it dropped to the floor. A severe blush spread from head to toe as I stood there in high heels and panties.

Clumsy with urgency, I tugged at his black shirt, and Jack moved to help me strip it off. His chest was powerful and emphatically defined, the large muscles mortared with smaller ones in between. Hesitantly I touched the rough dark hair on his chest, drew my fingers through it. He felt maddeningly good. I let him pull me closer, his arms wrapping around me, and my hands slipped around to his back. The tickling brush of hair against my breasts, the long, delicious kisses, flooded me with sensation.

Feeling the way I had molded myself against his body, my hips urgently cradling the shape of his erection, Jack eased me back with a smothered laugh. "Not yet."

"I need you," I said, red and shaking. It was something I had never said to a man before. And even as I said it, I remembered what Jack had said in the parking garage: "*. . . you know if you start something with me, it'll go to a place you and Dane never went.*" It was true. It was absolutely true. I was going to let Jack get close in much more than a physical sense. The enormity of the risk I was about to take scared the hell out of me.

Feeling the reverberations of my panic, Jack pulled me between his thighs and gathered me against his chest. He held me wordlessly, with infinite patience.

"I guess . . . ," I managed to say eventually, "I don't feel all-the-way safe."

"Probably because you're not." Jack hooked his fingers at the side of my panties, drawing them down. "But in a few minutes, darlin', you're not going to give a damn."

Feeling dazed, I let him take off the panties, and I obeyed his urging to sit on the edge of the bed. I tried to reach for one of the silver shoes.

"No," Jack murmured, sinking to his haunches in front of me. He pushed my thighs open with his hands, his face intent.

I tried to close against him. "The light," I said bashfully. But Jack pinned me in place, and despite my wriggling objection, he leaned forward and pressed his mouth against me, *there,* in a full searching kiss. In a matter of seconds I was moaning, frozen in place as the pleasure surged and buzzed with each silky flick of his tongue. It went on and on until the desire was too much, and I clutched his head hard and close. He took my wrists, pulling them down to my sides, and just held them there.

Manacled in his grip, spread open, I breathed in low cries as he gnawed and licked and ate gently into the softness, and the sensation built until my inner muscles began a frantic, involuntary clenching.

Jack pulled back, leaving me floundering. I was weak, desperate, my pulse brutal in its force. As he stood between my thighs, I reached for the front of his pants to unfasten them. My hands felt encumbered, as if I were wearing mittens.

Jack was heavily aroused, his erection taut and dusky. I touched him in wonder, gripped the pulsing heft, breathed against the engorged head. He went still, and I heard a faint groan. He tolerated my careful touch, the warm suction of my mouth as I tried to taste as much of him as possible. But in a matter of seconds he was easing me away, muttering, "No . . . I can't. I'm too close. I'm too . . . wait, Ella . . ."

Stripping off his clothes, he joined me on the bed and tugged me toward the center of the mattress. He took interminable minutes to remove my shoes, unbuckling the tiny straps when it would have sufficed to slip them over my heels. And then he was over me again, his mouth at my breasts, one of his thighs nudging insistently between mine. I reached up to him, my palm flattening on the flexing surface of his back. His mouth found mine, and I went pliant, supine, moaning and resistless. Clasping me securely, he eased us to our sides, his hands venturing everywhere.

Our entwined bodies turned in a slow revolution across the wide bed. It was a sensual altercation, the way we rubbed and slid, with me trying to entice him inside and Jack resisting. He delayed and teased and tormented my aching flesh until I begged him in a hoarse whisper to do it now, I was ready, now, *now*—

He rolled me to my back and spread my legs wide. I complied with an expectant groan, tilting my hips up.

He eased inside me, and the entire world seemed to stop as I felt the low, thick slide. I clutched at his shoulders, my nails indenting his skin. Pushing deeper into my shrinking body, Jack murmured that he would be gentle, just relax, relax . . . and he went deeper and held, while I felt myself yield by slow degrees.

His face was right over mine, his eyes as dark and bright as hellfire.

He stroked the hair back from my forehead. "You're gonna have to get used to me," he whispered. I nodded as if in a trance.

His lips caught at mine. He nudged within the wet constriction of my body, gentle in the way only a big man could be. He was sensitive to every breath and heartbeat, searching for a perfect bias of flesh and movement, and when he found it, I cried out helplessly.

Jack nearly purred in satisfaction. "You like it this way, Ella?"

"Yes. Yes." I gripped his back, my hips lifting into his weight. He was solid, heavy, impaling me with disciplined strokes, and I began to struggle beneath him, wanting it faster, harder. A quiet laugh filtered through his raspy breathing. He pinned me down and forced me to accept his pace, and after what seemed like forever, I found myself relaxing into the pleasure. My head tilted back as his arm slid beneath my neck, and his mouth wandered over my throat.

He thrust in a tireless rhythm, in and in, the friction slippery and sweet and carnal. I reached the height of the excruciating rise, and then it all began to fragment and I came in voluptuous jolts, my knees clamping on his hips. He rode it out until the last spasms had faded, and then he moved in a few final thrusts as he found his own release.

Afterward, I lay quiet and trembling in Jack's arms, feeling the hot slick of him between my thighs. I turned my face into his chest. My body felt heavy with satisfaction, tender as a fruit ripened to full-slip sweetness.

"Rest," Jack murmured, pulling the covers over my naked shoulders.

"Can't," I mumbled. "Downstairs. The babysitter . . ."

He kissed my hair. His voice was a stroke of raw velvet. "Just for a few minutes. I'll watch over you."

Burrowing against him, I dozed gratefully.

In a while, I blinked and stirred, filled with the dreamlike awareness that something had changed. Me. I felt uncertain, undermined, and yet it was a strangely good feeling.

Jack was propped up on an elbow, staring down at me with surprising gravity. One of his fingers came to trace the edge of my smiling lips. "That was the best I ever had, Ella. There's not even a close second."

I closed my eyes as he traced the wings of my brows. And I reflected that the difference between good sex and mind-blowing sex had been a quality of attention I'd never gotten from Dane. Jack had been wholly absorbed in me, intensely focused on my responses. Even now he touched me as if the contact between our bodies was a language all its own. His caressing fingers moved down to my throat. "Your skin is so soft," he whispered. "And your hair is so silky. I love the way you feel . . . the way you move . . ." His thumb ran slowly along the edge of my jaw. "I want you to trust me, Ella. I want every part of you. Someday you're going to let go with me."

I turned my face into Jack's hand, pressing a sideways kiss in his palm. I knew what he meant, what he wanted, and I didn't know how to convey to him that it wasn't possible. I would never be able to lose myself entirely in lovemaking—there was a guarded center to my personality that no one would ever be able to reach. "I just had sex with the light on," I said. "For God's sake, isn't that enough?"

He laughed and kissed me.

Even sated as I was, the feel of his mouth against mine was enough to start me simmering. Settling my palms on the angles of his shoulders, I followed the rises and curves of solid, efficient muscle. "I saw you with Ashley tonight at the party," I told him. "She's very beautiful."

Jack's mouth quirked without humor. "That fades the more you get to know her."

"What were the two of you talking about?"

"She's bitching to everyone about her problems with Pete."

"That's her husband? Was he there?"

"Yeah. They seemed to be doing their best to avoid each other."

"I wonder if she's been unfaithful to him," I mused.

"Wouldn't be out of character," Jack said dryly.

"That's sad. But it justifies what I've always thought about marriage: you can never promise to love a person forever. Because everything changes."

"Not everything." Jack eased back onto the pillows and I stretched against him, settling my head into the crook of his shoulder.

"Do you think she loved you?" I asked. "I mean, sincerely loved you?"

He sighed tautly. "I don't know if there was ever any love on her part." He paused. "If there was, I ruined it."

"Ruined it?" I sensed this was territory that had to be navigated with care, that remnants of pain, or regret, were still part of the landscape. "How did you do that?"

"When Ashley left me for Pete, she told me—" Jack broke off with an unsettled breath.

I climbed over him fully, draping myself over his hard, furry chest. "Trust works both ways, Jack." I reached to the ruffled disorder of his hair and slid my fingers through it gently. "You can tell me."

Jack looked away from me, his profile as hard and perfect as a face on a new-minted coin. "She said I wanted too much. That I was demanding. Needy."

"Oh." I knew that to a man with Jack's pride, that was about the worst thing a woman could say to him. "Were you?" I asked in a matter-of-fact way. "Or was Ashley trying to put all the blame on you for the fact that she cheated? Because I've never been a big fan of the look-what-you-made-me-do defense."

The tension eased from his body. "Ashley sure as hell never took responsibility for anything. But the truth is, I probably was a pain in the ass. I don't do things half-measure, including falling in love." He paused. "I have a possessive streak."

He seemed to believe he was telling me something new. I bit the inside of my lower lip to keep from laughing. "No kidding," I said. "The good thing is, Jack, I have no problem telling you where to draw the line."

"I noticed that."

We stared at each other as smiles started on both our faces.

"So," I said, "after Ashley cheated on you, you spent the next several years scoring with every woman in sight, to show her what she'd missed out on."

"No, that had nothing to do with Ashley. I just happen to like sex." His hand slid down to my bottom.

"No kidding." I rolled away from him with a gasp of laughter and hopped out of bed. "I need a shower."

Jack followed readily.

I stopped short as I flipped on the switch in his bathroom, an immaculate well-lit space with contemporary cabinetry and modern stone vessel sinks. But it was the shower that left me speechless, a room made of glass and slate and granite, with rows of dials and knobs and thermostats. "Why is there a car wash in your bathroom?"

Jack went past me, opened the glass door, and went inside. As he turned knobs and adjusted the temperature on digital screens, jets sprouted from every conceivable place, and steam collected in white drifts. Three rainfall streams came directly from the ceiling.

"Aren't you going to come in?" Jack's voice filtered through the sound of abundant falling water.

I went to the glass doorway and peeked inside. Jack was a magnificent sight, all bronzy and lean, a sheet of water glimmering over his skin. His stomach was drum-tight, his back gorgeous and sleekly muscled.

"I hate to be the one to tell you this," I said, "but you need to start exercising. A man your age shouldn't let himself go."

He grinned and gestured for me to come to him. I ventured into the maelstrom of competing sprays, battered with heat from all directions. "I'm drowning," I said, spluttering, and he pulled me out of the direct downpour of an overhead spray. "I wonder how much water we're wasting."

"You know, Ella, you're not the first woman who's ever been in this shower with me—"

"I'm shocked." I leaned against him as he soaped my back.

"—but you're for damn sure the first one who's ever worried about wasting water."

"How much, would you say?"

"Ten gallons per minute, give or take."

"Oh my God. *Hurry*. We can't stay in here long. We'll throw the entire ecological system out of balance."

"This is Houston, Ella. The ecological system won't notice." Ignoring my protests, Jack washed me and shampooed my hair. It felt so good that I finally shut up and just stood there, letting his strong, slick hands run all over me while I breathed in the steam-laden air. And I washed him, dreamily sifting my fingers through his soapy chest hair, tracing the wonderful masculine textures of his body.

There was a feeling of unreality about all of it, the muted light and water sluicing over our skin, the frank sensuality that left no allowance for modesty. His mouth fastened on mine with wet, sucking kisses, and his hand slipped between my thighs, the long fingers gently playful. I pressed my cheek against his shoulder, gasping.

"The first time I saw you," Jack murmured against my sodden hair, "I thought everything about you was so cute, I could hardly stand it."

"Cute?"

"In a sexy way."

"I thought you were sexy in a jerky kind of way. You're—" I paused, my vision blurring as his fingers slid inside me, "—not at all my type."

I felt him smile against my scalp. "Really? Because right now my type seems to be working for you." He lifted one of my knees until my foot was propped on a cypress shower stool. I held on to him, weak with lust. His body pressed against mine, length to length, and the desire was a back-and-forth current between us. Careful and intent, he stroked me open, positioned himself, slid deep. His hands gripped my bottom and compressed it in his fingers. For a moment we stayed like that, my body motionless and filled and possessed.

I stared, blinking, into his dark wet face. There was no rush toward quick satisfaction, only this leisurely discovery. My flesh throbbed around him as he held me steady against a slow, rolling rhythm. I felt as if I were the only fixed point of the universe.

Each time he drove in, I shivered and held his shoulders, and he gathered me closer. The accumulating pleasure seemed to dissolve my bones. I felt his tongue licking the hot mist from my neck, my ear. I writhed, my body sliding in his grip, limbs slick and protean.

But without warning the rhythm broke, and he withdrew, leaving me trembling, bewildered. "No," I said, clinging to him. "Wait, I didn't . . . Jack . . ."

He was turning off the knobs, the waterfalls disappearing.

"I wasn't finished yet," I told him woefully as he came back to me.

Jack had the nerve to grin. Taking my shoulders in his hands, he guided me out of the shower. "I wasn't, either."

"Then why did you stop?" Privately I excused myself for whining. Any woman would have whined in such circumstances.

He reached for a fluffy white towel and began to dry me efficiently. "Because you're dangerous when it comes to standing-up sex. Your leg muscles give out."

"I was still standing!"

"Barely." He scrubbed my hair with the towel, and reached for another to dry himself. "Face it, Ella—you're at your best horizontal." Throwing the towel aside, he pulled me back to the bedroom. In a matter of seconds, he had tossed me onto the bed as if I weighed nothing.

I squeaked in surprise as I bounced on the mattress. "What are you doing?"

"I'm fast-tracking this. It's twenty to eleven."

I frowned and pushed a tangle of damp hair back from my face. "Let's wait until we have more time."

But I found myself covered with nearly two hundred pounds of playful, aroused male.

"I can't go downstairs like this," Jack said.

"Too bad," I told him sternly. "You can either wait or do it a cappella."

"Ella," he cajoled, "let's finish what we started in the shower."

"You should have finished it right then."

"I didn't want you to fall and get a head injury. The afterglow never lasts as long in the ER."

I chuckled, and Jack pressed his cheek against the soft bounce of my breast. His hot breath rushed against the distended tip. Slowly his mouth opened over the rosy flesh, his tongue circling. Sliding my arms around his neck, I kissed the thick, damp locks of his hair. He lifted his mouth and took the nipple between his fingers, clamping softly while he moved to kiss the other breast, and my hips pressed upward into his weight. In a matter of seconds I was steaming. He browsed over me as if I were some lavish buffet, nibbling and licking and kissing, lifting and turning me to make certain there was nothing he had missed. I lay on my stomach, gripping fistfuls of amber quilt as he took my hips and hoisted them upward.

"This okay?" I heard him whisper.

"Yes," I panted. "God, yes."

His electrifying weight lowered over me from behind, and he nudged my stiff limbs apart. I groaned at the heavy penetration as he glided easily into the wetness. His hand slid beneath me, fingers going to the exact place I needed them.

Caught deliciously between his body and his hand, I pushed upward invitingly, and he went as deep as I could take him. His mouth went to my back, kissing the top of my spine. He waited until I pushed up again before he thrust. I realized he was letting me set the rhythm, his every motion a counterpoint to mine. I arched and gasped as I took him, worked him, feeling him shove deeper while those gentle fingers tantalized and teased. Sensations flowed together until I could no longer recognize their separate sources. I gripped his thick muscled wrists, one braced near my head, the other down between my thighs, and I held

him there as I went over the edge. The climax was lush and brimming, and each time I thought it had died down, it gave another voluptuous kick. I felt Jack shudder, the heat of him flooding me in violent pulses.

When he finally caught his breath, he muttered a few curses. I had to bury a shaky laugh in the covers, because I understood. It felt as if, somehow, a thing that was entirely ordinary had been reinvented, and the two of us along with it.

WE DRESSED CLUMSILY AND WENT DOWN TO MY APARTMENT, and Jack overpaid the babysitter, who pretended not to notice how disheveled we were. After checking on Luke, who was down for the count, I told Jack that he was welcome to spend the night with me, except the baby would probably wake him up.

"No problem," Jack replied, kicking off his shoes. "Wasn't planning on doing much sleeping anyway." He stripped off his jeans and T-shirt, climbed into bed, and watched me change into my pajamas. "You don't need those," he said.

I smiled at the sight of him leaning back against the brass headboard with his hands clasped comfortably behind his head. He was brawny and tan, incongruously masculine against all the frilly antique fabric and lace.

"I don't like to sleep naked," I told him.

"Why? It's a great look for you."

"I like to be prepared."

"For what?"

"If there's ever an emergency—a fire or something. . . ."

"Jesus, Ella." He was laughing. "Think of it this way—going to bed naked is better for the environment."

"Oh, shut up."

"Come on, Ella. Sleep green."

Ignoring him, I got into bed wearing a T-shirt and boxer shorts printed with penguins. I reached over to the nightstand and flipped off the lamp.

A moment of silence, and then I heard a lecherous murmur. "I like your penguins."

I snuggled back against him, and his knees tucked under mine. "I'm guessing your usual female company doesn't wear boxer shorts to bed," I said.

"Nope." Jack's hand settled on my hip. "If they wear anything, it's usually some kind of see-through nightgown."

"That sounds pretty pointless." I yawned, relaxing into the warmth of his body. "But I'll wear one someday if you want me to."

"I don't know." Jack sounded pensive. His hand circled my bottom. "I'm kind of partial to these penguins."

My God, I thought, *I love talking with you.* But I stayed silent, because I never used the word "love" with a man.

SEVENTEEN

I WOKE UP ALONE AND WORRIED, SITTING UP AND rubbing my eyes. The source of the worry was the bright glitter of sunshine coming through the shades. I hadn't heard the baby.

Luke never slept this long.

Galvanized, I leapt out of bed and flew to the main room, only to stop like a cartoon character quivering at the edge of a cliff.

There was a mug of half-finished coffee on the table. Jack was on the sofa, dressed in his jeans and T-shirt, with Luke cuddled on his chest. They were watching the news.

"You got up with him," I said bemusedly.

"I thought I'd let you sleep." His dark gaze slid over me. "I worked you out pretty good last night."

I leaned over both of them, kissing Luke and teasing a gummy smile out of him.

Luke had awakened once in the middle of the night, and Jack had insisted on getting up with me. While I had changed the diaper, he had warmed the bottle, and sat with us until Luke had finished feeding.

We had gone back to bed, and Jack had held me and caressed me with artful stealth. He had slid along my body, his lips parted, tongue stroking and darting for long minutes of refined torture. He had lifted me, turned me over and around, and we'd had sex in positions I wouldn't have thought were possible. As it turned out, Jack was an athletic and highly creative lover, and it was only at my insistence that we had finally stopped. Exhausted and sated, I had slept without stirring for the rest of the night.

"I haven't slept in this late forever," I told Jack earnestly. "This was the nicest thing you could have done for me." I went to pour myself some coffee. "I am chronically sleep-deprived. I can't tell you how good last night was."

"The sleep or the sex?"

I grinned. "The sex, of course . . . but by a narrow margin."

"What about getting your mom to help with babysitting?"

I stirred cream into my coffee. "She could probably be talked into it, especially if it's on the right day and it's not interfering with something else. But the amount of gratitude you have to shower on Mom for something like that is exhausting. I mean, you owe her *forever*. And the other thing is . . . I don't trust her with Luke."

Jack watched intently as I came to the sofa. "You think she'd hurt him?"

"Oh, not physically, no. Mom never hit me or Tara, or anything like that. But she was a drama queen, and she yelled a lot—which is why, to this day, I can't stand raised voices. I don't want her to do that to Luke. And basically, if I don't want to be alone with her, I can't imagine subjecting Luke to it." I set my mug on the coffee table and reached for the baby. "Here's my boy," I murmured, snuggling his warm, wriggly body against my chest. I glanced at Jack. "How often do you raise your voice?"

"Only at football games. No, that's not true—I also yell at contractors." He leaned over and kissed my temple. His hand closed lightly in my hair. "Do you have plans for the day?"

"No."

"You want to spend it with me?"

I nodded immediately.

"I'd like to take you and Luke to Lake Conroe," Jack said. "I keep a boat there. I'll call ahead to the marina and they'll pack lunch for us."

"Would it be okay to take Luke out on a boat?" I asked uncertainly.

"Yeah, he'd be safe in the cabin. And when he's on deck, we'll put him in a life vest."

"Do you have one his size?"

"We'll get one at the marina."

Lake Conroe was about forty miles north of the Metroplex, and it was unofficially known as Houston's playground. The lake was approximately twenty-one miles long, vaguely scorpion-shaped when seen from overhead, with a third of its shoreline bordered by the Sam Houston National Forest. The rest of the area featured high-priced residential communities and almost two dozen golf courses. I had never actually been to Conroe, but I had heard about the lavish watercolor sunsets, the luxury resorts and fine restaurants, and its reputation for world-class bass fishing.

"I don't have any experience with boats and fishing," I told Jack on the drive up. "So I'll help as much as I can, but I just want to make certain you understand that I'm flotationally challenged."

Jack grinned, setting his cell phone in one of the cupholders between the front seats of his SUV. Wearing black rimless aviator sunglasses, board shorts, and a fresh white polo shirt, he radiated sexy vitality. "There are boat valets to help us launch. Your only job is to have a good time."

"I can do that." I felt cheerful, alight with a sense of impatient happiness I had never felt before. I actually found it difficult to stay still in my car seat—I was tempted to wriggle like a child on the last day of school with five minutes to go before summer began. For the first time in my life, there was no other place I would rather have been and no one else I wanted to be with. I twisted around to look at Luke's car seat, which was facing backward.

"I should check on him," I said, reaching to unbuckle my seat belt.

"He's fine," Jack said, reaching over to take my hand. "No more crawling back and forth, Ella. Stay buckled in and safe."

"I don't like it when I can't see Luke."

"When do you get to turn him around?"

"He'll have to be a year old, at least." Some of my happiness dimmed. "I won't have him then."

"Have you heard from Tara lately?"

I shook my head. "I'm going to call her tomorrow. Not only do I want to know how she's doing, I want to give her an update on Luke." I paused reflectively. "I have to admit, I'm surprised by how little interest she seems to have in him. I mean, she wants to know if he's basically okay, but all the details—how he's feeding and sleeping, how long he holds his head up, that kind of stuff—she doesn't seem to care."

"Did she ever have an interest in babies before Luke?"

"God, no. Neither of us did. I always thought it was as boring as hell when other people talked about their babies. But it's different when it's your own."

"Maybe Tara didn't have him long enough to feel a bond with him."

"Maybe. But by the second day I was taking care of Luke, I'd already started to—" I stopped and flushed.

Jack glanced at me quickly, his eyes hidden behind the dark lenses. His voice was very gentle. "Started to love him?"

"Yes."

His thumb rubbed an easy circle over the back of my hand. "Why does that embarrass you?"

"I'm not embarrassed, it's just . . . it's not easy for me to talk about that kind of thing."

"You write about it all the time."

"Yes, but not when it involves my own feelings."

"You think of it as a trap?"

"Oh, not a trap. But it gets in the way of things."

I saw the flash of his grin. "What does love get in the way of, Ella?"

"When I broke things off with Dane, for example. It would have been messy and difficult if we'd ever gotten to the point of saying we loved each other. But because we hadn't, it was much easier to detach."

"You're going to have to detach from Luke at some point," Jack said. "Maybe you shouldn't have said it to him."

"He's a *baby*," I said indignantly. "He has to hear it from someone. How would you like to come into the world and not have anyone say they loved you?"

"My parents never said it. They thought you shouldn't wear out the words."

"But you don't agree?"

"No. If the feeling is there, you might as well admit it. Saying the words, or not saying them, doesn't change a damn thing."

It was a hot, hazy day. The marina was busy, the weathered gray docks creaking beneath the weight of hundreds of feet. There were boys in shorts but no shirts, girls in swimsuits made of strings and scraps, men wearing T-shirts featuring slogans such as "Shut up and fish" or "Kiss my Bass." Older men wore polyester shorts and Cuban-style shirts with embroidery running down both sides of the chest, and older women wore skorts and tropical-colored shirts and large brimmed sunhats. A few ladies with teased and frosted bouffants wore visors, over which hair billowed like little atomic mushroom clouds.

Smells of water and algae hung in the air, along with scents of beer, diesel, bait, and coconut sunblock. A busy dog trotted back and forth from the marina to the docks, appearing to belong to no one.

As soon as we entered the marina, a boat valet dressed in red and white came to greet us enthusiastically. He told Jack the boat was fueled and clean, the battery was charged, food and drinks were stocked, everything was ready to go. "What about the infant life vest?" Jack asked, and the valet told him they'd found one and it was on board.

The transom of Jack's boat was emblazoned with the name *Last Fling*. The vessel was about twice the size I had anticipated, at least thirty-five feet, sleek and white and showroom-perfect. Jack helped me through the open transom door, and took me on a brief tour. There were two staterooms and heads, a full galley equipped with a stove, an oven, a refrigerator, and a sink, a main saloon with gleaming woodwork and rich fabric, and a flat-screen TV.

"My God," I said, dazed. "When you said there was an indoor

cabin, I thought you meant a room with a couple of chairs and some vinyl windows. This is a *yacht,* Jack."

"More like what they call a pocket yacht. A nice all-around boat."

"That's ridiculous. You can have pocket change or a pocket watch. You can't put a yacht in your pocket."

"We'll discuss what's in my pockets later," Jack said. "Try the life vest on Luke and see if it's okay."

AT CRUISING SPEED THE RIDE WAS QUIET AND SMOOTH, the hull of the *Last Fling* cutting decisively through the dark blue water. I sat on the flybridge, one of the boat's two helms, on a wide cushioned bench seat next to the skipper's chair. Luke was bundled in a blue nylon life jacket with a huge rounded flotation collar. Either it was more comfortable than it looked, or the baby was distracted by the new sounds and sensations of being on a boat, because he was surprisingly unfussy. Holding the baby on my lap, I put my legs up on the bench.

As Jack took us around the lake, pointing out homes, mini islands, a bald eagle hunting for catfish, I sipped from a glass of chilled white wine that tasted like pears. I was overtaken by the kind of ease that could only come from being in a boat in sunny weather, the air humid and beneficent in my lungs, the warm breeze rushing continuously over us.

We anchored in a cove shaded by abundant pine and cedar, the shoreline still undeveloped. I unpacked an enormous picnic basket, discovering a jar of creamed honey, crisp pale baguettes, disks of snowy-white goat cheese and a wedge of Humboldt with a thin line of volcanic ash, containers of salad, sections of gourmet sandwiches, and cookies the size of hubcaps. We ate slowly and finished the bottle of wine, and I fed and changed Luke.

"He's ready for a nap," I said, cuddling the sleepy baby. We took him inside the air-conditioned cabin to one of the downstairs staterooms. I laid him carefully in the center of the double berth. Luke blinked at me, his eyes staying closed longer each time, until finally he was fast asleep. "Sweet dreams, Luke," I whispered, kissing his head.

Straightening, I stretched my back and glanced at Jack, who was waiting near the doorway. He had propped his shoulders against the wall, and stood with his hands in his pockets.

"Come here," he murmured. The sound of his voice in the darkness sent a pleasant shiver across my skin.

He took me to the other stateroom, cool and shadowy, and scented of polished wood and ozone and the slightest hint of diesel.

"I get a nap?" I asked, slipping off my shoes and crawling onto the bed.

"You get whatever you want, blue eyes."

We lay on our sides facing each other, skin releasing heat, retaining the flavor of salt as our perspiration dried. Jack stared at me steadily. His hand lifted to the side of my face, the tip of his middle finger following the wing of a brow, the soft ridge of a cheekbone. He touched me with absolute absorption, like an explorer who had discovered a rare and fragile artifact. Remembering the devilish patience of those hands, all the intimate ways he had touched me last night, I flushed in the semidarkness. "I want you," I whispered.

All my senses turned acute as Jack slowly undressed me. He covered the erect tip of my breast with his mouth, his tongue a soothing swirl. His hand moved to the small of my back, finding the sensitive hollows of my spine, caressing until I was filled with hot sparks.

Jack took off his own clothes, his body sleek and unbelievably strong. He arranged me in revealing positions, each one more open and vulnerable than the last, exploring with his hands and mouth until I was breathing in ragged gasps. Pinning my wrists to the mattress, he stared down at me. I moaned and tilted my hips upward, waiting tensely, my arms straining in his grasp.

I gasped as I felt the low, heavy penetration, his body sliding over mine until I was stroked inside and out. Hard flesh over pale curves, heat against coolness. Every thrust translated skin into sensation, form into fire. Jack held still, panting, trying to stave off the climax, make it last. Letting go of my wrists, he laced all of his fingers through all of mine with painstaking deliberation.

I lifted up against him, wanting to go on, and he inhaled sharply, trying to hold back. But I kept nudging upward, pushing him, until finally he lost all restraint and began to thrust deep and steady, taking my sobs into his mouth as if he could taste them. Since I couldn't hold him with my arms, I used my legs, twining them around his back. He gritted his teeth and buried himself over and over, stoking the sensation, driving me into long, silky spasms, and then he let himself come, too, growling his pleasure against my throat.

Afterward we lay together, limbs tangled, my head resting on his shoulder. How strange it was to lie there with a man who wasn't Dane. Stranger still was that it felt so natural. I thought of what Dane had told me, that although he didn't want a traditional relationship, it was okay if I wanted to explore that with Jack.

"Jack," I said drowsily.

"What?" His hand sifted slowly through my hair.

"Are we having a traditional relationship?"

"As opposed to what you had with Dane? Yeah, I'd say that's what we're having."

"So . . . it's sort of an exclusive deal, the two of us?"

Jack hesitated before replying. "That's what I want," he finally said. "What about you?"

"It makes me uneasy that we're doing this so fast."

"What does your gut tell you?"

"My gut and I aren't currently speaking to each other."

He smiled. "Mine's almost always right. And it's telling me this is a good thing." Jack traced the ladder of my spine, his fingertips raising gooseflesh. "Let's try it with just you and me. No other people, no distractions. Let's find out what that's like. Okay?"

"Okay." I yawned. "But just to be clear, I'm not going to get serious with you. There's no future in this."

"Go to sleep," he whispered, pulling the covers farther over my shoulders.

I couldn't keep my eyes open any longer. "Yes, but did you hear—"

"I heard you." And he held me as I slept.

My relaxed mood was shattered as soon as we got back to 1800 Main, and I listened to the messages on the answering machine. Tara had called three times, sounding increasingly agitated as she told me to call her back no matter what time it was.

"It's about our meeting with Mark Gottler," I told Jack glumly as he set down Luke's carrier and lifted the baby to his shoulder. "About the promissory contract. I'm sure of it. I wondered if he would say something to her."

"Did you tell her that we'd seen him?"

"No, I didn't want Tara to be bothered with it. She's supposed to be getting her head together . . . she's vulnerable. . . . If Gottler got her all upset about this, I'm going to kill him."

"Call her right now and find out," Jack said calmly, taking Luke to the changing table.

"Does Luke have a dirty diaper? I'll take care of it."

"Call your sister, darlin'. Believe me, if I can field-dress a deer, I can handle changing a diaper."

I gave him a grateful glance and called Tara.

Tara picked up on the second ring. "Hello?"

"Tara, it's me. I just got your message. How is everything?"

Her tone sounded like breaking glass. "Everything was great until Mark called and told me what you'd been up to."

I took a deep breath. "I'm sorry he bothered you with that."

"You should be sorry you did it in the first place! And you knew it was wrong, or you would have said something to me. What's going on, Ella? And what are you doing, dragging Jack Travis in on my business?"

"He's a friend. He was there for moral support."

"It's too bad you wasted his time, and your own. Because it was all for *nothing*. I'm not signing any contracts. I don't need your help, especially *that* kind of help. Do you know how much you've embarrassed me? Do you know what's at stake? You're going to ruin my life if you don't shut up and mind your own business."

I was silent, trying to regulate my breathing. Tara, when she was angry, sounded too much like our mother. "I'm not going to ruin anything," I eventually said. "I'm only doing what you asked, which is to take care of Luke. And I'm trying to make certain you get the help you're entitled to."

"Mark's already promised to help me. There was no need for you to get lawyers involved!"

I was astounded by her naiveté. "How much stock are you going to put in the promises of a man who cheats on his wife?"

I heard her gasp of outrage. "It's not your business. This is *my life*. I don't want you to talk to Mark ever again. You don't understand the situation at all."

"I understand a lot more than you do," I said grimly. "Listen to me, Tara . . . you need protection. You need guaranteed support. Did Mark tell you what we were negotiating for?"

"No, and I don't want to hear it. I know what he's promised me, and that's enough. Any contract you give me, I'm going tear it up and throw it away."

"Can I just tell you a few of the things we talked about?"

"*No*. I'm not interested in anything you have to say. I'm finally getting what I want, for once in my life, and you're judging and interfering and spoiling everything. Just like Mom."

I recoiled. "I'm not like Mom."

"You are! You're jealous like her—you're jealous of me because I'm prettier and I had a baby, and I have a rich boyfriend."

Right then I discovered that you actually could see red, if you were angry enough. "Grow up, Tara," I snapped.

Click.

Silence.

I looked at the dead phone in my hand. I dropped my head in utter defeat. "Jack."

"Yeah?"

"I just told my sister—who's in a mental health clinic—to grow up."

He came up to me with the freshly diapered baby. His voice was soft and amused. "I heard."

I looked up at him bleakly. "Do you have Mark Gottler's number? I have to call him."

"Got it right here on my cell phone. You're welcome to it." Jack studied me briefly. "Would you trust me to take care of it?" he murmured. "Can I do that for you?"

I considered the offer, knowing that even though I could handle Gottler on my own, this was precisely the sort of thing Jack was good at. And right now it was nice to have the help. I nodded.

He handed Luke to me, went to the table where he had left his wallet, keys, and phone. In about two minutes he had Gottler on the phone.

"Hey, Mark. How are you doing? Great. Yeah, things are okay, but we have an issue here, and we need to get it straightened out. Ella just got off the horn with Tara . . . about that meeting we had, the contract . . . yeah. Ella's not too happy, Mark. Tell you the truth, neither am I. Guess I should have made it clear that it was confidential. But I didn't expect you to go talking out of school." He paused to listen. "I know why you did it, Mark." His tone was quiet but blistering. "And now you got these sisters as aggravated as two cats in a bathtub. No matter what Tara says she wants right now, she's not in any shape to make those decisions. You don't need to worry about if or when she signs the contract. Once my lawyer sends it over, you have your boys look it over, you sign the fucker, and you send it to me." Jack listened for a moment. "Because Ella asked me to be in on it, that's why. I don't know how you usually handle these things . . . yeah, that's what I'm implying. . . . Fact is, Mark, I'm here to make sure Tara and Luke get their due. I want them to have what we talked over and what we shook on. And you know what it means to cross a Travis in Houston. No, of course that's not a threat. I consider us friends, and I know you won't back down from doing what's right. So let's be clear on how the next couple of months will play out: you're not going to bother Tara with this stuff again. We're going to nail down this contract, and if you cause any problems for our side, I guarantee you're going to have even bigger problems. And I don't think any of us want to go there. Next time you want to talk about any of this stuff, you call me or Ella. Tara's out of the loop until she gets well enough to leave that clinic. Good. I think so, too." He listened for a half minute or so, looked satisfied and said goodbye, and closed the phone with a decisive snap.

Looking at me, he raised an expectant brow.

"Thanks, Jack," I said softly, the tight feeling easing from my chest. "You think he was paying attention?"

"He was paying attention." Jack approached me as I sat on the sofa, lowered to his haunches, and looked into my face. "It'll be fine," he murmured. "You don't waste one minute worrying about it."

"All right." I reached out and stroked the dark layers of his hair. I felt oddly bashful as I asked, "Do you want to spend the night with me, or would you rather—"

"Yes."

A crooked grin spread across my face. "You want some time to think about it?"

"Okay." He squinted thoughtfully as if mulling it over, and a split second later, he said, "Yes."

EIGHTEEN

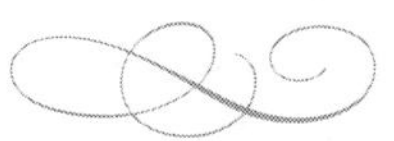

DURING THE NEXT MONTH WE SPENT EVERY NIGHT together, and all the weekends, and still it seemed that I could never see Jack enough.

There were moments when I hardly recognized myself, laughing and playing like the child I had never been. We went to a roadhouse honky-tonk, where Jack led me onto the wooden dance floor, sticky with the residue of beer and tequila, and taught me how to two-step.

Another day we went to an indoor butterfly garden and let hundreds of colorful wings flutter around us like confetti. "He thinks you're a flower," Jack whispered in my ear as one of the butterflies perched on my shoulder.

He took Luke and me to an arts and flowers market, where he bought me a huge basket of handmade soaps and two pails of melting-ripe Fredericksburg peaches. We dropped off one of the pails at his father's home and visited for about an hour, going out to the back with him to view a putting green that had just been installed.

Discovering that I had never played golf, Churchill gave me an impromptu putting lesson. I told him I didn't need to take on a new hobby that I was bad at, and Churchill told me that golf was one of the two things in life you could enjoy even if you were bad at them. Before I could ask what the other thing was, Jack shook his head with a groan and dragged me out of there, but not before his father had made him promise to bring me back soon.

There were elegant occasions when Jack and I attended a charity event for the Houston Symphony, or went to the opening of an art gallery, or out to dinner at a luminous restaurant located in a renovated 1920s church. I was amused and also annoyed by the reactions of other women to Jack, the way they fluttered and flirted. He was courteous but distant, but that only seemed to encourage them. And I realized Jack was not the only one with a possessive streak.

I relished the weekend afternoons when I hired a babysitter to look after Luke, and I went up to Jack's apartment. We lay together for hours, talking or having sex, sometimes at the same time. As a lover, Jack was inventive and skillful, guiding me into new levels of sensuality, easing me back carefully. Day by day I felt myself changing in ways that I couldn't bring myself to examine. We were getting too close, I knew that, but I couldn't think of how to stop it.

I found myself telling Jack everything about my past, things I had previously confided only to Dane, memories still painful enough to make my eyes water and my voice crack. Instead of saying something philosophical or wise, Jack simply hugged me, offering the comfort of his body. It was what I needed most. But I often felt the tension of conflicting desires when I was with Jack. I was so powerfully drawn to him, and yet also trying hard to maintain any fragile barriers I could. And he was so damnably smart, too smart to push me. Instead, he seduced me constantly, with gentleness and strength, with sex and charm and steely patience.

* * *

ONE DAY JACK BROUGHT LUKE AND ME TO GAGE AND Liberty's home in the Tanglewood subdivision, for an afternoon of swimming and relaxation. He explained that he would have to spend part of the time helping his brother Gage work on a twelve-foot salt bay skiff they were building in the garage. It had started as a project for Liberty's eleven-year-old sister, Carrington, whom Liberty had raised since birth. Gage was helping her to make the small boat, but they needed an extra pair of hands to get the job done.

Tanglewood was in the Galleria area, the residential lots generally smaller than River Oaks, the main boulevard lined with live oaks and wide paths and benches. Gage and Liberty had bought a tear-down property, one of the last few crumbling "rambling ranch" homes built in the fifties, and they had built a European-style mansion of limestone and stucco, with a black slate roof. The entrance featured a two-story rotunda and a curving staircase with a wrought-iron balustrade, and more ironwork at the circular balcony of the second-floor level. Everything was serene, agreeably textured and roughened, as though it was a centuries-old home.

Liberty welcomed us at the door, her hair pulled back in a ponytail, her slim but curvaceous figure dressed in a neat black swimsuit and a pair of frayed denim shorts. She wore flip-flops decorated with sequined fake flowers. Liberty had an interesting quality I could only describe as wholesome sultriness, a sort of clear-eyed, sexy niceness.

"I love your shoes," I said.

Liberty hugged me as if I were an old family friend. "My sister Carrington made them for me at summer camp. You haven't met her yet." She stood on her toes to kiss Jack's cheek. "Hi, stranger. We haven't seen much of you lately."

He grinned at Liberty while he held Luke against his shoulder. "Been busy."

"Well, that's good. Anything that keeps you out of trouble." She took the baby from him and cuddled him. "You forget how little they are at the beginning. He's adorable, Ella."

"Thanks." I felt a glow of pride, as if Luke were my own child instead of Tara's.

Two new figures entered the hall—Liberty's tall, black-haired husband, Gage, and a young blond girl. Carrington looked nothing like Liberty, which led me to conclude they were half-sisters.

"Jack!" she exclaimed, hurtling toward him, all skinny legs and flying braids. "My *favorite uncle*."

"I already said I'd help with the boat," Jack said ruefully as she tackled him.

"It's fun, Jack! Gage banged his finger and said a bad word, and let me use the cordless drill, and I got to hammer nails into the side boards—"

"Cordless drill?" Liberty repeated, darting a half-worried, half-chiding glance at her husband.

"She did great." Gage smiled and reached out to shake my hand. "Hi, Ella. I see your taste in company hasn't improved."

"Don't believe anything he tells you, Ella," Jack said. "I am and always have been an angel."

Gage snorted.

Liberty was trying to look at Gage's hand. "Which finger did you hurt?"

"It's nothing." Gage showed her his thumb, and she frowned as she inspected the place on the nail that had begun to bruise. I was struck by the way his expression changed as he looked at his wife's down-bent head, the way his eyes softened.

Retaining his hand in hers, Liberty glanced at her little sister. "Carrington, this is Miss Varner."

The girl shook my hand and smiled at me, revealing two crooked front teeth. She had porcelain skin and sky blue eyes, and a barely discernable tracery of pink lines on the bridge of her nose and her forehead, as if she'd been wearing a mask.

"Call me Ella, please." I glanced at Liberty and added, "She was wearing protective eyewear, by the way."

"How did you know?" Carrington asked, impressed and mystified. Before I could answer, she caught sight of Luke. "Oh, he's so cute! Can I hold him? I'm really good at holding babies. I help with Matthew all the time."

"Maybe later when you're sitting down," Jack said. "For now, we got work to do. Let's go have a look at the boat."

"Okay, it's in the garage!" She took his hand and tugged eagerly.

Jack resisted for a moment, looking at me. "You okay hanging out with Liberty by the pool?"

"There is nothing I'd rather do."

Liberty took me through the house and out to the back. She carried Luke, cooing to him, while I followed with the diaper bag.

"Where is Matthew?" I asked.

"He went down for his nap a little early today. The babysitter will bring him out when he wakes up."

We went through a kitchen that looked like something out of a rustic French chateau. A pair of French doors led to a fenced-in backyard, which was landscaped with a green lawn, flower beds, and a party deck with a grill. The dominant feature of the half-acre yard was a stone-and-tile pool made of two connecting lagoons, one shallow and one deep.

The end of the shallow lagoon ended in a sandy white shore with a real palm tree growing in the center. "Hawaiian sand," Liberty said, laughing as she noticed my interest. "You should have seen us picking it out—the landscaper must have brought twenty samples, while Gage and Carrington tried to figure out which kind would make the best sandcastles."

"You mean it was shipped all the way from Hawaii?"

"Yes. A truckload. The pool guy wants to kill us on a weekly basis. But Gage decided it would be fun for Carrington to have her own little beach. He would do anything for her. Here, let me hand the baby to you, and I'll turn on the misters."

"Misters?"

Liberty went to flip a switch near the barbecue pavilion, activating nozzles that had been recessed in the deck to create a light cooling mist around the pool.

I was very nearly awed. "That is amazing," I said. "Don't take this the wrong way, but your life is unreal, Liberty."

"I know." She made a face. "Believe me, this isn't how I grew up."

We settled into a couple of green cushioned patio chairs by the pool, and Liberty adjusted an overhead umbrella to shade Luke as I held him.

"How did you meet Gage?" I asked. Although Jack had told me their father Churchill had introduced Liberty to the family, I didn't know the particulars.

"Churchill got his hair cut at the salon where I worked, and we became friends. I was his manicurist for a while." Liberty glanced at me with a spark of mischief in her eyes, and I knew she was studying my reaction. No doubt most people made a lot of assumptions based on that information.

I decided to be blunt. "Was there anything romantic between the two of you?"

Liberty smiled and shook her head. "I loved Churchill immediately, but not at all in a romantic way."

"He was a father figure, then."

"Yeah, my own dad died when I was young. I guess I always had a feeling of something missing. After we'd known each other a couple of years, Churchill hired me as a personal assistant, and that was when I met the rest of the family." She laughed. "I hit it off with everyone *except* Gage, who was an arrogant jerk." A pause. "But very sexy."

I grinned. "I'll admit, the Travis men have some great DNA going for them."

"The Travis family is . . . unusual," Liberty said, kicking off her flip-flops and stretching out her tanned, gleaming legs. "They're all very strong-willed. Intense. Jack's the most easygoing of all of them, outwardly at least. He's sort of the mixer of the family—he keeps everything balanced. But he can be stubborn. He does things his own way, and he's willing to butt heads with Churchill when necessary." She paused. "You've probably figured out by now that Churchill is not the easiest of fathers to get along with."

"I know he has high expectations of his children," I said.

"Yes, and he has strong ideas of how they should live, what choices they should make, and he gets mad or disappointed when they don't do things his way. But if you stand your ground with Churchill, he respects that. And he can be incredibly caring and understanding. I think the more you get to know him, the more you'll like him."

I stretched out my legs and studied my unpolished toes. "You don't have to talk me into liking Churchill or the other Travises, Liberty. I already do. But this relationship between Jack and me isn't going anywhere. It's not going to last."

Liberty's green eyes widened. "Ella . . . I hope you won't let Jack's past reputation get in the way. I've heard some of the stories about him running wild around Houston. He's sown his oats, though, and I think now he's finally ready to settle down."

"It's not that—" I began, but she interrupted earnestly.

"Jack is one of the most loving, loyal guys you could ever meet. I think it's been hard for him to find a woman who could look beyond the money and the Travis name, and want him for who he is. And Jack needs someone who is strong and smart enough to handle him. He would be miserable with a passive woman."

"What about Ashley Everson?" I couldn't help asking. "What kind of woman is she?"

Liberty wrinkled her nose. "I can't stand her. She's the kind of woman who has no female friends. She says she just likes men better. And what does it say about a woman who can't be friends with other women?"

"It says she's competitive. Or insecure."

"In Ashley's case, probably both."

"Why do you think she left Jack?"

"I wasn't around at the time, but Gage was, and he says the problem with Ashley is that she can't ever stick with any guy for long. Once she gets a man, she's bored and wants to move on. In Gage's opinion, Ashley never meant to end up married to Pete. She would have divorced him right away if she hadn't gotten pregnant."

"I don't get why Jack fell in love with her in the first place," I grumbled.

"Ashley is good with men. She knows all the football stats, and she hunts and fishes, and she cusses and tells filthy jokes, and on top of all that she looks like a Chanel model. Men love her." Her mouth quirked. "And I'm sure she's great in bed."

"Now I can't stand her, either," I said.

Liberty chuckled. "Ashley is no competition for you, Ella."

"I'm not competing for Jack," I told her. "He already knows that I'm not interested in getting married, ever." I saw her eyes widen. "It has nothing to do with how great he is," I continued. "I have a lot of reasons for being this way." I gave her a sheepish smile. "And I'm sorry if I sound defensive, but telling a married person you never want to get married is like waving a red flag at a bull."

Instead of looking offended or trying to debate the matter, Liberty nodded thoughtfully. "That must be frustrating. It's hard to swim against the tide."

I liked her even more than I already did, for such ready acceptance of my feelings. "It was one of the great things about my boyfriend Dane," I told her. "He never wanted to get married, either. It was a really comfortable relationship."

"Why did you break up with Dane? Was it because of the baby?"

"Not really." I pulled out of the diaper bag an infant toy, a musical inchworm, for Luke to play with. "Looking back on it, I guess there wasn't enough to hold me and Dane together. Even after all the years we'd spent with each other. And when I met Jack, there was something about him—" I stopped, conscious that for all the variety of words I knew, there was no way to describe why and how I had been so completely captivated by Jack Travis. I looked down at Luke, stroking back the little dark feathers of his hair. "Hey, why are we with Jack?" I asked him, and he gazed back at me as if similarly mystified.

Liberty laughed gently. "Believe me, I know. Even when I couldn't stand Gage, it seemed like the temperature in the room went up about a hundred degrees whenever he was there."

"Yes. That's the fun part, the attraction. But I don't see the relationship lasting forever."

"Why not?" Liberty seemed genuinely puzzled.

Because I lose everyone I care about, sooner or later. I couldn't say that aloud—although it had a potent inner logic for me, I knew it would make me sound crazy. There was no way to explain that the very thing I craved, the intensity of a relationship with Jack, was what I feared most. It wasn't a rational fear, of course . . . it was purely visceral, which made it that much harder to fight against.

I shrugged and made my lips in the shape of a smile. "I think I'm just the flavor of the month as far as Jack is concerned."

"You're the first woman he's ever brought around the family," Liberty said in a low voice. "He could get serious in a hurry, Ella."

As I cuddled Luke and struggled with my thoughts, I was relieved when Liberty's nanny emerged from the house with a robust, handsome toddler. The boy was dressed in a swimsuit and a T-shirt printed with cartoon lobsters.

"Matthew, honey . . ." Liberty hopped up and went to get him, lavishing him with kisses. "Did you have a nice nap? Do you want to play with Mommy? We have a friend visiting, and she brought her baby . . . do you want to see him?" He responded with an enchanting wide grin, conversing with his mother in a few garbled sentences, his plump arms wrapped around her neck.

After giving us a cursory inspection, Matthew decided that playing in the sand was far more interesting than the new baby. Liberty stripped down to her swimsuit and took her son to the edge of the water, where they sat and began to fill a bucket with sand. "Ella, come put your legs in the water," she called. "It feels great."

I was dressed in a printed halter top and matching Bermuda shorts, but I had packed a swimsuit. Pulling it from the diaper bag, I said, "Give me a minute to go and change."

"Sure. Oh, this is our nanny, Tia . . . let her take care of Luke while you put on your swimsuit."

"Is that okay?" I asked Tia, who came forward with a smile.

"Yes, he's no problem," she exclaimed.

"Thank you."

"There's a guest bathroom off the kitchen," Liberty told me, "or if you need a little more space, go into any of the upstairs bedrooms."

"Got it." I went into the house, relishing the coolness of the kitchen, and found a small bathroom with earthy-hued striped walls and a stone vessel sink and a black-framed mirror. I changed into my pink swimsuit, a retro-styled one-piece. Padding barefoot through the kitchen, carrying my clothes, I heard the sound of voices, one of them Jack's deep murmur. The voices were accompanied by hammering and sawing, and the occasional squeal of a power drill.

I followed the sound to a partially opened door that led to the spacious garage, where a huge shop fan circulated the warm air. The space was brilliantly lit from the secondhand sunlight that bounced in through the open garage doors. Tapping the door a little wider, I watched unobserved as Jack, Gage, and Carrington worked on the wooden skiff, which was propped up on padded sawhorses.

Both Jack and Gage had removed their shirts in the heat. I wondered wryly how many women would have paid good money to see the two Travis brothers dressed only in jeans, all sun-burnished muscles and long, lean bodies. As my gaze lingered on Jack's sweat-glittered back, I had a flash of recent memory, my hands urgently gripping those hard muscles on either side of his spine, and a pleasant riff of awareness went through me.

Carrington was busy spreading a thick layer of glue on the last of three strips of wood that would be joined and fastened to the top edge of the skiff as a gunnel. I had to smile at the sight of Gage crouched beside her, murmuring instructions, holding back one of the braids that threatened to drag through the glue.

". . . and then at recess," the girl said, squeezing a huge bottle of wood glue with both hands, "Caleb wouldn't let anyone else play with the basketball, so Katie and I went and told the teacher—"

"Good for you," Gage said. "Here, put more glue on the edge. Better to use too much than not enough."

"Like this?"

"Perfect."

"And then," Carrington continued, "the teacher said it was someone else's turn to play with the ball, and she made Caleb write an essay about sharing and cooperation."

"Did that fix him?" Jack asked.

"No," came Carrington's disgusted reply. "He's still the terriblest boy you could ever meet."

"They all are, honey," Jack said.

"I told him you were going to take me fishing," Carrington went on indignantly, "and you know what he said?"

"That girls aren't good at fishing?" Jack guessed.

"How did you know?" she asked in amazement.

"He approves of Hardy, doesn't he?" I asked with a touch of concern.

"Yeah, he's given his blessing to the match," Gage said. "But Dad never misses the opportunity to turn a family event into a three-ring circus. He wanted to be in charge of it."

I nodded, understanding immediately why Haven and Hardy hadn't wanted their wedding to be a big production. For all that they were a friendly and gregarious couple, they were both protective of their private life. The feelings cut too deep for them to be put on display.

We all drank to the newlyweds and talked for a few minutes about Playa del Carmen, which apparently was known for its beaches and fine fishing, and was far less touristy than Cancún.

"Have you been to Mexico, Ella?" Liberty asked.

"Not yet. I've wanted to go for a while."

"We should go one of these weekends, all four of us, and take the kids," Liberty told Gage. "It's supposed to be a good place for families."

"Sure, we'll take one of the planes," Gage said easily. "Do you have a passport, Ella?"

"No, not yet." My eyes had widened. "The Travises have a plane?"

"Two jets," Jack said. A smile touched his lips as he saw my expression. He picked up my free hand and played with it lightly. I supposed that by then I should have been used to the little shock that occurred whenever I was reminded of the financial stratosphere the Travises occupied. "Gage," Jack said to his brother, still staring at me, "I think the mention of the planes is scaring Ella. Tell her I'm a regular guy, will you?"

"He's the most regular guy in the Travis family," Liberty told me, her green eyes twinkling.

I couldn't help laughing at the qualifier.

"Because I was a terrible boy once, and that's probably what I would have said. But I'd have been dead wrong. Girls are *great* at fishing."

"Are you sure about that, Uncle Jack?"

"Of course I—wait a minute." Together Jack and Gage lifted the assembled wood strips and fit them to the edge of the boat.

"Sweetheart," Gage murmured to Carrington, "bring that bucket of clamps over here." Carefully he placed clamps along the gunnel, pausing to adjust the wood strips when necessary.

"What were you saying, Uncle Jack?" Carrington pressed, handing him some paper towels to wipe up dripping glue.

"I was about to ask you: Who is the fishing expert in this family?"

"You."

"That's right. And who's the expert on women?"

"Uncle Joe," she said, giggling.

"Joe?" he asked in feigned outrage.

"Humor him, Carrington," Gage said. "Otherwise we'll be here all day."

"*You're* the expert on women," Carrington told Jack promptly.

"That's right. And I'm here to tell you, some of the best anglers in the world are women."

"How come?"

"They're more patient, and they don't give up easy. They tend to fish an area more thoroughly. And women can always find the spot with the hidden boulders or underwater weeds where fish are hiding. Men, we just look right past those spots, but women always find 'em."

As Jack spoke, Carrington caught sight of me in the doorway, and she threw me a grin. "Are you gonna take Miss Ella fishing?" she asked Jack, who had picked up a Japanese saw and was cutting off the protruding end of the gunnel at an angle.

"If she wants to," he said.

"Is she gonna catch *you,* Uncle Jack?" Carrington asked slyly.

"She already did, darlin'." At the sound of her titter, Jack paused in his sawing, followed her gaze and saw me standing there. A slow smile spread across his face, and his gaze turned dark and hot as he glanced over my pink swimsuit and bare legs. Dropping the saw, he muttered to the other two, " 'Scuse me, I've got to talk to Miss Ella about something."

"No, you don't," I protested. "I just wanted a peek at the skiff. It's beautiful, Carrington. What color are you going to paint it?"

"Pink like your bathing suit," she said cheerfully.

Jack was coming toward me. I retreated a few steps.

"Don't take him away for good, Ella," Gage said. "We still need to fasten the gunnel on the other side."

"I'm not taking him away at all, I . . . Jack, get back to work." But he headed for me without pausing, and I giggled and retreated into the kitchen. "Leave me alone, you're all sweaty!" In a few seconds, I found myself pinned against a countertop, his hands gripping the beveled granite edge on either side of me.

"You like me sweaty," he murmured, his denim-clad legs corralling mine.

I leaned backward to avoid contact with his damp chest. "If I have caught you," I told him, still giggling, "I'm going to throw you back."

"You only throw the little ones back, darlin'. The big ones you keep. Now give me a kiss."

I tried to stop smiling long enough to comply. His lips were warm as they moved over mine, the kiss erotic in its careful lightness.

* * *

After the boat-builders had finished gluing and nailing the gunnels in place, they cooled off in the pool, and we spent the rest of the afternoon lazing and swimming. Lunch was brought out, big bowls of field greens tossed with grilled chicken, red grapes, and walnuts, and we shared a bottle of ice-cold white burgundy in chilled glasses. The nanny took the children inside the cool house, while Gage, Liberty, Jack, and I ate at a table shaded by a huge umbrella.

"I'm making a special toast," Gage said, lifting his glass. We paused and looked at him expectantly. "To Haven and Hardy," he continued, "who by now have become Mr. and Mrs. Cates." He smiled as we all stared at him in surprise.

"They got married?" Liberty asked.

"I thought they were going to Mexico for a long weekend," Jack said, looking torn between pleasure and annoyance. "They didn't say anything to me about any wedding plans."

"They had a private ceremony at Playa del Carmen."

Liberty was laughing. "How can they get married without us? I can't believe they wanted privacy for their own wedding." She turned a mock-scowl on Gage. "And you didn't say anything to me. How long have you known?" But she was glowing with obvious happiness.

"Since yesterday," Gage said. "Neither of them wanted a big show. But they're going to plan a big celebration party when they get back, which I told Haven was a fine idea."

"I think that's great," Jack said, raising his glass to the unseen couple. "After everything Haven's been through, she deserves any kind of wedding she wants." He took a swallow of his wine. "Does Dad know?"

"Not yet," Gage said ruefully. "I guess I'm going to have to tell him . . . but he won't like it."

Liberty smiled. And I realized she understood how I felt. *It's okay,* her gaze seemed to say. *You'll be fine.* She lifted her glass again. "I've got some news to share, too . . . although it's not a surprise to Gage." She glanced at Jack and me expectantly. "Guess."

"You're pregnant?" Jack asked.

Liberty shook her head, her smile widening. "I'm going to start my own salon. I've been thinking about it for a while . . . and I thought before we had another child, I'd like to do this. I'm going to keep it small and exclusive, just hire a couple of people."

"That's wonderful," I exclaimed, clinking my glass with hers.

"Congratulations, Lib." Jack extended his own wineglass and followed suit. "What are you going to call the place?"

"I haven't decided yet. Carrington wants to call it Clippety-Do-Da or Hairway to Heaven . . . but I told her we have to be a little bit classier."

"Julius Scissors," I suggested.

"Hair Today, Gone Tomorrow," Jack joined in.

Liberty covered her ears. "I'll go out of business in the first week."

Jack raised his brows into mocking crescents. "The big question is, how is Dad going to get more grandchildren? That's a Travis wife's job, isn't it? You're wasting prime childbearing years, Lib."

"Stow it," Gage told him. "We're just now starting to catch up on our sleep, with Matthew getting a little older. I'm not ready to go through it again just yet."

"No sympathy from this side of the table," Jack said. "Ella's been going through all of it—the sleepless nights, the diapers—for a kid who's not even hers."

"He feels like mine," I said without thinking, and Jack's fingers tightened protectively on my hand.

There was silence except for the quiet spray of the misters, and the splashing waterfall.

"How long do you have left with the baby, Ella?" Liberty asked.

"About a month." With my free hand, I reached for my wineglass and drained it. Ordinarily I would have put up a bright false smile and diverted the subject. But in the company of sympathetic listeners, with Jack beside me, I found myself saying what I really thought. "I'm going to miss him. It's going to be hard. And lately it's started to bother me that Luke won't remember the time he spent with me. The first three months of his life. He won't know any of the stuff I did for him—I won't be any different to him than a stranger off the street."

"You won't be seeing him, after Tara takes him?" Gage asked.

"I don't know. Probably not often."

"He'll remember deep down," Jack said gently.

And as I looked into his steady dark eyes, I found solace.

NINETEEN

LUKE LAY ON THE FLOOR OF MY APARTMENT IN A baby gym, a floor quilt with two crossed arches featuring rattling beads, spinning birds and butterflies, crinkly leaves, and cheerful electronic music. He loved it nearly as much as I loved watching him. At two months, he laughed, smiled, made noises, and was able to raise his head and chest.

Jack lay on the floor beside him, lazily reaching up to flick the toys or to push a button for new music. "I wish I had one of these," he said. "Strung with beer cans, Cohíbas, and those little black panties you wore Saturday night."

I paused in the midst of putting away dishes in the kitchen. "I didn't think you noticed them, you took them off me so fast."

"I'd just spent a two-hour dinner looking at you in that low-cut dress. You're lucky I didn't jump you in the parking garage again."

I bit back a smile and stood on tiptoe to slide a glass pitcher on a tall shelf. "Yes, well, I usually like a little more foreplay than the jingle of car keys and two-and-a-half kisses, and—" I jumped as I felt him behind me, having moved so swiftly and silently that I hadn't even noticed him entering the kitchen. The pitcher wobbled in my grasp, and Jack reached up to push it firmly onto the shelf.

I felt his mouth at my ear. "I took care of you, didn't I?"

"Yes." I gave a throaty laugh as his arms closed around my front. "I'm not saying I was shortchanged. I'm just saying, you didn't waste any time getting down to business . . ." The words dissolved into a sigh as I felt him bite and lick my neck gently, his tongue playing in a gentle swirl that evoked scalding memories. My glasses slipped down my nose, and I pushed the frames back into place. One of Jack's arms crossed beneath my breasts, while his free hand slipped beneath the waistband of my shorts.

"You want foreplay, Ella?" His hips pressed against me from behind, and I felt the hard shape of him through the layers of our clothing.

My lashes lowered, and I gripped the edge of the countertop as his hands played over my body. "The baby," I said breathlessly.

"He won't mind. He's doing his workout in the baby gym."

Laughing, I pushed his hands away. "Let me finish the dishes."

Jack pulled my hips back against his, wanting to play.

But we were interrupted by the shrill ring of the phone. I reached for it and hissed, "Be still," to Jack before answering. "Hello?"

"Ella, it's me." The voice was my cousin Liza's, flat and sheepish. "I'm calling to give you a heads-up. I'm so sorry."

I stiffened, and Jack's hands went still. "What kind of heads-up?" I asked.

"Your mom is coming to see you. She'll be there in fifteen minutes to a half hour. Sooner, if traffic's good."

"No, she's not," I said, blanching. "I didn't invite her. She doesn't know where I live."

"I told her," Liza said guiltily.

"*Why?* What possible reason could you have for doing that to me?"

"I couldn't help it. She called me all fired-up because she just talked to Tara on the phone, and Tara told her she thought something might be going on between you and Jack Travis. And now they both want to know what's going on."

"I don't owe either of them explanations," I burst out, going crimson. "I've had it, Liza. I'm tired of Tara's messes, and I wish Mom was even half as concerned about her grandson as she is about my sex life!" Too late, I realized the slip, and I covered my mouth with my hand.

"You're having sex with Jack Travis?"

"Of course not." I felt Jack's mouth brush gently over the nape of my neck, and I shivered. Holding the phone against my chest, I twisted to face him. "You have to go," I told him urgently.

I brought the phone back up to my ear. ". . . he there with you?" Liza was asking.

"No, it's the UPS guy. He wants me to sign something."

"Down here," Jack murmured, pulling my free hand along his body.

"Go," I muttered, pushing hard at his chest. He didn't budge, only eased my glasses off and cleaned the smudged lenses with the hem of his T-shirt.

"Is it a serious thing?" Liza asked.

"*No*. It's a shallow, meaningless, purely physical relationship that's heading absolutely nowhere." I flinched as Jack leaned over to nip my earlobe in retaliation.

"Cool! Ella, do you think you could get him to fix me up with one of his friends? I've been having kind of a dry spell lately—"

"I've got to go, Liza. I've got to clean up and figure out what to . . . oh, hell, I'll talk to you later." I hung up the phone and grabbed my glasses from Jack.

He followed as I ran to the bedroom. "What are you doing?"

I yanked the sheets and covers over the unmade bed. "My mother's going to get here any minute, and it looks like we had an orgy in here." I paused long enough to glare at him. "You have to go. I mean it. There is no way you're meeting my mother." I tossed the pillows onto the bed. Hurrying back to the main room, I whisked clutter into a giant wicker basket and shoved it into the coat closet.

The intercom by the door beeped. It was the concierge, David. "Miss Varner . . . you have a visitor. It's—"

"I know," I said, slumping in defeat. "Send her up." Turning to Jack, I saw that he had picked up Luke and was cuddling him against his chest. "What can I do to get rid of you?"

He smiled. "Not a damn thing."

In about two minutes, I heard a determined knock at the door.

I opened it. There was my mother, in full-face makeup and high heels, and a snug red dress that displayed the figure of a woman half her age. She sailed in on a cloud of department-store perfume, hugged and air-kissed me, and stood back to give me an assessing glance.

"I finally got tired of waiting to be invited," she told me, "so I decided to take the bull by the horns. I'm not letting you keep my grandson away from me any longer."

"You're a grandmother now?" I asked.

She continued to look me over. "You've put on weight, Ella."

"I've lost a few pounds, actually."

"Good for you. A few more, and you'll be back to a healthy size."

"A size eight is healthy, Mom."

She gave me a fond, chiding glance. "If you're that sensitive about it, I won't mention it anymore." Her eyes widened theatrically as Jack approached us. "Well, who is this? Why don't you introduce me to your friend, Ella?"

"Jack Travis," I muttered, "this is my mother—"

"Candy Varner," she interrupted, going in for a hug, crowding the baby between them. "We don't need to bother with handshakes, Jack . . . I've always been crazy about Ella's friends." She winked at him. "And they've always been crazy about me." She pried the baby from his arms. "And here is my precious grandson . . . oh, I don't know why I let Ella keep you away from me this long, you little sugar lump."

"I said you were welcome to babysit any time," I muttered.

She ignored that, venturing into the apartment. "How cozy this is. I think it's so sweet, the two of you taking care of Luke while Tara is on her spa vacation."

I followed her. "She's at a clinic for psychologically and emotionally disturbed people."

My mother went to the windows to check out the view. "It doesn't matter what you call it. Places like that are so in, nowadays. The Hollywood stars do it all the time—they need a little escape from the pressure, so they come up with some made-up problem, and they get to relax and get pampered for a few weeks."

"It's not a made-up problem," I said. "Tara—"

"Your sister has stress, that's all. I was watching a program the other day about cortisol, which is a stress hormone, and they said coffee drinkers have a lot more cortisol than the average person. And I've always said you and Tara drink too much coffee, both of you."

"I don't think Tara's problems—or mine—occurred because of one too many lattes," I said darkly.

"My point is, you bring on your own stress. You've got to rise above it. Like I do. Just because your father's side was weak-minded, doesn't mean you have to give in to it." As my mother chattered, she wandered around the apartment, looking at everything with the attentiveness of an insurance assessor. I watched her uneasily, longing to take the baby back. "Ella, you should have told me you were living here." She cast a grateful glance at Jack. "I want to thank you for helping my daughter, Jack. She has a vivid imagination, by the way. I hope you don't believe everything she says. When she was a child, she'd make up such stories . . . if you want to get to know the real Ella, you need to talk to me. Why don't you take us all out to dinner, and we'll get better acquainted? Tonight would be fine."

"Great idea," Jack said easily. "Let's do that sometime. Unfortunately, tonight Ella and I have plans."

My mother handed the baby to me. "Take him, sweetheart, this is a new dress. He might spit up." She sat gracefully on the sofa and crossed her long, toned legs. "Well, Jack, I'm the last one to interfere in someone else's plans. But if you are getting involved with my daughter, I'd feel more comfortable about it if I knew you and your family a little bit better. I'd like to meet your father, to start with."

"You're too late," I said. "His father's already got a girlfriend."

"Why Ella, I didn't mean . . ." She laughed lightly and shot Jack a commiserating, conspiratorial glance—*look at what we have to deal with*—and her tone became maddeningly sweet. "My daughter has always resented that men like me so much. I don't think she brought a single boyfriend home who didn't make a pass at me."

"I only brought one home," I said. "That was enough."

She gave me a chilling glance and laughed, her mouth a wide, taut pouch. "No matter what Ella says," she told Jack, "don't take her word for it. You ask me."

Whenever my mother was around, reality took on the dimensions of a fun-house mirror. Insanity was simply a result of being a frequent Starbucks customer, size eight was a stage of obesity that required medical intervention, and any man I dated was clearly having to make do with a second-rate substitute for Candy Varner. And anything I had ever done or said could be conveniently rewritten to suit whatever spin she had chosen.

For the next forty-five minutes, it was the Candy Varner Show with no commercial interruptions. She told Jack that she would have offered to take care of Luke, but she was just too busy, and she'd already done her duty, working and sacrificing all those years for her daughters, neither of whom were appropriately grateful and were both more than a little jealous. And imagine Ella giving advice to people for a living, when Ella hardly knew what she was talking about—you had to do a lot more living than Ella had before you knew who was who and what was what. Whatever Ella knew about life, it had come from her mother's imparted wisdom.

Mom proceeded to present herself as the desirable original, the brand name, with me as a failed copy. She tried to do some heavy-handed flirting with Jack. He was polite and respectful, occasionally glancing at my stony expression. When Mom started to name-drop, pretending she knew some of the same rich people Jack did, it was so mortifying that I felt myself shutting down. I stopped protesting or correcting, just occupied myself with Luke, checking his diaper, putting him back into the baby gym, and playing with him. My ears felt hot, the rest of me ice-cold.

And then I registered that, like clockwork, she had shifted the conversation to the inappropriately personal, revealing that she'd recently signed on for laser hair-removal treatments from an exclusive Houston spa. "I've been told," she was telling Jack with a girlish giggle, "that I have the cutest coochie in Texas—"

"Mom," I said sharply.

She glanced at me, her eyes sly and laughing. "Well, it's true! I'm just saying what other people—"

"Candy," Jack interrupted briskly, "this has been fun, but it's time for Ella and me to get ready for our evening out. Great to meet you. Why don't I take you down to the concierge, and he'll show you out?"

"I'll stay here and watch over Luke while you're gone," my mother insisted.

"Thanks," Jack replied, "but we're taking him with us."

"I haven't had any time with my grandson," she protested, frowning at me.

"I'll call you, Mom," I brought myself to say.

Jack went to the door and opened it. Keeping it open, he stepped out into the hallway. His tone was friendly and inexorable. "I'll wait here while you get your purse, Candy."

I stood while my mother came to embrace me. The perfumed smell of her, the warm proximity of her, made me want to cry like a child. I wondered why I would always long for her to love me in a way she wasn't capable of, why Tara and I were nothing more to her than collateral damage from a marriage that had gone bad.

I had learned that there were substitutes for a mother who couldn't be a mother. You could find love with other people. You could find it in places you weren't even looking. But the original wound would never heal. I would carry it with me forever, and so would Tara. That was the trick . . . accepting it, going on with your life, knowing it was part of you.

"Bye, Mom," I said thickly.

"Don't give him everything he wants," she said in a low voice.

"Luke?" I asked, puzzled.

"No. Jack. You'll hold on to him longer that way. Don't be too smart with him, either. Try to put some makeup on. And take off those glasses, they make you look like an old maid. Has he given you any presents yet? Tell him you want big stones, not little ones—it's a better investment."

A brittle smile worked across my face, and I drew back from her. "See you later, Mom."

She picked up her handbag, and sauntered out into the hallway.

Jack looked around the doorjamb, his gaze sliding over me. "I'll be back in a minute."

By the time Jack had returned, I had downed a shot of tequila from the pantry, hoping the liquor would burn through my head-to-toe numbness. It hadn't. I felt like a freezer that needed to be defrosted.

Luke fretted in my arms, making impatient noises, wriggling.

Jack came to me and touched my chin, forcing me to meet his searching gaze.

"Now aren't you sorry you didn't take my advice and leave?" I asked morosely.

"No. I wanted to see what you grew up with."

"I guess you can tell why Tara and I both needed therapy."

"Hell, I need therapy, and I only spent an hour with her."

"She'll say or do anything for attention, no matter how embarrassing." I looked at him sharply as a hideous thought occurred to me. "Did she make a pass at you in the elevator?"

"Nope," he said, a little too smoothly.

"Yes, she did."

"It was nothing."

"God, how awful," I whispered. "She makes me so angry."

Jack took the fussing baby from me, and Luke quieted immediately.

"Not the regular kind of angry," I went on. "It's the kind that makes you tired and cold all the way through and you can't feel anything. Not even your own heartbeat. I want to call Tara and download on her, because I think she'd understand."

"Why don't you?"

"No, she's the one who sicced Mom on me. I'm mad at her, too."

Jack studied me for a moment. "Let's go up to my apartment."

"What for?"

"I'm going to thaw you out."

I shook my head at once. "I need alone-time."

"No, you don't. Come on."

"Dane always let me have alone-time when I needed it." I was in a terrible, sullen mood, and anything he did was only going to irritate me. "Jack, I don't need to be held or comforted, or have sex or talk. I don't want to feel better right now. So there's no point—"

"Bring the diaper bag." Still carrying Luke, he went to the door, held it open, and waited patiently for me to join him.

We went up to his apartment, and Jack took me straight to the bedroom. He turned on a lamp, and went into the bathroom, and I heard the sounds of water and steam. "I don't need a shower," I said.

"Get in there and wait for me."

"But I—"

"Do it."

I heaved a sigh. "What about the baby?"

"I'm putting him down. Go on."

I removed my glasses and stripped off my clothes, and trudged into the shower room. It was dimly lit and filled with a hot eucalyptus-scented mist. Jack had laid a fluffy white towel out on the long built-in tile bench. I sat and breathed deeply. In a minute or two, I began to relax. I was surrounded by fragrant steam, my pores opening, muscles softening, lungs filling with moist heat. The tequila hit my system, and my entire body seemed to sigh, and I felt my heart start again.

"Oh, this is better," I said aloud, and lay face down on the towel. There was no sound except the soft rush of steam. I felt color rising to the surface of my skin. I lay there tranquilized by the warm mist, losing all sense of time. I had no idea how many minutes had passed before I was aware of Jack sitting next to me, his hip lean and smooth next to mine.

"How's Luke?" I mumbled.

"Down for the count."

"I wonder if—"

"Hush." His hands settled on my back, sliding easily over the wet skin. He started at the shoulders, rubbing, drawing the soreness out of my tense muscles. The pressure deepened. I felt the circling of his thumbs against the muscles and connective tissue, working steadily, rolling out pleasure until a helpless groan slipped from my throat.

"Oh, that feels so . . . *Jack* . . . I didn't know you could do this."

"Shhh." He worked down my back, his hands gliding, sweeping in long strokes, then kneading in deeper, shorter strokes, coaxing out tension, easing the knotted muscles. I gave myself over entirely to those strong, deliberate hands, my body lost and flung and heavy. He worked on my bottom, thighs, calves, and turned me over and pulled my feet into his lap. I made a little sound of pleasure as I felt him run his thumbs along my arches.

"Sorry I was bitchy," I managed to say.

"You had cause, honey."

"My mother's awful."

"Yeah." He wiggled my toes individually. His voice was steam-blended and soft. "That advice she gave you was crap, by the way."

"You heard that? Oh, God."

"You should give me everything I want," Jack informed me. "You should spoil me rotten. And it's too late to play dumb, and you're cute as hell without makeup."

I smiled, my eyes still closed. "What about my glasses?"

"Definite turn-on."

"Everything's a turn-on for you," I said languidly.

"Not everything." Laughter thickened his voice.

"Yes. You're like one of those pharmaceutical commercials where they warn about four-hour erections. You need to go see your doctor."

"I don't find him all that attractive." He moved upward, parted my thighs, and I gasped as I felt his teasing fingers slide over me. "You ever been massaged this way, Ella?" he whispered. "No? Lie still . . . you're gonna like this, I promise. . . ."

And my body arched in response to his eloquent hands, the tile walls echoing with the muted sounds of my pleasure.

TWENTY

THE DAY AFTER MY MOTHER HAD SHOWN UP AT 1800, I felt uneasy, raw, deprived of necessary insulation. I put up a normal facade. My childhood had given me the ability to carry on as usual through anything, including a nuclear holocaust. But something about the visit, just the fact of having seen her, had set me off balance.

Jack was gone the first part of the day, visiting a friend who had landed in the hospital after a hunting accident. "Wild boar," Jack had told me when I'd asked what kind of game his friend had been hunting. "Lots of accidents happen on a boar hunt."

"Why?"

"You have to do it at night when most of the hogs are moving. So you've got a bunch of guys running around the woods shooting at stuff in the dark."

"Lovely."

Jack had gone on to explain that the friend had shot the hog with a twelve-gauge, approached him in deep brush thinking he was dead, and the hog had charged him before he could get out his sidearm. "Gored him near the groin," Jack said with a wince.

"Amazing, how testy those boars get when you're shooting at them," I said.

Jack had given me a playful swat on the bottom. "Have a little sympathy, woman. A groin injury's nothing to laugh about."

"My sympathy is entirely with the hogs. I hope you don't go boar hunting too often. I'd hate for my sex life to be compromised by your dangerous hobbies."

"I don't hunt boar," Jack told me. "When I bag a trophy at night, it's going to be in bed."

While Jack was gone, I worked on my column for a while.

Dear Miss Independent,

I got married five years ago to a man I didn't really love, because I was thirty and it was time. All my friends were married, and I was tired of being the only single one. The man I ended up marrying is a good guy. He's kind and sweet and he loves me. But there is no magic or passion in our relationship. I settled for him, and every time I look at him, I have to face it over and over again. I feel like I've been shut in a closet, and he's on the other side, and he doesn't have the key to unlock the door. We don't have any children, so I feel that if divorce him, I won't be hurting anyone outside the two of us. Something is holding me back, though. Maybe I'm afraid I'm too old to start over. Or maybe I'm afraid of the guilt I'll feel, because I know he really loves me, and he doesn't deserve this.

I don't know what to do. All I know is, I settled and I regret it.

—Restless Heart

Dear Restless,

We're all creatures of complex needs and desires. The only certain thing in a romantic relationship is that you will both change, and one morning you will wake up, go the mirror, and see a stranger. You will have what you wanted, and discover you want something different. You think you know who you are, and then you'll surprise yourself.

In all the choices in front of you, Restless, one thing is clear: love is not something to be thrown away lightly. There was something about this man, beyond coincidences of timing and opportunity, that drew you to him. Before you give up on the marriage . . . give him a chance. Be honest with him about the needs that aren't being met, the dreams you want to pursue. Let him find out who you really are. Let him help you in the work of opening that door, so the two of you can finally meet after all these years.

How do you know he can't satisfy your emotional needs? How can you be sure he doesn't long for magic and passion just as you do? Can you state with absolute certainty that you know everything there is to know about him?

There are rewards to be gained from the effort, even if it fails. And it will take courage as well as patience, Restless. Try everything you can . . . fight to stay with a man who loves you. Just for now, put aside the question of what you might have had with someone else, and focus on what you can have, what you do have, at this very moment. I hope you'll find new questions, and that your husband might be the answer.

—Miss Independent

I stared at the screen, wondering if that was the right advice. It occurred to me that I was worried about Restless and her husband. I seemed to have lost my grip on my usual position as dispassionate observer.

"Crap," I said softly, wondering how in the hell I had ever decided I should be advising people what to do with their lives.

I heard the sounds of Luke waking up in the crib, little baby-snuffles and yawns. Setting aside my computer, I went to the crib and looked in. Luke smiled up at me, excited to be awake, happy to see me. His hair was sticking up like a bird's crest.

I picked him up, hugging him close, and the contours of him fit me perfectly. Holding him, feeling his kitten-breath on my face, I was caught off-guard by a rush of joy.

BY FIVE IN THE AFTERNOON I STILL HADN'T HEARD from Jack. I was mildly concerned, since he always called when he said he would, if not sooner. We had agreed I was going to come up to his apartment and cook an old-fashioned Sunday dinner. I had given him a list of groceries to buy.

I dialed his number, and he picked up quickly, sounding uncharacteristically curt. "Yeah?"

"Jack, you didn't call."

"Sorry. I'm in the middle of something." He sounded weird, sort of gruff and pissed-off and harassed all at the same time. He had never used that tone with me before. Something was wrong.

"Can I help?" I asked softly.

"I don't think so."

"Do you . . . do you want to call it off for tonight, or—"

"*No.*"

"Okay. When should I come up?"

"Give me a few minutes."

"Okay." I hesitated. "Turn the oven on 375."

"Right."

After hanging up, I stared at Luke contemplatively. "What in the world could be going on? You think he's having family problems? Maybe business stuff? Why do we have to wait down here?"

Luke chewed thoughtfully on his fist.

"Let's watch the sock-puppet show," I said, and took him to the sofa.

But after about two minutes of classical music and dancing puppets, I was too impatient to sit. I was concerned for Jack. If he was confronting a problem, I wanted to be there. "I can't stand it," I told Luke. "Let's go up and see what's going on."

Slinging the diaper bag over my shoulder, I carried the baby out of the apartment, and we headed to the elevator. When we reached Jack's door, I pushed the doorbell.

The door opened promptly. Jack blocked me for a few seconds, his body conveying the tension of a man who badly wished he were somewhere else. I had never seen him look so upset. Beyond his shoulder, I saw the movement of someone else in the room.

"Jack," I murmured. "Is everything okay?"

Jack blinked, touched his tongue to his lips, started to say something, and stopped himself.

"Someone's here?" I suggested, trying to glance around him.

Jack nodded emphatically, with a flash of desperation in his eyes. I pushed past him and stopped as I saw Ashley Everson.

She was a gorgeous mess, her eyes smoked with heavy dark liner, cheeks slicked with tears, her slender fingers knotted around a wad of tissues. The pale, stick-straight locks of her hair needed a good brushing. I was struck by the contrast between her woeful little-girl expression and her stylish outfit, a short white skirt, a slim-fitting black top that conformed perfectly to her uplifted breasts, a neat little cropped jacket, and strappy sandals with four-inch heels. Photographed just this way, smudgy makeup included, she would have made the perfect perfume ad, a sexy waif.

I didn't think for one second that Jack had invited her there, or that he still wanted her. But I couldn't decide if this were a situation best left for him to handle alone, or if he needed backup.

I glanced at Jack with a quick grimace. "Sorry. Should I come back later?"

"No." He hauled me inside the apartment and lifted the baby from me as if he were taking him hostage.

"Who's she?" Ashley asked, eyes unblinking and round in a face so perfect, it might have been molded from Plasticine.

"Hi," I said, moving forward. "Ashley, right? I'm Ella Varner. We were both at Churchill's birthday party, but we weren't introduced."

She ignored my outstretched hand, glanced over my T-shirt and jeans, and spoke to Jack with patent bewilderment. "*She's* the one you left the party with?"

"Yes," I said, "Jack and I are together."

Ashley turned her shoulder to me, focusing entirely on Jack. "I need to talk to you," she said. "I need to explain some things and . . ." Her voice trailed away, syllables pressed flat by the weight of bewilderment as she saw the refusal in his cold face, the harsh grooves bracketing his mouth. From the subtle recoil of her body, I guessed she had never seen that expression from Jack before.

Faced with his impervious regard, she whirled around and finally spoke to me. "If you don't mind, I need some time with Jack. Alone. We have a history. There are issues. He and I are figuring things out."

Behind her, Jack was shaking his head and pointing at the sofa in a wordless command for me to stay.

The situation was teetering on the edge of farce. I gnawed delicately at the insides of my cheeks, contemplating her. From what I could tell, Ashley Everson had sped carelessly through life and never considered the damage she caused with her hit-and-runs. Now it was all catching up with her, and she looked so wretched that I couldn't help but feel a reluctant stirring of compassion. On the other hand, I wasn't about to let her mess with Jack. She had hurt him once, badly, and she wasn't going to get the chance to do it again.

Besides . . . he was mine.

"She's not going, Ashley," Jack said. "You are."

I spoke to her carefully. "This is about your problems with Pete?"

Her eyes widened until I could see the whites all around the irises. "Who told you?" She pinned Jack with an accusing stare, but he seemed deeply absorbed in adjusting one of the tapes on Luke's diaper.

"I don't know all that much," I said. "Just that you and your husband have hit a rough patch. It's not an abusive relationship, is it?"

"No," came her frosty reply. "We've grown apart."

"I'm sorry," I said, sincerely. "Have you gone to counseling?"

"That's for crazy people," came her disdainful reply.

I smiled slightly. "It's for sane people, too. In fact, the saner you are, the more you'll get out of it. And it might help you to figure out where the problems are coming from. You may need to adjust your ideas of what marriage should be. Or, it's possible that part of the problem is the way you and Pete communicate. If you want to stay married, you might want to take a look at those things and—"

"I don't." It was clear that Ashley loathed me, that I had been judged as an unworthy rival. "I don't want to fix anything. I don't want to be Pete's wife anymore. I want—" Ashley broke off and looked at Jack with ferocious, imperious longing.

I knew what she was seeing . . . a man who seemed to be the answer to all her problems. Handsome, successful, and desirable. A fresh start. She thought if she could get back together with Jack, it would erase all the unhappiness that had transpired since she had gotten married.

"You have children," I said. "Don't you owe it to them to try to save the family you've created?"

"Have you ever been married?" she demanded.

"No," I admitted.

"Then you don't know shit about it."

"You're right," I said calmly. "All I know is that getting back together with Jack won't fix you or your problems. What you had with him is in the past. Jack's gone on with his life. And I'm going to take the liberty of speaking for him by saying that I'm sure he still cares about you as a human being, but nothing more than that. So now, the best thing you can do for Jack, and yourself, and everyone, is to go home to Pete and ask him what you can do about your marriage." Pausing, I glanced at Jack. "Did I get all that right?"

He nodded, his face relaxing.

Ashley made an infuriated sound. She stared hard at Jack. "You told me once you'd always want me."

Jack stood, keeping the baby comfortably tucked against his shoulder. His eyes were opaque. "I've changed, Ashley."

"I haven't!" she snapped.

His reply was very soft. "I'm sorry to hear that."

She grabbed blindly at her handbag and headed to the door. I went after her, frowning as I wondered if she should be allowed to run off in such a distraught condition. "Ashley—" I said, reaching out to touch her skinny arm.

She shook me off.

I saw that she was angry but in control, her face taut, her forehead puckered as if it had been embroidered too tightly. Her gaze arrowed to Jack, who had come up behind me. "If you send me away now," she told him, "you'll never have another chance. Be sure of what you want, Jack."

"I'm sure." He opened the door for her.

She flushed in anger. "Do you think you've got what it takes to keep him?" she asked me scornfully. "He'll put lots of mileage on you, honey. He'll take you on a fast ride, and then you'll get dumped by the roadside." Her gaze switched to Jack. "You haven't changed at all. You think going out with someone like her will make everyone think you're all mature now, but the truth is, you're still the same selfish, shallow asshole you always were." She paused for breath, glaring at him. "I'm so much prettier than she is," she choked indignantly, and left.

As Jack closed the door, I turned to lean my back against it. Still holding Luke, Jack stared at me. He seemed bemused, as if he had found himself in unfamiliar territory and was trying to get his bearings. "Thanks."

I gave him a tentative smile. "You're welcome."

Jack shook his head, looking baffled. "Seeing the two of you together like that . . ."

"The past and the present?"

He nodded and sighed, the corners of his mouth pulling with a troubled grimace. Raking his free hand through his hair, he said,

"You look at someone like Ashley, and you know exactly what kind of guy would want her. And I used to be that guy, and that bothers the shit out of me."

"A guy who wanted a trophy?" I suggested. "A guy who wanted someone pretty and fun . . . I wouldn't be too hard on him."

"You're more of a woman than she could ever be. And a hell of a lot more beautiful."

I laughed. "You're just saying that because I got rid of her for you."

He came closer until the baby was caught between us, and he slid his hand around the back of my neck. His fingers were strong and slightly cool as they clasped my tender nape. The sensation, almost unbearably pleasant, made me shiver. "We don't have a problem?" he asked warily.

"Why would we have a problem?"

"Because any other woman I've ever known would have gone ballistic, coming up here and finding Ashley in my apartment."

"It was obvious you didn't want her here." My lips curved with a wry smile. "And for the record, Jack . . . whatever kind of man you used to be, you're not at all selfish or shallow now. I'll vouch for you any time."

Jack bent his head, his breath fanning hotly over my mouth. He kissed me, hard and sweet and long. "Don't ever leave me, Ella. I need you."

Abruptly I felt uncomfortable in his embrace. "Luke's getting squished," I said with a half-laugh, maneuvering away, even though the baby had been resting still and content between us.

TWENTY-ONE

I SAVORED THE TWO WEEKS THAT FOLLOWED WITH the bittersweet awareness that it was only a brief season in my life. Jack and Luke had become the axis on which the entire world spun. I knew I would lose them both eventually. But I pushed that awareness as far away as I could, and simply allowed myself to enjoy the near-magical quality of those blazing summer days.

It was a busy, bustling kind of happiness, my schedule filled with work, taking care of Luke, trying to keep up with friends, and spending every available moment with Jack. I had never suspected I could become so familiar with someone so quickly. I learned Jack's expressions, his favorite words, the way his mouth tightened when he was deep in concentration, the way his eyes crinkled at the outside corners right before he laughed. I learned that he kept a tight rein on his temper, that he was gentle with people he judged to be more vulnerable than himself, and that he couldn't abide pettiness or small-mindedness.

Jack had a wide circle of friends, two of whom he considered close buddies, but the ones he trusted most were his brothers, especially Joe. His greatest requirement of others was that they keep their word.

To Jack, a promise was a life-or-death matter, the greatest measure of a person.

With me he was openly affectionate, tactile, a physical man with a strong drive. He loved to play, to tease, and to coax me into trying things that made it difficult to face him in the bright light of morning. But there had been a time or two when sex was not playful at all, when we breathed and moved together until it seemed Jack had brought me to the brink of something, a kind of white-hot transcendence, that startled me with its force, and I drew back and broke the momentum, afraid of what might happen.

"YOU NEED A BABY OF YOUR OWN," STACY TOLD ME, when I called her one afternoon. "That's what your biological clock is telling you."

I had tried to describe to her how Luke, in his small and innocent way, had broken down my defenses. For the first time in my life I was experiencing an emotional connection with a child, and it was stronger than I ever could have expected.

I had told Stacy I was in terrible trouble.

I wanted Luke for a lifetime. I wanted to be there at every stage of his growing up. But soon his real mother would come for him, and I would be on the periphery.

It was one hell of a one-two punch, what Tara and Luke had done to me.

"It's gonna hurt bad when you give him up," Stacy continued. "You need to be ready for that."

"I know. But I don't know how you get ready for something like that. I mean, I've told myself that I've only had him for about three months. That's not a huge investment of time. But I've gotten attached to him all out of proportion."

"Ella, Ella . . . there is no proportion with babies."

I gripped the phone tightly. "What do I do?"

"Start making plans. Come back to Austin right after Luke is gone, and stop wasting time with Jack Travis."

"Why is it wasting time if I'm enjoying it?"

"There's no future in it. I admit he's hot, and I'd probably be hittin' that, too, if I were single. But Ella, keep your eyes open. You know that kind of man's not in it for the long haul."

"Neither am I. That's what makes it perfect."

"Ella, come back home. I'm worried about you. I think you're fooling yourself."

"About what?"

"About a lot of things."

But privately I wondered if just the opposite was true— that I had stopped fooling myself about a lot of things, and life had been more comfortable and less complicated when I had been mired in self-deception.

I TALKED WITH MY SISTER ONCE A WEEK. WE HAD A couple of long, fairly awkward conversations, littered with the inevitable psychospeak that you couldn't help but lapse into after having seen a therapist. "I'm coming to Houston next week," Tara finally told me. "Friday. I'm leaving the clinic. Dr. Jaslow says I've gotten a good start, but I should probably keep seeing someone if I want to make more progress."

"I'm so glad," I managed to say, feeling cold all over. "I'm glad you're better, Tara." I paused before making myself ask, "You'll want to take Luke right away, I guess? Because if not, I could always—"

"Yeah, I want him."

Do you really? I wanted to ask her. *Because you hardly ever ask about him, and you don't seem to find him all that interesting*. But maybe that wasn't fair. Maybe he meant too much to her . . . maybe she couldn't bring herself to discuss the source of such powerful longing.

I wandered to Luke's crib, where he was sleeping. I reached out to touch one of the honeypots on the mobile. My fingers were trembling. "Can I pick you up at the airport?"

"No, I'm . . . that's being taken care of."

By Mark Gottler, I thought. "Listen, I don't want to be a pest, but . . . that promissory contract we talked about . . . it's here at my apartment. I hope you'll at least take a look at it while you're here."

"I'll take a look at it. But I won't sign it. There's no need."

I bit my lip to keep from arguing with her. *One step at a time,* I told myself.

Jack and I argued over the prospect of Tara's return, because he wanted to be there, and I wanted to face it alone. I didn't want him to be a part of something so painful and personal. I had a pretty good idea of how much giving up Luke was going to hurt, and I would rather not have Jack see me at a moment of such weakness.

Besides, that Friday was Joe's birthday, and they had planned to go fishing on an overnight trip to Galveston.

"You have to be there for Joe," I told Jack.

"I can reschedule the trip."

"You *promised* him," I said, fully aware of the effect that word had on Jack. "I can't believe you're even thinking of backing out on your brother on his birthday."

"He'll understand. This is more important."

"I'll be just fine," I said. "And I need the private time with my sister. Tara and I won't be able to talk if you're there."

"Damn it all, she wasn't supposed to come back until the next week. Why the hell is she getting out early?"

"I don't know. I can't believe she didn't think to schedule her mental-health issues around your fishing trip."

"I'm not going."

Exasperated, I paced around his apartment. "I want you to go, Jack. I can be stronger about this without you. I need to do it alone. I'm going to hand off Luke to Tara, drink a big glass of wine, have a bath, and go to bed early. If I really need to be with someone, I'll go upstairs and visit Haven. And you'll be back the next day, and we can do the postmortem."

"I'd rather call it the postgame analysis." He watched me intently, seeing too much. "Ella. Stop that damn pacing and come here."

I was still for about ten seconds before I went to him. His arms went around me, and he pressed my resistant body against his at intervals: my shoulders, back, waist, hips.

"Stop pretending everything is fine," he said near my ear.

"That's all I know how to do. If you pretend everything's fine long enough, everything eventually becomes fine."

Jack held me for wordless minutes. His hand continued to move slowly over me, pressing me closer, squeezing, urging, like an artist molding clay. I breathed deeply, letting myself be petted and gently gripped, my nerves leaping as he pulled my hips against his, letting me feel how aroused he was.

He pulled off my clothes and then his own, every movement deliberate, and when I tried to say something, he took my head in his hands and kissed me, openmouthed and searing. Pulling me down to the floor, he straddled my hips, his mouth working at mine. I struggled upward, trying to get closer, straining toward the pleasure of his firm body. We rolled slowly, first me on top, then him, and he grasped my hips and slid inside me, deeper, deeper, until he was encompassed in wetness and heat. I groaned in satisfaction at the necessary weight of him anchoring me, the feel of his flesh pressing, mine opening.

He reached for a sofa cushion, shoved it beneath my hips, and took me in grinding thrusts, pushing, demanding, making me come with plangent cries. And even then he kept on, making it last, delaying release until it broke over him. He stayed in me for a long time, his strong fingers tangled in my hair, not letting me turn my mouth from his. It seemed as if he were trying to prove something, demonstrate something, that my heart and mind were unwilling to accept.

It was still dark when Jack left on Friday morning. He sat beside me on the bed and pulled my sleeping body upward, holding me. I awakened with a murmur, and he held my head in one hand, long fingers cupping firmly around my skull. His rich baritone was soft in my ear. "You do what you have to. I won't stand in the way. But when I come back, you're not shutting me out, you hear? I'm going to take you somewhere . . . a nice long vacation . . . and we're going to talk, and I'm going to hold you while you cry until you feel better. And we'll get you through this." He kissed my cheek and smoothed my hair, and lowered me back to the mattress.

I was silent, my eyes remaining shut. I felt a caressing stroke of his fingertips along the side of my face, over my body, and then he pulled the covers to my collarbone and left.

I didn't think there was any way to convince Jack that he wanted more than I had to give, that to people who'd been damaged the way I had been, fear and the will to survive would always be more powerful than attachment. I could only love in a limited way, except for Luke, and that had been the miracle I had never counted on.

But I was losing Luke.

I had learned this lesson so many times before. It was the great inner truth that didn't require the support of logic. Every time I loved, I lost, and I was diminished.

I wondered how much of me would be left after tomorrow.

As I dressed Luke in a sailor suit and tiny white sneakers, I tried to imagine how he would look to Tara, how many differences there were between a three-month-old and a newborn. Luke could now grasp an object in his hand, or bat at an object that dangled over him. He smiled at me, and he smiled at the sight of himself in a mirror. When I talked to him, he gurgled and made sounds in response, as if we were having a perfectly fascinating conversation. When I held him up and let his feet touch the floor, he pushed down with his legs as if he wanted to stand.

Luke was at the beginning of infinite discoveries and abilities. Soon there would be milestones such as his first word, the first time he could sit up, the first step. I would miss all of it. He wasn't mine anywhere except in my heart.

I felt the sting of incipient tears, like a sneeze that wouldn't quite happen. But it seemed the mechanism for tears had been shut off in me. It felt awful, wanting to cry but not being able. *You'll get to visit him*, I told myself sternly. *You can find a way to be part of his life. You'll be the really cool aunt who always gives him the best presents.*

But it wasn't the same.

"Luke," I said scratchily, fastening the Velcro tabs on his shoes, "Mommy's coming today. You'll finally have Mommy back."

He smiled up at me. I bent and brushed my lips over his petal-soft cheeks, and felt his miniature fingers grip in my hair. Gently disentangling his fists, I picked him up and took him to the sofa. I sat him on my lap and began to read his favorite board book, about a gorilla who let all the zoo animals out of their cages one night.

Midway through the story, I heard the intercom beep. "Miss Varner, you have a visitor."

"Please send her up."

I felt nervous and defeated. And somewhere deep inside, I was aware of lurking anger. Not a lot of anger; just a small, potent kindling, enough to burn out any remaining hint of optimism about my own future. Had Tara never asked me to do this, I would be unaware of this level of pain. And if I ever had to go through this again, someone was going to have to put me in a dirt-filled pot and start watering me three times a week.

A knock at the door, three soft raps.

Carrying Luke, I went to answer it.

And there was Tara, more beautiful than I remembered, with a few hard edges that didn't detract from her looks at all. She was slender, beautifully dressed in a white hammered-silk top and skinny black pants, and black flats with silver studs. Her white-blond hair fell loose in casual waves, and oversized hoops hung from her ears. And her wrist glittered with what had to be a fifteen-carat tennis bracelet.

Tara came into the apartment with a wordless exclamation, not trying to take Luke from me, just putting her long arms around us both. I had forgotten how much taller than me she was. I remembered the time in our teens when I realized she had shot up past me in height, and I had complained that she shouldn't have gotten a growth spurt before I had. And she'd teased me by saying she'd gotten both our growth spurts. The embrace reminded me of a thousand memories. It reminded me how much I loved her.

She drew back to look at me, and her gaze fell to the baby. "Ella, he's so beautiful," she said in wonder. "And so much bigger."

"Isn't he?" I angled Luke to face her. "Luke, look at your gorgeous mommy . . . here, hold him."

We transferred the baby carefully, and as Tara took him, I still felt the imprint of Luke's soft weight against my shoulder. She looked at me with a wet glitter in her eyes, the tops of her cheeks bright with color that burned through her makeup. "Thank you, Ella," she whispered.

I was vaguely surprised that I wasn't crying. It seemed there was a small but crucial distance between me and what was happening. I was grateful for that. "Let's sit down."

Tara followed me. "Living in 1800 Main and trading up for a rich guy like Jack Travis . . . you sure landed on your feet, Ella."

"I didn't start going out with Jack because of his money," I protested.

Tara laughed. "If you say so, I believe it. Although you got this apartment from him, didn't you?"

"It was a loaner," I said. "But now that you're back and I'm not taking care of Luke anymore, I'm going to live somewhere else. I'm not sure where yet."

"Why can't you keep staying here?"

I shook my head. "It wouldn't feel right. But I'll figure it out. A more important question is, where are you staying from now on? What are you and Luke going to do?"

Tara's expression became guarded. "I've got a nice house not far from here."

"Mark arranged it for you?"

"Sort of."

The conversation went on for a little while, with me trying to nail down any specifics of Tara's situation: her plans, her situation, how she was going to get money. She didn't want to answer me. Her evasiveness was maddening.

Sensitive to the tension between us, or perhaps tiring of the unfamiliar arms, Luke began to writhe and fret. "What does he want?" Tara asked. "Here, take him."

I reached out for the baby and settled him against my shoulder. He went quiet and sighed.

"Tara," I said carefully, "I'm sorry if you think I overstepped by getting that promissory contract from Mark Gottler. But I did it for your protection, to get you and Luke some kind of guarantee. Some security."

She gazed at me with baffling serenity. "I have all the security I need. He promised to take care of us, and I believe him."

"Why?" I couldn't help asking. "Why are you so willing to take the word of a man who runs around on his wife?"

"You don't understand, Ella. You don't know him."

"I've met him, and I think he's a cold, manipulative asshole."

That made her temper flare. "You're always so smart, aren't you, Ella? You know everything, don't you? Well, how about this? . . . Mark Gottler isn't Luke's father. He's covering for the real father."

"Who is it, Tara?" I asked with weary anger, covering the back of the baby's head with my hand.

"Noah."

I was silent, staring at her. I saw the truth in her eyes. "Noah Cardiff?" I asked hoarsely.

Tara nodded. "He loves me. He is loved by tens of thousands of people, he could have anyone, but it's me he wants. Or do you think it's impossible for a man like that to love me?"

"No, I . . ." Luke was falling asleep. I stroked his small back. Luke . . . his favorite disciple.

"What about his wife?" I had to clear my throat before continuing. "Does she know about you? About the baby?"

"Not yet. Noah's going to tell her when the time is right."

"When is that?" I whispered.

"Some time in the future, when his kids get a little older. He's got too many responsibilities now. Noah's real busy. But he's going to work it all out. He wants to be with me."

"Do you think he'll ever risk his public image by getting a divorce? And how often will he see Luke?"

"Luke's going to be little for a long time. He won't need a father 'til he's older, and by then Noah and I will be married." She frowned as she saw my face. "Don't look at me like that. He loves me, Ella. He promised to take care of me. I'm safe, and so is the baby."

"Maybe you feel safe, but you're not. You have nothing to bargain with. He can dump you at any time and leave you high and dry."

"And you think you've got a better deal with Jack Travis?" she asked. "What do you have to bargain with, Ella? How do you know you won't get dumped? At least I've got Noah's baby."

"I'm not dependent on Jack," I said quietly.

"No, you don't depend on anyone. You don't trust anyone or believe in anything. Well, I'm different. I don't want to be alone—I need a man, and there's nothing wrong with that. And Noah's the best man I've ever known. He's good and smart, and he prays all the time. And I bet he's got more money than Jack Travis, and he knows *every-one*, Ella. Politicians and businesspeople, and . . . just everyone. He's amazing."

"Will he put any of his promises in writing?" I asked.

"That's not what our relationship is about. A contract would make it cheap and ugly. And it would hurt Noah's feelings if he thought I didn't trust him. He and Mark know that contract was something you pushed for, not me." Reading my expression, she tried to set her mouth against a quiver of frustration. Tears weighted the delicate rims of her lower lids. "Can't you just be happy for me, Ella?"

I shook my head slowly. "Not like this."

She dashed at the moisture beneath her eyes with her fingertips. "You try to control people just like Mom does. Do you ever think about that?" Standing, she reached for Luke. "Give me the baby. I've got to go. I have a car and driver waiting."

I surrendered Luke, who had fallen asleep, and gathered up the diaper bag, tucking the board book inside. "I can help you get the stroller down to the car—"

"I don't need it. I've got a whole nursery filled with brand-new baby stuff."

"Don't leave angry," I said, suddenly breathless, my chest filled with cold, dry pain.

"I'm not angry. It's just . . ." She hesitated. "You and Mom are toxic to me, Ella. I know that's not your fault. But I can't see either of you and not remember the hell of our childhood. I need to fill my life with positive things. From now on it's going to be just me, Noah, and Luke."

I was so stricken that I could hardly speak. "Wait. Please." I leaned over the carrier and clumsily pressed my lips to the sleeping baby's head. "Goodbye, Luke," I whispered.

And then I stood back and watched my sister carry Luke away. She took him onto the elevator, and the doors opened and closed, and they were gone.

Moving like an old woman, I went back into the apartment. I couldn't seem to think of what to do. Mechanically I wandered into the kitchen and began to make tea that I knew I wasn't going to drink.

"It's over," I said aloud. "It's over."

Luke would wake up and I wouldn't be there. He would wonder why I had left him. The sound of my voice would fade from his memory.

My boy. My baby.

I accidentally scalded my fingers with the hot water, but the pain didn't really register. Some part of my mind worried over how badly I was dissociating. I wanted Jack . . . he might know how to break through the layers of ice around me . . . but at the same time, the thought of being with him filled me with dread.

I changed into my pajamas, and for the rest of the afternoon I watched TV without seeing or hearing anything. The phone rang, and the answering machine picked up. Before I glanced at the caller ID, I knew it was Jack. There was no way I could talk to him, or anyone, at the moment. I turned the volume down completely.

Recognizing that I needed to go through the motions of a normal routine, I made soup with powdered chicken broth and consumed it slowly, and followed it with a glass of wine. The phone rang again, and again, and I let the answering machine take it each time, until a half-dozen messages had been left.

Just as I considered going to bed, there was a knock at the door. It was Haven. Her dark brown eyes, so like her brother's, were filled with concern. She made no attempt to come inside, just slipped her hands in the pockets of her jeans and regarded me with infinite patience. "Hey," she said softly. "The baby's gone?"

"Yep. He's gone." I tried to sound matter-of-fact, but the last word stuck in my throat.

"Jack's been trying to call you."

The shadow of an apologetic smile crossed my lips. "I know. But I'm not in the mood for talking. And I didn't want to ruin his fishing trip with my bad mood."

"You wouldn't ruin his fishing trip—he just wants to know you're okay. He called me a few minutes ago and told me to come down here and check on you."

"Sorry. You didn't need to do that." I tried to smile. "I'm not outside on the ledge or anything. Just really tired."

"Yeah, I know." Haven hesitated. "Want me to stay with you for a little while? Watch a late show or something?"

I shook my head. "I need to sleep. I . . . thanks, but no."

"Okay." Her gaze was warm and searching. I shrank from it like a nocturnal creature avoiding sunlight. "Ella. I've never had a baby, and I don't know exactly what you're going through . . . but I do know about loss. And grief. And I'm a good listener. Let's talk tomorrow, okay?"

"There's really nothing to say." I had no intention of talking about Luke ever again. It was a closed chapter in my life.

She reached out and touched my shoulder lightly. "Jack's getting in around five tomorrow," she said. "Maybe even sooner."

"I probably won't be here," I heard myself say distantly. "I'm going back to Austin."

She looked at me alertly. "For a visit?"

"I don't know. Maybe for good. I keep thinking . . . I want to go back to the way things were before." I had been safe in Austin, with Dane. I had not felt too much, given too much, needed too much. There had been no promises.

"Do you think that's possible?" Haven asked softly.

"I don't know," I said. "I may have to try it. Everything feels wrong here, Haven."

"Wait before deciding anything," Haven urged. "You need time. Give it some time, and you'll know what to do."

TWENTY-TWO

In the morning I woke up and went into the main room. There was a protesting squeak beneath my foot. I reached down to pick up Luke's stuffed bunny. Holding the bunny tightly, I sat on the sofa and wept. But it wasn't the good, gusty cry I needed, only a slow anguished drizzle. I took a shower, standing in the hot water for a long time.

I realized that no matter how far away from me Tara was, no matter where she and Luke were or what they did, I would still love them. No one could take that from me.

Tara and I were fellow survivors, responding to our wasteland of a childhood in opposite ways. She feared being alone just as much as I feared not being alone. It was entirely possible that time would prove us both wrong, and the secret of happiness would always elude us. All I knew for certain was that the boundary of isolation was the only thing that had ever kept me safe.

I dressed and put my hair in a ponytail, and I began to fold my clothes in neat piles on the bed.

The phone stayed silent. I guessed that Jack had given up on calling me, which made me perplexed and uneasy. As much as I didn't want to talk about Luke, or how I was feeling, I wanted to know how Jack was. As the local news came on, the weather forecast showed a storm pattern forming in the Gulf. That would make it a bumpy return ride for the Travis brothers, unless they had gotten in front of the system. A half hour after the first report, the tropical depression had been upgraded to a forty-five-mile-per-hour storm.

Worrying, I picked up the phone and called Jack, and got his voice mail. "Hi," I said, when the beep signaled to leave a message. "I'm sorry I didn't answer last night. I was tired, and . . . well, anyway, I saw the weather report, and I want to make sure you're okay. Please call me."

There was no return call, however. Was Jack mad that I hadn't talked to him the previous night, or was he simply busy trying to get the boat safely to harbor?

When I heard a ring early in the afternoon, I hurried to the phone and picked it up without even checking the ID. "Jack?"

"Ella, it's Haven. I was wondering . . . by any chance did Jack leave a copy of the float plan with you?"

"No. I don't even know what that is. What does it look like?"

"Nothing fancy, just a couple of pieces of paper. It's basically a description of the boat, and it tells where you're heading, the rig numbers along your course, and what time you expect to get back."

"Can't you just call Jack and ask him?"

"He and Joe aren't answering their cell phones."

"I noticed that. I tried to call Jack earlier because of the weather report, but he didn't pick up. I thought he was probably busy." I hesitated. "Should we be worried?"

"Not really, it's just . . . I'd like to find out what their exact schedule is."

"I'll go up to his apartment and look for the float plan."

"No, that's okay, I already did that. Hardy's going to call the harbormaster at the marina they left from. They probably left the information with him."

"Okay. Call and let me know, will you?"

"Absolutely."

Haven hung up, and I stood frowning at the receiver in my hand. I reached up and rubbed the back of my neck, which was prickling. I dialed Jack's cell phone again, and his voice mail picked up immediately. "Just checking in again," I said, my voice taut. "Call and let me know how you are."

After watching the weather channel for a few more minutes, I picked up my purse and left the apartment. It felt weird to go out without all the paraphernalia I usually dragged around because of Luke. I went up to Haven and Hardy's apartment, and Haven let me in.

"I'm really getting worried," I told her. "Has anyone gotten hold of Jack or Joe?"

She shook her head. "Hardy's talking to the harbormaster, and they're looking for the float plan. And I talked to Gage, and he said he thought they should have been back by now. But the marina guys said the boat slip is still empty."

"Maybe they just decided to prolong the fishing?"

"Not with the weather. Besides, I know for a fact that Jack was planning to come back early today. He didn't want to leave you alone for too long, after what you went through yesterday."

"I really hope he's okay, so I can kill him when he comes back," I said, and Haven managed a laugh.

"You may have to get in line for that."

Hardy hung up and reached for the TV controller, turning the volume up as another weather report came on. "Hey, Ella," he said absently, his gaze on the TV. Contrary to his usual relaxed charm, Hardy looked troubled, the lines of his face hard and stern. He half-sat on the back of the sofa, his long form tensed as if ready for action.

"What did the harbormaster say?" Haven asked.

His tone was even and reassuring. "They're trying to reach them on the VHF radio. Nothing on 9—that's the distress channel—and no Maydays have come in."

"Is that good?" I asked.

Hardy glanced at me with a slight smile, but a pair of notches had settled between his brows. "No news is good news."

I knew nothing about boats. I didn't even know what questions to ask. But I was trying desperately to think of an explanation for why Jack and Joe were missing. "Could the boat just lose all power or something? And at the same time they could coincidentally be out of cell range?"

Hardy nodded. "All kinds of fuck-ups, coincidental and otherwise, can happen on a boat."

"Jack and Joe are really experienced," Haven said. "They know all about safety procedures, and neither of them would take unnecessary chances. I'm sure they're okay." She sounded as if she were trying to convince herself as well as me.

"What if they didn't manage to outrun the weather?" I asked with difficulty.

"It's not a bad storm," she said. "And if they got caught in it, they would just batten down and ride it out." She hunted for her cell phone. "I'm going to call Gage and see if anyone's with Dad."

For the next half hour Haven and Hardy stayed on their cell phones, trying to get information. Liberty had gone to River Oaks to wait with

Churchill as events unfolded, while Gage was already heading to the Coast Guard offices in Galena Park. A couple of patrol boats had been sent out from Freeport to find the missing vessel.

That was all we heard for a while.

Another half hour passed while we watched the weather channel, and Haven made sandwiches that none of us ate. There was a quality of unreality to the situation, the tension growing exponentially as time passed.

"I wish I was a smoker," Haven said with a brittle laugh, walking around the apartment with jittery energy. "This is one of those times when chain-smoking seems appropriate."

"Oh, no you don't," Hardy murmured, reaching out to catch her wrist. "You got enough bad habits already, honey." He drew her between his thighs as he leaned against the sofa, and she nestled against him.

"Including you," she said, her voice muffled. "You're my worst habit."

"That's right." He combed his fingers through her dark curls, and kissed her head. "And there's no getting over me."

The phone rang, making both Haven and me jump. Still holding his wife in one arm, Hardy picked it up. "Cates here. Gage, how's it going? They found 'em yet?" And then he went very still and silent in a way that made every hair on my body lift. He listened for several moments. My heart thudded heavily, making me light-headed and nauseous. "Got it," Hardy said quietly. "Do they need more choppers? Because if so, I can get as many as . . . I know. But it's like trying to find two fucking pennies someone dropped in the backyard. I know. Okay, we'll sit tight." He closed the phone.

"What is it?" Haven asked, her small hands gripping his shoulders.

Hardy looked away from her momentarily, his jaw so taut that I could see the strain of a small twitching muscle in his cheek. "They found a debris field," he finally brought himself to say. "And what's left of the boat is submerged."

My mind went blank. I stared at him, wondering if he had just said what I thought he'd said.

"So they're doing a search and rescue?" Haven asked, her face drained of color.

He nodded. "The Coast Guard is sending out a couple of Tupperwolfs—those big orange choppers."

"Debris field," I said dazedly, swallowing against rising nausea. "As in . . . as in an explosion?"

He nodded. "One of the rigs reported smoke in the distance."

All three of us struggled to take in the news.

I put my hand up to my mouth, breathing against the screen of my fingers. I wondered where Jack was at that very moment, if he was hurt, if he was drowning.

No, don't think about that.

But for a second it felt as if I were drowning, too. I could actually feel the cold black water folding over my head, pushing me down where I couldn't breathe or see or hear.

"Hardy," I said, surprised by how rational I sounded, when there was chaos inside me. "What would cause a boat like that to explode?"

He sounded excessively calm. "Gas leaks, overheated engine, buildup of vapor near fuel tank, exploding battery. . . . When I was working on the rig, I once saw a fishing boat, over a hundred-footer, explode when it ran across a submerged fuel line." He looked down at Haven's face. She was flushed, her mouth twisting as she tried not to cry. "They haven't found bodies," he murmured, pulling her closer. "Let's not assume the worst. They might be in the water waiting for rescue."

"It's rough water," Haven said against his shirt.

"There's a lot of movement out there," he conceded. "According to Gage, the captain who's coordinating the rescue operation is looking at a computer model to figure out where they might have drifted."

"What are the odds that both of them are okay?" I asked unsteadily. "Even if they survived the explosion, is it likely that either of them was wearing a life jacket?"

The question was greeted with a frozen silence. "Not likely," Hardy said eventually. "Possible, though."

I nodded and sat heavily on a nearby chair, my mind buzzing.

You need time, Haven had told me, when I'd confided my thoughts about going back to Austin. *Give it some time, and you'll know what to do.*

But now there was no time.

There might never be.

If I could only have five minutes with Jack . . . I would have given years of my life for the chance to tell him how much he meant to me. How much I wanted him. Loved him.

I thought of his dazzling grin, his midnight eyes, the beautiful severity of his face when he was sleeping. The thought of never seeing him again, never feeling the sweetness of his mouth against mine, caused an ache I could hardly bear.

How many hours I'd spent with Jack in silence, resting together, all words restrained by the limits of what my heart would allow. All those chances to be honest with him, and I'd taken none of them.

I loved him, and he might never know.

I understood finally that the thing I should have feared most was not loss, but never loving. The price for safety was the regret I felt at this moment. And yet I would have to live with it for the rest of my life.

"I can't stand waiting here," Haven burst out. "Where can we go? Can we go to the Coast Guard office?"

"If you want to, I'll take you. But there's nothing we can do there except get in the way. Gage will let us know the minute something happens." He paused. "Do you want to go wait with your dad and Liberty?"

Haven nodded decisively. "If I'm going to go crazy waiting, I may as well do it around them."

We started on the drive to River Oaks in Hardy's silver sedan, when we heard the ringtone of his phone. He reached toward the center console where he had stashed it, but Haven snatched it up. "Let me, sweetheart, you're driving." She held the phone up to her ear. "Hi, Gage? What is it? Have you found out anything?" She listened for a few seconds, and her eyes went huge. "Oh my God. I can't believe—which one? They don't know? *Shit.* Can't someone—yes, okay, we'll be there." She turned to Hardy. "Garner Hospital," she said breathlessly. "They found them, and picked them up, and they're medevacing both of them straight there. One of them seems to be in good condition, but the other—" She broke off as her voice fractured. Tears sprang to her eyes. "Other one's in bad shape," she managed to say.

"Which one?" I heard myself ask, while Hardy maneuvered the car through traffic, his aggressive driving eliciting indignant honks from all around us.

"Gage doesn't know. That's all he could find out. He's calling Liberty so she can bring Dad to Garner."

THE HOSPITAL, LOCATED IN THE TEXAS MEDICAL Center, was named after John Nance Garner, the Texas-born vice president for two terms of Franklin Roosevelt's administration. The 600-bed hospital was home to a top-notch aeromedical service, with the second busiest heliport for a hospital of its size. Garner also had one of the only three level-one trauma centers in Houston.

"Skybridge parking?" Hardy asked as we drove through the huge sprawl of buildings in the medical center. We were passing the thirty-story Memorial Hermann tower sheathed with spandrel glass, one of a multitude of offices and hospitals in the complex.

"No, there's a valet at the main entrance," Haven said, unbuckling her seat belt.

"Hold on, honey, I haven't stopped yet." He glanced over his shoulder at me and saw that I was out of my seat belt, too. "Y'all mind waiting 'til I put the brakes on before you jump out?" he asked ruefully.

As soon as the car was in the hands of the valet, we went through the hospital entrance, both Haven and I hurrying to keep pace with Hardy's long strides. As soon as we gave our names at the information desk, we were directed to go up to the Shock Trauma Center on the second floor. All they could tell us was that the chopper had arrived safely at the heliport, and both patients were in the hands of a trauma resuscitation team. We were ushered into a beige waiting room with a fish tank and a table piled with tattered magazines.

It was unnaturally quiet in the waiting room, except for the drone of a news channel on the small flat-screen TV. I stared blindly at the TV, the words meaning nothing to me. Nothing outside this place had any significance.

Haven seemed unable to sit still. She paced around the waiting room like a tiger in a cage, until Hardy coaxed her to sit beside him. He rubbed her shoulders and murmured to her quietly, until she relaxed and took a few deep breaths, and blotted her eyes surreptitiously on her sleeve.

Gage arrived nearly at the same time Liberty and Churchill did, all three of them looking as haggard and distracted as the rest of us.

Feeling like an interloper in a private family matter, I went to Churchill after Haven had hugged him. "Mr. Travis," I said hesitantly. "I hope you don't mind that I'm here."

Travis seemed older and more fragile than I had seen him on previous occasions. He was facing the possible loss of one or both of his sons. There was nothing I could say.

He surprised me by reaching out and putting his arms around me. "'Course you should be here, Ella," he said in his gravelly voice. "Jack'll want to see you." He smelled like leather and shaving soap, and there was a faint tinge of cigars . . . a comforting fatherly smell. He patted my back firmly and let go.

For a while Gage and Hardy talked quietly, mulling over what might have occurred on the boat, what could have gone wrong, all the possible scenarios of what might have happened to Joe and Jack, and all the reasons to hope. The one scenario they didn't discuss was the one most on all of our minds, that one or both of the brothers had been fatally injured.

Haven and I went out into the hallway to stretch our legs and get her some coffee from a vending machine. "You know, Ella," she said hesitantly as we headed back to the waiting room, "even if they both make it, there could be a rough time ahead. We could be talking amputation, or brain damage, or . . . God, I don't even know. No one would blame you if you decided you couldn't handle it."

"I've already thought of that," I said without hesitation. "I want Jack no matter what shape he's in. Whatever's happened to him, I'll take care of him. I'll stay with him no matter what. It doesn't matter to me, as long as he's alive."

I hadn't meant to distress her, but Haven surprised me by giving a few muffled sobs.

"Haven," I began in contrition, "I'm sorry, I—"

"No." Regaining control, she reached out and took my hand, squeezing tightly. "I'm just glad Jack's found a woman who will stand by him. He's been with a lot of women who wanted him for superficial reasons, but—" She paused to fish a Kleenex from her pocket and blow her nose, "—none of them loved him just for being Jack. And he knew it, and he wanted something more."

"If only I—" I began, but through the open doorway, Haven caught sight of movement in the waiting room. A door on the opposite side had opened, and a doctor came in.

"Oh God," Haven muttered, nearly dropping her coffee as she hurried into the room.

My stomach dropped. I was paralyzed, the fingers of one hand digging into the door frame as I watched the Travis family gather around the doctor. I watched his face, and their faces, trying to divine any reaction. If either of the brothers had died, I thought the doctor would say so immediately. But he was speaking quietly, and no one in the family revealed any emotion other than bleached anxiety.

"Ella."

The sound was so quiet, I barely heard it through the blood-rush in my ears.

I turned to look down the hallway.

A man was coming toward me, his lean form clad in a pair of baggy scrub pants and a loose T-shirt. His arm was bandaged with silver-gray burn wrap. I knew the set of those shoulders, the way he moved.

Jack.

My eyes blurred, and I felt my pulse escalate to a painful throbbing. I began to shake from the effects of trying to encompass too much feeling, too fast.

"Is it you?" I choked.

"Yes. Yes. God, Ella . . ."

I was breaking down, every breath shattering. I gripped my elbows with my hands, crying harder as Jack drew closer. I couldn't move. I was terrified that I was hallucinating, conjuring an image of what I wanted most, that if I reached out I would find nothing but empty space.

But Jack was there, solid and real, reaching around me with hard, strong arms. The contact with him was electrifying. I flattened against him, unable to get close enough. He murmured as I sobbed against his chest. "Ella . . . sweetheart, it's all right. Don't cry. Don't . . ."

But the relief of touching him, being close to him, had caused me to unravel. Not too late. The thought spurred a rush of euphoria. Jack was alive, and whole, and I would take nothing for granted ever again. I fumbled beneath the hem of his T-shirt and found the warm skin of his back. My fingertips encountered the edge of another bandage. He kept his arms firmly around me as if he understood that I needed the confining pressure, the feel of him surrounding me as our bodies relayed silent messages.

Don't let go.

I'm right here.

Tremors kept running along my entire frame. My teeth chattered, making it hard to talk. "I th-thought you might not come back."

Jack's mouth, usually so soft, was rough and chapped against my cheek, his jaw scratchy with bristle. "I'll always come back to you." His voice was hoarse.

I hid my face against his neck, breathing him in. His familiar scent had been obliterated by the antiseptic pungency of antiseptic burn dressings, and heavy saltwater brine. "Where are you hurt?" Sniffling, I reached farther over his back, investigating the extent of the bandage.

His fingers tangled in the smooth, soft locks of my hair. "Just a few burns and scrapes. Nothing to worry about." I felt his cheek tauten with a smile. "All your favorite parts are still there."

We were both quiet for a moment. I realized he was trembling, too. "I love you, Jack," I said, and that started a whole new rush of tears, because I was so unholy glad to be able to say it to him. "I thought it was too late . . . I thought you'd never know, because I was a coward, and I'm so—"

"I knew." Jack sounded shaken. He drew back to look down at me with glittering bloodshot eyes.

"You did?" I sniffled.

He nodded. "I figured I couldn't love you as much as I do, without you feeling something for me, too." He kissed me roughly, the contact between our mouths too hard for pleasure.

I put my fingers to Jack's bristled jaw and eased his face away to look at him. He was battered and scraped and sun-scorched. I couldn't begin to imagine how dehydrated he was. I pointed an unsteady finger at the waiting room. "Your family's in there. Why are you in the hallway?" My bewildered gaze swept down his body to his bare feet. "They're . . . they're letting you walk around like this?"

Jack shook his head. "They parked me in a room around the corner to wait for a couple more tests. I asked if anyone had told you I was okay, and nobody knew for sure. So I came to find you."

"You just *left* when you're supposed to be having more tests?"

"I had to find you." His voice was quiet but unyielding.

My hands fluttered over him. "Let's go back . . . you may have internal bleeding—"

Jack didn't budge. "I'm fine. They already did a CT, and it was clean. They want to do an MRI just to be sure."

"What about Joe?"

A shadow crossed Jack's face. Suddenly he looked young and anxious. "They won't tell me. He wasn't doing well, Ella. He could hardly breathe. He was at the wheel when the engine exploded . . . he may be really fucked up."

"This is a world-class hospital with the best doctors and the best equipment," I said, one of my hands settling carefully on his cheek. "They'll fix him. They'll do whatever they have to. But . . . was he burned badly?"

He shook his head. "The only reason I got singed a little was because I had to push through some burning debris to find him."

"Oh, Jack . . ." I wanted to hear everything he'd been through, every detail. I wanted to comfort him in every way possible. But there would be time for that later. "The doctor was talking to your family in the waiting room. Let's find out what he said." I gave him a threatening glance. "And then you're going back for the MRI. They're probably looking for you right now."

"They can wait." Jack slid an arm around my shoulder. "You should see the redheaded nurse who was wheeling me around. Bossiest woman I ever met."

We went into the waiting room. "Hey," I said in a wobbly voice. "Look who I found."

Jack was immediately surrounded by his family, Haven reaching him first. I stood back, still breathless, my heartbeat galvanized.

There were no wisecracks as Jack embraced his sister and Liberty. He turned to his father and hugged him, his eyes glittering as he saw the runnel of a tear down Churchill's leathery cheek.

"You okay?" Churchill asked in a rusted voice.

"Yeah, Dad."

"Good." And Churchill touched his son's face with a sort of gentle cuffing pat.

Jack's jaw quivered, and he cleared his throat roughly. He seemed relieved to turn to Hardy, with whom he exchanged a manly half-hug back-pat.

Gage was last, taking Jack by the shoulders and surveying him intently. "You look like shit," he commented.

"Fuck you," Jack said, and they embraced each other roughly, the two dark heads close together. Jack gave him a few forceful thumps on the back, but Gage, mindful of his brother's condition, was far gentler.

Jack swayed a little and was immediately pushed in a chair.

"He's dehydrated," I said, going to the water dispenser in the corner and filling up a paper cup.

"Why aren't you on an IV?" Churchill demanded, hovering over him.

Jack showed him his hand, where an IV needle was still inserted and anchored with tape. "They used a fourteen-gauge needle, and it feels like a six-penny nail was shoved into my vein. So I asked them for something smaller."

"Pussy," Gage said affectionately, rubbing the top of Jack's rough, salt-stiffened hair.

"How's Joe?" Jack asked, taking the water from me and drinking it in a few gulps.

They all exchanged glances—not a good sign—and Gage answered carefully. "The doctor said Joe has a concussion and a mild case of blast lung injury. It may take a while for the lungs to get back to speed, maybe up to a year. But it could have been a lot worse. Joe's in respiratory distress and has borderline hypoxia—so they're treating him with supplemental high-flow oxygen. He'll be spending some serious time in ICU. And he can hear out of one ear, but not the other. At some point a specialist will tell us if the hearing loss is permanent."

"That's okay," Jack said. "Joe never listens anyway."

Gage grinned briefly, but sobered as he stared at his younger brother. "He's going in for surgery right now, for internal bleeding."

"Where?"

"Abdomen, mostly."

Jack swallowed hard. "How bad?"

"We don't know."

"Shit." Wearily Jack rubbed his face with both hands. "I was afraid of that."

"Before they corral you again," Liberty said, "can you tell us what happened, Jack?"

Jack gestured for me to come to him, and he pulled me into his warm side as he spoke. It had been a clear morning, he said. Fishing had been decent, and they had gotten an early start back to the marina. But on the way they'd seen a huge brown seaweed mat, about an acre in size. The mat had formed its own ecosystem with algae, barnacles, and small fish, all living amid the accumulated driftwood and mermaid purses.

Figuring there was good fishing around or under the mat, the brothers had killed the engine and glided up to the seaweed. In just a few minutes Jack had hooked a Dorado, the rod nearly doubling and the reel screaming off a bunch of line as the acrobatic fish took off. It leapt from the water, revealing itself to be a five-footer, a monster, and Jack had followed around the boat to keep the line from catching. He had shouted to Joe to start the boat and go toward the fish, otherwise it would gain too much line. And just as he started to reel it in, Joe had started the engine and there had been an explosion.

Jack fell silent at that point, blinking as he struggled to recall what had happened next.

Hardy murmured, "Sounds like a buildup of fumes."

Jack nodded slowly. "Maybe the bilge blower cut out? Hell knows with all that electronic crap . . . anyway, I don't remember anything about the explosion. All of a sudden I was in the water, and there was debris everywhere, and the boat had turned into a fireball. I started looking for Joe." He looked agitated, his words coming in choppy bursts. "He'd grabbed on to a floating cooler—remember the orange one you got me, Gage—so I looked over him. I was afraid he'd gotten a leg blown off or something—and he was all in one piece, thank God. But he'd gotten one hell of a knock on his head, and he was struggling. I got hold of him and told him to relax, and I towed him to a safer distance from the boat."

"And the weather came in," Churchill prompted.

Jack nodded. "Wind picked up, water got rough, and we were getting pushed away from the boat. I tried to stay with it, but it took too much energy. So I just held on to Joe, and the cooler, and I swore I wouldn't let go no matter how long it took for someone to find us."

"Was Joe conscious?" I asked.

"Yeah, but we didn't talk much. The waves were too rough, and Joe was having a hard time breathing." Jack worked up a rueful smile. "The first thing he said to me was, 'Guess we lost that Dorado?' " He paused as everyone chuckled. "And later on he asked if we should worry about sharks and I said I didn't think so, since it was still shrimp season and most of the sharks go offshore to pick off throwbacks." A stark, endless hesitation. He swallowed hard. "After we'd waited a while, I could tell Joe was getting worse. He told me he didn't think he was going to make it. And I said—" His voice broke, and he dropped his head, unable to finish.

"You can tell us later," I whispered, putting my hand on his back, while Haven handed him a wad of Kleenex. It was too much, making him relive it so soon.

"Thanks," Jack said gruffly after a minute, blowing his nose and letting out a sigh.

"Here you are." A strident, accusatory voice came from the doorway, and we all looked up to behold a stout, redhaired nurse with a ruddy complexion, pushing an empty wheelchair into the waiting room. "Mr. Travis, why did you run off like that? I've been looking for you."

"I took a break," Jack said sheepishly.

The nurse scowled. "That's the last break you'll get for a while—you're getting a new IV needle put in, and you're going for your MRI, and I may think up some extra tests to pay you back for scaring me half to death. Disappearing like that . . ."

"I completely agree," I said, urging Jack to stand. "Take him. And keep an eye on him."

Jack shot me a narrow-eyed glance over his shoulder as he shuffled to the wheelchair.

The nurse stared incredulously at his scrub pants and T-shirt. "Where did you get those?" she demanded.

"Not telling," he muttered.

"Mr. Travis, you need to stay in your hospital gown until we're finished with all your tests."

"Bet you'd like that," Jack retorted, "me wandering bare-assed around the hospital."

"With all the backsides I've seen, Mr. Travis, I doubt I'd be impressed."

"I don't know," he said reflectively, easing into the wheelchair. "Mine's pretty good."

The nurse wheeled him around and pushed him through the doorway while they began to trade insults.

TWENTY-THREE

AFTER JACK'S TESTS WERE FINISHED, THE HOSPITAL kept him for six hours of observation. After that, the nurse promised, he could go home. They let him shower and wait in a private suite, one of their VIP rooms. It was decorated with maroon wallpaper and a mirror with an ornate gold frame, and a TV housed in a Victorian armoire.

"This looks like a bordello," I said.

Jack irritably flipped his IV lines so they didn't catch on the bed rail. One of the nurses had detached him from the IV long enough to let him take a shower, and then she'd hooked him up again despite his protests. "I want this needle out of my hand. And I want to know what the hell's going on with Joe. And I've got a bitch of a headache, and my arm hurts."

"Why don't you take one of those pain pills they keep trying to give you?" I asked gently.

"I don't want to be out of it, in case there's news about Joe." He flipped through the TV channels. "Don't let me fall asleep."

"Okay," I murmured, standing beside him. I reached out to stroke his clean, damp hair, letting my fingernails lightly scratch his scalp.

Jack sighed and blinked. "That feels good."

I continued to sift through his hair, scratching gently as if he were a big cat. Not two minutes later, Jack was completely out.

He didn't move for four hours, not even when I periodically smoothed more salve onto his lips, or when the nurse came in to change the IV bag and to check the monitor readouts. And I sat and watched him the entire time, half-afraid I was dreaming. I wondered how I had fallen so deeply in love with a man I had known for such a short time. It seemed my heart had been set on full throttle.

By the time Jack finally woke, I was able to tell him that his brother was out of surgery, and was in stable condition. In light of Joe's age and health, the doctor said, he had a good chance of recovery without complications.

Overcome with relief, Jack was unusually quiet as we went through the discharge process, signing a stack of forms and receiving a folder filled with burn-care instructions and prescriptions. He had dressed in a pair of jeans and shirt Gage had gotten for him, and then Hardy drove us to 1800 Main. After dropping us off there, Hardy would return to Garner to wait with Haven, who wanted to stay in the ICU with Joe for a while.

Jack's quietness persisted as we went up to his apartment. Despite the rest he'd gotten at the hospital, I knew he was still exhausted. It was half-past midnight, the building hushed, the elevator beep piercing the stillness.

We entered the apartment, and I closed the door. Jack seemed dazed as he glanced at his surroundings, as if he'd never been there before. Feeling the need to comfort him, I went up behind him and slid my arms around his waist. "What can I do?" I asked softly. I felt the rhythm of his breathing, faster than I'd expected. His body was tense, every muscle knotted.

He turned and stared into my eyes. Until then I'd never seen Jack, so eternally self-assured, look so lost and uncertain. Wanting to comfort him, I stood on my toes and brought my mouth to his. The kiss was off-center at first, but he gripped the back of my neck in one hand, and slid the other low on my hips, pressing me against him. His mouth was hot, urgent, tasting of salt and need.

Breaking off the kiss, Jack took my hand and pulled me to the dark bedroom. Panting, he tugged at my clothes with a frenzy he had never shown before.

"Jack," I said in concern, "we can wait until—"

"Now." His voice was strained. "I need you now." He tore at his own shirt, flinching as it caught at the burn wrap.

"Yes. All right." I was afraid he might hurt himself. "Go slowly, Jack. Please—"

"Can't," he muttered, reaching for the waist of my jeans, fumbling in his roughness.

"Let me help," I whispered, but he shoved my hands aside and dragged me to the bed. His self-control had vanished, eroded by exhaustion and emotion. My jeans and panties were stripped away and tossed to the floor. Kneeing my thighs apart, Jack lowered between them. I lifted willingly, opening to him, both of us intent on one goal.

He thrust strongly, rooting deep, a primal sound vibrating in his throat. His shaking hands clenched in my hair, and he took my mouth with bruising kisses. The rhythm began with a hammering, almost vicious power, and I answered every visceral stroke with tender acceptance. Grasping his head in my hands, I pulled his ear close to my lips, and I whispered how much I loved him, loved him beyond anything. He tensed and gasped out my name, his body shuddering with the violence of his release.

Some time before morning I woke with the hazy awareness of warm hands drifting over me, fingertips gliding and playing. Jack was cuddling me from behind, his knees drawn up beneath mine as we lay on our sides. In contrast to his earlier ferocity, his touch was extraordinarily light, teasing out sensation. I felt the hardness of his chest against my back, the soft mat of hair brushing my shoulder blades and raising gooseflesh. His mouth touched the back of my neck, teeth closing tenderly on the thin, hot skin, sending a shiver along my spine.

"Easy," Jack whispered, soothing me with his hands, kissing my nape, stroking it with his tongue. But it was impossible to stay still as he caressed my breasts and stomach and between my thighs, long fingers slipping into the core of my body. I moaned and reached blindly for his wrist, gripping it, and feeling the subtle, clever play of muscle and bone. His lips curved against my neck.

He eased his hand away, and his strong arm hooked beneath my top thigh, levering it upward. Positioning himself, he shunted deep and easy, whispering, *I love you, just let go, Ella, let me have you. . . .* He was so deliberate, the pace dreamy and delayed, and the more I struggled, the more time he took. We began the incremental climb, rising gradually on every throb, pulse, breath.

Withdrawing slowly, Jack turned me onto my back. He spread me wide and helpless beneath him. Incoherent sounds rose in my throat as he entered me again. His mouth took mine with erotic gentleness, while the urgent cadence of our bodies never ceased, the sleek undulations drawing out more pleasure, and more.

Our gazes locked, and I sank into the darkness of his eyes, feeling him all around me, inside me. He quickened, deepening the strokes, following the inner pulse of my body, pursuing my pleasure with hard, assuaging thrusts until he had driven me into a climax higher and stronger than anything I had ever felt. I cried out at the summit, twining my limbs around him, while Jack breathed my name and tumbled with me in the rush, the voluptuous undertow, the slow, rich ebb.

For a long time afterward, Jack held my shivering body and stroked me into stillness.

"Did you ever think it could be like that?" I whispered.

"Yes." He smoothed my hair and kissed my forehead. "But only with you."

WE SLEPT UNTIL HOT BLUE MORNING PRESSED AGAINST the shuttered windows, light filtering into the bedroom. I was dimly aware of Jack leaving the bed, the sounds of a shower, coffee being made in the kitchen, his quiet voice as he called the hospital to check on Joe's condition.

"How is he?" I asked drowsily when Jack returned to the bedroom. He was wearing a plaid flannel robe, carrying a mug of coffee. He still looked a little worse for wear, but sexier than any man had a right to be after what he'd been through.

"Stable condition." Jack's voice was still roughened from the ordeal. "He's going to be fine. Tough as hell."

"Well, he's a Travis," I said reasonably. Climbing out of bed, I went to his dresser and pulled out a T-shirt, which hung past the tops of my thighs when I put it on.

When I turned to face Jack, he was standing right there, tucking a lock of my hair behind my ear, and gazing down at me. No one had ever looked at me with such tender concern. "Tell me about Luke," he said gently.

And as I stared into those velvety-dark eyes, I knew I could share anything with him. He would listen, and he would understand. "Let me get my coffee first," I said, and went to the kitchen.

Jack had set a cup and saucer beside the coffeemaker. I saw a piece of notepaper, folded lengthwise, standing in the empty cup. Perplexed, I opened the note and read:

Dear Miss Independent,

I've decided that of all the women I've ever known, you are the only one I will ever love more than hunting, fishing, football, and power tools.

You may not know this, but the other time I asked you to marry me, the night I put the crib together, I meant it. Even though I knew you weren't ready.

God, I hope you're ready now.

Marry me, Ella. Because no matter where you go or what you do, I'll love you every day for the rest of my life.

—Jack

I felt no fear, reading those words. Only wonder, that so much happiness could be within my reach.

Noticing something else in the cup, I reached in and pulled out a diamond ring, the stone round and glittering. My breath caught as I turned it in the light. I tried on the ring, and it slid neatly onto my finger. Picking up a nearby pen, I turned over the paper and wrote my answer in a flourishing scrawl.

I poured my coffee, added cream and sweetener, and went back into the bedroom with the note.

Jack was sitting on the edge of the bed, his head tilted slightly as he watched me. His simmering gaze took me in from head to toe, lingering at the diamond sparkling on my hand. I saw his chest rise and fall with a quick breath.

Sipping my coffee, I approached him and handed him the note.

Dear Jack,

I love you, too.

And I think I know the secret to a long and happy marriage—just choose someone you can't live without.

For me, that would be you.

So if you insist on being traditional . . .

Yes.

—Ella

Jack let out a pent-up sigh. He took my hips in his hands as I stood before him. "Thank God," he murmured, drawing me between his thighs. "I was afraid you were going to give me an argument."

Taking care not to spill my coffee, I leaned forward and pressed my lips against his, letting our tongues touch. "When have I ever said no to you, Jack Travis?"

His lashes lowered as he glanced at my damp lower lip. His accent was as thick as sorghum. "Well, I sure as hell didn't want you to start sayin' it now." Taking the coffee from me, he finished it in a few swallows and set the cup aside, disregarding my laughing protest.

He kissed me until my arms were twined around his neck and my knees threatened to buckle.

"Ella," he said, finishing the kiss with a gentle nuzzle, "you're not going to take it back, are you?"

"Of course not." I was filled with a sense of rightness, of calm certitude, and at the same time I was as giddy as a kaleidoscope of butterflies. "Why would I?"

"You told me you believed marriage was for other people."

"You're the only man who could make me believe that it's for me, too. Although when you get down to it, love is what's real. I still say marriage is just a piece of paper."

Jack smiled. "Let's find out," he said, and he pulled me down to the bed with him.

IT OCCURRED TO ME MUCH LATER THAT THE PEOPLE who said marriage was just a piece of paper were usually people who had never done it. Because that cliché discounted something important—the power of words . . . and I, more than anyone, should have understood that.

Somehow the promise we had made on that piece of paper gave me more freedom than I'd ever known before. It allowed both of us to argue, to laugh, to risk, to trust—without fear. It was a confirmation of a connection that already existed. And it was a bond that extended far beyond the borders of a shared living space. We would have stayed together even without a marriage certificate . . . but I believed in the permanence it represented.

It was a piece of paper you could build a life on.

At first my mother had been incredulous that I had managed to catch a Travis, and she had tried to descend like a plague of Egypt in hopes of profiting from my new connections. But Jack handled her adroitly, using a mixture of intimidation and charm to keep her in line. I didn't see or hear from her often, and when she did get in touch, she was oddly subdued and respectful.

"I wonder what's going on with her," I told Jack in bemusement. "She hasn't said anything about my weight or my hairstyle, and I haven't had to listen to any gross stories about her sex life or grooming habits."

"I promised her a new car if she managed not to piss you off for six months," he said. "I told her if I ever saw you frowning or unhappy after you got off the phone with her, the deal was off."

"Jack Travis!" I was amused and indignant. "Are you going to start buying her big-ticket items every six months as a reward for impersonating a decent human being?"

"I doubt she'll last that long," he said.

As for Jack's side of the family, I found them colorful, affectionate, argumentative, fascinating. They were a real family, and they made a place for me, and I loved them for it. I quickly grew fond of Churchill, who was a kind and generous soul despite the fact that he didn't suffer fools gladly. We debated various subjects and annoyed each other with dueling political e-mails, and we made each other laugh, and he insisted that I sit right next to him at family dinners.

After two weeks at Garner Hospital, Joe came home to recuperate at the mansion in River Oaks, which delighted Churchill nearly as much as it aggravated his son.

Joe said he wanted privacy. He didn't like it that when anyone came to see him, they visited with his dad first. But Churchill, who hardly minded having so many attractive young women come to the house, retorted that if Joe didn't like it, he'd better get well faster. As a result Joe was a model patient, determined to recover his health as soon as possible and get away from his interfering parent.

I married Jack two months after he proposed, which shocked all of my friends and most of his, who had come to think of him as a perennial bachelor. I'd heard some speculation that his near-death experience had helped him to readjust his priorities. "My priorities were fine," Jack told everyone innocently. "It was Ella's that needed straightening out."

The night before the wedding, my sister Tara came to the dinner for out-of-town guests. She was beautifully dressed in a pink suit, her hair upswept, diamond studs sparkling at her ears. And she was unescorted. I wanted to ask her how she was, if she was being treated well, if she was happy in her arrangement with Noah. But all thoughts of Tara's relationship with Noah Cardiff disappeared as soon as I realized she had brought Luke.

He was a gorgeous blue-eyed cherub who reached and grabbed for things, grinned, and drooled, and looked too adorable for words. I held out my arms eagerly, and Tara handed him to me. The cuddly weight of Luke on my chest, the scent and warmth of him, the round, searching eyes that tried to take everything in, all of it reminded me that I would never be quite whole without him.

During the two months we had been apart, I had tried to console myself with the thought that in time the pain of Luke's absence would fade, that I would forget and move on. But as I snuggled him close and smoothed his soft black hair, and he smiled as if he remembered me, I knew nothing had changed. Love didn't move on.

I held Luke in my lap all during the formal dinner, once getting up to walk around with him, another time taking him upstairs to change his diaper, despite my sister's protest that she could do it. "Let me," I told her, laughing as Luke grasped the strand of pearls I was wearing and attempted to cram some of them into his mouth. "I don't mind at all, and I want to spend every possible second with him."

"Be careful," Tara warned, giving me the diaper bag. "He rolls over now. He'll roll right off the bed."

"Do you?" I asked Luke, enchanted. "Can you roll? You'll have to do it so I can see, sweet baby."

He gurgled in agreement, gnawing on the pearls.

When Luke was freshly diapered, I took him toward the stairs, heading back down to dinner. I paused as I saw Jack and Tara ascending to the top of the flight, both of them absorbed in conversation. Jack glanced at me and smiled faintly, but his eyes were alert, and intent, and it seemed there was something he wanted to tell me. And Tara looked guarded.

What in the world could they have been talking about?

"Hey," I said, forcing a smile. "Were you afraid I'd lost my touch?"

"Not at all," Jack replied easily. "You've changed enough diapers, I didn't think you'd forget so soon." He came to me and brushed a warm kiss on my cheek. "Darlin', why don't you let me take Luke for a few minutes? He and I got some catching up to do."

I was reluctant to let the baby go. "Maybe a little later?"

Jack looked directly into my eyes, his face right above mine. "Talk to your sister," he murmured. "And tell her yes."

"Tell her yes about what?"

But he didn't answer. He pried the baby away from me, laid him against his shoulder, and patted his diapered bottom. Luke conformed to him bonelessly, content in Jack's secure grip.

"This won't take long," Tara told me, looking uncertain and almost bashful. "At least, I don't think it will. Is there somewhere quiet we can talk?"

I led her to a little upstairs sitting area, and we settled into soft leather-upholstered chairs. "Is it about Mom?" I asked in concern.

"Lord, no." Tara raised her eyes heavenward. "Mom's fine. She doesn't know about me and Noah, of course. All she knows is that I've got a rich boyfriend. She's telling everyone that I'm secretly dating one of the Astros."

"How are things with Noah?" I hesitated, uncertain if I should use his name.

"Wonderful," she said without hesitation. "I've never been so happy. He's real good to me, Ella."

"I'm glad."

"I have a house," Tara continued, "and jewelry, and a car . . . and he loves me, he says it all the time. I hope he can keep his promises to me . . . I believe he wants to. But even if he can't, this has been the best time of my life. I wouldn't trade it for anything. It's just . . . I've been thinking about things lately . . ."

"You're going to leave him?" I asked hopefully.

A wry smile curved her lacquered lips. "No, Ella. I'm going to be spending more time with him. He's started traveling a lot . . . he'll be going across the country to present programs in big stadiums, and he'll also be touring in Canada and England. His wife is staying here with the kids. I'll be going as part of his entourage. And I'll be with him every night."

I was speechless for a moment. "You want to do that?"

Tara nodded. "I'd like to see some of the world, learn new things. I never had the chance to do anything like this before. And I want to be with Noah and help him any way I can."

"Tara, do you really think—"

"I'm not asking for permission," she said. "And I don't want your opinion, Ella. I'm making my own decisions, and I have the right to do that. After growing up with Mom, you know how important it is to get to decide things for yourself."

That quieted me as nothing else could have. Yes, it was her right to make her own decisions, even her own mistakes. "Are you telling me goodbye?" I asked huskily.

She smiled and shook her head. "Not yet. It'll take a few months to arrange. The reason I'm telling you now is . . ." Her smile faded. "God. It's not easy to say what I really feel, instead of what I think I should feel. But the truth is, I've been taking care of Luke, spending a lot of time with him, and it's still like it was in the beginning. He doesn't feel like mine. He never will. I don't want children, Ella. I don't want to be a mother . . . I don't want to relive our childhood."

"But it's not like that," I said urgently, taking her long, slim hands in mine. "Luke has nothing to do with that old life."

"That's how you feel," she said gently. "It's not how I feel."

"What does Noah say?"

Tara looked down at our entwined hands. "He doesn't want Luke. He's already got children. And having a baby around makes it hard for us to be together."

"Luke'll get older. You'll change your mind."

"No, Ella. I understand what I'm doing." She gave me a long, bittersweet glance. "Just because a woman can have children, it doesn't make her a mother. You and I know that, don't we?"

My eyes and nose stung. I swallowed against the tightness of my throat. "Yeah," I whispered.

"So what I'm asking, Ella, is if you'd like to take Luke for good.

Jack said he thought you might. It's the best thing for Luke, if you're willing."

The world seemed to stop. I was caught up in a suspended moment of wonder and fearful longing, thinking maybe I hadn't heard right. She couldn't really have offered me something so precious. "If I'm willing," I repeated thickly, fighting to control my voice. "How do I know you won't want him back someday?"

"I wouldn't do that to you, or the baby. I know what Luke means to you. I see it on your face whenever you look at him. But we'll make it a legal adoption. We'll have all the papers drawn up. I'll sign everything, and so will Noah, as long as his part of it's kept private. Luke is yours if you want him, Ella."

I nodded, covering my mouth to hold in a sob. "I do," I managed to say between sharp breaths. "I do. Yes."

"Don't, you'll ruin your makeup," Tara said, using her finger to swab a pooling tear beneath my eye.

I reached for her, and hugged her fiercely, heedless of makeup and hairstyles and outfits. "Thank you," I choked.

"When do you want to take him? Some time after you get back from the honeymoon?"

"I want him now," I said, and burst into tears, unable to hold them back any longer.

Tara let out a startled laugh. "The night before your wedding?"

I nodded emphatically.

"I can't think of worse timing," Tara said. "But it's fine with me, as long as Jack agrees." She fished in the diaper bag and found a dry burp cloth, and handed it to me.

As I blotted my eyes, I was aware of someone approaching. I looked up and saw Jack coming back with Luke. His gaze read every detail of my face as if it were a familiar and beloved landscape. He saw everything. A smile crept into the corners of his mouth, and he whispered something in the baby's miniature ear.

"She wants him right now," Tara told him. "Even though I told her we can wait 'til after the wedding."

Jack came to me and lowered Luke into my waiting arms. His long fingers slid beneath my chin, tilting my face upward, thumb gently brushing away a lingering streak of dampness on my cheek. He smiled down at me.

"I don't think Ella wants to waste time," he murmured. "Do you, sweetheart?"

"No," I agreed in a whisper, the world around me shimmering through a hot ebullient glaze, the sound of his voice and my own ragged heartbeat mingling like music.

EPILOGUE

JACK PICKS ME UP AT THE AIRPORT AFTER MY conference in Colorado, where I attended some workshops, pitched ideas to magazine editors, and sold a freelance piece tentatively titled, "Six Strategies for Finding and Keeping Happiness." It was a good conference, but I'm more than ready to go home.

After nearly a year of marriage, these four days have been the longest separation Jack and I have ever gone through. I have called him frequently, told him about the people I've met, the things I've learned, my ideas for future articles and columns. In turn, Jack has told me about the dinner he had with Hardy and Haven, and that Carrington just got her braces on, and Joe's checkup went well. Every night, Jack gives me a detailed account of Luke's day, and I am hungry for every bit of news.

My breath catches as I see my husband waiting for me at baggage claim. He is handsome and sinfully sexy, the kind of man who attracts female gazes without trying, but he is oblivious to everything except me. As he sees me walking toward him, he reaches me in three strides, and his warm mouth crushes mine. His body is hard and sheltering.

And although I don't regret having gone to the conference, I realize I haven't felt this good since I left him.

"How is Luke?" is the first thing I ask, and Jack entertains me with a story of how he was spoon-feeding applesauce to the baby, and how Luke took a handful and smeared it into his own hair.

We collect my luggage, and Jack drives me back to our apartment at 1800 Main. We can't seem to stop talking, even though we've talked every day we've been apart. I keep my hand on Jack's arm the whole way, and I notice that his bicep feels huge. When I ask him if he's been working out harder than usual, he says it was the only way to deal with his pent-up sexual frustration. He says I'm going to be busy for a while, making it up to him, which I say is just fine.

I stand on my toes and kiss him during the entire elevator ride, and he kisses me back until I can hardly breathe.

"Ella," he murmurs, holding my flushed face in his hands, "four days without you, and it felt like four months. All I could think was, how did I make it for so long before I met you?"

"You went out with a lot of placeholders," I tell him.

A grin crosses his face before he kisses me again. "I didn't know what I was missing."

While Jack carries my suitcases, I hurry down the hallway to our apartment, my heart beating in anticipation. I ring the bell, and the nanny opens the door just as Jack catches up with me.

"Welcome home, Mrs. Travis," she exclaims.

"Thank you. It's good to be back. Where is Luke?"

"In the nursery. We were playing with his trains. He's been a good boy while you were gone."

Dropping my purse beside the door, tossing my suit jacket onto the sofa, I go to the doorway of the nursery. The room is painted in pale shades of blue and green, one wall a mural of cars and trucks with cheerful faces, and a rug printed with roads and train tracks.

My son is sitting up by himself, gripping a wooden train engine in his hands, trying to spin the wheels with his fingers.

"Luke," I said softly, not wanting to startle him. "Mommy's home. I'm here. Oh, I missed you, sweet boy."

Luke looks at me with round blue eyes and drops the truck, his small hands remaining suspended in midair. A wide grin spreads across his face, revealing one pearly tooth. He lifts his arms to me.

"Mama," he says.

I thrill to the word. And I go to him.